Strange Companions

Chronicles of the Dawnblade Book 2

Andrew Claydon

Strange Companions

By Andrew Claydon

Published by Andrew Claydon

Copyright © 2022, Andrew Claydon

Edited by Danielle Fine

Cover Design by MiblArt

All Rights Reserved. This book may not be
reproduced, transmitted, or stored in whole or part in any means, including
graphic, electronic, or mechanical without the express written consent of the
publisher except in the case of brief quotations embodied in critical articles and reviews.

Written in UK English

Just because you're chosen, doesn't mean you want to be.

A month ago, Nicolas Percival Carnegie was chosen to deliver a message, but circumstances spiralled far beyond his control, and he ended up dodging danger, death, and vampires to try to save his kingdom.

Returning home, he had one comfort, beyond having done the right thing, which was that his adventuring days were one and done.

But then a strange creature attacks his village, and he has to set out into the world to try to find the source of this creature before more are unleashed.

Still haunted by the events of his previous journey, Nicolas must take to the road again with old companions and surprising new ones as he somehow finds the fate of another kingdom resting in his hands.

At least this time he has his own sword.

But will it make a difference when the forces of evil have a minotaur?

Dedicated to my wife Shona, who found her own *strange companion* in me.
And to everyone who loves a good adventure.

Guest starring: Wade Leibeck as *Wade LeBeck*
Thank you for the contribution to my kickstart campaign.

'I was once advised that it was better to stay silent than to speak ill of a place. As sound as that counsel may appear, unfortunately the fellow who imparted that wisdom has never tried to sell a book.
Therefore, my choice with Sarus City is thus, give the reader a thorough and accurate account of the place, or leave this section of the book blank.
On the assumption that you, dear reader, will not purchase a work of blank pages, allow me to tell you of Sarus City...'

Etherius, A Travellers Guide – Dieter Von Ostric

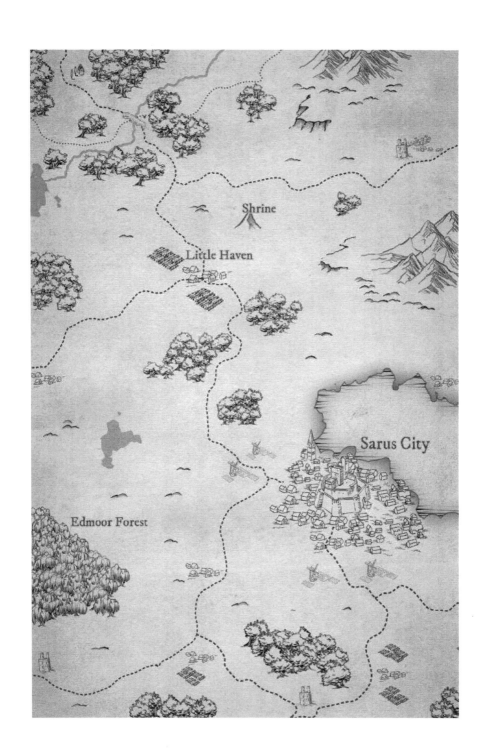

Chapter 1

There are no monsters out there.

Nicolas had told himself that five times now but still wasn't convinced. It had become almost a routine: the trepidation as he woke, the anticipation as he walked down the stairs, the minutes his hand hovered over the door handle before he finally opened it. Then the anxious staring into the shadowed trees and bushes. *What could be waiting amongst them?* The problem was he'd seen first hand some of the horrors that Etherius had to offer. And so he began his mantra.

Today, he was almost certainly late, so he didn't have the luxury of searching for phantom enemies.

Why is it always so hard to take that first step?

Because the dark can conceal some very terrible things. That was why he stood before the front door as if it were potentially a portal to terror itself.

There are no monsters out there.

He began to slow his lungs, forcing them into a more regular rhythm until his thumping heart beat followed suit.

There are no monsters out there.

In his mind he chased away the mental images of unholy creatures with pleasant memories of his family, and fluffy animals.

There are no monsters out there.

Flexing his fingers he finally managed to stop the tremble in his hand.

There are no monsters out there.

With a single deep breath he grabbed the handle and turned it, pulling the door open before he had time to second guess it. The cool night air instantly caressed his face as he looked out into the dark.

Keeping close to the house, he made his way towards the mill, where work seemed to be commencing in earnest. He was definitely late, a common occurrence in the month since he'd returned from his task to deliver a message to a hero. That supposedly simple job that had turned into something much worse. Surviving vampires—and more—should've made every day feel like a gift. Instead, all he'd brought back with him was the fear of what could be lurking around each corner. He'd been bad enough before he actually *knew* what was out there. As his mind drifted back to those few days, familiar faces began to form in his mind.

Nicolas shook himself, banishing the images again and instead focusing on the softly creaking, weather-beaten blades of the mill.

The smell of freshly baked bread met him halfway to his destination, filling his nostrils and tantalising his stomach. But it wasn't time to eat; it was time to work. That gave him something concrete to focus on that ensured the three faces on the edge of his mind stayed away.

The wave of heat that greeted him as he opened the mill door was reassuringly familiar, engulfing half his body and warming him to the core. After taking a second to enjoy the contrast between the warm air on his front and the cold on his back, he entered the mill, where work was indeed already in full swing.

By the old stone ovens, his father was busy pulling out fresh, golden-crusted loaves with his trusty wooden paddle, adding them to the others cooling on the table. Nicolas's nose tingled from the flour dust in the air and there were already tell-tale signs of the perspiration to come.

Shouldn't I be used to these things by now?

'You're late.' The brief look his father gave him made his manhood retract slightly. The blast of cool air he'd let into the room must've given away his entrance.

'Sorry.' As much as he kept promising himself he'd do better the fear wouldn't leave him. Every night was the same: lying in bed afraid to sleep for the images that awaited his closed eyes — the fanged creatures waiting to attack his dreaming mind. Even lying awake, they still slipped in. *Was that his heartbeat thumping or footsteps creeping toward him? Had that shadow just moved?* When sleep eventually took him against his will, he found it hard to wake. So, yeah, late.

At least here he could lose himself in the work for a few hours. There were orders to fill, and time was the eternal enemy.

The work itself passed quickly, as well-practised things always did. Mixing and kneading and baking consumed the senses so well that concepts like time were really lost. The only evidence of its advance was the morning light creeping through the windows. By the time it had, the table was overflowing with loaves and other, smaller delicacies, making his stomach growl in longing.

'Breakfast.' He allowed himself a sigh of relief at his mother's call. A rumbling tummy was more easily fought than fear.

He looked around the bakery. Production was finished for the day, but there was still much to do, because of his tardiness. The place was a mess of flour dust, dough pieces, and tools in need of cleaning. On the other hand, he was really hungry. Probably another effect of so little sleep, his body requiring much more energy to run itself.

'Go,' his father said from out of the blue. 'Get some food in you before we begin loading the cart.'

'Are you sure?' Turning up late, leaving early, and saddling his father with the cleaning...he was hardly the model apprentice.

'Go. You can thank me by doing most of the loading.' His father looked at him and must've seen the guilt written over his face. 'Ask me a third time and you can stay and clean up while I eat.'

That was enough for Nicolas. Quickly he walked toward the door, only stopping to wash off the dough and flour encrusted on his hands at the water bowl beside it. Once he was clean, he hung his apron back up and sprinted towards the house and the inviting smells emanating from it.

'Good morning, Hero.' His mother smiled as she placed the last of the plates on the table.

Ever since he'd returned from delivering his message, his mother had taken to affectionately referring to him as *Hero* in private. He'd said nothing about what had really happened during his time away, simply stating that he'd completed his task, which he had. He'd just omitted the parts about the necromancer, the vampire army, and helping save the kingdom. Telling the full story would come with the kind of fuss he wanted to avoid. Besides, who would believe him anyway? Truly, he just wanted to forget all about it...but it was proving more difficult than he'd ever imagined.

However, his mother knew more had happened than he let on. It was obvious, really, when a single day's task took him several days and he'd returned looking like he'd been to war. Hence his new nickname. He'd tried correcting her the first few times but given up when he realised she wasn't going to let up.

'Thanks.' Sitting at the table, he had no idea where to start. It all looked so inviting. It was an issue that didn't last long.

Everything tasted as great as it smelled. There was something about a good meal after hard work that felt well earned, making the taste sweeter, the food more filling. His mother sat across from him and sipped her tea while studying him with an affectionate smile.

'Okay?' Crumbs fell from his mouth—probably why people shouldn't talk with their mouth full.

His mother hesitated before answering, as if she were unsure as to say what was on her mind or not. 'It's just that you're here today,' she answered finally. 'It's nice.'

'I'm always here.' Other than *that* time away.

'Your body is, but your mind has been elsewhere.' Her smile was heavy. She probably didn't like being kept in the dark. 'Don't pretend it hasn't. I see you drifting away every now and then, or you're doing things but just going through the motions. It's getting better, though, which is nice.'

'I'm—'

'Don't apologise.' His mother waved away his explanation.

Maybe he *had* left a part of himself there, with them. Or what he'd brought back with him had overshadowed everything else. It certainly hung over him like a storm cloud, ready to surprise him with a fierce clap of thunder at any moment.

Not knowing what to say, he instead reached across the table and held his mother's hand for a moment. That was enough.

'Did he tell you what happened when he was away yet?' His father sat next to him as if he'd asked a casual question, instead of being more overt about his curiosity than his mother.

'We're respecting the fact that he doesn't want to talk about it,' his mother chastised firmly.

'I respect it,' his father protested, before adding with a smile, 'but I'm damn curious all the same. Especially about where that sword in your room came from.'

With a hacking cough he spat the water he was drinking back into the cup, not needing to see his own face to know that it was reddening. This couldn't have been more awkward if they'd found some smutty parchments. The sword. He'd thought he'd hidden it well enough.

Why did I even keep it?

He'd asked himself that repeatedly, but never came up with a legitimate answer. It wasn't like he ever planned on needing it again. Yet it stayed.

He needed a way out of this conversation. Lacking any subtler ideas, he simply changed the subject. 'We all ready to go?'

'Once the wagon is loaded.' His father clicked his fingers as if remembering something, then gave him a wide smile. 'Once *you* load the wagon.'

'Another day in our quiet village.' Nicolas rolled his eyes. 'Same old bread and rolls to sell.'

'It's called supply and demand, son.' His father chuckled. 'I would make the fanciest breads and cakes in all the Nine Kingdoms, but folks round here won't buy them and then I can't afford lavish breakfasts for my ungrateful and tardy son.'

'I do like a nice breakfast,' he mused as he took another bite and chewed it thoughtfully.

****

An hour later, the high morning sun cast golden light over the fields of corn that bobbed slightly in the breeze, looking like the spears of a marching army. Their wagon travelled down the road between those fields, loaded with baked goods for the morning market. One month on and being on the wagon still made him uneasy. Being thrust into a world of vampires, ghostly heroes, and necromancers had all started with a wagon ride.

It's daytime, and you're home, he reminded himself. *It's safe.*

The wooden cart rocked gently as wheels turned over the track, pulled slowly by the family's horse. Lounging in the back of the cart, he looked over the lip of the wagon at the outlines of buildings that made up the village square. Hablock was a very rural community, with homes spread far from each other, so people only really congregated at the village square for the morning market or evening social events. It was—

What was that?

His eye caught movement to his left. Carefully, he scanned the cornfield. *Something* had moved. He knew it. A bead of perspiration ran down his temple as his heart beat faster. His right hand twitched as he pulled a knife from his boot. *Just a precaution*. There were no vampires in the cornfield. They'd all died in Yarringsburg. Besides, it was daytime.

Despite his pep talk, a quick glance down confirmed the whiteness of his knuckles as he gripped the small blade.

Bursting from the cornfield, a bird cawed. The wagon shook as he fell back, a small cry escaping his lips as he brought the knife up in front of him. The bird flew past, ignorant of the threat.

First he's jumping at brushes that fall from cupboards and doors that're closed too hard, and now it's at birds.

Stupid winged idiot.

Market was still setting up as the wagon pulled into the village square, folks going about their business, though still finding time to exchange the latest gossip. With quick and practised ease, Nicolas and his family set up their table of bread and cakes. There were quite a few people bustling around already this morning. It should be a good day.

'Morning, sunshine.' The familiarity of the voice made him smile. 'And how is Mister Nicolas Percival Carnegie today?'

Potter stood behind him, a rakish grin beaming from beneath his bushy beard. They'd initially met on the wagon ride to the *Tower of the Oracle* a month ago. Since Nicolas had returned from his adventure, he and Potter had struck up a friendship, though he had no idea why. The pair were vastly different, and quite frankly, Potter could be pretty irksome at times. However, there was a roguish charm to him that outweighed some of his more annoying qualities. Nicolas took the proffered hand.

'Good haul this morning?' He pointed to the limp rabbits in his friend's hand.

'Of course.' Potter winked smugly. 'No rabbit is safe from the best bowman in the Nine Kingdoms.'

Potter was a very skilled archer, and a very boastful one. He'd taken Nicolas out with him once, but the arrow had ended up on the floor by his feet more than in the bow. One time it'd nearly ended up in his foot, so he'd decided to leave the archery to the expert. The rabbits had had it easy that day.

'Just a shame you have to dress like that to catch them.' Potter's green tunic and breeches were a little snug in the wrong places.

'It's called camouflage.' Potter chuckled. 'Can't let them see you coming.'

'You should try. They may die from the embarrassment of being seen with you.'

'See, Nicky, that's why I hang around with you: to make me look good.' Potter grinned before making a mock-serious face. 'So…are you going to tell me today then?'

This was one of Potter's more annoying qualities. Since his return, most people had accepted his story that nothing interesting had happened on his journey, save delivering his message. Potter, however, sometimes seemed almost desperate to know.

'What would you like to hear?' he asked, 'About how many times I tripped in the forest or how many fish I saw in the river?'

Potter made a tutting noise and smiled. 'You'll tell me what really happened one day,' he chided, wagging an accusing finger. 'You'll need to talk about it at some point, and I'll be your shoulder to cry on.'

'And risk wetting that fashionable tunic of yours?' Nicolas laughed. 'I could never do that to you.'

'Thank you, my friend.' Potter put his hand on Nicolas's shoulder. 'Everyone knows ladies don't like a man with wet shoulders. My reputation as a lover will be in tatters.'

The pair's laughter was interrupted when a flock of birds flew overhead, cawing urgently at the top of their lungs.

Stupid birds. Hadn't they annoyed him enough for one day?

Still, Nicolas took the opportune moment to deflect the conversation. 'When are you going to go and make your own stories?'

Many nights in the tavern—after numerous ales—Potter told of his big plans to leave Hablock one day, to go out into the world and make something of himself. He believed he had some grand destiny awaiting him. Initially, he'd hoped that being Chosen would be the stepping stone to greater things and had been pretty jealous when Nicolas had become the Word Bearer over him, but he'd gotten over it.

'My mother's still unwell.' Potter seemed awkward at the omission. 'I'm just waiting for the right opportunity.'

Still? 'Oh I'm sorry.' He didn't really know the best words to comfort his friends. 'Did the healer...'

That was when the screaming started.

Chapter 2

Nicolas would never know where they originated, but when the screams reached the square, they spread like a contagion. Conversations were cut off and people dropped what they carried as they began to flee, only adding to the chaos and confusion. Craning his neck, he tried to look over the crowd for the source of the panic. All he could see was the human stampede, filled with frightened faces.

There was throbbing in his temples as his heart raced. His vision tunnelled as the fleeing villagers seemed to slow. Running his shaking hands over his head, he hoped to somehow banish the disorientation creeping up on him. Yet, there was something about it that was almost funny. All of the times he'd *thought* he been scared lately by the most ridiculous things, like birds in a corn field, he'd forgotten what it *really* was like to be in peril. Something was here. This was *real*.

He looked to Potter. 'What are they running from?'

His friend looked as confused as he did. 'I don't know.' Potter had to shout to be heard.

Needing answers, he grabbed several of the fleeing people as they passed him, but all they would say was *'run'* or *'get away'* as they pulled and fought to break his grip and get to safety. It suddenly occurred to him that maybe he should be following them.

Why am I just standing here waiting for whatever it is to come? It wasn't safe for him or his...*oh no*.

'Mum! Dad!' He cupped his hands to his mouth as if somehow that would help over the background noise as he frantically searched the sea of faces for his parents.

Nothing. No sign. What he did have was Potter. Maybe, between the two of them, they could—

His train of thought was broken by the strange look on his friend's face as he peered up into the sky. In the bright blue sky was a black shadow, a dark blob with large wings protruding from its sides, coming from the south. Though it was hard to make out properly, whatever it was didn't seem to be flying, per se, more bobbing randomly in the air with great flaps of its wings. Either way, it was headed towards them.

'That's an odd-looking bird.' It had to be a bird. There was no way in all Etherius it was what he thought it was. Cupping his hands over his eyes, he attempted to discern more detail.

'That's no bird.' Potter ran his hand down his beard, his eyes wide.

It wasn't possible. Not here. There must be another explanation.

Two bursts of flame emerged from the shadow, and his worst fears were confirmed.

'*Dragon!*' Potter was already turning in the general direction of the exodus.

Yet he didn't move, and had no idea why. He wasn't rooted from fear nor was he bravely standing down the monster. He was just *curious*. Something in his gut told him something wasn't right, beyond the general fact of a dragon in these parts at all. The nagging idea that it wasn't a dragon just wouldn't go away. He *had* to know for sure. The irony of him standing in the path of an approaching dragon when he'd nearly had a panic attack due to a bird in a field wasn't lost on him. Indeed, his curiosity had only dampened his panic, not extinguished it.

Closing on the square at speed, the shadow glided haphazardly over the buildings, emitting a shriek as it did. *By the Deities', that things fast.* The blur moved over Nicolas, blotting out the sun for a second and bathing him in a backwash of blown-up dirt and debris. Still, he didn't move. For a second, he'd seen the creature as it passed over him.

Or did I?

What he saw made no sense. Curiosity became outright confusion.

The creature—for he certainly wasn't comfortable calling it a dragon anymore—rose high into the sky before almost seeming to drop back towards the earth, swooping low over the village square again. There was an inhuman scream, and several of the market stalls combusted into flames. Flinging himself away from the centre of the square, he slipped down a nearby alley, pressing himself to the wall of the tavern. Waves of heat washed over him from the blazing stalls even here. Between the billowing smoke and the buildings around him, he lost sight of the creature. A heavy charred smell made his nose wrinkle.

The new heat in the air made everything hazy. Vaguely, he made out Potter ducking into an alleyway across the square from him, crouching low with his bow in hand. Those who hadn't been so quick to flee were taking any available shelter, be it behind a barrel or underneath a wagon. All around, fearful eyes looked to the sky.

For a moment, the world spun dizzyingly, and he struggled for air, his right hand shaking. In slow motion, another flame lit up the street. Terror promised to consume him.

No.

He didn't have the luxury. This creature wasn't just going to fly away, and soon people would start getting hurt, or even die. By some terrible leap of logic, stopping it had become his responsibility. Why? Because of his previous experience? Going from killing a single vampire to slaying a dragon was a massive leap. He didn't want to take it, but if not him then who?

Resolution fought back reluctance, and Nicolas forced his breathing to slow, closing his eyes so that he could focus on calming his mind. Slowly but surely, he regained some semblance of self, though his hand still jittered and he might soil himself at any second. Good enough. Now he just needed a plan.

He tried to form one, urging his mind to think fast. Those people hidden under wooden wagons weren't going to last long once... He was leaning against a wooden building with a creature flinging fire around.

Move!

His panic caused impulsive rather than considered action, and he threw himself back into the street, just as the creature made another dive.

This time, it came in really low, almost lower than it seemed to want to as it continued its erratic flight. But leaping from his hiding place in such a foolhardy way caused Nicolas to land hard on the dirt floor, his body rolling with the momentum so that he ended on his back just as the creature passed over him.

Way too close.

He got his first clear view of the creature. It was what he'd thought it was.

How can that be?

More surprising was the moment of eye contact they'd shared the second before it whooshed over him.

Those aren't the eyes of a rampaging monster.

As it rose back into the sky with difficulty, an idea came to mind. It was a stupid idea, a crazy idea, a quasi-suicidal idea, but he had no time to debate the pros and cons or come up with anything better. The village was burning, and something needed to be done, *now*. In the back of his mind, the image of a certain spirit giving him an impressed nod appeared. Maybe a stupid, off-the-cuff plan was better than no plan at all?

He pushed up from the floor and bolted for the door of the tavern, his fear at being in what essentially was a big pile of kindling overridden by his need to act swiftly. After bursting through the swinging doors, he ran past abandoned tables with discarded glasses. The tavern was one of the few buildings in the town square more than a single storey high. Wood thumped in protest as he bounded up the stairs and to the hallway window that looked out over the square.

Wrestling with the catch proved fiddly with his sweat-soaked hands, but eventually the window opened, and putting one foot on the windowsill he leaned out, craning to see where the creature was.

The large shadow rose high into the sky before dropping again as if gravity were asserting itself. *Please come in low again.* The creature's descent was heralded with cries of fear from the people below. That gave him just enough drive to do what he was about to do.

Keeping one hand on the rough wooden frame, he put both feet tentatively on the sill, trying to keep his balance whilst ignoring the demands from his survival instinct to know exactly what he thought he was doing. He wasn't sure he could explain it to himself if he tried. Instead, he watched his incoming target, and waited.

The creature came in low with a shriek, just a metre above the ground, which was perfect. Praying to the Deities that his timing would be right, Nicolas tensed his legs and launched himself from the window, reaching out with his hands.

'Craaaaaaaaaaap.' As his body flailed through open air he finally considered the possibilities if he missed. In truth, there was only one: a painful drop to the floor. The shadow approached, and their paths began to intersect.

It's going to be close.

The collision almost winded him as he scrabbled wildly for a handhold, threatening to roll right back off again. Finding a tuft of hair, he held onto it for dear life. Unsurprisingly, the creature didn't care for having someone fling itself onto its back, and it jerked wildly to the side. In that second, an arrow sailed through the sky, barely missing its neck. With an angry shriek, it rose back into the sky. The odd bouncing nature of its movement threatened to make his hearty breakfast rise up from his stomach as the wind whipped his face and the rhythmic beat of the large wings deafened him. Shuffling carefully, Nicolas manoeuvred himself into a more stable position, wrapping his arms around its neck and gripping its sides with his legs as hard as he could. The creature cried and bucked and swooped in an attempt to dislodge him, but he held firm with clean breeches. Just.

'Shhhh,' he whispered in its ear. 'Shhhh. It's okay. You're safe. You can stop now.'

This seemed to go on for hours as he was propelled through the sky, trying to ignore the blurred scenery, which went from a couple of buildings to miles of countryside and back again as his mount rose and fell at speed. He focused instead on the creature itself, whose bucking and jerking lessened with every minute until its flight levelled out. With a wince, he swallowed the sick in his mouth. He doubted throwing up on this beast would be good for their already tenuous relationship. Fortunately, the feeling of descent negated that issue. He didn't want to look down, so he shut his eyes tightly, all the time whispering in soothing tones. Eventually, a slight bump signalled that they were settled on the ground.

With all haste, but trying not to spook his mount, he slid down from it, only to end up in a crumpled heap on the floor when he discovered that his legs wouldn't hold him. Fear, and the jarring experience of his unplanned trip into the sky had turned his body to jelly. He was sure that his stomach was still up there somewhere, hanging around with the clouds. Somehow, he managed to keep his palm on the creature, stroking it softly to ensure that it stayed calm. At the moment it was compliant, but with something like *this*, that could change in an instant.

It was only now that he could take in the true horror of what stood before him. It had long green, reptilian wings with sharp, curved talons, just like you'd expect from a dragon. Slightly *less* expected was the body, which was…a cow. Just a regular, run-of-the-mill black-and-white cow, except four times the size and with certain alterations, such as random patches of green scales or the odd horn bursting from its skin. Thank the Deities he hadn't landed on any of those. Smoke trails danced lazily into the sky from its udders, of all things.

But the worst thing about it was easily its eyes, and the fear and pain he saw in them. The creature was in agony, knowing it shouldn't exist. It wanted to die. The movements of its head and the awkward way it still jerked from side to side while at rest spoke of deep inner pain.

How did this poor creature end up like this?

People began to creep from the buildings around them and gather at the edge of the village square. They were hesitant at first, knowing, like him, that the beast could turn at any moment, yet they came anyway, curiosity overcoming fear. Of course it noticed them, rearing a little at the newcomers, but Nicolas calmed it. The people gawked at the horrendous looking thing.

'What is it?' asked Billy Bagrad, owner of the tavern, as he stepped out in front of his establishment. The thickset man was tough as they come but still kept his distance from the cow.

'I...I don't know.' Nicolas knelt beside its head, continuing to soothe it. 'Some horrible amalgamation of cow and dragon.'

'How is that possible?' Gretta Hourox, the produce lady, asked.

'It's not,' he said, more to himself than anyone. 'You can see just by looking at it that it's not supposed to be.'

The creature seemed to understand what Nicolas had said and turned its large bovine head towards him. Those eyes. They told him *exactly* what it wanted. Automatically, he reached for the knife in his boot. He didn't want to kill the frightened animal—it felt wrong—but letting it suffer would be a crueller fate. He also couldn't risk it going crazy again and finishing the job of burning down the whole square.

Slowly, he brought the knife up, tears welling in his eyes. The creature looked at him before turning its head to present its neck. The blade shook in Nicolas's hand. 'I'm so sorry this happened to you.'

Placing the tip of the blade against the bovine skin, he took a deep breath and put pressure on the hilt of the knife. There was resistance, but the blade penetrated flesh.

The worst part about the whole thing was that it didn't make a sound. Flesh cut and blood flowed, but it didn't cry out. It simply stared at him for a moment, making its unspoken thanks more than clear, showing its relief at not having to exist anymore. After a few moments, the creature's knees trembled and it collapsed to the floor, dead. A single tear rolled down its cheek, but it finally looked at peace.

Nicolas's hand was covered in blood. Quickly and furiously, he cleaned it on a patch of nearby grass before standing properly.

Why did I have to do such a terrible thing?

The sound of hissing drew his attention back to the creature, just in time to see the beast dissolve like butter in an oven. Its solid form disintegrated until it was no more than a large green puddle on the floor. It was only then he realised the size of the crowd that had gathered around him.

All the faces wore variations of the same look: fear and awe. Billy Bagrad clapped fiercely, his meaty hands slapping together and resonating through the silence of the square. Soon a spattering of claps joined in, which gathered pace and mass until it became a crescendo of cheers and whoops, people asking each other *'Did you see what he did?'* There was even some chanting of his name. He didn't know how to react so defaulted into standing there sheepishly. Fortunately for his social awkwardness, there were more pressing matters for the villagers to attend to, such as the multiple fires. The crowd dispersed quickly to tackle the blazes. As much as Nicolas hoped they'd forget about this, he knew they wouldn't.

Holding the knife, he looked from the blade to the pile of bubbling ooze that had once been the creature. Some kind of dark magic had been involved in this. How else could something like *that* come into being? The beast had meant no real harm; it had been scared and in pain. Hopefully no one had paid for that with their life.

'By the Deities, lad,' Billy Bagrad bellowed from beneath his walrus-like moustache, slapping him on the back as he ran by carrying a bucket of water. 'That was some display of balls. Never seen anything like it.'

Even if he'd had a reply, at that moment his parents ambushed him from the side. He'd survived a ride into the sky on a cow-dragon hybrid, but he wasn't sure he'd be so lucky against the tightness of their embrace. When it ended, his mother patted him down, seemingly searching for wounds, but there were none—being shaken and nauseous was the worst he'd gotten from the encounter. He'd been lucky, stupidly lucky, but both his parents' faces gave off pride like the sun gives off light.

'Take a moment.' His father obviously saw how shaken he was.

It was sage advice. He needed to come to terms with what had just happened. After sitting him carefully on the grass, his parents reluctantly moved away to help fight the fires.

His mind was swirling.

Did I actually jump on the back of a flying creature?

That didn't sound like him. It sounded more like a certain spirit he'd been acquainted with, who would've been telling him a hundred stories of dragons *he'd* slain, though

Nicolas was willing to bet none of them had been part cow. Breathing deeply, he tried to fight off the panic building inside him. It was over. Everyone was safe.

Calm down.

'Upstaged again.' The voice brought him back to the present, and he looked up. Standing beside him was Potter, bow in hand and half-smile on his face.

'I had him, you know.' Potter's smile was fixed. 'My arrow would've done for that creature. Just didn't reckon on you diving from a window like a crazy man to throw my shot off.'

'Sorry.' Nicolas shrugged. 'I didn't know. Next time a cow-dragon attacks the square, we'll coordinate better. In fact, you can definitely take the first shot at it. You can take all of them, if you like.'

Potter sat down next to him and sighed. 'Well, you can make it up to me.' His friend looked at the still-bubbling remains of the creature.

'How's that?' Nicolas asked with a raised eyebrow.

'Tavern, tonight.' Potter smiled. 'They'll be singing songs about you and buying you drinks all night. Least you can do is let me get a bit of reflected glory, since you stole mine.'

Nicolas laughed aloud. Several of the townspeople running around with buckets of water looked at him sharply, obviously disapproving of laughter while fires still raged.

'It's a deal,' he said, offering Potter his hand. 'I'll do you one better. I'll tell everyone that stupid stunt was your idea.'

'That'll do nicely.' Potter grinned.

Chapter 3

Potter hadn't been wrong about either the song singing or drink buying. The saving of the village square was a cause for celebration, and naturally the person who'd *'slayed the beast'* was the focal point of that, much to Nicolas's dismay. All he'd done was put a creature out of its pain, and only because it'd allowed him to do so. Sipping his ale, so as not to rouse the nausea that hadn't left his stomach since the incident, he couldn't help but glance at his hand. Really, he knew there was no blood left on it. He'd cleaned both of his hands thoroughly and obsessively, several times since. Yet some trick of his mind made his eyes see the blood as if it were still fresh. Quickly he put down the tankard and moved his hand out of his line of sight.

Fortunately, the blood on his hands had been the only blood of the day. It was a miracle no one had been killed, though he guessed no one had been hurt, save the odd minor burn, because the creature hadn't wanted to hurt anyone. *Maybe all the chaos it created was just to give someone cause to kill it?* The worst the people had dealt with was the stress of the encounter and the exhaustion of having to fight the fire. If not for those, all of Hablock would've probably been in the tavern tonight.

In the spirit of celebration, everyone around him drank, danced and sang, as he continued to fake smiles whilst listening to the compliments of those who wanted to heap praise on their *'saviour'*. He exchanged pleasantries and gave thanks for the kind words, but it was all lip service. He couldn't stop turning it over in his mind. *Where had the creature come from? How had it come to be?* Hablock was a safe area and had been so for…ever—and now they're attacked by a *cow-dragon,* of all things. Everyone else was just so pleased it was dead that they didn't need to know anything else about it. Not too long ago, he would've been of the same opinion, but now he'd seen things that had taught him to take nothing for granted.

His money was no good in the tavern that night, others insisting on buying him drinks, whether he wanted them or not. Not being a big drinker, he instead slipped unwanted drinks to Potter, who was more than happy to have free ale. Though the insistence that he repeated the tale of what'd happened again and again was beginning to make his throat raw, so the occasional beverage was necessary. He made a big deal of Potter's involvement, trying his best to make it sound like a team effort, which, judging by the beaming smile when that part of the story came up, pleased his friend no end. People nodded along amiably to those parts of the story, but he could tell most didn't buy it.

Darkness was beginning to settle into the sky when he made to leave the tavern. Groans of protest greeted his decision, but he held firm, citing his exhaustion from the encounter. In his absence, he directed people towards Potter, who was more than happy to continue telling the story for free drinks. As he looked back from the tavern door, several of the young ladies who'd been making awestruck eyes at him all night had already turned their attentions to his friend, much to Potter's unsubtle delight.

In truth, he wasn't tired at all, though he ought to have been dead on his feet by now. He was leaving because being the centre of attention in such a crowd was more exhausting than his stunt today. Also, he wanted to properly ponder what had occurred without off-key singing distracting him. Mainly, though, he didn't want to be out after the sun went down. Walking through the arch that marked the edge of the village square, he anxiously eyed how low the sun was. It was later than he'd believed.

Walking in the centre of the road, he cursed as darkness consumed the scenery around him. He cast wary glances at the shadowy foliage, looking for any glint of a fang or other sign of danger. There almost certainly wasn't anything around him worse than the things he conjured in his mind, but still he took a moment to remove the knife from his boot and conceal it in his sleeve before going back to his musings.

'It must be magic,' he muttered to himself as he thought of the unnatural creature.

It was the only answer. He could see no situation in which a cow and a dragon would mate, and from the way the creature had moved, it hadn't known how to use its wings—meaning they were new.

So magic then.

He sighed. The only person in the region who knew anything about magic was the Oracle. Beloved by the people of Hablock and shrouded in mystery, he'd turned out to be a cantankerous old man who didn't care for visitors and lived in a squalor Nicolas wanted to stay well clear of, if at all possible. But he needed answers before another strange creature attacked the village.

What if the next one's less inclined to let me euthanise it?

'I won't know if he has any answers until I check.' Nicolas sighed again, rallying himself to visit the Oracle the first chance he got. He couldn't put it off or let his dislike of the man dissuade him from going. This was urgent. There was a feeling in his gut, more than simple paranoia, telling him this wouldn't be a one-time occurrence.

Snap.

He stopped dead in his tracks. Alert, he scanned the side of the road from which the noise had come. Even straining his eyes, he could see nothing in the darkness save the shadowed branches and leaves that framed it. He shook himself.

It was just an animal.

Preferably a small one. Yet he went on his way at a slightly faster pace, praying that the eyes he felt on him were just his imagination.

Random noises followed him down the road: a rustling of leaves here, a snapping twig there. Suddenly, the road felt both closed in and endless. In his mind, he saw clearly the *rabbit-trolls* or *horse-spiders* hunting him to avenge their fallen friend. Normally, he would've laughed at such images, but he'd killed a cow-dragon today.

The frequency of the sounds matched the pace at which he moved down the road.

Dammit, that's no coincidence.

He was in a tight spot. Home was still too far away to run without the possibility of being caught and he didn't want to lead whatever was pursuing him to his parents. That left one option—one he didn't relish because of the danger involved. But if it was the only choice then so be it.

Spinning on his heel, he let the knife slide from his sleeve into his hand, almost missing the catch as his hand trembled. Holding the blade in front of him, he tried his best to scowl fiercely, if he could pull off such a look?

'Okay.' He knew that his attempt to deepen his voice to sound intimidating was a failure from the outset. 'Whoever, or whatever, you are, show yourself. If you're here looking for trouble, I have some for you.'

Brandishing the knife, he waited. There was no sign of anything now. Whatever was after him had stopped.

What's it waiting for?

How long could he hold his faux-intimidating posture? Already the knife was starting to shake slightly. Looking down at his hand, something odd caught his attention. Though it was dark, he could vaguely make out his shadow, cast by a dim light behind him. He swung around, knife ready.

'Boo.'

Crying out, he stumbled back a few steps, dropping the knife and nearly falling, much to the amusement of the figure who'd been standing behind him.

Who was...

Suddenly he recognised the familiar face. 'You dick.' Nicolas put his hand on his chest just to be sure his heart stayed in there. It was pounding wildly.

The incandescent form of Auron wore a broad grin on his face. Nicolas had never known Auron of Tellmark—better known as *The Dawnblade*—in life, meeting him only shortly after he'd been murdered. Nicolas's moment of confusion had come from a very obvious change to his companion. When they'd last been together Auron's spiritual form had been made up of swirling bright blue mist. Now, he was more like a hazy reflection of the man he'd been in life, there, yet at the same time, not. An aura of light surrounded him but he was much easier to look at directly, thankfully. Auron's bright white eyes were still full of life for someone so dead.

'Well, hello to you too, kid,' Auron said, not losing his smile, 'Can I just say that your tough talk needs a lot of work. *If you're here looking for trouble, I have some for you.* Really?'

'I thought I'd graduated from being called *kid*?'

'Yeah, well.' The spirit shrugged. 'That was a while ago now, and I need to see if you still have the stuff. I am yet to be impressed, especially by you dropping your knife. Good job I wasn't dangerous.'

'No, just annoying.' Was it the release of tension, or pleasure to see his old companion that made him laugh aloud? Either way, Auron was quite happy to join in. There was a definite relief that something hadn't been chasing him to....

'Hang on.' A thought had occurred to him. 'How were you making all that rustling? You can't touch things.'

Auron's smile broadened with more than a touch of smugness to it. He blatantly knew something Nicolas didn't.

'Well met, Nicolas Percival Carnegie,' said a deep, familiar voice behind him.

Turning, he smiled broadly. This was becoming quite the reunion. 'Garaz!' he cried happily.

The large orc stood as if he'd been there all along, proud and upright. He, too, was just as Nicolas remembered him, wise face upon a muscular green body surrounded by his tattered red cape. He offered Nicolas a bow.

Oh, he's let his hair grow out. It suits him.

As Garaz rose, he took the orc's hand and shook it happily.

'Is Shift with you too?' His eyes darted around, looking for the third companion from their previous adventure. Spooking him like this would be just their sort of idea.

'It's just us, kid.' There was a slight sadness in Auron's response.

That was a shame. Still, this was a good moment, despite the way they'd snuck up on him.

'So, I take it you two being here the day my village is attacked by a cow-dragon isn't a coincidence?' It was more of a statement than a question.

'Astute observation,' Garaz replied with a smile.

'We were right behind the thing when it got to your village,' Auron said. 'By the time we got there, you had it well in hand... Well done, by the way, mighty tamer of cow-dragons. Throwing yourself out the window was pretty impressive, even if you looked like you were about to cry whilst doing it. Need to work on your action face, kid.'

He ignored the jibe. It'd worked out well enough without the added theatrics Auron was so fond of.

'If you were there, why didn't you—'

'Everyone was in a heightened state, as is only natural,' Garaz interrupted. 'And an orc shaman turning up just after a strange creature attacked the village might have led to some very incorrect assumptions.'

The orc wasn't wrong. The people of Hablock would've definitely jumped to the wrong conclusions had they seen Garaz just after the attack. He would've done the same had he not known the orc personally. How was there a time he was so narrow minded?

Nicolas looked back at Auron, a question popping into his mind. 'How are you still here? We finished your unfinished business. I thought you said you felt yourself being called to the other side?'

The group had believed that avenging Auron's murder at the hand of hero-turned-mercenary Silva Destrone would free his spirit to the next life. The overly armoured mercenary had drowned, thanks to Nicolas causing her partner Grimmark Bear Slayer to knock her off a bridge with his oversized hammer.

'I honestly don't know, kid.' Auron looked awkward. Maybe a little sad too. 'I do know we have a lot to catch up on.'

****

Aside from the visible draining of colour from his mother's face when she opened the door, he thought his parents handled him returning home with an orc in tow very well, certainly a lot better than most around these parts would. There was a consequence of this action however, one he wasn't fond of at all. It was finally time to tell his parents what'd *really* happened when he'd gone to deliver the message.

Their faces gave away nothing as he recounted the events to them. Any sort of reaction would've been nice so he knew what to expect when he was done. But no, neutral faces stared back at him as he spoke of necromancers, mercenaries and vampires. He'd half an idea to sugar coat the whole thing, downplaying the more *perilous* parts of the journey. But once he'd begun it all came flooding out regardless, as if he needed to say it all aloud. Not necessarily to his parents, but to simply help him come to terms with it himself.

But did they believe him, or did they think he'd gone mad? It *was* a crazy tale. Why were they giving nothing away?

'…and then I returned home.' He sat back and exhaled with satisfaction, surprisingly relieved to not have it bottled up inside him any longer. Now to see how is parents took it.

'Oh.' His mother looked as if she was having trouble taking it all in. He could hardly begrudge her that.

'So, you saved the world.' Was his father asking him or trying to explain it to himself?

'Well, really only the kingdom, actually.' He found that he couldn't meet their eyes. He should've told them this a lot sooner. 'But it may have spread to the rest of the world, so I suppose technically, yes. But then King Eldric was the one who killed the necromancer so, not really. Let's just say that I helped a bit and leave it there.'

'Oh,' his mother said again.

'When we heard of the disaster in Yarringsburg, there was no mention of you.' There was no suspicion or accusation in his father's tone; he simply wanted clarification. 'All we heard was that King Eldric broke the necromancer's spell and saved the city.'

'He did, but we were there. We were edited out of the official story.' *Thankfully.* 'Which was fine with me because I just wanted to come home.'

'I can assure you that your son was very brave,' Garaz offered from the other end of the table, where he'd been quietly observing until now. 'He showed true courage against things he had no experience with.'

His mother cast a wary glance at Garaz, who for his part, took it in stride. He'd told Nicolas before that he was unfortunately used to it, even from his days at the Academy of Magic.

'And the ghost of *The Dawnblade* is here too?' His father looked around the room warily.

'He prefers to be called a *spirit*,' Nicolas corrected.

'Damn right I do.' Auron sniffed.

'I didn't realise there was a difference.'

Nicolas wasn't sure there was, but his friend seemed to think being a ghost was a bit common, or beneath him, or something, so he respected his wishes. It was easier that way.

'Hello, by the way.' Auron waved heartily, knowing they couldn't see him.

Now they were starting to look at him as if he was crazy. That was understandable. He was insisting a person was there that they could neither see nor hear. Not knowing how he could prove it, he looked to Auron for help.

The spirit nodded in understanding. Leaning forward, Auron extended a single finger. With what appeared to be great concentration and effort, he pressed the finger against one of the cups on the table, which shook slightly.

His mother stifled a cry, hands to her mouth.

'You can touch things now?' Nicolas cried.

'Little things,' Auron confirmed, with no modesty whatsoever. 'It takes a lot out of me, but Garaz and I have been working on it.'

His mother began to pale further. If she kept this up she'd be mistaken for a ghost herself. His father must've noticed it, too, because he rose from his chair. 'I'm going to take your mother to get some fresh air,' he said calmly. 'This is a lot to take in, and I'm sure you need to catch up with your friends.'

His mother attempted to wave off his father's helping hand, but when she wobbled a little trying to stand up, she relented and took his arm. As his father led her towards the door, they stopped beside him, looking at him as if he were someone new.

Is that a good or bad thing? He swallowed hard.

'I *knew* you were a hero.' His mother embraced him tightly, the gesture saying a lot more than words could easily convey. Returning the hug, he fought back the tears that welled in his eyes, a weight falling from his shoulders. Though he'd still never use *that* word to describe himself.

A hand touched his shoulder. From beyond his mother's bushy hair he saw his father staring at him with pride. 'Well done.' Seeing his father this emotional made him uneasy, the tears threatened to make their presence known again. 'We're both so proud of you.'

As his mother let him go, she brushed his arms, as if trying to remove creases from his sleeves. 'You talk to your friends. We will be outside. I really do need that fresh air.' She took his father's arm again and allowed him to lead her to the door.

After the door closed behind them, Garaz looked at him seriously. 'We do have much to discuss.'

'Like, how are you still here?' He indicated Auron, who seemed to be exploring the room, trying to poke things and make them wobble.

'No idea, kid.' Auron seemed more intent on his task than answering questions. 'When we finished up in Yarringsburg, I thought I could feel the pull. I thought that I was due to go to the other side for sure. The next day the feeling was gone.' The spirit shook his head before gesturing indignantly to his new form. 'Not only am I still here, I appear to be settling in.'

It's an improvement. Nicolas wasn't about to say that aloud.

'But Silva is dead, and so is Grimmark. And the necromancer.' The memories those names evoked made him shiver slightly.

All Auron could offer him by way of response was a shrug.

'So, you two have been travelling together ever since?'

'I had concerns about the events in Yarringsburg,' Garaz replied solemnly. 'I wanted to know where the spell and the crystal the necromancer used to channel it had come from and who else might know of it.'

'He did mention that he had friends during his self-indulgent monologue,' Auron interrupted.

'Indeed,' Garaz agreed. 'So I decided to seek out any leads to find these associates of his and whatever else they may possess. That magic was serious, and such things cannot be allowed in the hands of crazy men like Avus Arex again.'

'And...?'

'Nothing,' Garaz admitted. 'Yarringsburg was in too bad a state to get any real information, and no one wanted to talk to an orc. We looked beyond the city and explored the area, hoping for some kind of clue. We even revisited the fort and the Crag, but nothing.'

The city of Yarringsburg had suffered for the defeat of the necromancer, Avus Arex. The spontaneous combustion of hundreds of vampires at the same time had caused a raging fire that cut through the city. It would take years to bring it back to its former glory.

'Eventually, we heard of strange events in Sarus,' Auron explained.

'The neighbouring kingdom?'

'You actually know the name of the neighbouring kingdom?' the spirit commented glibly, mocking Nicolas's general lack of knowledge of anything outside Hablock. 'But yeah, there were whispers of odd events, potential magic misuse. Nothing clear, but it was enough. We were on our way there when a cow-dragon creature flew overhead, burning up the countryside. Thought it best to follow it before it hurt anyone. You got to it first.'

'That creature was unnatural.' He tried not to remember the look in its eyes. 'It wanted to die.'

'I could not get close enough to make a full assessment, but it was definitely magic born,' Garaz confirmed with a nod.

'Do you think it's related to what happened in Yarringsburg?'

The large orc shrugged, an almost comical motion for a body so muscular. 'I cannot say.' The fact seemed to irk Garaz. 'But whatever made it bears investigating. Hablock was lucky to have you to defend it. If another one of those things or something similar made it to an undefended village, many innocent people may be hurt. We need to track it back to its source and ensure that nothing else comes of this.'

We? Oh crap.

'You want me to go with you?' The room began to feel very enclosed.

Garaz nodded.

The room shrank again.

'I...I can't.' He needed a decent excuse, quickly. 'I'm needed here. I have work to do, and responsibilities. And I'm not exactly handy in these situations. Surely there's someone more suitable.'

His former companions looked bemused.

'We need you, kid,' Auron stood next to Garaz. 'All I'm good for is wobbling the odd vase, and Garaz needs better backup than that. You have experience and while not a natural to it, you're better than you give yourself credit for. For example, you jump out of windows onto the backs of flying magical creatures that shoot fire. That'll come in handy.'

The orc nodded in agreement.

Are they mad?

He wasn't fit for this. He was barely over his last *adventure*. Yet there was a surprising nagging part of him that yearned to go, to do good again. However, the part of him riddled with fear and a desire to continue living was much louder. He started making a mental list of well thought out reasons why he couldn't go, but before he could launch into it, Garaz cut him off.

'People could get hurt.'

Inwardly, he cursed. That was the one thing he hadn't wanted to hear, because it was the one thing he couldn't ignore. At what point in his life had he suddenly started walking toward danger the minute he knew people might be harmed? It was completely contrary to his view of himself. *And yet I'm going.* Which meant another awkward talk with his parents. He could imagine his mother pleading with him to stay, his father forbidding him to walk into unknown peril. He wasn't looking forward to it.

Rising from the table, he prepared himself for that conversation, as much as one could. Turning, he walked to the door. Opening the only thing separating the warm house from the cold night air beyond, he nearly jumped when he found both his parents standing directly behind the door. Having intended to talk to them outside, it seemed strange now to have that conversation on the doorstep, plus it was bloody cold, so he gestured them into the house. They sat quietly back at the table, his father's arm around his mother's shoulder. Again, they were frustratingly unreadable. He'd known them all his life, you'd think he'd have an idea what they were thinking by now.

Here we go then.

He opened his mouth to speak.

'So, people could get hurt then?'

He closed his mouth, surprised by his father's sudden interruption. Nodding, he found he'd lost the fortitude to speak.

'It's decided then,' his mother said firmly. 'You can help, they need your help, so go help.'

That wasn't right. They weren't supposed to be telling him to go. His parents were meant to plead with him to stay, to lay out the potential dangers that awaited him, to forbid it even. Part of him wanted a reason to stay. Yet he knew he would've argued against it because he needed to go. But at the same time…Deities, he was so confused.

'What about the bakery?' he asked finally.

His father let out a sudden and hearty laugh. 'I think I can cope without an apprentice who's constantly late and quite lackadaisical.'

And there it was. The last obstacle gone. The part of him that had wished they'd forbid it so he must stay home went to sulk in the corner of his mind. It was done. He'd join the quest. He tapped his hand on the table to drive away the tremor in it.

'And your companions will do their utmost to keep you safe?' The question was directed at him, but his mother's gaze was firmly on Garaz.

'I will do everything in my power,' Garaz vowed solemnly with a bow.

'Then it's settled.' There was note of finality in his mother's voice.

'Adventure time.' Auron looked almost giddy.

'Just one more,' he added cautiously.

'Just one more, he says.' Auron smiled. 'But look at the glow on him. He can't wait.'

Glow? How could he be glowing when he was about to throw himself out into the world again, whilst the horrors of what he'd seen the last time still haunted him?

But he'd bested those things. He'd helped save the kingdom. He'd saved his village. And he'd have Garaz and Auron with him. The ember of excitement burned brighter as he fed it reassurances. His doubts and fears moved to the dark corners of his mind, chased away by the flames of anticipation. Yeah, it was adventure time.

Chapter 4

The next morning, the scene in Nicolas's home echoed the one from the night before, with Garaz, his parents, and himself sitting around the dinner table while Auron prowled the room, interesting himself in attempting to poke objects and make them wiggle, with varied success. This time, however, there was a large breakfast arranged on the table, his mother wanting to be sure that the travellers departed on full stomachs. There were also packed travel bags by the front door, next to which rested a sword with a rising sun carved into the hilt.

'I owe you an apology.' His mother had been eyeing Garaz since she sat down, obviously choosing her moment.

Garaz put his cup down on the table. 'I do not understand?'

'There is a certain stereotype attached to your ki…to orcs,' she admitted sheepishly. 'And—'

Garaz raised his large, clawed hand gently. 'Please, Madam.' The orc's tone was soft and his expression amiable. 'I am aware of the reputation of my people, which I am sad to say is well earned. There is a lot of blood between our two peoples. Indeed, there is a lot of blood between my people and every other people in Etherius. It is a reaction I am used to. I take no offence.'

'Thank you.' His mother nodded, her bushy hair bouncing with the bobs of her head 'You've taught me a lesson on judging I won't soon forget.'

Garaz chuckled. 'I am glad to have been of service.'

If only the people of Yarringsburg had been so tolerant after the orc had helped save their city. But no, Nicolas had seen the suspicion with which the humans of the city had treated any non-human resident once the fires had been quenched. He still couldn't get his head around why. The necromancer had been human and the vampires had been human, once. The people of Yarringsburg's definition of what did and didn't count as human was confusing and pretty ignorant.

'If you head south, you should reach the main road in a few hours,' his father told him confidently, most likely having poured over maps most of the night to learn this. 'Once you're on the main road, you'll reach the border by evening. There's a tavern close by, the Pixie...something. You can stay there overnight. Maybe even find out some information.'

'The way he's talking and with your mother preparing your bags, I half expect them to be coming with us.' Auron chuckled as he flicked at a candle, his finger passing through it to his obvious frustration.

'Thank goodness they can't hear you say that. They may like the idea.' When he turned, both his parents were looking at him strangely. He pointed in Auron's general direction and shrugged.

'Hopefully whatever this is will be easy to track down,' Garaz said thoughtfully. 'It is hardly being discreet.'

'Always worry about the ones that don't feel the need to be discreet, as they tend to be dangerous.' Auron counselled absentmindedly. 'But sometimes they're not. There was a goblin king called Snot summit-or-other. Got himself a magic sword that could pierce any armour and made a lot of noise about being the next big deal, undefeatable *blah, blah, blah.* Trouble was, the sword was twice the size of him. Little idiot couldn't even lift the thing, let alone swing it. He was still huffing and puffing trying to raise it from the ground when I ran him through. Not one of my more glorious victories. Still, I think someone wrote a poem about it or something. I'm sure there was some artistic embellishment from the bard.'

'What a fascinating anecdote that we don't really learn anything from.' Nicolas wasn't sure if he'd missed Auron's stories or not.

'Don't try to pick up a sword too heavy for you.' Auron pointed at him and winked.

Nicolas glanced towards the door at the *Dawn Blade*, resting in its sheath. During his previous adventure, he hadn't had a great deal of success with the legendary sword. He'd managed to behead a single vampire, yes, but mostly he'd stood around holding it, not sure what he was supposed to be doing, or dropping it. It wasn't a start that inspired confidence.

It was strange though. Once he'd returned home he'd planned on never needing the sword again. He was unsure why he'd even brought it with him. And yet, every so often he'd find himself taking it to a quiet spot where he could practise swinging it. Perhaps it was the need to protect himself from the things he'd seen, or maybe he somehow knew this day would come.

Maybe I'm an Oracle? No, he was too clean for that.

But taking the sword came with implications. That at some point he may need to use it in a life or death situation – which is really the only kind of situation in which you'd need a sword. Could he do it? Could he harm another? Maybe the blade wouldn't be needed. Maybe this could be solved simply, without fighting or exposing himself to danger.

Wow, you're trying hard to delude yourself.

Of course there would be danger. He just hoped he could face it, for all their sakes.

'You'll be fine.' His father's morale boost was appreciated, even if he wasn't so convinced. It's strange how parents can read your minds sometimes.

'Our village could be in peril, son,' his father continued. 'And like it or not, you have experience in these matters. I guess you're chosen again, if you care to call it that.'

I don't.

'Kid, you've fought vampires and helped save the world once.' Auron made it sound so breezy. 'Anything after that should be simple stuff.'

'You will probably not even need to draw your sword.' Garaz had the same easy confidence.

As uncertain as he was, he allowed the confidence of those around him to bolster his own. He'd stood against an army of the undead. What were some odd creatures compared to that? He could do this. A quiet tapping drew his focus away from his growing excitement. On the table his hand was trembling slightly. He put it on his lap and forced it still.

****

An hour later, the company of three were enroute to their destination and whatever awaited them. Goodbyes had taken longer than he'd expected, to the point he'd been unsure his mother was ever going to let him go, stalling him with bag checks and last-minute advice. It wasn't like the last time, when he'd left to deliver the ill-fated message, because this time, danger was almost certain, but neither of them spoke about it openly. His parents had stayed by the door of the house until Nicolas could no longer see them when he looked back. Probably long after that, too.

The air was crisp and fresh, and he felt ready to go out and see more of the world. Deciding that the straightest possible line to their destination was the best, the group stuck to the main roads, which were quiet save for one wagon whose driver gawked so hard at Garaz that he nearly drove it right off the road. Beyond that, it was just golden fields and the occasional livestock and birds.

'So, there I was...' Auron began on his third story of the trip.

'I see he hasn't run out of anecdotes,' he commented quietly to Garaz as the spirit recounted his deeds with gusto.

The orc sighed. 'He has certainly led an eventful life.'

'What happened with Shift?' It was a question he'd been meaning to ask, but for some reason he'd been putting it off. Did the answer worry him?

'They left Yarringsburg the day we did, headed south,' Garaz answered. 'I know not where exactly. I asked and got a sarcastic response.'

That sounded about right. Still, though...south, the same way they were headed. He found himself hoping they would cross paths, though there were a lot of things south of Yarringsburg, so it was unlikely.

'They said they were going to see some old friends about work.' Auron glared at the pair irritably for not paying attention to his story. 'I'm assuming that means stealing stuff.'

Shift used their unique gift, the ability to change form, as a way to relieve people of their goods and gold. It seemed to him they could've used it for so much more, but it wasn't his choice to make.

'We asked them to travel with us, but they declined,' Garaz added. 'They are *'not one for prancing around the countryside doing quests,'* apparently.'

Thinking of Shift caused memories to stir. In keeping with how his brain usually worked, the memories it brought forth were all those in which he'd embarrassed himself in front of them. Too many for such a short acquaintance. Maybe a reunion wouldn't be such a good idea, after all.

And yet, look how natural it was to have the three of them together again. Once upon a time, the idea of him travelling with an orc and a spirit would've been laughed off as ridiculous. But here he was, walking into who knew what with a sword on his hip and two people he barely knew. He couldn't deny the bond that facing danger together had created, and the confidence that came from having them at his side again.

'You will be happy to know I have expanded my magical repertoire somewhat, Nicolas,' Garaz said matter-of-factly as he stared at the clouds above them.

Previously, Garaz had taught him that magic was much less of an all-encompassing term than he'd been led to believe. It turned out most wizards only had enough power to learn a single magical discipline, maybe knowing a thing or two about another. Garaz had chosen to become a healer, which had come in quite handy considering the various injuries he'd sustained during their last adventure.

'I can now create a respectable looking fireball.' The pride in the orc's voice was well earned. He wished he could throw fireballs.

'A bit at odds with his healer philosophy, but I have no doubt we'll find a use for it.' Auron's smile suggested this was an ongoing jest between the two.

'Indeed.' Garaz rolled his yellow eyes, confirming his suspicion. 'If my time with you has taught me anything, it is that there are situations which require an unfortunate measure of violence, as much as I detest it. If only the hordes of the undead yielded to a well thought out argument.'

'Yes, he is a bad influence.' Nicolas's grin warmed his face.

Auron feigned hurt. 'You could use a bad influence.' The spirit smiled back. 'Bring out your inner *Nick Carnage*.'

Now it was his turn to eyeroll. The last time they'd travelled together, Auron had suggested he create a heroic identity for himself, with *Nick Carnage* as a perfect hero name. He didn't care for it. It irked him when people got his name wrong. He was Nicolas Percival Carnegie. That was his given name, and he was quite happy with it. Funny, though, that the name had been first brought up by Potter in the fateful wagon ride to the inaptly named *Tower of the Oracle*. Was that moniker dogging him somehow? A paranoid fellow, like himself, could make up all sorts of nonsense about *chosen ones* and *destiny*. But he wasn't going to. *Nick Carnage* wasn't who he was or who he was going to become.

With all the easy camaraderie it seemed as if the tavern had only been up the road. Time passes quickly in good company. Yet it was already late in the afternoon, the air cooling and the sky threatening to darken any time now. From the outside, the tavern had a cosy look to it. The border of stone masonry gave way to thick, deep brown timber atop which sat a thatched roof. Smoke idly climbed from the tavern's chimney, promising heat and maybe a warm meal. From the look of the several horses tied to the post in front of the attached stable, they seemed busy. Strange there was no sound of revelry as they approached. It must still be early for it.

The Pixie's Wing. The well-weathered sign was difficult to read. 'What an odd thing to name a place after.'

'Taverns all have daft names,' Auron stated. 'Who knows why? Maybe they think it'll ward off evil spirits?'

'Do you think that would work?'

'If I were an evil spirit, I wouldn't want to be caught undead in a place called *The Pixie's Wing*.' Auron chuckled.

'Good thing you're just an irritating spirit then.'

'Ha, ha, kid.' Auron gave him a mock-glare.

'So, we are staying here tonight?' Garaz probably wished to press on with things rather than dally outside all night exchanging barbs.

'Yeah,' Auron replied. 'We'll cross into Sarus in the morning when you're fresh. I do want to pick up any information we can while we're here, however. That's up to you, kid.'

'Me?'

'Yeah,' the spirit replied as if it were the most obvious thing in the world. 'I don't want to take a chance that this place is less than amenable to orcs, which is very likely, so you do the talking. I'll tell you what to say, you say it, right?'

He knew how to ask questions. 'Why can't I just talk for myself?'

'Because you aren't exactly...'

'Worldly,' Garaz finished Auron's thought, probably more politely.

Cheeky pair of troll droppings. They weren't entirely wrong, but it still stung.

'Fine.'

It turned out Auron's fears about the tavern were unfounded. Once they entered, no one seemed to bat an eye at Garaz. The tavern obviously catered to various travellers, as evidenced by the pair of dwarves by the hearth and the kascat serving maid. In the corner sat a man in green, patched clothing talking to several others. Good clothing for blending into forests, but not so much in here.

The air in the tavern was close, and beads of sweat immediately broke out on his forehead. It didn't seem necessarily busy, but the air was smoky and thick. The atmosphere was muted, everyone engrossed in their hushed conversations.

Good luck getting information out of any of this lot.

'You still do the talking,' Auron declared as they approached the bar. 'You need the practise.'

Behind the bar, a slender man in an apron that had once been white, with hair that was very white, wiped down a tankard with an old rag. Despite the fact that he worked in a place frequented by the public, everything about this man suggested that he didn't like dealing with people. Maybe it was the way his beady eyes sized them up as they entered, looking at them like they were sources of profit rather than welcome customers.

'What'll it be, gentlemen?' His voice was unenthused.

Auron looked the barman over with distaste. 'Kid, lean on the bar and repeat after me...'

Nicolas leant forward, intending to look casual but completely overthinking it and ending up in an awkward position that he couldn't change without looking more of a fool. Auron audibly sighed. Then the spirit began to speak, and he repeated his words as if they were his own.

'We're looking for some food, drink, and a room for the night.'

'We have those things, if you have coin.' The barman pointed to a slate on the wall that listed the prices for rooms. 'We have a hot stew, and I can get you some ales. Anything else?'

Nicolas slid some coin across the counter as Auron instructed then added two more in a very particular manner. The barman looked at the coins then back at Nicolas with a quizzical eyebrow raised.

'Information.' He tried to say it casually. Auron's look suggested that he'd failed.

The barman took the coins and slid them into his apron. 'About?'

'Anything strange happening in Sarus lately.'

The barman picked his teeth with his tongue and looked off at the corner of the room for a second before answering. 'Hard to say.' Nicolas nearly gagged as the man spat in the tankard then wiped it. He hoped he wasn't drinking out of that one. 'They've shut the border, which is pretty strange itself. Usually do a decent trade from the soldiers on the border post, but the last few days, nothing. No one in or out.'

'That all?'

'All I know, unless you want me to make some stuff up,' the barman replied testily. 'No one's coming out so there's no one to tell me anything.'

'Thanks.'

Reaching behind him, the barman took a key from several hanging on a wall and handed it to Nicolas. 'I take it you want two beds, not one?' There was a cheeky glance in Garaz's direction as he let the key dangle in the air for a second.

Nicolas took the key. Yeah, this guy was a bit of a jackass.

'Go get settled, and I'll send the girl up with the beer and stew.' Judging from the barman's smile, they were being dismissed. He was quite comfortable with that.

Thanking the barman, he followed the others to the stairs in the corner of the bar. While Garaz and Auron made their way up the stairs, a sudden feeling of being watched made him stop. Attempting to be casual, he scanned the tavern to see if he was correct. He was. Near the door, a woman sat eyeing him intently. She was clearly a warrior, with slicked back, shoulder-length blond hair and an intent and serious face. After making eye contact with her, he looked away awkwardly, blood rushing to his cheeks. She was very attractive, in a harsh sort of way. Nicolas steeled himself to look back and give the woman what he hoped would be a dashing smile. However, when he did, the look she was giving him was one a predator would offer its prey, so he quickly followed his companions up the stairs before the predator had a chance to strike.

Auron waited for him testily atop the landing. 'Hurry up, kid. You've got the key.'

What did it matter to him? He could just walk through the bloody door anyway.

Chapter 5

Judging by the state of the room, Nicolas quickly managed his expectations with regards to the food to come. He hadn't expected grandeur of any sort, but had hoped for a decent space and a comfortable bed, only to be disappointed on both counts. When the food did arrive it was lukewarm and bland, but at least the cold piss ale was the perfect accompaniment. He wasn't sure of the going rate for room and board, but had an idea that this place wasn't worth what he'd paid. Though he doubted the barman took complaints in a constructive manner. So it was a case of put up and shut up.

As darkness fell, the poor excuse for a bed dashed his hopes of a decent nights sleep. Turning over again, he tried to find a spot that didn't have a lump. Between that and what he knew awaited him in his dreams, his attempts to rest were doomed to fail. The hulking orc a foot or two from him seemed to have no such difficulty as he snored with passion, further embuggering his effort to sleep.

In frustration, he hit the bed, his fist coming worse off in the encounter as it struck one of the unidentifiable lumps. *Maybe I should just go outside and try and calm myself?* Would that help him sleep? Rising, the bed gave a deep groan of protest as his weight shifted on it. He cast a worried look at Garaz, but doubted a calvary charge through the room could wake the orc, so he was content to put on his boots and walk out the room without the need to creep around.

Maybe he could find Auron. The spirit had left to explore the area as they'd called it a night. At the time, he'd appreciated it, as he hadn't liked the idea of the sleepless spirit stood around watching him, but now he fancied some company.

At the bottom of the stairs he came to a halt. It was eerie seeing the tavern, a room built to be full of people and merriment, so deserted. And there were shadows everywhere. For a moment he thought about going back, but he was in the middle of an adventure, he couldn't allow himself to be spooked by an empty room. Walking to the tavern's door, trying not to cast wary glances around him as he did, he reached for the handle. His hand stopped short.

Oh, for Deities' sake.

And so he began to act out the scene that had become so familiar to him.

There are no monsters.

It was driving him insane, but it had gotten to the point where he couldn't *not* do it. He needed that reassurance. Or did he? He'd jumped on the back of a cow-dragon, for Deities' sake, and here he was, scared of the dark. Steeling himself, he grabbed the handle, opened the door and strode out into the night. There was nothing to be scared of.

He'd made it just past the door when an arm wrapped around his neck, and his legs were kicked out from under him.

He tried to cry out as he fell back, but a meaty paw covered his mouth, turning his shouts into mumbles. Flailing, he tried to grasp his attacker, strike him even, but there was no firm footing and the man was behind him. Yet desperation kept his limbs thrashing. His throat fought to take in air as the grip around it tightened. The edges of his vision began to blur despite his eyes being wide. Slowly his efforts to fight became less and less.

Each breath he did manage to take was now laced with the smell of horse manure. Was he being taken to the stable? The hand came away from his mouth abruptly before he was spun around and slammed against the wall. A strong hand around his neck pinned him in place whilst the tip of a sharp blade hovered before his eye.

There were three of them, and enough moonlight coming through the stable doors to make them out. Each had the look of men not unused to fighting and killing, but other than that, the only distinguishing thing about them was the small anvil with a sword through it tattooed under each man's right eye.

'You've been asking questions.' Ale-scented breath hit him in the face as the man holding him spoke. The look in his eye suggested that he would be more than happy to use his blade. Nicolas needed to be very careful what he said next.

The pressure on his neck made it hard to form words, but knowing an answer was required, he persevered. 'Y...yes.'

'We don't like questions,' the man snarled. 'Do we, boys?'

The two men flanking him made affirmative grunts. This wasn't going to end well. His mind, flustered and fearful, tried to think of a way out. Taking on three burly men, one armed with a knife, wasn't a scenario he believed he would come out on top of even if he'd had his sword. But he'd left it in the room. Again.

'So,' the man continued, quite at his leisure. 'You're gonna tell us who you are and why you're asking around, and then I'm going to decide whether or not to let you walk out of here. Understood?'

These men had no intention of letting him walk out of here. This fact only added to his panic. His hand trembled as he looked his attacker in the eye.

The man sneered happily at the fear in Nicolas's eyes. 'So what's it gonna b—'

A horseshoe struck him hard in the temple. Making a strange grunting sound, the knifeman took a couple of dazed steps back, his head cut and bleeding. The hand dropped from Nicolas's throat, and he attempted to breathe normally again, clutching his sore neck. The other two men looked around in confusion for a second, not having paid enough attention to see where the horseshoe had come from. The flinger of the horseshoe soon remedied that for them.

It was the warrior woman from the bar. She charged into the fight, face set in a fierce expression. Nicolas got the impression from the way she moved that despite their numbers, the thugs didn't stand much of a chance.

The simple chest plate she wore allowed her to flaunt a lean, muscled stomach that matched her arms and legs. Her short leather skirt was covered in metal plates, the same as her boots and gauntlets. There was no fancifulness to any of the armour; it was all about business. She came at the men silently but bringing with her a fury that almost made him feel sorry for his attackers.

Before the knifeman's first companion had finished turning to meet the threat, the warrior had kicked him in the side of the knee, collapsing him before striking his jaw with an open palm. The force of the strike caused the ruffian to spin, spittle flying from his mouth, until he faced away from the warrior, who brought her booted leg up high to kick him in the side of the neck. He fell headfirst into the straw with an angry-sounding *thud*.

Now they knew who they were fighting, the second man came on with a roar, lashing out wildly with a fist. The woman parried inside his punch, striking him under the chin with her rising elbow, following it with a mean-looking cross to the same area. Reeling back, the ruffian tried to recover his wits. The woman didn't give him the chance, kneeing him in the stomach then wrapping her muscled arm around his neck as he buckled forward. Dropping herself back, the woman drove her attacker's head into the stable floor.

There he stayed as the warrior flipped to her feet in a way that made Nicolas gasp. He winced as the action caused a burning sensation in his abused throat. For a moment he'd been so engrossed in the fight he'd managed to forget that he'd nearly had his throat cut only moments ago

By now, the ruffian with the knife had recovered, despite the bloody wound to his temple. Seeing the fate that had befallen his companions, he stalked the woman cautiously, knife held before him to ward off attack. The warrior circled him slowly, eyes fixed on the man in an emotionless stare. Eventually, the knifeman made his move, lunging forward and stabbing with his blade. The woman sidestepped the attack as if it were nothing, gripping the ruffian's knife hand and bringing her free hand upwards, striking under his elbow. The arm bent inwards with a sickening snap. For a second, Nicolas could've sworn he saw protruding bone. Crying in pain, the man stumbled back, cradling his now limp arm before turning and fleeing. His comrades, having picked themselves up and assessed their chances of continuing the fight, soon bolted after him, stumbling drunkenly after the beating they'd received.

What do I do now?

His limbs wouldn't move. The warrior woman stood with her back to him, her body rising and falling in time with her breathing, which gradually slowed. She faced the direction in which the men had fled, probably to ensure they stayed gone. Considering that thrashing, he doubted they'd be back any time soon, though he was glad she was being thorough. He just wanted to know what this meant for him.

Who is she?

Was she a danger to him too? And why was her body so mesmerising?

As she turned back towards him, his attention became immediately focused on her hard, yet attractive, face. If the men who'd grabbed him had the look of men used to violence, she looked like violence personified. Half of him wanted to thank her for saving his life, while the other half wanted to beg for mercy. She took several steps toward him, completely invading his personal space, but he didn't say a thing. His life might still be hanging by a thread. The way she scrutinised him almost gave him the impression that they knew each other, but that couldn't be. This woman…he'd have remembered.

What's that tapping sound? He didn't have to look far for the source. It was his hand, again. This time against the wall of the stable. With a deep breath he stilled it.

'Th…thank you,' he stammered, wishing to break the tense silence between them.

'It's the least I can do for my saviour.' The voice was oddly familiar.

'Your what?' He was completely lost. 'I don't know who you think I—'

'*Silva!*'

The warrior's head turned in the direction of the stable door in time with his, where Auron stood, glaring furiously at her, his aura reddening with each passing second. The last time he'd seen the spirit react like that was in the presence of the woman who'd killed him.

Hang on a minute. What was that name Auron just said?

As the realisation of who this was set in, he pressed himself against the wall harder, looking at the woman through wide-eyes, bowels threatening to loose at any second.

****

Silva Destrone, known in many parts as *The Rose of the Southlands*, sat on a chair against the back wall of their pokey room, face unreadable as he stared at her warily. Garaz shared his expression while Auron continued to glower at the warrior. As paranoid and anxious as he was, he was right to be wary around Silva. Not only had she been the one to uncermoniously murder Auron with a crossbow while he answered the call of nature, she had, in service of a certain necromancer, attempted to kill him and Garaz several times.

How in the Underworld is she alive?

He'd fought her and her partner Grimmark Bear Slayer on a bridge outside the fort of said necromancer. Well, fought was perhaps not the right term. He'd dodged Grimmark's hammer until it had struck Silva and knocked her from the bridge. From there, her excessive armour had dragged her to the bottom of the moat, with no indication that anything else but her drowning had occurred. And yet here she was, alive, and having evidently learned her lesson about over-armouring.

'Why did you call me your saviour?' Maybe he had more than one question, after all.

'How can you see me?' Auron demanded at the same time, his face grim. Also a good question.

The pair looked at each other, the spirit looking furious at the interruption. Nicolas gestured for him to go first.

'I think the first question has to be *how are you alive?*' Garaz interjected. The orc's calmness was impressive, considering he'd been woken to find someone who'd tried to kill him stood in his bedroom.

They all looked at her and awaited an answer.

'I remember being stuck underwater and thinking I would die. It was...horrible, being trapped, struggling to breathe, the water pressing down on me. From what I can gather, I managed to unstrap my armour enough to wriggle free.' Her brow furrowed and mouth thinned, as if she had to force the memories to come. 'I think I'd been underwater a while by the time I did, and I lost consciousness. I awoke on the edge of the moat almost half a day later. I think I passed over, which is most likely why I can see...' The emotion of her last statement was betrayed by a tiny break in her otherwise cool tone and her refusal to use Auron's name.

'You murdered me.' The spirit's voice was a low growl.

'I—'

Auron approached Silva, leaning so close to her that the red of his aura illuminated her face. 'You *murdered* me.'

They were on the cusp of losing their companion. The last few times Auron had been confronted with Silva, his rage had consumed him, and all he'd been able to do was scream at his murderer. Understandable, really. He was impressed the spirit had maintained his composure for this long, but if he went down that path again, they would learn nothing, and it would only cause his companion more pain.

Maybe this time he won't come back from it?

A realisation hit him. Auron would've gladly torn Silva apart himself if he could've, but he couldn't. Which meant the spirit would inevitably ask *him* to fulfil his promise and kill her. Nicolas didn't look forward to that conversation.

'Okay, Auron.' As much as he didn't want to make himself the focal point of Auron's wrath, someone needed to say something. Usually, he would've left it to Garaz, the general voice of reason but...well, he didn't know why he'd spoken up. It just needed to be done.

Auron spun round, and he shrank under his glare, which held for a few moments before the spirit visibly sagged. With a cry of frustration, Auron stomped to the corner of the room, or would have had his ethereal feet made contact with the floor. He must've been feeling pretty impotent right now.

'As for you being my saviour.' Silva's attention was back on him as if the outburst hadn't occurred. 'You are, and because of that, I am yours.'

There was a moment of confused silence in the room.

'You what?'

Why does nothing make sense anymore?

'I am yours.' Silva stood, and he took a step backwards. They'd disarmed Silva, of course, but that didn't make her any less dangerous. He'd seen that first-hand in the stable.

'Noooooo, you aren't.' Nicolas needed to be careful here. It seemed likely he was walking into a conversational trap.

'I died and came back.' Silva's voice broke slightly. 'As soon as I awoke, I was faced with the things I have done. Despite a few *gaps* in my memory, I know the deeds I took part in before and that they have tainted my soul.' The warrior looked away for a moment, as if composing herself. 'I think I've been given a second chance—a chance to atone for my sins.'

'This bitch gets resurrected but I stay dead.' Auron was outraged. He wasn't wrong.

'For a time, I wandered, not knowing how to do what I was meant to do,' Silva continued. 'Then I saw you in the tavern and it became clear. I need an example to follow. Who better than the village boy who, with no skill, vanquished me because he was standing up for what was right?'

That had a terrible logic to it. Responsibility had just been dumped on him like a snowy avalanche. How was he supposed to help a professional killer cleanse her soul? He barely knew how he was going to look after himself on this adventure, never mind helping Silva atone for what he imagined was a pretty long list of bad things.

'Whoa.' He needed to nip this in the bud. 'You don't belong to me or anything, and I can't help you with your new life.'

'Yes, you can,' Silva replied firmly. 'You are the perfect person to guide me on my new path. Us crossing paths like this can't be a coincidence. It has to mean something.'

'Are you sure you don't just want revenge?' Auron's idea seemed much more likely.

'I want you to guide me.' Silva looked at him intently. He really wished she wouldn't. 'I was good once, but I've forgotten how to be that person. I need you to show me how I can be that again. Please.'

'Garaz?' Unable to make sense of anything, Nicolas looked to the orc.

'The memory loss could be due to being underwater for too long, which may also explain her change in personality. It sounds like she may have actually died for a moment or two, which may go some way to explaining how she can see Auron.' The orc stroked his chin thoughtfully. 'Maybe I could heal the damage...'

'Would you want to?' Auron cried.

The others turned and looked at the spirit, except Silva, whose eyes were focused completely on Nicolas.

'Maybe you restore her memory,' Auron continued, 'and restore her previous character with it.'

'In the sense of her becoming a murdering mercenary again?' Nicolas asked, which Auron confirmed with a vehement nod.

'But it doesn't seem right to leave her like this if we can help her.' As much danger as that may put them in.

Maybe she'd had some kind of epiphany or simply an extended lack of oxygen to the brain, but there *was* something markedly different about her from the last time he'd seen her. Less hateful. Was that a good or a bad thing? Or maybe the whole thing was a ruse and she planned to kill them in their sleep? No. That didn't make sense, when she could've killed him in the stable.

'She does seem to think of you as a role model of sorts, which may indicate how bad the trauma is.' Garaz didn't seem to be being sarcastic, which was worse.

'Ha, ha,' he laughed dryly. 'We should do our best to restore her to her true self. Then at least we know if this need to atone is a real thing.'

'Or we do the obvious thing and just put her down.'

There it was. He looked at Auron, somehow shocked the spirit had said it aloud, despite expecting it. Garaz reacted less, though the orc wasn't as prone to outbursts of emotion as he was.

'You're not serious?' A stupid question.

'She's a murderer.' Auron shook his head, as if frustrated he even had to remind them. 'As evidenced by my standing here. Broken brain or no, she's still a killer. Either way, the humane thing, the right thing, to do would be to finish it.'

'Oh, that's the best thing, is it?' There was no high-minded sense of justice here.

'Yes.'

'And this wouldn't have anything to do with you being one of her victims?'

'I'm glad you finally remembered.' There was venom in the spirit's voice. 'She killed me. *Murdered* me. While I was taking a dump, no less. Are you at all surprised I want her dead? You promised me you'd avenge me, and yet here we are, weighing the pros and cons of making her *better*.'

'My friend,' Garaz's tone was soft. Probably necessary, given the sensitive situation. 'I understand how it must feel seeing her here. But I cannot simply murder this woman, and I doubt Nicolas can either.'

Silva took another step towards him—a simple, elegant movement that killed their debate. Nicolas had been so busy talking about her, he'd forgotten she was actually in the room. When the warrior drew a small dagger, he made an *'eep'* sound. Where had she hidden that? They'd searched her, twice.

Before she could advance further, he found himself doing something very out of character: he stepped towards her, hands raised to show he was no threat. Of all the things he'd randomly worried about killing him, here he was about to talk down someone who'd already tried. 'If you want to go about redemption, drawing a knife on us isn't the way to do it.' Trying to keep his voice calm took colossal effort.

Behind him, he heard Garaz picking up his sword from beside the bed. Looking back, he shook his head at the orc, who looked at him as if he were insane. Maybe he was.

Silva grabbed his hand before he could protest or pull it back and pressed the hilt of the dagger into it. She put the blade of the weapon to her throat, her eyes locked with his so intently that he couldn't look away, though it was all he wanted to do.

'I don't want who I was back.' Silva's voice was a hoarse whisper. 'If you want to heal me, this is the way. If death is how I atone, so be it, but I would rather you be the one to do it.'

'So would I,' Auron muttered darkly.

Looking from the blade in his hand to the person against whom it was pressed, he remembered the cow-dragon. The poor creature had been in pain and wanted to die because it should never have been, and he'd obliged. Here was another creature in pain asking him to put it out of its misery. The difference here was that they both had a choice. Maybe healing her mind was the wrong course, but he wouldn't cheat her of the chance to heal her soul.

Auron let out a cry of exasperation as he put the knife back into Silva's hand. 'If you want to atone, you have your chance.'

For a moment, he could've sworn he saw a flash of disappointment in her eyes.

'Or maybe you just aren't man enough to do it.'

Auron's words cut him quite deeply. Without even looking, he could feel the judgement of those white, ethereal eyes on him. He wouldn't turn to look into them; he couldn't. Was cutting someone's throat in a tavern bedroom a mark of manliness? Killing the cow-dragon haunted him when he closed his eyes, and occasionally he could still swear there were traces of its blood on his hands. But this time, it didn't matter, because this was the right thing to do.

'You live.' His mind was set. 'Make it count.'

Silva's eyes became hard with determination. 'I will not let you down.'

He really hoped not. It would be dangerous for all of them if she did. Nodding, he finally turned to face Auron's wrath, but the spirit had vanished.

'He will be back,' Garaz said softly. 'I think you are making the right decision.'

The fact that his companion agreed with him banished any lingering uncertainties that nagged at the back of his mind.

'Perhaps now we should discuss those men who attacked you?' Silva suggested.

What did she mean? Who'd attacked him? It only took a second for him to remember In all the fuss, it had actually slipped his mind that a group of men had nearly killed him. He truly wished he knew how his brain worked sometimes.

'You were attacked?' Garaz asked, looking him over with concern.

'I'm sure I mentioned it?'

Garaz raised an eyebrow. 'I was awoken by you shaking me, Auron screaming, and a woman standing beside me who had previously tried to kill me. You will have to forgive me if I missed some of the finer details of the story.'

'A group of men outside grabbed me.' He rubbed his neck. 'They wanted to know why we were asking questions. I think—'

A thought popped into his mind. A ridiculous thought, most likely, but once it was there, he had to say it aloud, just to be sure.

He turned to Silva. 'You didn't...well...hire those men to attack me so you could save me, did you?'

Silva's incredulous expression was all the answer he needed.

'They all had this tattoo under their eyes,' he continued. 'A small black anvil with a sword through it, I think.'

Garaz mulled over this piece of information for a moment. 'Sounds like a gang marking, but I am not familiar with it. If our questioning has provoked a reaction, though, it suggests that whatever is happening, someone is behind it, or has a vested interest in it. I think this journey may be more perilous than we first thought.'

Nicolas found himself looking at Silva. Now he knew a gang might be after him, he was suddenly glad of the extra muscle. And who knew? Maybe, somehow, he *could* help her redeem herself.

Chapter 6

The look of surprise on the barman's face the next morning suggested he hadn't expected them to still be here. It didn't take a wizened scholar to see the connection between that and what had happened last night. Quietly, he mentioned his suspicion to Garaz and Silva.

Several seconds later, he was still trying to dislodge Silva's arm from around the windpipe of the barman, who was turning a dark shade of blue.

'Let him go!' She wouldn't give despite his best attempts. Deities', her arm was toned.

'He tried to have you killed,' Silva replied. 'We need to know who those men were.'

'And how do you intend to question him while choking him?'

The warrior mulled this over for a moment or two before finally releasing her grip. The barman stumbled back, knocking several tankards to the floor, coughing and spluttering as he attempted to breathe again.

Though he didn't care for Silva's questioning style, the barman was surprisingly open to talking, once he could form words again. 'Don't know who they were.' The man was shaken, eyeing Silva fearfully as he spoke. 'They were from Sarus, I know that. Gang boys by the look of 'em. Had some meetin' or other going on but slipped me some gold to point out anyone asking around about Sarus. That's all I know. I swear.'

Judging when people were lying was not in his skill set. He seemed genuine enough, but how could they be sure? As if reading his mind, Silva took a single step towards the barman, who looked as if a full-grown dragon stood before him, mouth open and flames ready. Repeatedly, he reassured the group that he knew nothing more. As reparation for the attack, the barman said he'd put the coin they'd given toward a slap-up breakfast for the trio, with a couple of extra rashers thrown in to boot. Seemed like the least he could do, though a single glare from Silva got an extra sausage added to the plate as well. Once he'd produced the breakfast, the barman made himself scarce.

The food was very welcome after a night of sleeping with one eye open. At least the warrior had agreed to stay out in the hall. Part of him had felt bad about that, but she was a known murderer.

Nicolas looked at Silva sitting nonchalantly across from him. 'You shouldn't have done that.'

'It worked,' the warrior replied simply.

'That's not really the point.'

Silva looked at him blankly.

How to explain it?

'What young Nicolas means is that you have to give him the chance to answer of his own volition before applying force,' Garaz interjected levelly.

'I doubt you would have answers or extra food on your plate if you had just asked nicely.' Silva seemed genuinely confused, and maybe a little indignant.

'Look.' Nicolas spoke slowly, not entirely sure where his words were leading. 'You want to learn how to be a better person, to atone, right? Well, then you have to follow our lead. If you go around choking out anyone you think knows something or looks at you funny, atoning is going to be a long road for you.'

She appeared unconvinced.

He looked to Garaz for help.

The orc wasn't happy about being included mid-mouthful, having to take a moment to chew and swallow. 'Until you develop better judgement,' the orc began with a slight cough, 'we will be your better judgement for you.'

Silva seemed to mull this over for a few moments before giving a half shrug and returning to her food. This was already proving troublesome.

With a wash of light, Auron appeared through the door. '*That* is still here then?'

'Look, Auron...' So far, the theme of his day was dealing with unreasonable people, and spirits, and he'd barely been awake for half an hour.

'You won't kill her, and I can't.' The resentment was thick in his aura. 'So she comes with us. I don't like it, but I guess I don't get a vote.'

'Auron—'

'I'll be outside when you're done eating.' The spirit cut him off before phasing back through the door, a slight shimmer on the wood marking his passage.

That wasn't going away any time soon.

****

It seemed strange that their trio was now a quartet, especially considering the disruption this new companion was causing. Nicolas's hope was that Auron would watch her like a hawk for the first sign of danger, and the spirit seemed intent on doing just that as he followed Silva closely, the burnt edges of his aura increasing and receding like waves on a beach. Silva, for her part, seemed be to ignoring the constant glare on the back of her head.

Whereas their journeying the day before had been full of easy camaraderie, today the tension was palpable in the air. He didn't wish to speak for fear of Auron's reaction. The spirit was mad at him, and he completely understood why. He would've been the same if the roles were reversed. Hopefully, in time, Auron would come to forgive him, if not see it his way. Garaz was also keeping to himself, most likely for the same reason. Auron's displeasure hung over them all like a storm cloud.

'The border is near,' Silva declared, pointing ahead of them.

After an hour of silence, it was a shock to hear someone speak. But finally, they had something to focus on other than the interminable awkwardness.

Nicolas had seen the forest ahead of them a while back, the trees getting bigger and clearer the closer they got to it. What Silva had been pointing at was a bridge over a stream just before the forest itself.

Another bridge.

Twice before he'd been in a life and death fight on a bridge. Both times with the woman ahead of him. He dearly hoped this one didn't continue the trend.

The road beyond the bridge was blocked by a small gate with a building at its side. Several figures milled around the bridge. Even from here, he could tell they were soldiers. Something about their posture. Or *possibly* the halberds they carried. Seeing their approach, the soldiers formed up on their side of the gate. Were a couple of them facing inwards? That was odd. The soldiers wore old plate armour, which was in line with what he knew of Sarus, the kingdom being poorer than Yarringsburg. A lot of their economic issues came from wide-scale corruption and the criminals who had the kingdom in a vice-grip. Lovely place they were about to visit.

'Borders closed,' bellowed the captain of the guard as they reached the centre of the bridge. 'By order of Chancellor Lorca.'

'Does the king not close borders?' Garaz's manner was politely inquisitive, but the captain bristled at the question, his furry moustache twitching angrily under his lip like a roused animal.

Behind the captain, his men were ready for action—a little too ready. They looked tense. Fearful, even. With a gesture from their captain, the soldiers facing them presented their halberds point first towards them. They weren't messing around, which was tricky because his group needed to get across the border.

'I think we've gotten off on the wrong foot.' Nicolas was very aware that Silva's hand was on the hilt of her sword, awaiting the slightest nod from him. 'But we aren't here for any trouble.'

'You can take both your wrong feet and walk back the way you came,' the captain barked back at him.

When he looked to Auron for help, the spirit simply stared back at him petulantly.

'May we ask why the border is closed?' Garaz asked, raising his hands to show that he meant no harm.

Below the captain's nose, his moustache went into wild fits, accompanied by several *humph* noises. Obviously, he was unaccustomed to follow-up questions. His face started to redden. They were on thin ice, and Nicolas could hear the cracks beneath his feet.

'Because,' the captain began slowly, as if talking to village fools, 'High Chancellor Lorca, who speaks for King Silus himself, has commanded the border closed. Now, if you do not step back, we will consider you a hostile force and take appropriate action.'

The soldiers reinforced their leader's point, taking a collective step forward with their weapons.

'Okay.' This was escalating far too quickly. 'There's no need for violence...'

'Are you sure?' Silva whispered in his ear.

He quickly looked at the warrior and shook his head.

She didn't look satisfied with the answer, but stayed put, much to his relief.

'We're leaving.' He began to back away from the border, Garaz following his example. If need be, they could find another way in that didn't entail getting stabbed.

'Someone takes their job very seriously,' Auron remarked, finally deciding to contribute something, which was thankfully unheard by the soldiers. 'We can find another way in—'

His words were cut off by a yelp from one of the guards behind the gate. The other soldiers turned and readied their halberds as if a horde of barbarians was charging them. What could spook trained soldiers so easily?

Manoeuvring himself to try to see past the soldiers, he finally spied something beyond them. 'It's just a squirrel.' *A big one, mind you.*

Sitting in the centre of the road, the unassuming squirrel tilted its head to the side to regard the men pointing weapons at it. Why were some of them shaking? Were they worried about death by furry cuddles? Maybe the soldiers had been out in the sun too long?

'Easy, lads.' The captain slowly drew his sword. 'Easy.'

In confusion, Nicolas looked at his companions. 'That *is* just a squirrel, right?'

Garaz shrugged while Silva drew her own sword.

Hissing, the squirrel's jaws opened out to the sides, impossibly wide, presenting rows of fangs dripping with green venom. Eight spindly legs appeared from beneath its fur, raising it to the height of a man. One of the soldiers cried out just as the creature leapt. Covering the distance between them in an easy bound, it landed on the soldier's chest, sinking its fangs into his neck as he screamed. Though he couldn't see the man's face, what parts of the soldiers skin Nicolas could see began to turn grey as the creature slurped greedily at his throat.

It also turned out to be an excellent multitasker. Two of its legs shot out to either side as th dead soldier fell, impaling the necks of those standing beside their falling comrade. As the three men hit the ground, it raised its head and let out a scream of delight that stung Nicolas's ears.

Crying in fear, two of the soldiers dropped their weapons and bolted down the road, the captain cursing in their wake as the squirrel-spider busily slashed the throats of two more of the border guards. In that moment of distraction, the monster leapt toward the captain, fangs bared. He screamed in a very unmanly fashion and continued to do so even after Silva's sword flashed in front of his face and sliced the squirrel-spider creature clean in half. The two halves fell to the floor with a wet *thud*, pumping blood onto the dirt floor until its body dissolved into green ooze, just like the cow-dragon.

After a moment of silence, the captain, face pale and visibly shaking, turned to look at Silva. Slowly, she cleaned her sword on the captain's cape before sheathing it. 'Can we come in now?'

The captain passed out.

'I take it *that* violence was acceptable? There wasn't time to ask permission.' Silva's question seemed matter of fact, but could've been sarcasm.

'That was...fine.' None of what he'd just witnessed was fine. Not at all.

'I guess we let ourselves in then.' Auron passed through the gate, eyeing the unconscious captain with a smirk.

Silva and Garaz followed dutifully, leaving Nicolas alone on the other side of the border. His body trembled as he looked at each of the dead soldiers, the puddle of the creature that had killed them so quickly, and the unconscious captain slumped against the gate. That squirrel-spider hadn't been some poor creature that had wanted to die; it was a monster that enjoyed killing. Beads of sweat ran down his temple as his shaking right hand clenched and unclenched.

Auron turned back to him, looking irritated to find he hadn't moved. 'Coming?'

'In there?' Nicolas pointed in the direction they were heading.

'Well, yes,' the spirit replied. 'That was the general idea.'

'But...' Words failed him, so he gestured to the smoking green puddle on the floor, which bubbled slightly as if aware it was being talked about.

'If you didn't know this would be dangerous then you're pretty naïve.' Auron's voice was stern as the spirit stared at him dispassionately.

Sure, he'd known it would be dangerous, but there was knowing and there was watching a crazed creature kill a load of soldiers right in front of him.

'That is enough, Auron,' Garaz chided before addressing him. 'You faced down a cow-dragon. We assumed there would be more, so this does not change the nature of our mission. If anything, it makes it more urgent. People are dying.'

He wasn't likely to forget that with still-bleeding corpses right in front of him.

'Yeah,' he protested. 'But I wasn't prepared for squirrel-spider.'

'How could you prepare for such a creature?' Silva asked calmly, seeming genuinely confused.

'How can you all be so calm after...*that*?' Whatever their secret was, he hoped they imparted it, because he needed something.

'Look, kid.' Auron's tone finally softened slightly. 'I get it. That was all pretty horrific. I guess I'm just professionally numb to the stuff and forget that you aren't. But you didn't seriously think it was going to be all jolly adventure and no danger?'

'I'd hoped.' Deluded himself, more like.

'The only way to stop these creatures is to continue with our quest.' Nicolas hated it a little that Garaz could be so right in such a matter-of-fact tone.

But people would die if he didn't act. That thought let him gather enough fortitude to step around the gate and into the kingdom of Sarus.

'I will protect you,' Silva whispered as she walked in synch with Nicolas.

That was...kind of reassuring. But he'd keep his hand on his sword, just to be sure.

'Whatever is going on must be more widespread than I first imagined for them to lock down the entire kingdom,' Garaz mused as they continued down the road, leaving the border behind them.

'Yeah,' Auron agreed. 'The border being closed, and the way the soldiers reacted to us and to that animal before it went crazy *spider monster* on them suggests we're pretty late to the party.'

'Then information will be easy to gather,' Silva interjected. 'We should ask at the first village we find.'

Auron threw Silva a filthy glare, one of the numerous ones he'd unleashed on her so far that day. He did not, however, argue. How could he when she made a good point? Surely people would know enough to at least point them in the right direction, which meant not having to worry about wandering around the kingdom for months on end with nothing to show for it.

As it turned out, he had no idea exactly how unforthcoming the first village they found was going to be, and how unfriendly.

Chapter 7

Almost half an hour down the road from the border, and thankfully without a crazy creature in sight, the group emerged from the edge of the forest onto an open plain with buildings in the distance—a collection of about thirty small, thatched dwellings with smoke emerging from the chimneys. The worn wooden sign on the road read *Little Haven 1/2 Mile*.

'Looks promising,' Nicolas suggested as they passed the sign.

'Well, they haven't encountered a cow-dragon.' Auron studied the village ahead of them. 'I'm pretty sure there wouldn't be much of those straw-roofed houses left if they had.'

'It does not mean they do not know anything,' Garaz offered.

'Maybe they have plenty to say on the subject of squirrel-spiders.' Nicolas shivered.

'Maybe they made the squirrel-spiders,' Auron teased, shooting him a smug grin. As much as he appreciated that the spirit was talking to him again, there was still a sharp edge to Auron's voice that let him know all was not forgiven.

'Then they will have to die.'

As simple as that is it Silva? Just like 'I'm hungry, so I'll eat.'

'No.' His tone was more abrupt than he'd meant it to be, and his testicles retracted as the warrior looked at him. As much as he didn't like it, he was responsible for her rebirth,—another duty chosen for him—and he was determined to make good on it.

'We don't go around randomly killing people.' He kept his tone firm, no matter the reaction it received. 'If they *are* making these creatures then we find out why and how to stop them, preferably without ending any lives. You want to be a better person? Think first, kill later.' Even to him that sounded lame.

'Very well.' Was the testy edge in her voice from annoyance or confusion? 'Whether I get it or not, I will comply. I did ask you to guide me in such matters.'

'If the people making these creatures do not respond to reason,' Garaz whispered, 'then I am quite happy to have Silva on hand.'

So was he, truth be told. Provided she didn't turn on them first chance she got. He wasn't sure he'd get lucky and beat her a second time.

Approaching the village, he could see figures in the distance—people going about their daily chores. Which meant the villagers could also see them. A cry of alarm rose, and the figures scurried like panicked ants until they'd all disappeared from view. The sound of slamming doors reached them.

'That's odd.' And a little unfriendly.

'Maybe not so odd when strange creatures abound,' Garaz suggested.

When they entered the village, he would've believed it deserted if not for the people they'd seen. And the feeling of fearful eyes watching their every move.

After making it to what they thought was roughly the centre of the village, the group waited for someone to come and talk to them, hoping that standing around looking nonthreatening would encourage a conversation. Although…looking at Garaz and Silva, there was a chance their group couldn't pull off a nonthreatening appearance. Either way, it was very apparent there would be no welcome for them in Little Haven.

Nicolas cupped his hands to his mouth, his patience wearing thin. 'Hello. Can anyone talk to us?'

'Bugger off,' someone shouted from one of the dwellings to their left.

'Looks like at least one person has something to say.' Auron strode towards the house.

In a motion he wasn't sure he'd ever get used to seeing, the spirit walked up to the stone wall of the house and then straight through it, leaving a ripple of light in his wake.

'Some old guy just behind this window.' Auron indicated the opening with his thumb as he emerged a second later. 'You talk to him, kid. He's more likely to open up to you than the orc or the filthy murderer.'

Dutifully, he walked to the house, hoping to contribute more to the group than just being the least threatening.

'Hello, I'm Nicolas Percival Carnegie.' He kept his voice warm and light.

'You're someone who doesn't know the meaning of *bugger off*,' the voice bit back.

Okay, at least the man was talking, even if it was just to insult him.

'We aren't staying.' He hoped he sounded reassuring. 'We just need a direction to go in.'

'Any'll do, so long as you bugger off.' This guy *was* committed to his train of thought. *Tough luck, old man, because so am I.*

'Why do you want us to leave so badly?'

Silence. For a good long time.

'Okay, fella.' Time to take a different tack. 'You want us to bugger off and I want to bugger off, but until we have some idea of which direction to go in, we are buggering nowhere.'

After a moment, there was a sigh from the other side of the window. 'You want to know about the terrible creatures, don't you?' he asked in a resigned tone.

'Yes, please.' Finally, he was getting somewhere. 'Do you know where they come from.'

'The Deities.'

This was like pulling teeth. And from the sound of his voice, the old man didn't have many teeth left to pull.

With a deep breath, he composed himself. 'That's not very specific,' he ventured. 'I'm looking for a more...North, South, East, West kind of answer.'

'We've angered the Deities,' the voice insisted. 'We haven't been devout. First the lights over the shrine a couple of weeks ago then the business in the castle with our poor king... We're cursed. Cursed, I say.'

Lights over the shrine sounded like the most promising piece of information the old man had given him so far, though the thing about the king was also pretty intriguing. He didn't, however, care much for the word *cursed*. 'Look, we're here to help and—'

'*Cursed*, I say.' The voice had become shrill and grating.

'Can you at least point me in the direction of this shrine?' He really wanted to swear, but it'd be unproductive.

'I've told you enough,' the old man's voice snapped. 'Now bugger off.'

This time he did as bidden. At least he had something to go on, vague as it was. As he began to walk away from the house, the voice spoke again.

'Leave this kingdom while you can. You go to that shrine, and you'll be cursed as well, Nick Carnage.'

Why do people keep calling me that?

It wasn't as if he were less than formal when introducing himself. He even gave them his bloody middle name, for Deities' sake.

'Did you get any information?' Garaz didn't sound hopeful, most likely because of the way he trudged back to the group.

'Not much. He reckons the kingdom is cursed. There are problems at the castle and something with the king, but he was most vehement about a nearby shrine.'

'Probably up there.' Auron pointed toward a large hill a few miles away from the village. 'They're usually built high so they can be a bit closer to the Deities. Like it makes a difference to beings who can supposedly see all.'

'*Supposedly?*' Somehow that word shocked him. 'You aren't a believer?'

'I'm a practical guy. I believe in what I can see,' the spirit replied with a shrug. 'And if they do exist then I don't see them ever lifting a finger to help us...though I am a believer in the afterlife now.' Auron gave a sardonic smile.

'But they do lift a finger,' he protested. 'The whole reason we first met was because they sent me to give you a message.'

'Yeah, and if they were so intent on me receiving that message, they should've stepped in before a crazy bitch crossbowed me to death answering the call of nature.'

Okay, he had a point.

'Are you a devout believer?' Silva asked, scrutinising him in a very uncomfortable manner.

'Well...I...' He struggled to collect his thoughts while feeling like a piece of meat. 'I mean, I'm not crazy devout or anything. My family go to the services and do the offerings and, like...usual stuff.'

'If your human Deities have cursed a kingdom with bizarre murderous creatures, it may take more than a simple offering to appease them,' Garaz noted dryly as he looked towards the hill.

'So, you think it is a curse?'

'It is definitely something.' The orc shrugged. 'And as unforthcoming as the villagers are being, some superstitions are rooted in fact. Maybe there is something to this shrine that we need to look into.'

The hill was a simple green mound in the earth like any other. So why did looking at it make him so uneasy?

Chapter 8

Apparently, the hill was not accepting visitors today. Before the group stood three heavy-looking standing stones that created an arch over what they assumed was a path leading up the hill. None of them could tell for sure, because the opening was covered by a thick wall of wooden branches emanating from the old tree stood at its side. It looked completely impenetrable, as did all the terrain around it.

Beside the arch sat a stone table on which offerings had been set. Or at least what had once been offerings. Time and weather had taken its toll on the flowers and produce, turning them to wilted, mouldy husks.

Silva touched the tip of her sword to a brown, wrinkled apple, which disintegrated under the slightest pressure. 'If this is the quality of their offerings, I see why the village is cursed.' It might've been a joke but for the voice in which it was delivered.

'So, how do we get up there then?' Nicolas pushed against the branches; the rough bark didn't move an inch.

Garaz carefully examined the archway. 'I am unsure,' he said finally.

'You could just ask nicely.'

After a couple seconds of fumbling, Nicolas drew his sword in response to the unseen voice. 'Hello?' he said tentatively.

'Greetings,' the voice responded pleasantly.

He was getting quite tired of disembodied voices.

'Is someone there?' Garaz asked.

'Yup,' the voice replied.

'Do you care to show yourself?'

The voice laughed like a joke had been told. He had a bad feeling the joke was on them. 'If you can't see me, you must be blind.' It chuckled. 'I'm right here.'

He looked around. Nope, nothing.

'Maybe you should *branch* out in your search.' There was whimsy in the voice, like a child at play.

His gaze went up into the branches of the tree, looking for signs of life. *Please no squirrels.* All he found were green leaves, not known for their conversational skills.

'I don't see anyone up there.' He was already tired of this kingdom. 'Someone's messing with us.'

Auron sighed as if something had just dawned on him. 'The voice isn't coming from in the tree...it is the tree.'

What is he talking about?

He was about to ask when the tree began to shake, leaves rattling rhythmically. 'Ho, ho, ho,' the tree boomed. 'The see-through fellow is a smart one.'

Jumping back in surprise, he tripped over a root jutting from the ground, falling on his rump. From his seated position, he could see the tree from a different perspective, the light catching contours in the bark that mapped out a mouth and nose and brow. The mouth was curved upwards in a warm smile.

'No one expects a talking tree,' the tree said gleefully. That was very true.

'How can a tree talk?' Nicolas looked to each of his companions for some sort of answer then settled on Garaz, as he was generally the wise one.

'Hey,' the tree interrupted. 'I have ears, you know? Well, I don't have *ears* exactly, but I can hear you.'

'Oh, sorry.' He rose, brushing himself off. 'Hello, tree, I'm Nicolas.' He forewent his usual formal greeting as it seemed silly doing it to a tree.

'I haven't named myself,' the tree said thoughtfully. 'Maybe I should? I was only born recently. It didn't occur to me to pick a name. Do you think I should? Or maybe it's a waste of time as I may go as quickly as I came?'

'Maybe you could tell us how you came to be?' Garaz walked around the tree, evidently fascinated.

'That is a good question, orc. But one to which I do not have the answer.' The tree's branches moved in something that approximated a shrug.

'You don't know how you came to be?' Auron asked.

'No, ghost.' Auron winced at the use of the *'G'* word. 'One day I was not here, then I was. It felt strange suddenly popping into being, with all this knowledge and no idea where it came from. I know that these two are human and that is an orc, but I do not know how I know.'

'Nothing at all you can think of?' Nicolas asked hopefully.

The tree went quiet for a moment, seeming to be in deep contemplation, its branches curled in slightly as if it were trying to focus.

'It was night,' it replied finally, as if having difficulty recalling the details. 'I woke up, and there were some figures in front of me. I don't remember much as I was quite stunned at suddenly being alive. I think one was very short. The short one waved something, and I felt my roots stretching until they covered the entrance to the shrine. It wasn't pleasant. Since then, you are the only conversation I've had. I've seen creatures passing, things that ought not to be, but that's all.'

Well, this certainly seemed like the right place.

'You're not going up there, are you?' the tree asked.

'It's our quest,' Auron replied with a tight smile. 'Those creatures you saw are hurting people. We need to find out how and reverse it.'

The tree went silent for another moment. 'When you find out…can you reverse me?' Its voice was low and serious.

'You want to die?' Nicolas was shocked. For a talking tree, it seemed so…nice.

'I do. Well, not die, per se, as that sounds pretty terrible. I just want to…not be,' the tree admitted. 'I didn't ask to be, but I am. And now that I am, I don't care for it. I cannot move and besides you, there is no one to talk to. The birds and squirrels run when I try. It's lonely, and I'm sad. And my bark itches constantly.' Again the branches shook, as if the tree were trying to reach and scratch that itch. 'I know that I shouldn't be as I am. Promise to unmake me, and I'll let you pass.'

'We'll see what we can do,' Auron said solemnly.

'Not very committal, ghost,' the tree said. 'But I will accept it, and wait, and hope.'

Auron bristled slightly at being referred to as a *ghost* again but kept it to himself.

With a creaking and groaning, the thick roots separated, just enough for them to pass through. It seemed to take a toll on the tree.

'Is there anything else we can do?' Nicolas patted the rough bark thankfully. The question was strange, but no less strange than this whole interaction.

'No,' the tree replied jovially. 'I shall wait and see what fate has in store. Maybe more people will come and talk to me. Thank you for this good conversation.'

'You are most welcome.' Garaz gave the tree a small bow, which both Auron and Nicolas copied.

****

The hill turned out to be a much steeper climb than he'd anticipated as they followed a rough path marked by stone tiles. Whichever Deity this shrine belonged to, and there were plenty to choose from, they evidently wanted their pilgrims to work for it.

As they rose, vast green plains swept from all around the hill, marking out the kingdom of Sarus. Below him, he could make out the ramshackle collective of buildings that made up Little Haven.

The further up the hill they went—though could this still justly be called a *hill?*—the more evidence there was that they were in the right place. Strange flora and fauna bordered their trail, though fortunately the odd hybrid creatures he briefly glimpsed seemed fearful of the newcomers, giving them a wide berth. That was just fine by him, as he had no wish to tangle with a *bird-centipede* or *goat-bat*. Or worse.

What's waiting atop the hill?

Maybe he would end up being turned into some strange creature? He didn't want to be a crab or something. He voiced his fear aloud.

'Nick Crabbage.' Auron laughed unhelpfully.

'It has occurred to me as well, Nicolas.' Garaz, as usual, was more helpful. 'But we came here for answers, and answers are at the summit of this hill. Whatever the outcome, we must press on.'

As much as he understood that, he just hoped to come back down again with two legs instead of four or eight...or none.

Another stone arch marked the peak of the hill, leading to an open clearing circled by trees, reminding him of the clearing in which the *Tower of the Oracle* was situated. But instead of housing a crappy cottage, this clearing was dominated by a twenty-foot statue carved from fine marble. The figure it depicted looked proud and powerful as it held a staff aloft towards the sky. The staff appeared to be a long piece of knotted wood with an eye carved into its tip.

'That's T'goth.' He recognised the face from his studies as a child. 'The Deity of Change, Growth, and Evolution.'

'Makes sense, I suppose.' Auron shrugged, approaching the statue.

His nose wrinkled at the charred smell that permeated the clearing, the source of it being very obvious. From the stone offering table in front of the statue outward there was a pattern burnt into the grass—circular and filled with spirals and what looked to be runes. Garaz immediately got down on his knees to study them, while Auron and Nicolas looked for further clues. Silva stood guard by the entrance arch, weapon thankfully ready.

'Fascinating,' Garaz muttered as he traced the runes with his thick green finger.

'I think this was definitely where it all began.' Auron eyed a plant with its own eye at the centre of its petals. The petals closed and opened as the eye blinked.

'What do you think, Garaz?' Nicolas looked over the orc's shoulder at the blackened grass. He was by far the expert in such matters.

'Something magical happened here. But the symbols are burnt and mostly indecipherable. The ones I can make out I do not recognise.' The orc informed them with a huff, suggesting the frustration of not having a decent answer.

They were all looking at the grass so intently that it was a complete surprise when someone jumped on Garaz's back.

Rising to his full, imposing height, the orc roared and shook his body fiercely. No matter how much he bucked and thrashed, the figure on his back clung on with thin, bony arms wrapped around the orc's neck. Sword in hand again, he readied himself, Silva at his side. But neither could do anything without the risk of hurting their flailing companion, or him hurting them.

Between Garaz's shouts and curses, he heard something out of place: laughter. Whoever was on Garaz's back was whooping and laughing as if they were having a merry old time. Slowly, the orc ran out of steam, until he fell to his knees, panting heavily, at which time the figure simply hopped off.

The man was so frail, Nicolas was surprised he'd managed to jump on the orcs back, much less hold on while Garaz thrashed around. Though the man's cheeks were gaunt and his face lined like a piece of knotted wood, his eyes were full of life and an almost youthful exuberance.

'That was fun.' The old man spun on the spot, cackling and whooping gleefully. 'Rest up, orc, then we shall do it again!'

'What is the meaning of this?' Garaz demanded in a growl, obviously not caring for being ridden and yet not recovered enough to stand. Probably good for the old man; those yellow eyes were furious.

'Mistook ya' for a goat.' The old man pointed an accusing finger at Garaz. 'Shouldn't go round on all fours on the grass pretending to be a goat, or yer gonna get ridden. Though turns out orcs are more fun to ride than goats.'

'I was *not* pretending to be a goat,' Garaz protested, his voice uncertain at the strange response.

The old man dismissed the orc with a wave of his skeletal hand. '*Pfft*, heard ya' bleating. Yer a goat.' If there was anything else he'd wanted to add, it was lost as he became preoccupied with a passing butterfly, following its trail with his bobbing head.

Whatever he'd expected, a crazy old man who mistook orcs for goats wasn't on the list. His companions seemed equally as confused as the man danced after the butterfly, imitating the flapping of its wings with his thin arms and making swooping noises. Sheathing his sword, he motioned for Silva to do the same. It took her a moment to relent, but eventually she returned her blade to its sheath. He doubted this man was a danger to anything other than Garaz's pride, which seemed seriously dented.

Taking a cautious step toward the old man, Nicolas waved politely. 'Hello, I'm Nicolas Percival Carnegie.'

Turning, the old man beamed at him with a gnarl-toothed smile, taking his waving hand and shaking it enthusiastically. 'Good to know ya, Nick Carnage.'

That damnable name again. He was about to correct the old man but was cut off.

'Nice to meet someone who doesn't pretend to be a goat.' The old man glared at Garaz.

'I did not—' the orc began to protest until Auron motioned for him to leave it alone.

'And you are?' Nicolas prompted.

'I'm an old man.' Nicolas had hoped for something more than that.

'Do you have a name?' Garaz asked.

The old man looked at Garaz suspiciously for a second then simply shrugged. Was every conversation they had in this kingdom destined to be a frustrating one?

'How long have you been here?' Garaz continued trying to press the man for more information, or at least some useful information.

Evidently disliking being questioned, the old man put two fingers to his head as faux horns and made bleating noises at Garaz, which understandably confused the stoic orc.

Despite himself, Nicolas stifled a laugh.

'Damned nosey goat impersonator.' The old man spat on the floor. Nice.

With a sigh, Nicolas asked the old man the same question.

'Can't 'member, young'un.' The old man seemed genuinely confused. Sad, almost. 'Maybe couple o' weeks now.'

'And how about how you got here?'

Though he looked away, Nicolas could see the visible strain on his wrinkled face as he tried to recall something that evidently would not come. He then became distracted again, wandering off to play with a rabbit with hoofed feet.

'The old man is useless.' Silva looked at the capering man with contempt. Maybe not all her former meanness had gone.

'Be nice,' he chided, causing the warrior to huff but thankfully offer no further comment.

'Come here.' Auron stood in front of the statue, looking up at it curiously.

Both he and Garaz approached their companion, while Silva continued watching the capering old man suspiciously.

'What is it?' Nicolas was really in no mood to appreciate art, as finely carved as the statue was.

'Does he remind you of anyone?' Auron asked, pointing to the old man.

As he watched the strange fellow wander from here to there with no seeming reason beyond some random thing catching his interest, he could see nothing he recognised.

'Look at the statue,' Auron prompted.

Nicolas focused on the statue's proud stone face. At first, he didn't understand what his companion meant, but then a slight crack on the cheek of the statue changed his perspective. Add wrinkles to the unmoving face, recede the line of curled hair on its head. Now the statue looked exactly like the old man.

Wait, what? No, that's not...really...it couldn't be. Could it? Surely there's no way he was...

The jumble of his thoughts began to slow and calm as the realisation set in. He felt like he was blinking a lot. Did that help him comprehend? Oh, and his mouth was open. Quickly he closed it.

'Auron's right.' It still sounded strange, even said aloud.

He'd always assumed these statues were based on imagination, as it seemed unlikely that a Deity would nip down to Etherius to pose for a carving. Yet the man and the statue were almost the spitting image of each other, age difference aside.

Turning back to the old man, Nicolas tried something. 'T'goth?'

'Yes?' the old man answered, his face lighting up. 'Yes, T'goth.' He danced in victory, pumping weathered fists into the air. 'That's my name. *T'goth, T'goth, T'goth.*'

So this crazy old man is actually an all-powerful Deity? He still couldn't marry those two concepts to each other.

Garaz looked at the old man with a raised eyebrow. 'You humans worship some strange gods.'

'He isn't supposed to be like that,' Auron scoffed. 'Look at the statue and look at him. Someone has done something to him.'

'Or the statue is a massive over exaggeration,' the orc noted. 'Wouldn't be the first time.'

'If Auron's right, that would mean somehow someone turned a Deity, *a Deity*, into a crazy old man? That can't be right.'

The idea of this crazy old loon as a Deity was even more preposterous than a cow-dragon.

A sudden cry made him jump. The old man reared his head back, making some kind of repetitive animalistic noise. After a moment Nicolas realised it was just an oncoming sneeze and let go of the hilt of his sword. Jerking with the force of it, T'goth let out mighty *'achoo.'* The sound was accompanied with a blinding flash of light. Once it receded the tree next to which the old man had stood had writhing snakes for branches.

It took a good few moments for Nicolas's jaw to close again. 'Okay then.'

'I suppose those symbols on the grass may be a summoning or binding spell of some form.' Garaz scratched his green chin. 'But why summon a god, much less try to bind him?'

'To take his power,' Auron said.

'That can't be possible,' Nicolas protested. 'He's a Deity. You can't just…call him and pinch his power.'

'Yet here he is.' Auron gestured to the old man. 'And I don't think he would choose to come to Etherius and manifest in the form of an old man who mistakes orcs for goats or sneezes crazy creatures into being.'

'As strange as it is, he has a point,' Garaz confirmed. 'I do not know how someone would go about doing this, but it is what the evidence suggests. It would seem someone has bound him, robbed him of his power, and left him here in this…form.'

Nicolas looked back up at the statue. 'The staff. He's making a big deal of it in that pose, and I can't see it around here. Didn't the tree say the short guy waved something at him?'

In a senseless situation, it made a strange kind of sense. He couldn't imagine the kind of power, let alone the size of the testicles on someone who would trap a Deity and steal his power. This quest was getting more dangerous in a gradient as steep as the hill they were on.

'That's what I was thinking too, kid,' Auron confirmed. 'It's the only missing piece of the puzzle. Which means we have to get it back.'

'It could be anywhere,' Garaz said. 'It is a big world. Where do we go?'

'The old man in the village who kept telling me to bugger off mentioned that something had happened at the castle with the king,' Nicolas recalled. 'That can't be a coincidence.'

'I doubt our crazy Deity has left this area at all,' Auron said with a raised eyebrow. 'And the creatures around here seem pretty docile compared to the ones we've seen previously. So someone has the staff and is using it. I think the castle's our best bet for a lead.'

'So, what do we do with him?' Nicolas looking uneasily at the old man—T'goth, Deity of Change, Growth, and Evolution.

Oh, for the days when the worst I had to worry about was being late for work.

'He stays here,' Auron's voice was firm. 'We don't want him with us, sneezing and turning your arms into tentacles at the wrong moment.'

'Is there ever a right moment for that?' Garaz mused.

'I'm coming with you,' T'goth suddenly cried as if he'd been part of the conversation all along instead of picking petals off a daisy. 'I had a stick. It's gone now. I need my stick back.'

'Now, sir—' Garaz began.

T'goth shot up from the floor and did a strange shuffling run towards Garaz with his robe pulled up to his knees. The old man got nice and close as he glared up at Garaz, wagging a bony finger under his chin.

'I'm coming,' T'goth declared with finality. 'And I won't stand for none o' yer objections or yer goat-pretending antics. We need to get my stick back. It's a good stick. And if ye say no, I'll just follow ye anyways.'

Garaz, who was several feet taller than the old man and much bigger built, looked almost intimidated and raised his palms in a conceding gesture.

Auron rubbed his hand over his face and sighed.

Well, they had a former murderer with them, they may as well add a demented Deity to the group.

Chapter 9

Though, generally speaking, going downhill is faster than going up, the trip down the hill was the longer of the two for the group. This was because their strange new companion insisted on wandering off to investigate each and every thing he saw. Nicolas had suggested that Silva escort the old man/Deity in order to keep him on the right track, but she'd refused point blank, so it'd been left to him.

At the bottom of the hill, he breathed a sigh of relief as the stone archway came into view ahead. But the second they passed the arch's threshold the old man gasped and went limp. Impressing himself with his reflexes, Nicolas managed to catch the former Deity before he crumpled to the ground, gently lowering him to rest against one of the standing stones.

'Is he okay?' the tree asked.

He really wasn't. Somehow, his face had aged, his skin growing greyer, and the light in his eyes fading a little. Nicolas was at a loss of how to help. All he could do was hold T'goth's hand for reassurance, which seemed appreciated.

'Maybe his remaining power is linked to the shrine?' Garaz suggested after trying to inspect the Deity but being waved away by the old man who didn't require '*goat medicine*'. 'If we leave the area then he loses what little link he has to his former life.'

'Then maybe he ought to stay here.' Silva obviously had no patience for him.

'Gotta go find my stick,' T'goth wheezed as some of the colour came back into his cheeks, possibly due to being aggravated. 'I'm comin' with ye or I'm goin' alone. Anyways…I'm goin'.'

'It's not like we can just tie him to the tree and leave him here.' Nicolas shrugged.

'I wouldn't care for that,' the tree and T'goth said in unison.

It was a bad idea anyway. It was doubtful the Deity would be too pleased to find himself tied to a tree if they restored his power and might take issue with them for doing it. Nicolas wanted to take no chances when it came to invoking a Deity's wrath.

'We're going to need transport.' Auron seemed frustrated, shaking his head at the scene. 'It's taken us an age just to get down the hill with him in tow, and as much as I'd like to, we can't exactly leave him. But we can't continue at this pace either.'

'Agreed,' Garaz confirmed as he eyed T'goth, 'If we are to walk to the capital, it will take us many days with all the…interruptions,' he finished diplomatically.

'Little Haven would be the quickest place to arrange transport.' Silva was right; it was their only option.

Nicolas didn't relish the prospect of returning to that place, assuming the reception on their return would be worse than the first time. 'They're hardly friendly.'

Auron seemed almost pleased about that. 'That means they'll want us gone quickly so we can hopefully get a good deal on a wagon. We can make up some time before we find a rest stop for the night.'

Helping T'goth back to his feet, he was surprised when the former Deity pulled him in close.

'The see-through fella,' he whispered conspiratorially, 'is he real or am I making him up?'

'He's real…enough,' Nicolas confirmed.

'Hmm,' the old man mused. 'I don't like see-through people any more than I like people who pretend to be goats. I'm gonna ignore him and pretend he ain't even there.'

'Okay.' What else was there to say?

****

The sun was beginning to lower in the sky as the group returned to Little Haven. Once again, the residents barricaded themselves in their homes, turning the village into a ghost town, with an actual ghost wandering the streets.

Nicolas gestured to the empty streets. 'Told you.'

'Do you think *'I told you so'* advances our quest any?' Auron looked at him with a deadpan expression.

'At least there is a wagon.' Garaz pointed to one already hitched up. 'You can speak to the owner and purchase it for us.'

As rickety as the wagon looked and as old as the nag that pulled it seemed, it was ready to go, and he had no wish to linger here longer than necessary. Happily, the house it stood next to wasn't the one whose resident he'd conversed with on their last visit, so hopefully being told to *'bugger off'* would be kept to a minimum.

Nicolas was about to ask Garaz to keep an eye on T'goth when he suddenly realised the old man wasn't with them. *Dammit.* Considering all the trouble he could possibly get into/cause, that could be a very bad thing. Luckily, he hadn't gone far.

T'goth stood a little way back down the well-travelled dirt road. The old man was looking down at a chicken. Calling to the Deity and getting no response, he trudged back towards him with a sigh.

On closer inspection, the powerless Deity wasn't just looking at the chicken, he appeared to be having a staring contest with it. He had no idea why or who was winning, but T'goth seemed very invested in it, standing bolt upright, chest puffed out, hands on his hips, one eye closed and the other burning a hole into the bird. The chicken looked back at the Deity in a very chicken-like way, bobbing its head back and forth.

'What're you doing?' Nicolas tried not to sound as irritated as he was. 'We have things to do.'

T'goth hocked and spat on the ground. 'I don't like this chicken.' The Deity refused to take his open eye off the animal, 'Summit 'bout it ain't right.'

He regarded the animal to humour the Deity. It looked like a regular run-of-the-mill chicken to him. T'goth suddenly began to dance, flapping his arms to try to shoo the bird away. It didn't budge. With a snarl, T'goth got on his hands and knees and went nose to beak with the animal.

Is this really my problem right now?

'We don't have time for this,' Nicolas pleaded, looking briefly back at his other companions for help. Auron was smirking, Garaz appeared hesitant to intervene and Silva looked as if she may persuade T'goth with her fists if she came over. This was *his* problem then.

'Think yer a big chicken, don't ya...chicken?' T'goth snarled at the animal.

The chicken clucked in response.

'Why you cheeky lil...'

Before Nicolas could react, the old man jumped to his feet, swinging a kick at the chicken. The bird squawked in alarm and flapped its golden wings, getting out of the way just in time. Nicolas grabbed T'goth before he fell to the ground, again.

A roar of outrage came from the houses directly around the group. As he looked from house to house in confusion, the overlapping shouts and curses coalesced into a cloud of angry noise that buzzed around them. To the group's left, a door swung open to reveal a man wielding a pitchfork standing in the doorway. He was seething about something, and Nicolas really hoped it was nothing to do with him.

With an angry shout, the man drowned out all the voices around him. '*Chicken attackers!*'

This declaration seemed to be a battle cry, which rallied the rest of the village, the shout spreading from house to house until it had passed right through the community. The people of Little Haven made themselves known. Doors opened, and villagers appeared from dwellings carrying all manner of improvised weapons—pitchforks, hammers, rolling pins, chair legs. Red-faced and outraged, they charged furiously at Nicolas and his companions.

'*Run!*' Nicolas's shout was directed mainly at Silva, who'd drawn her blade ready to fight, a battle he didn't want to see.

'I will hold them at bay and cover your escape.' The warrior readied herself in a fighting stance. Well, that was suicidal.

'No, you will bloody not,' he told her firmly. 'You are running.'

Hesitantly, the warrior complied.

Running past a house just as the door opened, Nicolas barely dodged the wooden ladle swung at his head by a washerwoman far burlier than he. Her curses followed him as he fled.

Dodging individuals emerging from their houses as he retreated down the road, T'goth beside him, he glanced back to find the villagers quickly merging into a rampaging mob. Weapons raised, the mob stormed them with as much spirit as armoured knights.

'It's a race.' At least T'goth was happy about it, working his bony arms and legs at speed. His enjoyment probably wouldn't last once the mob caught them.

'We cannot outrun them forever.' Garaz was spot on.

Already Nicolas's legs burned, and he was struggling to breathe.

Behind them, the mob showed no evidence of stopping or wavering. These people were certainly animated over a chicken, which T'goth had missed anyway. Eventually, the mob would overrun them, and though he was unsure whether they would be killed, by the look of the villagers, they were at least in for a savage beating.

'We could split up and make for the wagon, if you won't allow me to fight them.'

How does Silva look so fresh when Garaz and I are nearly spent?

Perhaps all those years encumbered in armour had given her really good stamina.

Though he wasn't sure if the horse had it in him to outrun the mob, it was better than nothing. It was definitely better than standing and fighting. Silva could almost certainly cut through them, but they were just everyday people...who wanted to lynch them for trying to kick a chicken.

'Split up.' Nicolas veered hard to the left, pulling the fussing T'goth with him. Garaz and Silva went right, and they all disappeared between the old houses.

Running in the maze of walkways between the village buildings, he hoped their sudden change of direction would buy them a few precious seconds as their pursuers worked out which way to go. The momentary quieting of the mobs baying seemed to suggest success. However, the noise soon grew again, as people began angrily shouting directions to each other to fan out and find the chicken attackers. The fact that they were organising so well made his stomach knot.

Making a broad circle around the village before coming back upon themselves, Nicolas and T'goth began to move with more caution, stopping at the edges of houses to check the coast was clear before charging across the gap. At first, T'goth wasn't interested in doing this, until he explained to the old man that they were playing hide and seek. He peered around corners, his legs shaking and breath ragged. The villagers were spreading out into search parties to corner their prey... Them.

'Are we winning?' T'goth whispered as Nicolas drew himself back into cover.

They hadn't been caught yet. 'I think so. But we wouldn't need to if you hadn't fallen out with a farm animal.'

'Stupid chicken,' T'goth spat, a little too loudly for Nicolas's tastes.

'Stupid you,' he retorted testily. 'You didn't need to try to kick it. It's only a bloody chicken.'

'Chicken disrespected me,' the old man huffed haughtily. 'I don't take disrespect from no one, least of all some damn chicken.'

'Well, I hope your honour was worth it.'

The villagers moved clear, and he pulled T'goth across the opening.

Reaching the edge of the next house, he looked out to check that the coast was clear before continuing. While there were no villagers in sight, the chicken stood watching them at the mouth of the alley. It started squawking loudly.

'I hope yer happy, ye damn stupid chicken!' T'goth roared as Nicolas cursed under his breath.

Between the noisy chicken and the disempowered Deity's outburst, the far end of the alley became much more occupied, angry villagers homing in on the sounds with frightening speed. Grabbing T'goth, he pelted in the opposite direction. Luckily, the gap between the houses was so small and cluttered that the advancing villagers got in each other's way, tripping over discarded objects and themselves in an attempt to catch them. Nicolas wasn't about to waste the precious seconds bought for him.

Making a quick decision, he yanked the old man with him, and they broke for the main road of the village, bursting out of the alley to cries of alarm. The villagers who spotted them tried to rally their fellows for the pursuit, and some of them said very unpleasant things about Nicolas's lineage.

'Over here, kid!'

Auron stood atop the wagon they'd hoped to purchase before the world went mad, waving at them—which seemed a little redundant, as his bright form was well illuminated against the dimming evening sky.

Running to the wagon, Nicolas skidded to a halt at it's side before turning and helping T'goth board it. The Deity secure, he jumped up and scrabbled quickly towards the drivers seat, the baying of the mob getting ever closer. His motion was suddenly impeded by a hand grabbing his ankle. When he turned, a toothless old man was glaring at him in disgust, a small scythe raised and ready.

'I told you to bugger off!' the old man snarled. 'Shoulda done it while ya still had two legs to do it on.'

Yes, I do have two legs. He used his free one to kick the old man in the face. The grip slackened as his attacker fell back into the mud. Moving toward the driver's seat, he felt bad that he felt good about kicking the old man. In all fairness, he was very rude and had tried to cut his leg off.

'You bugger off,' he muttered as he grabbed the horse's reins.

Trying to still his shaking hands, he snapped the reins and cried to the horse, which thankfully proved to be a lot faster than it looked. The sudden motion pushed him back into the seat as the horse gave a startled whinny and charged down the road. Still, he goaded it faster with the liberal application of the word *'yah.'* As the wagon pulled away, several thumps signalled improvised projectiles striking the wooden transport.

'*Silva*! *Garaz*!' The world moved fast around him as he searched for some sign of his companions.

Spying the pair standing tentatively on a nearby roof, he made to slow the wagon, but Garaz gestured for him to continue. He directed the horse to pass as close to the house as possible, and then the wagon suddenly bucked hard, signalling new occupants. The weight of the orc and the warrior caused an echoing thud, spooking the horse to greater speed.

'I will try not to take offence that you called her name before mine.' Garaz appeared in a much more jovial mood than expected from someone who'd very nearly been lynched.

Leaving Little Haven at speed, they were followed by the curses of the village folk.

'What in the Nine Kingdoms was that about?' *Surely all that wasn't over a chicken?*

'That did escalate quickly,' Auron mused as he looked back towards the village.

'Apparently, people here are quite precious about their poultry.' Garaz lay across the back of the wagon, recovering his strength.

Nicolas's body yearned for the same opportunity.

'Told ye that chicken was trouble.' T'goth was draped over the side of the wagon like a pouty child.

'Allow me to correct you.' His tone was sharp, but then he'd nearly died. 'The chicken was not the problem. You taking a swing at the chicken was the problem.'

'I could've controlled the situation.' Silva spoke as if it were simple. 'Just make an example of a couple of them and the rest would've calmed down.'

'And that *example* may have gotten the local militia on our backs,' Nicolas retorted. 'They didn't want us in their kingdom in the first place, never mind if we go around kicking livestock and roughing up locals.'

'Kid's got a point.' He was thankful for Auron's support. 'If we're going to help this senile old Deity get his powers back, the last thing we need is soldiers pursuing us, or to be lynched by crazy, chicken-loving villagers.'

'It was a fun race.' T'goth seemed to be talking more to himself than any of them.

'We are most definitely unwelcome recently,' Garaz said, ignoring the random comments of the powerless Deity. 'Even before we reached the kingdom itself, there was the incident with those men with the anvil tattoos.'

T'goth suddenly sat bolt upright, making everyone, even Auron, start. The Deity stared at the orc with a raised eyebrow. 'Anvil tattoos?'

'You know that?' Nicolas asked.

'I remember summit.' T'goth creased his face as he struggled to recall. 'When I woke up in that clearing, I saw a group of figures. There was a short one with them. Don't remember faces…but I remember seeing an anvil tattoo just under the eye.'

'Narrowing down the bad guys.' Auron appeared pleased. 'That's always a step in the right direction.'

About to say something, he lost his train of thought completely when a clucking sound distracted him. Sitting in the corner of the wagon was the chicken. Though it looked just like any other chicken, he knew it was *the* chicken. T'goth had come to the same conclusion, judging by the stream of curses coming from the powerless Deity's mouth. At least he wasn't attempting to boot it this time.

Chapter 10

Night fully claimed the sky again, the darkness much more peaceful than the world beneath it was turning out to be. Arriving at a forested area with a small stream nearby, the group decided to make camp for the night. Both food and rest would be very welcome right now.

Garaz went to forage for food, leaving Nicolas and Silva to set up camp and ensure that a certain old man didn't cause anymore mischief. Auron decided to take a supervisory role, which apparently meant criticising everything Nicolas was doing in a haughty tone that rankled. It was more like being ridden than guided, which caused him to make silly mistakes, increasing both the spirit's scrutiny and scorn.

T'goth sat by the campfire, which Nicolas had finally set after many abortive attempts and bouts of ethereal huffing and tutting. The old man appeared dedicated to keeping an eye on the chicken. The poultry seemed to care not a bit as it pecked the surrounding ground for worms.

'We should cook it,' T'goth exclaimed from nowhere, snarling at the animal across from him. 'But I bet it tastes sour. It looks like a sour chicken.'

'No.' Nicolas continued to arrange the extra kindling for the fire but gave T'goth a stern look. 'Bad enough when you tried to kick it. If we eat it and someone finds out, we'll have an army after us.'

The Deity snorted and wrapped his arms around his bent legs like a scolded child, but at least he seemed to listen. 'Stupid cursed chicken,' he muttered petulantly.

'When will we make it to the capital?' He found himself already eager to get this adventure done, but more because of the burdens they now carried instead of any desire to speed justice along.

'If we get some decent rest and an early start, I would say midday,' Auron answered as he fruitlessly attempted to pick up a stick to add it to the kindling by the fire.

'What's the capital like?' he asked, less out of interest and more in a bid to distract Auron.

He'd been trying to pick up small items for the last few minutes, his visible despondency growing with every failed attempt, and if Nicolas knew anything about the spirit, it was that he liked to impart wisdom.

'I don't want to use the word *dump*, but it's not inaccurate.' Auron took the bait. 'Either way it's a bit of a hole. I'm not sure if Sarus is a poor kingdom because of the crime and corruption, or if being poor made them all crooked. The city itself is nowhere near as grand as Yarringsburg. It's the best place in the Nine Kingdoms for whores or gaming, though. Also, the best place to get beaten and robbed if you keep your full purse where people can see it. Maybe if you were a bit more worldly, you wouldn't need to ask?'

That was a cheap dig. Nicolas was well aware of his sheltered life, thank you very much.

'Though I did hear that Sarus had been on the up of late,' Auron continued thoughtfully. 'King Silus led the kingdom into a more prosperous era, shutting down the various dens of vice that plagued the place and practically drove the mob out, or so I heard. Since then, the kingdom's been getting back on its feet and life has generally improved. Until now.'

'King Silus?'

Glowing white eyes were rolled at his ignorance—a little unfairly, he thought. 'King Silus has only been in the job for about a year, since the royal family were lost at sea.' As much as he liked storytelling, Auron seemed aggravated at having to lay out every single detail. 'Before that, he was a bit of a layabout and party boy, by all accounts, but he was next in line, so they had to crown him. He wasn't keen on the role, but that's duty for you. They call him *King Silus the Unwilling*. Turns out the people love that humble *I don't want the job* attitude. Coupled with the fact that he actually does a decent job means he's pretty well loved by the people.'

'Ah, the tale of *Silus the Unwilling*,' Garaz said as he appeared from the woods carrying a curved piece of bark on which the achievements of his foraging expedition sat. It didn't look like a filling meal for one of them, let alone four. 'The man who has a job most covet, but he does not want.' The orc set his dubious bounty down by the fire.

That was something Nicolas could relate to. 'I don't think I'd want to be a king.' He tried to picture himself in a crown. He didn't think it'd suit him. 'I can't imagine the responsibility involved.'

'Trust me, kid,' Auron scoffed, 'no kingdom would want you as their king.' There had been more than a little venom in that statement.

Nicolas looked away from Auron for a moment.

'Indeed, you wouldn't know where anything was and complain every time a decision was required.' Had Garaz noticed the tension and was trying to lighten the mood?

'Oh, you too?' Nicolas threw a stick in the orc's general direction.

'*King Nicolas the Clueless.*' This time, Auron smiled slightly.

'*King Nicolas Percival Carnegie the Formal,*' Garaz offered.

Even though he was having insults levelled at him, he couldn't help but chuckle, and Garaz joined him. T'goth, who'd given every sign he was oblivious to the whole conversation, began to laugh, a cackling from the belly that soon infected both Nicolas and Garaz. Only Silva didn't join in, watching them with a curious expression, matched by the chicken at her side.

****

Nicolas had no idea what time it was, but he knew what had woken him—a feathered menace running past him, clucking. He opened his bleary eyes to the starry sky in the breaks of the forest canopy above him. It was as stunning as ever and he couldn't help but smile at the stars. Getting up, he stretched and looked around the camp, it was chickenless.

The fire had dwindled but still gave off heat. Garaz and T'goth slept, apparently deep in a competition to see who could snore in the most obnoxious way possible. Auron was nowhere to be seen. He'd probably gone for a wander, as he didn't sleep. Considering the unspoken animosity Auron had for him at the moment, he was glad the spirit wasn't around. Well, that wasn't exactly true. The animosity was very clearly spoken.

Running his hands over his face to ward off the last, lingering sleepiness, he turned his head to follow the rustling of branches. *That must be where the chicken's gone.* He hesitated for a moment as he looked at the dark foliage, but then took a deep breath and walked towards the sound.

'Waking up randomly in the middle of the night and following a chicken into the woods,' he muttered to himself. 'This is the part where you get attacked.'

It did seem to be becoming a bit of a habit. There was the tavern, of course, and on his last adventure, he'd woken randomly to find the barracks in which he slept had a vampire infestation.

No. It was just the chicken. *Stop being ridiculous.*

The tremor in his hand stopped. Now just to find the bird.

Maybe it's making its way back to Little Haven to lead the lynch mob to us?

He must still be half asleep to be giving a chicken so much credit.

With every step he took towards the bushes his full bladder demanded his attention more urgently, until finding the chicken was no longer his priority.

'Where are you going?'

With a start, he spun around, reaching for the sword that wasn't on his belt. Silva was nestled between the nearest tree and a bush, barely visible in the moonlight.

'What are you doing?' Nicolas thought his heart was going to pound right out of his chest.

'Keeping watch,' Silva replied in her usual simple manner.

An uncomfortable question sprang to mind. 'You haven't been watching me sleep?'

'I mostly watch for danger.'

Mostly? If he didn't care for a spirit watching him sleep, he certainly didn't want a former mercenary who'd tried to kill him multiple times doing it.

'You did not answer my question,' Silva stated.

What was the least embarrassing way to explain it? 'I'm going to...urinate.'

'Do you wish me to accompany you?'

No, no, he did not. Silva may have had him mostly convinced that she'd changed, but he couldn't help but remember that the whole reason a spirit was part of their group was that he'd answered the call of nature while Silva was near. Plus, it was just plain weird.

'I can manage, thanks.' He moved away before Silva could say something else unnerving.

The warrior said nothing but watched him leave.

It took a few minutes of clambering, carefully, through the foliage until he found a place discreet enough to pee comfortably, ensuring that he was far enough from camp that Silva couldn't see or hear him. Facing a tree, he lowered his breeches and waited.

Cluck.

The chicken was down by his leg, watching him. Why did everyone suddenly want to watch him pee? Nicolas raised his breeches, looking at the bird.

'Don't watch me.'

The chicken didn't move.

'Go away,' he commanded.

The chicken didn't move.

'*Shoo.*' He waved his hand at it.

The chicken didn't move.

'Will you bugger off?' He was starting to understand why T'goth hated it so.

The chicken didn't move.

Bending down, Nicolas tried to push the stubborn bird away so he could finally finish his business, which was on the cusp of happening whether he was ready or not.

Thunk.

Still bent over, he turned his head and looked up. The tree in front of which he was just standing, at about the height of his head, now had a crossbow bolt protruding from it, quivering slightly. Several flakes of bark rained on his back. After a second of stunned shock, Nicolas reached for his belt. No sword. *Dammit.* That left him one option...

'*Heeeeeelp!*' he yelled.

Nicolas attempted to run, but already off balance, he fell over instead then crawled on all fours through the undergrowth. A brief whistling sound was the only indication that another bolt was incoming. It pinged from the rock a couple inches from him, before ricocheting to the floor right next to his hand. A single name ran through his mind.

Silva. This was exactly what she would do. *How could I have been so naïve?*

He was going to die just like Auron had.

Where did she even conceal the crossbow?

Her skimpy armour was not conducive to hiding weapons that large.

A third arrow whizzed by, the angry rustling of leaves marking its passage.

Must find cover.

It was only a matter of time before her aim improved. Desperate, he grabbed a nearby rock and threw it into the bushes away from him before getting up and bolting for the nearest tree.

As he ran, he prayed to the Deities, even the crazy one he was travelling with, that his distraction had worked. There was no immediate arrow in his back, but a mere second after he'd concealed himself behind the thick trunk of the tree, another arrow flashed past, perilously close. Pressing himself to the rough bark and breathing heavily, Nicolas gave thanks for that small moment of deliverance.

Trying not to give into the panic curling around him like a giant snake, ready to squeeze the life out of him, he desperately scrabbled for an idea of what he should do next. His rock-throwing gambit was single-use, and there was nothing practical around with which he could defend himself. A couple of broken twigs probably wouldn't match up to a crossbow well. Maybe he could break off a piece of bark to use as a shield? No, he didn't want to trust his life to a piece of bark. *What then?*

He sighed. It was hard to think when his shaking hand kept distracting him.

Where was that help he'd called for?

Nicolas was so engrossed in how to get out of this dire situation, preferably in one piece, that he nearly jumped back out of cover when something bumped against his leg. It was the chicken. He could've kissed the bird. Had it not interrupted him trying to pee, he would've been dead. They were now even for the village thing. Sadly, that didn't improve his current situation.

In the back of his mind, some primal sense for danger gave Nicolas a poke, and he looked up. Not far from him, the leaves rustled. He cursed himself. While he was procrastinating, Silva was circling around the tree to get a better shot. Grabbing a nearby rock, for want of anything better, he tentatively peered out.

There was a blur of motion, a flash of pain, and he hit the ground hard.

With no bright light to go towards, he was presumably still alive...but he didn't want to open his eyes. Not just yet. His temple burned with pain, and his forehead was wet with what he guessed was blood. A presence stood over him. Silva was ready to finish the job.

Why isn't she?

Only one way to find out.

Oh.

It wasn't Silva.

At the trigger end of the crossbow pointing directly at him, a man looked down at him with a self-satisfied smile that raised the sideburns on either side of his head and caused wrinkles to pass through several of the many scars on his face. Something about his clothing, a patchwork of greens and browns, was familiar, but he couldn't put his finger on why.

Devious eyes assessed Nicolas. 'What have I caught here?'

All he wanted to do was curl into a ball and sob, cold fear gripping his heart as death stared him literally in the face. Fighting to control himself, he tried to think like someone else, because thinking like himself was getting him nowhere.

In his head, a faux-Auron voice spoke. *'Overconfidence, that's the key to this guy.'*

True enough. The man assumed the crossbow gave him all the advantage, so he'd gotten way to close. The crossbow only had one arrow loaded. He could work with that.

Acting quickly, Nicolas rolled to the side, buckling the man's leg as his entire body-weight collided with it. Cursing, the man jerked and so did his trigger finger, the bolt implanting harmlessly in the ground. Nicolas leapt to his feet, using his momentum to shove the man away...and then everything started spinning. For a moment, it seemed the ground itself was moving, but no, it was him. The head wound must be worse than he'd thought. He was in a very dangerous situation; he didn't have the luxury of being dizzy.

His vision unblurred just in time to see his attacker rising. Launching himself forwards, Nicolas grabbed the man's shirt, attempting to force him back to the ground. As the man fell back, his boot connected with Nicolas's stomach, driving the air from him and propelling him overhead. His shoulder jarred badly against the forest floor as he landed. Soon enough he'd be in agony...if he lived that long.

Winded and in pain, he somehow managed to stumble to his feet. The man had already risen, shaking his head and chuckling.

'Some fight in you yet, eh, boy?' The man's haughty accent was made worse by the smarmy tone of his words. 'Didn't figure that when you screamed for help just now.'

Not taking his eyes from his opponent, Nicolas crouched and swept up another rock from the forest floor. Having some kind of weapon in his hand was a relief. It was just a shame his opponent had a much better one. The man examined the thick blade of his hunting knife almost lovingly.

Though the knife should've been his main focus, Nicolas couldn't help but notice the necklace the man wore: a simple piece of string adorned with teeth of various shapes and sizes. The sight doused the final embers of his courage. Hands soaked in fear-induced sweat dropped the rock, and he fell to his knees. They both knew Nicolas was no match for his attacker. The man looked at him as a lion might do a zebra before feasting.

Finally, he remembered where he'd seen those clothes before. 'I saw you at the tavern,' Nicolas murmured.

'That you did, boy.' The man pointed to him with the tip of the blade. 'It is unfortunate for you that we should meet again under such circumstances...but such is life.'

The man took a step forwards, and Nicolas hoped his death would be quick.

'Nicolas...Nicolas, where are you?'

Garaz was near—very near, judging by how clear his voice was. His companion calling to him distracted his attacker, the man looking irritably in the direction of the sound that had ruined his moment. Maybe he had one more chance left? Grabbing the rock from the floor, he swung his arm and launched it with what strength he had left.

The rock flew through the air, his aim true. It was an impressive shot, even if Nicolas did say so himself. Except, even though he wasn't looking, the man somehow stepped out of the way in time.

'Nice try, boy.' The words were not sincere. 'But my peripheral vision is excellent.' He tapped his eye with the tip of his knife to reinforce the point then frowned and looked in the direction of Garaz's call. 'I think I have just enough time to finish you.'

He raised the blade and took a step towards Nicolas…only to be blocked by Silva, who'd jumped between them, crouched in a fighting stance, sword in hand. Which put his eyes right at the level of her rear. Nicolas quickly stood, his legs wavering and causing him to stumble against the nearby tree.

'You will not touch him,' Silva snarled at the attacker. 'But I invite you to try.'

For a moment, the man seemed to weigh his options.

Why had Silva given him that chance? Surely she could've struck him from behind?

'Next time,' he declared, gesturing to Nicolas and Silva with his knife.

The man produced a small ball from a pouch on his belt, which he threw to the ground. Hitting the floor, it exploded in a large puff of smoke that made Nicolas's eyes tear. Once the smoke had cleared, the man was gone.

Garaz burst from the bushes, sword in hand. 'Nicolas, are you okay?'

'I am.' He didn't know why he'd said that; it was blatantly untrue. Nevertheless, he was alive, and he turned to thank Silva for it, but she was staring grimly at his headwound.

'I do not think you are.'

Before Nicolas could respond, his eyes rolled back into his head, and he slumped against the tree. The rough bark scraped his back as he slid down the trunk to the ground, and into the dark.

Chapter 11

When he opened his eyes, the glaring morning sun was a bit of a shock, and he closed them again quickly. After a moment, he opened them more tentatively, using his hand to shield him from the sun's glare. Nearby, Garaz and Silva were dutifully packing their camp, ready to travel. T'goth was busying himself throwing handfuls of leaves in the air then spinning in them, giggling with childlike glee.

'You're awake then.'

On his other side, Auron was sitting on a tree stump. *Or was he? He couldn't touch the thing, so how could he sit on it?* Thinking caused a sharp pain in his temple so he stopped.

'Seems so.' Even to Nicolas, his voice sounded weak. 'I had a pretty close call.'

'So I heard.' Between his tone of voice and the intent look he was giving him, Nicolas was concerned.

'You have something to say?' Nicolas really hoped not.

Auron huffed and shook his head. 'Does it need saying?'

'I think so.'

'And that's the problem,' Auron whispered sternly. 'You don't know. You don't know anything about the world around you or how to survive in it. You're like a baby wandering around a kitchen, just as likely to start playing with a knife as find a toy.'

Wow, that cut deep. 'Why don't you say what you really think?'

'What I really think is that you aren't cut out for this and that we shouldn't have brought you. I thought after our last adventure you would've become more worldly, but I was wrong.' The reply was as sharp as it was blunt. 'And as we can't send you home for fear of you getting eaten on the way, we're stuck with you…unless you go and get yourself eaten anyway. Which is very likely.'

His hand was shaking again, the edges of his vision blurring. Auron had confirmed his worst fears, pulling back the veil of his fake confidence to reveal the same village boy he'd been last time. The only change was that now he knew exactly what to be scared of, instead of imagining all kinds of impossible threats. Auron was right. He was unworthy to continue, but couldn't go back.

'You are awake!'

Garaz's voice snapped him back to a reality he no longer cared for. The orc's voice also seemed to quiet Auron, who stood and walked off. Nicolas watched the spirit leave, hoping Auron would turn and command him to run home, because he had no idea what to do. His mind was wracked with indecision.

'Ah, that looks much better already.' Garaz smiled triumphantly as he inspected Nicolas's temple. 'It was quite a nasty wound, young Nicolas. I closed it with a healing spell then dressed it with moss and herbs to dull the long-term pain. Have I succeeded?'

There was only a slight ache now. He hated to imagine how much pain he would've been in if not for the ministrations of his companion. But Auron had ensured the physical pain was replaced with an emotional one that no moss would dull.

'Yeah, you have, thank you. I'm okay.' For now. It was just a matter of time.

'You are lucky to be alive,' Garaz continued. 'It appears we cannot leave you for a moment without someone trying to attack you.' Though the orc chuckled at the notion, for Nicolas, there was too much truth in it to find humour.

'Was it the same men who accosted you at the tavern?' Garaz asked.

He pictured his attacker...but no, there'd been no anvil tattoo under his eye. That was worse. Now, he potentially had two groups of people after him, and both might've succeeded had it not been for Silva. Closing his eyes, he cursed himself for ever believing she'd been his attacker, whom he began to describe to Garaz.

'Wade LeBeck.' Auron had evidently not wandered out of earshot.

'What?' Nicolas hadn't heard the spirit properly. Everything seemed so surreal.

'Not what, *who*,' Auron corrected. 'Wade LeBeck is a famous hunter. He specialises in exotic and dangerous stuff. Quite the legend, apparently, and a bit of a dick. But what do you expect from someone who hunts animals for fun.' Said the guy who hunted monsters for glory. 'I've never met him, but I've heard enough tales about him to be pretty certain that's the guy.'

The implications of this took a second to sink in. 'Hunter? You mean I'm being *hunted*?' This just kept getting worse. 'Why am I being hunted?'

'Not for the challenge.' Even Garaz noticed the spite in Auron's voice, shooting him a stern look. 'Someone must've put him on to you. But he's not a guy that goes after any old thing, and I can't imagine he's cheap. Strange.'

'It must've been the men at the tavern then.' That made sense. *Something has to.* 'After Silva beat them up, they hired him to get answers from me.'

'That doesn't sound likely,' Auron scoffed. 'Like I said, this guy isn't exactly the *hired muscle* type.'

'Whatever his motive, this quest has become even more dangerous.' Garaz seemed perturbed by this. Thank the Deities he wasn't the only one.

'Surely he's hunting all of us?' That was a fool's hope.

'Doubtful.' Garaz seemed to understand the thought behind his question. 'Otherwise, he could have easily killed us all in our sleep.'

'And you wouldn't have known it,' Auron added. 'He's supposed to be that good.'

If only he'd stayed home. All these anxieties he had and he didn't think to listen to a single one of them just in case they were actually right.

'Will ye all quieten down?' T'goth snapped from the other side of the camp. 'Tryna talk to this here tree and can't make out a word it's saying with all yer yappin'.'

Garaz ignored the Deity. 'And there was no sign of him during the rest of the night?'

'I patrolled the area all night,' Auron replied thoughtfully. 'There was no sign of him, but again, if he's as good as they say, there wouldn't be.'

'Fantastic, not only am I being hunted, but I'm being hunted by a man who can out-ghost a gh…spirit,' Nicolas corrected himself quickly thanks to Auron's glare.

Considering the frosty nature of their relationship at the moment, he didn't want to keep adding to the grievances his deceased companion had with him. So he rose, carefully, and headed for the far side of the camp. He had a more pressing matter to attend to.

Silva watched him approach through narrowed eyes. 'Don't.'

'Don't what?'

'You were about to thank me, most likely in the long-winded, emotional way you favour. It is unnecessary. I have selected you to teach me how to be…better. I am therefore bound to be your protector, which you need. I was doing my duty. Thus, no thanks are required.'

It meant a lot more to him than that, but he thought he understood. Hard warriors like Silva weren't ones for the kind of—admittedly flowery—words he'd been about to say.

'Thank you.' Nicolas didn't want to leave without at least acknowledging the fact that she'd stood between him and certain death. He owed her that, especially as he'd believed it was her trying to kill him.

Silva took the thanks with a simple nod.

He was about to walk away, but stopped himself. There was something else that needed saying. 'I'm sorry.'

Silva looked about to ask what he was sorry for, but stopped, her mouth becoming a thin line. She looked almost…hurt.

How could I have believed it was her? Easily really, but that didn't make it right.

The warrior looked away for a moment. 'I understand,' she said when she finally looked back. 'Thank you.'

'Nicolas,' Garaz called from beside the wagon. 'I suggest we pack up with haste. I do not want to linger here any longer than necessary.'

Nor did he. Walking over to help Garaz he broke step for a single second as the hairs on the back of his neck rose slightly. He was being watched. There were eyes on him as sure as if he could see them. Knowing that even if he looked, he wouldn't be able to see his stalker, he instead hurried to help Garaz so they could finally leave this forsaken place.

****

Between worrying about being attacked by more strange creatures, stopping T'goth from wandering off whenever he fancied, and keeping an eye out for crossbow-wielding madmen who might want his teeth for a necklace, Nicolas was mentally exhausted. Whenever there was a lull in this worrying his brain filled it, posing questions about the long-term damage a hard blow to the head may have created, and he found himself trying to remember facts of his life such as his parents birthdays to reassure himself.

But by the time the City of Sarus came into view on the horizon, they were all still alive and together. As much of a blessing as that was, the fact they hadn't seen any other odd creatures was interesting.

'Maybe they are mostly nocturnal?' Garaz hypothesised.

'The squirrel-spider was happy to run around killing during the day.' The recollection made Nicolas gulp involuntarily.

'Then maybe they simply are not as numerous as our worst theories suggested?' Garaz voiced his own hopes.

'They're numerous enough that they caused an entire kingdom to lock down,' Auron replied. 'It's likely they would've spread out anyway and not all clumped together. I can't imagine those things forming a pack and staying together.'

'I'm happy to just call it good luck and be thankful for it.' He kept his eye on the horizon. It'd be typical for that luck to run out so close to safety.

As they closed on the city, the road began to show more signs of life, though by the look of it, this wasn't the route to a thriving, prosperous metropolis. The smattering of mills and farm buildings peppering the area around the city all had the same dilapidated look as Little Haven. Even the crops surrounding them seemed withered and pitiful, with those meant to tend them having abandoned them at the sight of the travellers approaching. More closed shutters greeted them.

Of the city itself, Nicolas could see nothing over the wall that surrounded it—but even that formidable structure showed signs of wear and required patching in several places. It had definitely looked more impressive from a distance. The other downside of getting closer was the smell. It took Nicolas a while to figure out that the damp, musky odour came from beyond the wall. He wasn't looking forward to entering a place that created such an aroma, save for the safety it promised.

As the group finally got a decent view of the giant wooden gates to the city, Nicolas became more concerned that the danger was ahead of them, instead of behind. 'We didn't think this through.'

The kingdom had proven itself unwelcoming to travellers on multiple occasions already, and the capital was a beacon of this inhospitality. The road ahead of the wagon disappeared under the formidable gate, before which sat rows of spiked pickets. Around these were at least two score of soldiers with pikes. Troops of archers patrolled the walls between the large, mounted ballistae that moved as their operators scanned the horizon. From the angle of the weapons, they seemed mostly focused on the sky. All in all, Sarus City was closed for business.

'I think we should go back, get off the road, and see if we can sneak in,' Auron suggested.

Nicolas wasn't keen on that idea, not with Wade LeBeck still out there. And the hunter was most definitely out there. All of them had had the feeling of being pursued or watched at some point during their journey to the city, though they hadn't seen anything. He was probably waiting for the opportune moment to strike, and Nicolas didn't plan on giving him that moment. However, moving straight toward the fortifications didn't seem like a promising idea either.

'You there, on the wagon. Move forward and be known,' a voice bellowed, amplified by some kind of speaking horn.

Oh no, they'd been spotted. Nicolas chided himself as he looked around him. Of course they'd been spotted, they were in the middle of the open road in a wagon.

At the gate, the soldiers marched forwards and prepared themselves in a defensive formation, pikes ready. Archers nocked bows and ballistae turned to target them. It seemed like their minds had been made up for them.

Slowly, Garaz urged the wagon forward, showing none of the fear and anxiety that was gripping Nicolas tightly by the balls. Part of him wanted to grab the reigns and turn the wagon around, but the defenders of the city were unlikely to take kindly to that. Even from a distance, the soldiers' tension was as clear as the wall they stood before. One wrong move, and the wagon, and by extension *them*, would be peppered in arrows. Briefly he pictured what it'd be like to watch sticks of death raining down upon them.

They stayed silent, the only sound the creaking of the wagon wheels on the track. Once the soldiers decided they were close enough to the city gates, the unseen voice commanded them to stop. Garaz pulled gently on the reins and the horse came to a halt.

There was silence and stillness. Even T'goth, who seemed unlikely to understand the seriousness of the situation, stayed put. Finally, five men broke from the troop of soldiers and cautiously approached the wagon. As they grew closer, Nicolas couldn't help but notice the sweat on the brow of the officer whose hand never left the hilt of his sword. Indeed, all the soldiers were showing signs of nerves as they spread out, surrounding the wagon.

'What is your business here?' The officer tried to evoke authority but was undermined by the slight tremor in his voice.

That did nothing for Nicolas's own nerves.

'We seek aid for an injured companion.' Garaz pointed to the bandage around Nicolas's head, which fortunately still had crusted blood around it.

He had to credit the orc for that quick thinking; it almost sounded plausible.

'How was he injured?' the officer asked, not even trying to cover the suspicion in his voice.

'There was a strange creature on the road,' Nicolas answered. 'Like two creatures stuck together. It came at me. I...I barely got away.'

The officer was silent for a moment. 'There is a lot of that around,' he said finally, before asking, 'Where are you from?'

He'd obviously picked up on Nicolas's accent, a note above the low, almost monotonous drone of the Sarus accent. There were only so many lies he could get away with in one conversation. 'Yarringsburg.'

'And why are you and your...companions, here in Sarus?' The inflection on the word *companions* was one of distaste. Most likely due to Garaz.

'We are—' Nicolas didn't even know how his own sentence would end before the officer cut him off.

'I should inform you that the city is off limits to travellers, as is the rest of the kingdom. The border being closed by order of High Chancellor Lorca on the authority of King Silus himself.' Now he'd seen no sign of danger, the officer was becoming quite haughty. 'That also means that travel within the kingdom is restricted, so I would like to know what you and your friends are doing here when you ought not to be.'

They were in trouble. What sounded plausible? 'Well, we—'

'Taking this into account and on authority of the City Guard, we will be taking this wagon and yourselves into custody for questioning until your motives can be determined.'

It seemed that the officer had no intention of letting Nicolas answer.

'Any failure to comply with this will be answered with lethal force. Am I understood?'

It didn't take a genius to work out that *lethal force* would involve a lot of stabbing with pikes and getting shot with arrows. Maybe the occasional sword slice thrown in for variety.

'But...' Garaz began to protest until two pike blades pointed directly at the orc reinforced the command.

Nicolas didn't even need to hear anything to know that Silva was drawing her sword; it seemed standard practice for the warrior. Turning slightly, he gestured for Silva to stop. The warrior looked at him like he was mad and she was mad at him, but complied. Waving her sword around wouldn't help this delicate situation one bit.

As prompted, Garaz moved to the back of the wagon, and one of the soldiers jumped into the driver's seat, grabbing the reins. Another collected their weapons. He was loath to part with the *Dawn Blade*, but he was more loath to get stabbed. With a bump, the horse began to move, towing the wagon towards the city gates, which towered over them, unmoving despite how close they got. Maybe they wouldn't actually open the gate and just let them drive the wagon slowly into it.

Is this all some elaborate practical joke?

However, at the last second, the heavy timber doors parted with the deep creaking of wood. Obviously, the defenders of the city were leaving nothing to chance. Even after they'd passed through the gate into the city, archers tracked their progress. An escort of ten soldiers flanked them.

Sarus City was simply Little Haven on a grander scale. The empty streets were littered with tell-tale signs of life, and fearful eyes followed their progress from behind closed shutters and curtains. The people he did see were dour, hollow-eyed folk who gave them a wide berth. Shabby rags seemed to be the fashion of choice for the city dwellers.

Poverty and disrepair were obvious with even a casual glance—from the garbage carelessly left in the streets to the missing tiles in the road, the signs of neglect were all around them. The musky odour that had teased them on their way to the city outright assaulted their noses now. Several times, Nicolas found himself nearly gagging as they rounded a corner, and a delightful new smell, such as the scent of rotting cheese, greeted them warmly. Other than the soldiers, who patrolled in abundance, there were mainly animals roaming the streets of this city—lean, almost feral creatures foraging for whatever scraps they could find. Down one avenue Nicolas saw a dog that turned out to be a rat.

This was not a thriving capital city.

'I thought you said the kingdom's fortunes were on the rise?' Nicolas wrinkled his nose at yet another foul smell as he whispered to Auron.

'It was.' The spirit seemed as shocked as he was. 'Before, when the gangs had control, it was rough, but not like this. I'd heard that when Silus came to power, he was cleaning the streets, literally. Now the place is…a pit.'

Nicolas had to agree. He knew a certain Oracle that might feel right at home here.

'Economic and social reforms take time, and their results are not always visible for a good while.' Garaz looked sympathetically at the conditions in which the people were living, while pulling his cloak tightly around himself to shut out the squalor.

After passing through the outskirts of the city, the wagon entered a more commercial district. Here the streets were lined with taverns, gaming halls, and brothels, all closed and boarded up. Maybe the people looked so sour because there was no fun to be had in Sarus anymore? Even the few markets they passed were rife with empty stalls and the mouldy remnants of produce left to rot. One thing the City of Sarus had no shortage of was flies, the annoying little buggers buzzing everywhere. Swatting them away became an exercise in frustration and stamina.

'It seems there was a time when there was no shortage of money for gaming.' How could one city have so many gaming houses? Surely there were only a finite number of people to wager on a finite number of games?

'Woah.'

With a yank on the reins, the horse was pulled to a sudden stop, bringing Nicolas's attention back to what lay ahead of them as the escort stood to attention sharply. Before the wagon, a lone rider blocked the road—a soldier of some rank, judging by the amount of gold gilding his armour, the sheer size of the plume on his helmet, and the unmistakable look of someone who outranked ninety percent of those he met. Judging by the immaculate armour and girth of the fellow, Nicolas would've been very surprised if he'd set foot on a battlefield or patrolled anything for a good long time.

With an easy stride, his horse approached the wagon.

'General,' the driver of the wagon greeted with a salute.

Acknowledging the salute with a casual one of his own, the general looked over Nicolas and his companions. For a moment, he could've sworn a smirk crept out from behind his large handlebar moustache.

'I'll take it from here, soldier,' the general commanded dismissively.

'Sir?' The soldier was visibly confused, as were those escorting the wagon.

'These people are here at my express invitation,' the general continued breezily. 'I'm assuming by the armed guard that my message didn't reach the gate. Typical.'

The driver seemed very uncertain, looking to his comrades for support but finding none. 'No, sir. We received no message.'

Shaking his head, the general muttered to himself before speaking up again. 'I shall be having words about this,' he snapped. 'But I'm here now, so no harm done. You men may return to gate duty, and I shall escort them the rest of the way. You can give them back their weapons while you're about it.'

'But, sir...' the driver said warily. 'Our orders were—'

'Were your orders given by a general?'

'No, sir.'

The general gave the driver a withering glare to make the rest of his point for him, which worked like a charm. Nicolas took the reins of the horse as the driver dropped down. Another handed them back their weapons before the group of soldiers made their way back towards the city gates. As they disappeared from view, the general gestured for Nicolas to get the wagon moving, riding alongside them as he did.

'Um...hello,' Nicolas said with a polite cough, glancing at the stony-faced general. 'I'm—'

'Nicolas Percival Carnegie.' The general's interruption was curt. 'I know well who and *what* you are, boy.'

Oh no, how does a general know my name?

His stomach churned as he searched his brain for an answer. He'd never seen this man before in his life.

'What I am?' Nicolas feared the answer but had to ask the question.

The helmed head turned slowly and locked eyes with him, face unreadable. 'What you are...' the general said slowly before his voice took on a more natural tone, '...is a travelling fool who still needs my help.'

That...was a very un-general like thing to say. Nicolas gawked at the broad grin coming from a face obviously unused to smiling. As he looked into the general's eyes, they flashed green for a moment, with a very familiar twinkle in them.

'Shift?' It was an educated guess.

The general looked impressed. 'The one and only.'

He went from fearful to elated in a second. Behind him, Garaz and Auron both chuckled in surprise.

'What are you doing here?' Despite the situation, he found himself excited to see his companion again.

Shift raised an eyebrow from under the ornate helm they were wearing. 'Do you think this is the best time for catch-up stories?' They gestured with their eyes to a group of soldiers on patrol, marching past them in two neat columns, throwing a salute to the person they thought to be their general.

'Fair point,' he replied uneasily. 'We're okay, aren't we?'

'You are riding with a general.' They were obviously impressed with their own antics. 'If I wanted to, I could get these men to march before you like we were in a parade. Maybe even with a banner or two because I'm such a good friend.'

'Maybe not this time,' Garaz whispered as his head appeared between the pair's shoulders. 'Discretion would be better, I think. It is good to see you again, my friend.'

Shift turned to Garaz and winked at the orc playfully before facing forward and putting on their most general-like expression.

Chapter 12

After passing through a commercial district, Shift directed the wagon away from the main thoroughfare heading to the castle and towards the city docks. All around them were blocky warehouses, storing who knew how many goods for import and export. Judging by the lack of activity, trade wasn't currently booming in Sarus. The few people they did actually see were too preoccupied to care about them, dourly going about their business. The reek of hopelessness in the city was nearly worse than the actual odour.

Several side streets later, Shift called them to a stop before a warehouse that was boarded up. Dismounting their horse, they approached the building's double doors. 'Garaz, give me a hand.'

The orc obliged, the weight of the wagon shifting abruptly as he jumped out. Quickly, the pair heaved the double doors open whilst Nicolas warily kept an eye out for watchers. The doors opened, he directed the wagon in, nearly driving it into the door frame as he failed to stop glancing around and concentrate on his driving.

The interior of the warehouse was dim, illuminated only by the shafts of light breaking through the numerous gaps in the boarding. The cobwebs on every conceivable surface made Nicolas's skin crawl as he thought of the creatures that had made them. What shelving was left was covered in a thick layer of grey dust that T'goth immediately amused himself by drawing in. The few boxes that still populated the place were broken and empty. Jumping down from the wagon, he walked around to the horse, giving it a thankful pat before hitching it to one of the sturdier shelves and going to greet his friend.

As Nicolas approached, the face of the general distorted, the features moving and rearranging. It became narrower and the skin tighter and younger as the moustache receded into the lip. Old brown eyes were replaced by bright green ones with dark lashes while short auburn hair emerged from under the helm, which now drooped slightly over a head too small for it. The thin mouth became a full pair of lips as limbs shrank and shortened. The display was disconcerting, to say the least. Soon, Shift stood before him in the form he remembered, though looking more comical for the now very ill-fitting armour.

'Much better.' Shift stretched their limbs with a broad grin. 'Having to walk around with such a stern face was starting to give me jaw ache.' They took their now oversized helmet off before it fell over their eyes and ran their hand through their hair.

'You've changed your hair.' When he'd met them last, Shift sported shoulder-length auburn hair. Now, it was neatly cropped at the back and sides and stylishly messy on top. 'It's nice.'

'Fancied a change,' Shift gave him an impressed half-smile. 'You noticed that quickly. Someone's been paying close attention to me.'

His cheeks flushed. 'Well...' he stammered. 'It's an obvious change.'

'No, no,' they protested with a grin. 'Don't be modest. Please continue telling me how pretty you think I am.'

'Maybe later,' he mumbled sheepishly.

'It's great to see you again.' Auron looked like he wanted to hug their companion, but for obvious reasons kept his impulse in check. Nicolas wanted to hug him for the interruption.

'You, too,' Shift replied. 'Though I'm surprised to see you. I thought you were due for the...' They pointed upwards.

'I did too,' the spirit replied quietly, with a spiteful glare towards Nicolas. 'It seems my business here isn't quite as finished as I thought.'

The excitement of seeing his companion again was churned into shame. Before Auron could say any more, Garaz strode to Shift and wrapped his large green arms around them in a warm embrace, lifting them from the floor slightly.

'I missed you too, big boy.' Shift patted the orc's arm as best they could.

Finally, Garaz let Shift down, and they turned to him. 'So, Nicolas Percival Carnegie...or is it officially *Nick Carnage* now you're adventuring once more?' The sentence came with a playful punch on the arm. 'How did they get you out of the village again? I thought you were all done with the adventuring malarky?'

'Well, my home was attacked by a strange creature, Auron and Garaz appeared soon after and...you can guess the rest.'

'Nice to see your *'I don't know what I'm doing here'* expression hasn't changed a bit.' Shift looked past him. 'Who are the new muscle girl and crazy grandad?' A brief look of confusion crossed their features. 'And why do you have a chicken with you?'

'That's the Deity T'goth, who's been robbed of his powers,' he replied, pointing at the old man who was following a spider's progress along the wall. 'That's Silva. And the chicken...I just have no idea.'

Shift nodded at this information and made a humming noise. 'You're messing with me, and it's a weak try at best. That old man is not a Deity. I've seen the statues and... Wait, did you say *Silva?*'

Nicolas nodded.

'As in *'wears lots of armour and goes around killing people'* Silva? The one who killed...' They very unsubtlety pointed at the scowling spirit in the room, their other hand creeping towards their sword.

'She claims to have changed,' Garaz soothed. 'Apparently, a near-death experience has left her wanting to atone for her sins. She is sworn to Nicolas because she judges him a good example of how to be a better person.'

Shift looked at Nicolas with an open mouth and raised eyebrow. All he could do was shrug.

'She seems sincere,' he managed. 'And she's saved my life already...twice.'

Shift made several scrunching actions with their face as they took this in before looking at Auron. 'And you're okay with this?'

'Not even slightly.' The spirit's face was hard and his pupilless eyes fierce.

Shift looked back at Nicolas, an exaggerated wince on their face, but thankfully knew when to leave a conversation alone.

'What about you?' Nicolas asked, wanting to change the subject quickly before Auron's unfinished business got brought up again. 'What're you doing here?'

For a moment, Shift looked like a giddy child. 'You're kidding, right?' The excitement in their voice rose to fever pitch. 'I had to come and see the site of the robbery of the century.'

Shift's ability to change form was something they'd always had, though they could only remember their life from a certain point; everything before that was blank. Not remembering who they were or where they came from, they did the most obvious thing someone with their gift could do: steal things.

'What robbery?' Garaz asked.

Shift looked between Nicolas, Auron, and Garaz in confusion. 'How do you not know?' they exclaimed finally. 'I mean, I'd expect Nick not to know…'

'Hey,' he protested.

'…but you guys?' Shift scoffed at their blank expressions before continuing. 'So, someone broke into the treasure vault in the castle and disappeared with the *entire* treasury. All of it. One moment it was there, the next it was gone. No one knows who took it or how, it's just gone. I know you've got all kinds of crazy creatures running around at the moment, but I couldn't resist trying to take a peek at the vault. Professional curiosity.'

'So, you're some sort of *crime tourist* now?' He couldn't hide the distaste in his voice.

'Some of us need more stimulation in our lives than milking the cows and churning the butter in our little backwater village, Nick,' Shift bit back. A part of him wanted to correct them about the fact that he was a baker, not a farmhand, but he didn't think it'd do him any favours saying it.

'Wow.' Auron raised his ethereal eyebrows in surprise. 'This kingdom's having a tough time of it. That explains the state of the place. The kingdom must be broke.'

'Yeah, they're taxing the people like crazy to try and make it back up.' Shift seemed thoughtful. 'Apparently, something happened with the king too, but no one's really talking about it. But between all that and these weird creatures appearing across the kingdom, everyone thinks the place is cursed.'

'Those creatures are the ones who brought us here,' Garaz interjected. 'We tracked them back to their original source.'

Shift followed the orc's pointing finger to T'goth, who was amusing himself by drawing in the dust again—this time, it was phalluses as he giggled like a child. Taking a moment to process the information, Shift shook their head. 'So that really is T'goth?'

'Yes,' Nicolas cut in testily. *Why is it more believable when Garaz says it?* 'Someone stole his powers, and is using it to create all kinds of hybrid monsters, and people are getting hurt.'

As if to punctuate his point, the dust caused T'goth to sneeze. There was a flash of light, and when it receded, the large cobweb above him was the colours of a rainbow. Less impressive than his last sneeze, but maybe that was due to leaving the shrine. The old man appeared to weaken and pale after the exertion, holding the shelf to steady himself for a moment before it passed.

'That. Is. Crazy!' Shift exclaimed as they looked at the cobweb in fascination.

'This has all got to be related,' Auron said. 'Someone steals the powers of a Deity and then someone steals the kingdom's entire treasury. That can't be a coincidence. No way. I'd bet my lif...' The spirit caught himself midsentence, '...a lot of gold on it.'

'We came here in hopes of a lead to find the culprits behind the creatures, and I believe we are on the right track,' Garaz mused.

'So, I have some company on my trip to the treasury then?' Shift asked with an expectant half-smile.

'Seems so,' Nicolas confirmed. 'Though how long do you think you can swan around as a general before bumping into the real one?'

Shift put their hand on his shoulder and shook their head like a disappointed parent. 'Give me some credit,' they scoffed. 'The real general *accidentally* took a sleeping draught before I nabbed his armour. I should've been in and out by now, but I was on my way to the castle and spied you guys in need of saving. *Again*.'

'Good job you did.' Auron laughed.

'Risky plan, though.' Just walking into a castle pretending to be someone else seemed more than risky; it seemed suicidal.

'Better than turning up at the city gates with all my friends and hangers-on in an old wagon and asking nicely to be let in.' Shift smirked.

That was fair.

'So the fellowship's back together then?' Auron sounded pleased, which was surprising given his vocal opinion of Nicolas's use to the group.

'Don't call us that.' Shift rolled their eyes theatrically. 'It makes us sound like a group of traveling minstrels.'

Nicolas chuckled at the thought of them as bards.

'So, we need to accompany you to the castle and—' Garaz began.

'Nick and Auron need to accompany me,' Shift interrupted. 'Sorry, big guy, but you stick out like a sore green thumb. And someone needs to stay here with the others. The old man is the most likely to get us caught, and I'm not having Silva walking behind me. I don't care how many times she's saved Nicky's life.' *Nicky?* 'I have a very clear memory of her trying to kill him and planning on doing the rest of us, too. Plus, she kidnapped me that time.'

Silva stared at Shift for a moment as if trying to remember them. 'Sorry,' the warrior offered finally.

'Not forgiven,' Shift replied snottily.

Garaz was clearly unhappy at being left babysitting a reformed murderer, an old man who insisted on referring to him as a goat, and the chicken, but he said nothing. With his facial expression, he didn't need to. Shift was right, though—no way they could walk an orc into the castle without questions being asked. T'goth ignored the whole conversation, but at least he'd gotten bored of drawing men's privates in the dust. For now.

'They have a point,' Auron conceded, 'I can't be seen anyway, and if we can find the kid here a uniform, no one will question a general walking with his adjutant.'

'You happy to be beneath me?' Shift suddenly asked Nicolas.

His cheeks flushed and his mouth opened but only stammering came from it. As the initial wave of awkwardness receded, it dawned on him that he was being teased and finally responded with a simple, but rude, gesture.

'Bet you didn't learn *that* in the village.' Shift smiled.

'I believe we are starting to be a bad influence on young Nicolas,' Garaz mused. 'Mostly you two, though, as I am a great example to follow.'

Again, they laughed, and Silva watched their interaction with confusion.

As terrible as this situation was, he was so pleased to see Shift again.

'That's settled then,' Auron declared. 'We shall investigate, and Garaz can babysit the rest of our ever-growing group.'

'We've taken down a necromancer and an army of vampires...what else can dare stand against us?' Shift declared boldly, slapping their chest plate a little too loudly for Nicolas's comfort.

This adventure was rapidly spiralling out of control. Starting out, all they'd needed to do was find who or what was making strange creatures and stop them. Now, they had to restore the power of a Deity, return a castle treasury, and maybe save a king too? It just kept piling on, one new dangerous task after another. How many more before his legs gave out, metaphorically speaking? He tried to get his mind around the enormity of what they needed to achieve, but all it did was cause his head to begin to throb. As the edges of his vision blurred he closed his eyes, trying to take slow, even breaths without making it obvious to everyone else that's what he was doing. Even with the calming breaths, his hand continued to tremble. It was getting worse.

Should I tell them? Would I be able to if I tried?

No matter how close to the brink he was, this kingdom was closer. Despondency was thick in the air. These people were suffering and in need of aid, and they were the best placed to do it. Part of him thought about suggesting they just handed all they'd learned, and T'goth, to the kingdom's army and let them deal with it. But the army knew the problems already and seemed to be doing little save locking everyone down and threatening any well meaning traveller they came across. If not the soldiers, then who was actually going to help the people? Looking at his companions, he guessed it was them. Stilling his hand, he let the thought settle in his mind.

'We need to help these people.' The determination in his voice surprised him. 'Whatever it takes.'

'We shall,' Garaz said, patting his shoulder. 'We will do all we can to heal this kingdom.'

'I was going to the treasury anyway, so I might as well help save the kingdom.' Shift shrugged playfully. 'Shame to let you guys have all the fun.'

Whatever Auron thought of Nicolas's statement, he kept it to himself, though he stared at Nicolas with that uncomfortable, unreadable face. Beside the spirit, the chicken also watched the proceedings.

Nicolas just wished he knew how they'd accomplish this feat. There were way too many unknowns for his liking. What he was sure of was that they needed to move quickly, as someone was bound to notice the wagon not arriving at the castle eventually. Plus, who knew when the real general would wake? Time was against them as sure as any opponent.

'Shift, what can you tell me about the layout of the city?' Now Auron had a clear objective he seemed in his element. It was refreshing after their companions recent behaviour.

Nicolas, who found conversations about street layouts difficult to follow and thus very uninteresting, decided the best method of navigation would be to simply follow those who knew where they were going. Wandering back to the wagon with the idea of grabbing something edible and hopefully tasty before they left on the next phase of their quest, he found Silva, hands on hips, blocking his way. The lithe warrior made for an imposing roadblock as he tried really hard not to pay too much attention to the muscle definition around her abdomen or her tightly moulded chestplate.

'My eyes are up here.' Obviously, his attempts had failed.

'I...uh...' Nicolas stammered. At least his tone was apologetic.

'I should go with you,' the warrior declared, changing the subject, much to his relief.

'Shift said you need to stay.' He didn't relish the prospect of this argument.

'She does not command me.' Silva's face was set.

'Firstly, it's *they* not *she*,' Nicolas corrected. 'And secondly, Shift is crucial to the mission, and if they cannot trust you, it will make our task much harder.' Maybe talking to Silva in terms of missions and objectives would make her understand his point better.

The former mercenary mulled it over for a moment or two. 'How am I to observe you and better myself if you are not around to observe? And how am I to protect you?'

Nicolas was about to say he didn't need protection, but it sounded stupid before he even opened his mouth. 'Well, you have saved my life twice, so I think you're off to a good enough start that a couple of hours without me won't harm you, and I think I can manage an hour or two in a castle surrounded by soldiers without getting in any serious danger.' *Time for a new tactic.* Nicolas dropped his voice low. 'Besides, someone needs to stay and guard the others. Garaz is nice and all, but he's a wizard, not a fighter, and T'goth is, well...' It was a simple gambit, but it was all he had.

Silva seemed to consider this for an overly long moment before nodding in satisfaction. 'It shall be done.'

Nicolas tried to stifle his sigh of relief.

Walking off without making a single sound, Silva moved to the window of the warehouse that faced the main street. Standing close to the wall to lessen her silhouette, she kept watch through a gap in the boarding.

As Nicolas turned, he found Garaz behind him, arms folded. 'I can fight better than you,' the orc commented dryly.

Chapter 13

Finding a uniform for Nicolas turned out to be a much easier task than he'd anticipated. Shift simply walked into the nearest guardhouse and demanded one, obviously having resumed the form of the general first. Apparently, all it took was the correct amount of bluster and bravado and the assumption that no common soldier dared question anyone way, way up the chain of command from them.

And yet, the further they got, the more he worried. Yes, Shift looked flawless as the general and carried themselves perfectly, but at some point, they would push their luck, and when they did, the results would be potentially lethal. Security in the castle was bound to be tighter than a simple guard house by a tavern, and though he wasn't up to date on the laws of Sarus, he assumed impersonating a general to infiltrate the castle was well into the realms of treason and espionage, and most likely earned you a one-way ticket to the executioner's block.

'It's all a matter of confidence,' Shift reassured him when he voiced his worry. 'Walk in like you own the place, and no one will say anything.'

Walking a couple of steps behind the mounted Shift, as an adjutant should, Nicolas wished he could be convinced so easily. The armour they'd found for him was actually a decent enough fit, but the helmet shifted position whenever it fancied, causing him to fidget with it, while the chest plate cut into his armpits in time with the movement of his legs.

'Once, I strode into the lair of Gragus Gut-ripper simply by painting myself green and snarling at anyone who looked at me funny. He lived in an underground cave, so it was dark, and I didn't fancy fighting my way through a horde of goblins to get to him. Spindly, annoying creatures, but pretty deadly in numbers,' Auron told them both. 'I was a good six feet from Gragus with sword in hand before anyone even realised. Gragus was dead before anyone could draw a weapon, and other than a couple brave ones who joined their master on the floor dead seconds later, the rest of the goblins legged it. Most sensible move they'd made since before joining up with the idiot.' Auron had an almost dreamy half-smile.

'I'm not sure Garaz would be happy to hear about you painting yourself green.' Nicolas tried to alter the strap on his helmet to keep the damned thing in place. 'He might not think it's very...appropriate.'

Auron looked at Nicolas for a second. 'I'm sure the Gut-ripper's past victims and the people he was going to kill wouldn't begrudge a little *greening up* for the greater good,' the spirit stated, before adding. 'Sometimes you have to get your hands dirty to do what's right.'

Subtle, Nicolas thought to himself sourly.

Locking down a whole city did make travelling anywhere thankfully simple. With no pedestrians or traders or playing children to hamper their progress, the trio made good time getting to the castle. Passing through the deathly quiet streets of what should've been a bustling city reminded Nicolas of his first foray in Yarringsburg. Though that city's streets were deserted due to a horde of vampires killing anyone who wasn't locked behind a sturdy door. This city was also under the grip of something malevolent, just less obvious. It felt as if the soul of the city itself was being drained, leaving despair in its place. Hopefully, this expedition proved fruitful and they could find something to help these poor people. Maybe if they got the treasury back, they would invest in a street cleaner or two. At the moment, it was a choice between trying not to breathe and gagging on the filth along every path. No choice at all then.

Even the finer dwellings near the castle, which should've been where the city's well-to-do lived, were but a shade of the lavish town houses he'd seen in Yarringsburg, and in a state of repair in keeping with the rest of the city. The fine topiaries left to wither as thorned, tentacle-like weeds protruded and strangled them was a good metaphor for what was happening to the rest of the city.

Beyond the homes of the city's elite sat Sarus Castle, in the dead centre of the city, somehow looking elderly and infirm. But just like the gates to the city, this aging citadel was heavily defended., Bristling battlements looked ready to unleash their fury at a moment's notice, and he could clearly see why. One of the castle's domed towers showed signs of damage—blackened where flames had struck stone and gouged by what could only be claws. Whatever had made them was a lot bigger and fiercer than a cow-dragon, though judging by the bloodstains splattered around it, the city's defenders had made a good account of themselves. No wonder it was on such high alert.

'Let me do the talking,' Shift whispered as they approached the heavy portcullis barring entry to the castle itself.

'Like I was planning on doing anything different,' he whispered back.

The trio, though only two of them were visible to the guards, stopped just short of the gate, Shift sitting astride their horse with what Nicolas assumed was a commanding posture, featuring a lot of chest puffing and chin raising. The guards before them wore finer armour than the ones he'd seen in the city thus far, obviously some kind of elite palace guard. Their commanding officer stepped forward and exchanged salutes with the general.

'Castle is on lockdown, General,' the officer said apologetically. 'None are permitted to pass since the...attack last night.' He glanced nervously at the damaged tower.

Shift stayed silent for a moment, glaring at the officer from beneath bushy black eyebrows.

Nicolas's limbs shook with nerves, and he had to physically force them to stay still. It wouldn't be him who blew their ruse, no matter how much of a burden he was to the group.

'Where did this order come from, Captain?' Shift finally asked in a tone of temporary indulgence.

The captain looked confused for a moment, as if trying to work out whether this was a trick question. 'From the High Council, sir.'

'And how was this order relayed to you?' Shift continued, keeping the same tone.

'Um...down through the chain of command, sir.' The captain was definitely out of his comfort zone now.

'Excellent.' Shift smiled thinly. 'And therefore, as a general and your superior in this chain of command...'

'You can countermand that order and be allowed access to the castle?'

General Shift smiled thinly. 'Correct,' they said. 'Now, get that gate open, son, and I will pretend this conversation never happened.'

The captain, now quite pale, quickly strode off and ordered the gate open.

Nicolas didn't envy his position. 'Nice work.'

General Shift turned to Nicolas and gave him a cheeky wink, which seemed too daring with so many potential eyes watching them. Though he had to admit he was impressed at the power one person could wield over another.

Moving through the now-open gate, they only broke pace slightly so the general could compliment the gate guard on doing their duty effectively.

****

The castle itself was as deserted as the rest of the city. Where there should've been servants bustling around and courtiers doing whatever it was they did, there were only silent corridors. It was as eerily quiet and empty as the last castle he'd visited, but he hoped for a very different reason.

'This will be easier than I thought,' Auron stated boldly as they walked through drab passageways of grey stone.

'We aren't there yet.' Nicolas didn't want to let his guard down too soon. *That's when fate gets you.*

'You're just as jumpy as I remember,' Shift commented, though with their back to him, he couldn't tell whether this was said in jest.

The trio looked for the first staircase leading down, working on the assumption that the treasure vault would be beneath the building itself. Shift assured the others that was where they generally were. Descending the stairs into the bowels of the castle, they finally came across some people, passing a pair of jittery-looking men in robes talking in hushed tones, who only paused briefly to nod to the general.

Nicolas picked out bits of their conversation as he passed.

'…luck locating the king…could be anywhere…tragedy for the kingdom…'

Looking briefly at his companions, he could tell they'd picked up on the conversation as well.

Reaching the bottom of the lowermost staircase in the castle, with some excellent guidance from Shift, the trio found themselves before a large iron door that seemed more formidable than the castle in its entirety. How had someone managed to get this far *and* steal an entire kingdom's wealth?

The five men guarding the door stood at attention with crisp salutes. The sergeant stepped forward. 'What can we do for you, General?'

'I'm here to examine the vault,' Shift replied in an authoritative tone.

'Hoping for another clue after your last visits, sir?' the sergeant enquired.

Nicolas's stomach clenched. Though the question had been breezy enough, it was a sign their deception might be starting to unravel.

'Coming back with fresh eyes may help us avenge this wrong that has blighted our kingdom,' Shift replied instantly, indicating Nicolas, who stood there attempting to do his best to look like he belonged and actually knew something. He tried to ignore the sceptical look from the spirit to his left.

'Very good, sir.' The sergeant seemed less than taken with Nicolas but turned and gestured to the two men standing directly by the door.

The sergeant took a key from a string around his neck, put it in the lock, and turning it as the two men worked the large circular handle on the door. After a deep clicking sound from somewhere inside the wall, the men heaved, pulling the door open and presenting a short corridor beyond.

'Will you need accompanying, sir?' the sergeant asked.

'No, no.' General Shift gave a dismissive wave of their hand. 'No assistance is required.'

'Very good, sir.'

Stepping back, the soldiers cleared the way, and the trio entered a long passageway, which led to a vast open room. Just like the rest of the architecture in Sarus, the treasury was designed purely for function. And that function was to be filled with treasure, making the fact that it was currently bare disconcerting. Plinths and raised platforms which should've contained valuable works of art and chests of gold sat empty. Walking into this room when it was filled with the wealth of a kingdom must've been awe inspiring. Now it just looked bleak and sad.

'I think we're on the right track.' Auron strode to the back of the room, and Nicolas and Shift followed.

Nicolas found the echoing of their steps throughout the room – save Auron's – unnerving. Despite himself, he glanced back several times to make sure they weren't being followed. As Nicolas approached the back of the chamber he made out a large shadow in the wall, a hole, leading to a dark tunnel beyond. What made the hole interesting was that the edges were lined with plant matter—what appeared to be vines that had been cut through to allow access to the treasury. The floor was still covered in rotting plants, creating a horrible sickly-sweet smell in the room.

'They must've used T'goth's stolen power to turn part of this wall to vegetation and simply cut through it.' Auron examined the opening carefully. 'Smart.'

'Is smart the right word?' Nicolas asked. 'You get the power of a Deity, and you use it to rob people. Is that the best you can do with it?'

'Sometimes people don't have a choice how they use their power. They just have to do the best they can with whatever fate deals them.' There was genuine offence in Shift's eyes.

He hadn't meant to include them in what he'd said, though it was pretty rich to be high and mighty about stealing from people. Feeling the need to defend himself, he was about to reply when he noticed a hint of regret in those green eyes, stopping the words before they came out of his mouth.

'Sorry,' he said instead.

For a moment, it seemed Shift didn't want to accept the apology, as if they had something to say. Then their brow furrowed momentarily before they shook it off. Maybe they weren't as happy-go-lucky as he'd always assumed. They were so engrossed in their moment that when they heard an unexpected noise, they both jumped. Nicolas wheeled round and drew his sword instinctively, a reaction he was quietly quite pleased about. Even Auron seemed to start.

The sword went from a ready position to hanging at his side as Nicolas stared in surprise.

'How in the Underworld did *that* get in here?' Shift asked with an expression of utter confusion.

Standing on the stone floor before them, as if it were the most natural thing in the world, was the chicken. The bird wasn't doing anything, just looking up at them in a creepy way.

'It must've followed us in.' The fact that this chicken's random appearance usually coincided with danger wasn't a good sign, and his heartbeat quickened as his hand tremored.

'So much for the security in this castle.' Auron snorted. 'They can't even keep a chicken out.'

'And well done to Garaz.' Shift smirked. 'He had one job.'

After staring blankly at them for a moment, the chicken tilted its head curiously. Then several things happened at once. The chicken screamed at the top of its avian lungs, a piercing screech that made Nicolas wince. Shift suddenly fell forward as if struck from behind, landing hard on the stone floor. When Nicolas wheeled around, the tip of a familiar crossbow was aimed directly between his eyes.

'We meet again, boy,' Wade purred from the trigger end of the crossbow. 'And once again you're in my way. Tut, tut.'

The hunter had only a single eye open—the one looking down the sights of the crossbow at Nicolas. He doubted it was really worth the effort of aiming at this distance; the hunter couldn't miss if he tried.

'Sorry it's for the last time.' Wade pouted insincerely.

Nicolas's bowels readied to empty, his world narrowing until all he knew was the crossbow. His chest tightened and his lungs pumped like dragon's wings. The tremor in his hand became a full shake, and with a clang, he dropped his sword. The hunter's face was covered in spots, and Nicolas swayed, his legs threatening to betray him at any moment and drop him to the ground.

Auron appeared beside Wade, regarding the hunter through narrowed eyes. 'Time to be useful.'

Though Wade could neither see nor hear Auron, the spirit's training had paid off, and the hunter most definitely felt the ethereal finger poke him on the side of his nose—the tip bent under the sudden pressure. Yelping in surprise, Wade wheeled around with the crossbow, looking for a target.

'Now, kid!' Auron cried.

He didn't move. Couldn't. He was going to die, and that was that. In fact, he was already dead, events just hadn't caught up to him yet. Images of vampires flashed in front of his eyes.

'For Deities' sake,' Auron cried before a second finger poke hit him directly between the eyes, jarring him back into the room as if he'd been shot from a catapult. Present again, he saw and understood what was happening, not wasting the opportunity he swung his fist with everything he had towards the distracted hunter.

Wade recoiled from the impact as the blow caught him hard in the cheek. Spittle flew from his mouth as he staggered back, dropping his weapon to the floor. Nicolas had hoped to floor the hunter, but his inexperience had made the punch less spectacular than he'd planned. Trying to follow up his momentum with a left hook, he found his arm caught mid-air in a vice-grip.

Snarling, Wade struck Nicolas with an uppercut that sent him reeling backwards. For a second, the whole world went black. His neck pulled taut as his head snapped back, the impact jarring his teeth. His body went limp, the only thing keeping him from falling completely being the hunter still gripping his arm. Blood poured from his mouth over his chin.

Yanking him painfully to a standing position, Wade followed up by grabbing Nicolas around the throat and driving him into the nearest wall, his head striking it with a dizzying smack. Leering over the still dazed and now-choking Nicolas, the hunter drew his knife with his free hand and ran it down Nicolas's cheek like a twisted lover's caress. His eyes followed the knife down as far as they could, his skin shivering at the cold touch. He tried to plea for his life, but his throat was held too tightly for words to escape. He was getting really sick of being choked against walls.

'What's going on here?' The noise of the infernal, now blessed, chicken had brought the guards upon them, weapons drawn and ready as they took in the scene before them.

The sudden burst of relief made tears well up in his eyes.

'Arrest this assassin,' Shift cried, raising themselves from the floor and pointing at Wade.

The palace guard didn't obey. Probably because the voice issuing the command wasn't the voice of their general, but Shift's actual voice. When he glanced at his companion, they'd reverted to their preferred form—probably a side effect of being hit from behind by Wade. The guards stared at the scene for a moment, the sergeant slack jawed at the sight of the slight female-looking figure in the general's uniform.

'Intruders. Spies,' he cried. 'Arrest them all.'

With a cry, the guards charged forward, Nicolas's relief turning back to despair in an instant.

Wade looked from Nicolas to the charging guards and furrowed his brow in frustration. 'Lucky boy,' the hunter snarled as he dropped him, before reaching for his crossbow, obviously intending to flee.

There was something about the casualness of Wade's manner that riled him.

He just hurt Shift, he's going nowhere.

Grabbing a handful of the hunter's cape, Nicolas yanked with all his might. There was a strangled choking sound before Wade toppled backwards, landing on the floor and cracking his head on the stone. The crossbow slipped out of the hunter's hand and landed at Nicolas's feet.

Scooping up the weapon, he wheeled round to face the charging guards. 'Stay where you are!'

His attempt to sound commanding wasn't what he hoped, but the guards still stopped instantly, glaring at him menacingly, clearly ready to advance again at the slightest opening. His arms, the weight of the crossbow unfamiliar to them, were already starting to shake. Fiercely he fought it back. His attempts to threaten the guards with the weapon would be undermined if said weapon started trembling in his hands.

How do you even work the damned thing?

Not that he intended to use it, but he needed to know. Carefully feeling around, so as not to alert the guards to his action, his finger finally came to rest on what he assumed to be the trigger.

'Calm down now, son,' the sergeant said with a more commanding voice than his. 'No one has to get hurt here.'

For a moment, he almost felt the need to respect the man's authority and hand over his weapon.

But then how will I explain all of this?

Not in any way he imagined would be either believed or accepted.

'No one will get hurt if you stay where you are.' Nicolas gestured with the crossbow for emphasis.

The soldiers clearly wanted to make a run for him, but none of them wanted to be the first to risk getting shot with an arrow.

'Think about this, son,' the sergeant continued. 'If you surrender now, you and your friends will be treated leniently.' The look on the sergeant's face said differently.

'Just remember, kid,' Auron whispered in Nicolas's ear. '*You* are in control of this situation. *You* are the one with the crossbow. You got this.'

Auron was right that he had the crossbow, but he certainly didn't feel in control of anything. He needed to make the most of the situation, though, especially as his arm felt like it would give out any second from the weight of the weapon. How did Wade carry it around all the time, let alone shoot it accurately?

'Drop your weapons,' he demanded.

'Not going to happen, son,' the sergeant replied firmly.

He had only a second to think *'oh no'* as he finally felt his arms give. The tip of the crossbow dipped against his will, to point at the blasted chicken, who squawked in alarm, causing the guards to finally notice it.

'No!' the sergeant cried, holding his hands up. 'We'll drop our weapons. Do not shoot.'

What?

The soldiers wore panicked expressions.

What's with Sarus folk and their chickens? Are they a holy bird?

The chicken certainly didn't look holy as it gave him a lopsided look.

'Wow, they really love their chickens here.' Shift rubbed the swelling on the back of their neck tenderly.

Whatever the reason, it was a fact, one that gave him leverage in a bad situation. So he kept the weapon pointed at the chicken. 'Weapons on the ground,' he reiterated, emboldened by his new power. 'Now!'

Surprisingly, the men slowly lowered themselves to the ground and laid their swords on the stone floor, albeit grudgingly. None seemed to want to risk the chicken. The problem they had now was they were stuck. If he went to leave, the soldiers would pick up their weapons and pursue them, but he couldn't stand here forever and wasn't about to kill soldiers doing their duty. Or the chicken, annoying as the thing may be.

There was a moment of tense silence in the treasury.

'Keys,' Shift demanded suddenly. 'Throw the keys to the door over to us then make your way outside the vault.'

For a moment, the sergeant seemed unwilling to relent, until Nicolas persuaded him with another gesture towards the chicken with his weapon. He removed the key from around his neck and threw it to the floor by Shift's feet. Then, at his nod, the men backed slowly out of the room.

'Don't think this is over, son,' the sergeant snarled. 'Your life isn't going to be worth spit from now on. You and your little girlfriend are going to be hunted down, and you'll both hang for—'

'Firstly, I'm not his girlfriend,' Shift interrupted. 'And secondly, I am not a *girl*.'

The sergeant's last words before he closed the door made Nicolas's stomach knot. 'The executioner won't care, love.'

Shift grabbed the key from the floor and ran to the door, locking it with a definite *click*.

'That won't hold them for long.' Shift's cool exterior melted, and Nicolas saw the urgency in their eyes. 'They'll have a ram or something down here soon. We have to move.'

'What about him?' he asked, pointing to Wade, who was beginning to stir.

'Leave him.' Auron seemed reluctant. 'We need to move fast, and if we try to take him with us, he'll be a liability.'

Nicolas had to agree. The hunter would either try to escape or be too dazed to move quickly. Worse, he might try to kill them again. Either way, they couldn't take him. But before they left, he had a question. Standing over Wade, Nicolas watched the hunter's eyes open slowly as he began to regain consciousness. They opened a heck of a lot wider when they noticed the crossbow pointed directly at his face.

'One question.' Nicolas put on his best tough voice. He doubted it was effective, but it didn't need to be with the crossbow. 'Why are you hunting me?'

Now fully alert, the look of surprise from Wade melted into one of professional detachment, his mouth forming into the smug grin of a man who knew Nicolas wouldn't kill him in cold blood. Still, he had the sense not to try anything funny. Trigger fingers could twitch.

'Who said I was after you, boy?' the sneering hunter answered slowly and deliberately.

About to ask what he meant, Nicolas was interrupted by a loud thump at the vault door.

Firing the bolt harmlessly into the nearest wall, he threw the crossbow away and grabbed his sword, following Shift and Auron as they ran through the opening in the wall, leaving Wade LeBeck where he lay in the hope that he would be caught by the guards and thrown into a deep dark hole.

'Did you see what I did back there with the finger?' Auron asked with a beaming smile as he ran beside Nicolas.

'Yes.' Mostly, he remembered how badly he'd frozen. He was getting less useful by the hour. 'Thanks.'

'I think I'll have to name that move,' the spirit mused to himself. 'I'm thinking *finger poke of doom*. What do you reckon?'

What he reckoned, as the echoes of the battering against the vault door rang through the tunnel, was that they didn't have time for conversations like this.

Chapter 14

The sound of the alarm bells that had begun to toll throughout the city reverberated through the earth until it was carried to them, almost drowning out the squelching as they crushed decayed plant matter underfoot. It was a call to arms for every soldier in Sarus, all of whom would now be looking for him and Shift. That fact made the claustrophobia of the slim tunnel a secondary concern.

When they finally emerged, it was into a warehouse similar to the one in which their companions awaited their return. Why had no one bothered to guard the end of a tunnel that led directly into the castle itself? They must've known it was there, unlike the tunnel he and his companions had used in Yarringsburg.

His question was soon answered when they discovered two dead soldiers heaped lazily behind some storage crates.

'Wade must've seen us enter the castle and knew of this access point.' Auron looked solemnly at the dead soldiers, who'd been stabbed in the back.

Two men didn't seem enough to guard a tunnel that led directly into the castle. It just seemed wrong. Even so, how had Wade managed to get the drop on them so well? Yes, the hunter was quiet, but surely after he'd killed the first soldier the other would've noticed?

'Shame we didn't have a chance to question him.' Nicolas hated the unknown; it went against his sense of preparedness. Though it was all he'd known since meeting Auron.

'I doubt he'll just go away, so we'll get another chance.' As much as Nicolas hoped Wade was being thrown into a cell right now, the spirit was almost certainly right.

'Yeah, I need to pay him back for my headache,' Shift said. 'But right now, we've got to move. Those bells aren't sounding for daily services. And they know exactly where we came out.'

Once Auron assured them the way ahead was clear, they made a fast exit from the warehouse and found cover in an alleyway directly across from the building. And just in time. Moments later, a troop of soldiers charged the warehouse and crashed through the door as if storming a castle. From the sound of it, they were equally heavy handed inside—shouts and the crunch of breaking wood reached them in their hiding place. Leniency was definitely out the window.

Quickly, Nicolas and Shift removed their armour, since it would slow them down and draw the wrong attention. After some struggle, Nicolas finally managed to free himself from his chest plate, only to find the chicken by his boot again. Looking up at him, the bird opened its beak.

'No, you bloody don't.' He grabbed the struggling animal and tucked it under his arm.

'We need to move before they're through in there,' Shift whispered, gesturing towards the sounds of crashing as the soldiers turned the warehouse upside down looking for them. Moving off, they heard a distinctive shout from inside the building. The soldiers had found their comrades' bodies. That was bound to be attributed to them.

Making their way through the warehouse district was a game of cat and mouse as they constantly stopped to avoid the patrols Auron scouted. The sigh of relief Nicolas breathed when they finally entered their hideout again became a yelp of fear as he found a blade at his throat, again.

'Ah, it is you.' Silva sheathed the knife. 'I am glad you are back.'

'I'm quite happy about that too.'

'What happened?' Garaz looked at their injuries with concern. 'Considering the city is in uproar and there are soldiers everywhere, I assume the mission did not go to plan?'

'We might've been caught sneaking into the castle treasury, and Nick might've threatened some soldiers with a crossbow.' Shift winced as Garaz touched their swollen neck.

'Nicolas?' Garaz said, shock evident in his voice. He'd been pretty shocked about it too.

'I didn't have a choice,' he said. 'We were doing fine then that idiot Wade jumped us again and things got a little...out of hand.'

'And then some.' Shift was peering carefully out the warehouse window. 'We need to move. It'll only be a matter of time before the search patrols get to us.'

'I don't think impersonating a general is going to work anymore,' Auron said thoughtfully. 'But we can't stay.'

'Well, unless you have a better idea...' Shift began, before something caught their attention. 'What's he doing?'

The Deity was standing in the corner of the room whistling merrily to himself. He held one of his hands in the air in front of him while moving the other up and down rhythmically. Whatever he was doing, the Deity was having the time of his life, though he looked older and greyer than he had before they'd left.

'Is he okay?' he asked Garaz.

'I believe his body is failing.' The orc was solemn. 'This is just a hypothesis, but I believe the shrine was keeping him alive with some kind of residual power. Now that he is away from it, he seems to be deteriorating, becoming weaker and less lucid. He has sneezed twice in your absence and there was no effect to the environment. He is dying.'

Does he even understand what's happening to him? Is this our fault for removing him from the shrine?

The knowledge that he would've followed them anyway didn't ease his guilt.

What even happens when a Deity dies?

After putting the chicken down, he approached the old man as the bird irritably scratched the ground.

'What are you doing, T'goth?' he asked.

Cloudy and unfocused eyes looked at him, as if the old man didn't recognise him. After a second, life came back into them and T'goth smiled weakly. 'I'm being a blacksmith. Look at the sword I made,' he declared, proudly holding up thin air for the group to look at. 'That picture gave me the idea.'

'Picture?' Garaz asked.

T'goth pointed vaguely to the back wall near where he stood. Though it was easy to miss at a glance, a tiny picture of an anvil with a sword through it had been carved into the wood at the very base of the wall. It looked exactly like the tattoos of the men who'd assailed him outside the tavern.

'The *Forged*,' Shift said as they appeared over Nicolas's shoulder and scrutinised the carving.

'The who?'

'The Forged,' Shift repeated. 'You've not heard of them?'

'Don't ask what the kid hasn't heard of. Just assume he doesn't know.' Auron huffed. Pretty rich considering he blatantly didn't know either.

'The Forged are a criminal gang that operate hereabouts,' Shift explained. 'They had this place in a stranglehold of corruption until King Silus came to power and started cleaning up the streets. Drove them right out of the city, so I heard. Like all gangs they're part of the Criminal Guild. This crew is run by a guy who calls himself *Big Boss*.'

'There's a *Criminal Guild?*' Garaz asked, sounding a little outraged.

'There's a guild for everything nowadays.' Auron shrugged.

'Who refers to themselves as *Big Boss?*' Someone with inferiority issues, Nicolas guessed.

'The Criminal Guild put him in charge of the rackets in Sarus, and they milked this place like a cow. Gaming, robbery, you name it,' Shift continued, ignoring him.

'And smuggling.' Auron's comment was pointed.

'And smuggling,' Shift repeated with a big grin. 'I bet this warehouse has a smugglers' tunnel. That's why the marking's here.' They searched feverishly around the carving, pressing the wall, pulling things, and moving boxes.

It was funny—after everything that had happened since the tavern, the ruffians seemed so inconsequential by comparison. He'd put them out of his mind.

Oh for the days when being roughed up outside a tavern was the worst part of this quest.

His reminiscences were interrupted by a clicking, followed by the sound of creaking wood. As the tunnel opened, Shift gave them all an exaggerated bow. 'Smugglers' tunnel-finder extraordinaire,' they announced with no attempt whatsoever at modesty.

After the whole affair with the vampires, the group had become a dab hand at navigating dimly lit tunnels. The one running under the warehouse was sturdy and well-supported, with a neatly flattened trail through it, giving it the dubious honour of being the best tunnel Nicolas had been in. As they travelled, the sound of chicken clucks echoed around, the persistent bird determined to follow them wherever they went. And the bells were still ringing.

When the tunnel came to an abrupt dead end panic came on instantly. Looking around the dirt walls they seemed to shrink towards him. *A trick of the eye, surely?* What his eye couldn't see, was a door. *Will we be trapped in here forever?* Whilst Nicolas worried, Shift did something practical and found the chain to open a secret door. Counterweights ground as stone slid away to flood the dark tunnel with eye-watering light and let fresh air mute the earthy smell around them. Nicolas uttered a small prayer as he let the light wash over him.

They emerged into the day—what was left of it, anyway—and a graveyard. The stone concealing the tunnel's entrance was a large, ornate gravestone reading *'Mr S Muggler, Beloved Father and Husband, Died of plague.'*

'Cute,' Auron remarked, reading the name.

They were well beyond the city limits, on a small hill far from the wall circling Sarus. Even here, the sound of the bells reached them. Surely there were no soldiers left to alert by now?

As the others milled around dusting dirt from their clothes—or mostly naked body, in Silva's case—Auron sidled up to Nicolas.

'What was that in the treasury?' the spirit asked.

'What?' Shame made him play dumb.

'When I distracted Wade, you nearly didn't do anything...what was that?'

That same shame made his voice a hoarse whisper. 'I just froze.'

Auron looked levelly at him. 'I have a lot of experience in seeing you freeze,' the spirit declared hurtfully. 'That wasn't freezing. That was something else. You weren't even in the room anymore.'

He'd hoped no one had noticed. His hand began to shake again. If it hadn't been for Auron, he would've been dead. Shift too. 'I...I...I don't know.'

He knew, he very much knew, but he was ashamed to say it aloud. From the look on his companion's face, the spirit didn't want to hear it either. 'Look kid, I know I've been harsh with you, but it's only because I'm starting to realise how much you aren't cut out for this.' More because of his refusal to kill Silva, he suspected. 'And that's on me too for convincing you to come along. But it's not just your life in danger, it's theirs too. If you really can't handle this...' the spirit paused as if reluctant to speak. Nicolas was reluctant to hear what he knew was coming. '...then maybe you ought just go. Slip away, before a lot of people you care about get hurt.'

'What's going on?' Shift came up to them, concern on their face.

'Just making sure the kid's okay.' Auron half-smiled before walking away.

Nicolas went to move but Shift took his hand. 'Whatever happened in there, I trust you.'

When he looked up at Shift, words tightened his throat, but he couldn't say them. What he really wanted to do was run home, but he was too frightened to even do that alone. Instead, he pulled away.

He turned...and there was a man standing in the middle of the graveyard, looking at them slack jawed, flowers in his hand.

How did we not notice him?

'Uh, hi there,' Nicolas said awkwardly.

The rest of his group turned to stare at the man, who was staring back at them.

'So,' Shift began, just as awkwardly, 'I know this looks a bit strange, but...' They looked to the others for help.

'We are doing nothing untoward. I can assure you, sir,' Garaz jumped in, his statement contradicted by the echoing of the alarm bells in the distance.

The man said nothing, continuing to stare at the group with surprise.

Eventually, just as Nicolas was about to speak again, he spoke.

'You have a chicken.'

Five people emerged from a hidden tunnel beneath a gravestone as the city's alarm bells went crazy and *that* was what he focused on? Bloody Sarus folk and their bloody chickens.

'Yes,' he replied. 'About that—'

Silva appeared out of nowhere and struck the man from behind. Crumpling to the floor, he dropped the flowers, which spread across the grass.

'*Silva!*' Nicolas shouted, running to the man and checking his limp body.

'He is still alive,' the warrior stated matter-of-factly.

'That's not the point,' he cried. 'You can't just go around knocking out anyone you fancy. I thought we'd talked about this?'

'He would have given us away to the city guards.' Silva was resolute. 'At least now we have a head start, and he cannot see which way we go.'

'That's a good point,' Shift agreed, reluctantly. Well, okay, there was a logic in making the cleanest getaway possible. He didn't fancy being run down by a troop of knights before teatime. But he didn't want to give Silva the satisfaction of confirming it aloud. Instead, he rolled the man into a comfortable position on the long grass.

Garaz loomed over Nicolas's shoulder, casting his own, more professional healer's eye over the man. 'He will be fine.'

'Shouldn't be out here when the city is locked down anyway,' Auron said unsympathetically.

'Yeah, out here paying respects to his dead relatives.' Nicolas snorted. 'What a goblin turd.'

Auron shrugged. 'He's probably up to no good.'

'With a bunch of flowers?'

'One day, I'll tell you about the old hag and the bag of apples, kid, but now isn't the time.' They were pressed for time indeed when Auron wouldn't tell a story. 'The question now is where do we go?' Auron looked at the horizon. 'We can't stay here but wandering around randomly might be just as bad.'

'Easy, the Forged aren't exactly hiding,' Shift said breezily. 'We need to go to *The Temple of Champions.*'

'And that is?' Nicolas asked since Shift was clearly dying to show off their knowledge.

'Not far from here is an enchanted forest,' Shift told the group. 'In it's centre is an old temple, just like in all the other enchanted forests in Etherius. Big Boss repurposed it as a gaming hall. Apparently you can bet on anything there, but they specialise in gladiatorial combats.'

'*Sacrilege.*' Garaz's brow was dark and his teeth were bared. 'He *dares* disregard the old laws and sully such an ancient site?'

'I'm missing something,' Nicolas said, raising his hand instantly to stall whatever smart remark Shift looked to make in reply.

'The enchanted forests of Etherius are supposed to be the sites where life first flourished on this world,' Auron explained. 'Each has a temple at its centre, built as a monument to the preservation of that life and gratitude for it.'

'And so he stains the very essence of Etherius itself by turning it into some giant *'gaming hall'.*' Garaz growled with a ferocity that made Nicolas back away slightly.

'The profaning of the temple aside,' Shift said, casting a wary look to the orc. 'The place is Big Boss's seat of power. If he's anywhere, it'll be there.

'And you know this because of your long criminal past?' Nicolas asked with a hint of sarcasm.

'Exactly.' Shift ignored the jibe.

'Okay, we have a destination.' Auron nodded. 'The only thing will be getting in when we get there. Fine for me, but I doubt that sort of establishment lets in just anyone.'

'Don't worry.' Shift said with a half smile. 'I have an idea about that.'

'Which you are not going to share because you love keeping us in suspense?' Garaz said.

'Exactly..' Their smile became a broad grin. 'The idea is part of my *'long criminal past,'* as funny man here puts it.'

'Lead the way then,' Auron said with a smirk.

Shift went west, followed by Auron and Garaz. Nicolas walked with T'goth to prevent him getting distracted and wandering off while Silva brought up the rear of the party, scanning for danger. The chicken walked at Nicolas's feet. As the group approached the opening in the iron fence that led out of the graveyard, Nicolas looked back at the man lying on the grass and then at the chicken.

'What is it with these people and chickens?' he muttered to himself.

'That chicken is full of secrets,' T'goth whispered, tapping his nose with his finger knowingly.

Nicolas looked down at the bird, who returned his gaze. It was just like any other chicken he'd ever seen. Except...

Why is it following us around so doggedly?

Chapter 15

When Shift had used the term *enchanted forest*, Nicolas had been sceptical, assuming it was simply applied to regular forests to make them seem mysterious and exotic. Now that he stood in one, *wow*, how wrong he'd been. He was only vaguely aware that he was still moving as he looked around, enthralled, trying to take in every amazing detail.

Shards of sunlight weaved through the high branches of old trees, illuminating what he first took to be large dust motes, but the intentional patterns of their movements suggested they were something more. Beneath impossibly old trees grew red mushrooms as big as Nicolas's head and as bright as Auron. The air was filled with a sweet humming, as if the whole forest was vibrating in unison to create a single pleasing harmony. This was nature at its absolute best and most mystical. Caressing a low-hanging leaf gently, he couldn't help but gasp as the veins glowed and pulsed at his touch.

'Tourist.' Shift chuckled.

'At least he's stopped complaining about how much his legs hurt,' Garaz smiled.

'And that we lost the wagon,' Auron added.

He was going to pretend he heard none of that. 'How can a place like this hold a seedy gaming den, arena, or whatever you said?' The sheer notion of it was completely ridiculous to him, like a cow-dragon.

'Never underestimate the tenacity of corruption,' Garaz replied sombrely.

'But if everyone knows this is where the Forged are, then why does no one do anything about it?' he asked, inspecting the bark of a tree which was surprisingly soft to the touch. 'Does the magic of this place protect them?'

'Not exactly,' Auron replied, holding his hand out and watching whatever the dust motes really were pass through them. 'Like I said before, these are sacred places. They aren't in the jurisdiction of kingdom's they inhabit.'

That wasn't really an explanation.

Garaz gave him a better one. 'When the elves left, it must have been coming up to a thousand years ago, they lay down edicts to the younger races, to ensure that Etherius thrived in their absence. One of those was the protection of forests such as this, that they be left untouched by the rest of the world. And thus, the life force, the essence, of our world would be preserved.'

'Wow,' Nicolas replied. 'I can see why you got so upset about the temple being defiled by criminals.'

'Indeed,' the orc snarled.

'And why it also makes it an ideal hiding place,' Shift added. 'No army can set foot here to remove them.'

'Places like this should be protected.' Nicolas looked up at the canopy above. Even the rustling of the leaves in the branches sounded melodious. If he'd had the choice, he would've happily stayed here. The glow of the place filled him with a warmth he hadn't felt in a good long while. Like his soul was being tucked into bed and sung a sweet lullaby to aid it to its rest.

'Welcome to Edmoor Forest.' Shift grinned, obviously amused by his dreamy state.

Walking at a dogged pace, they'd made good time, only having to circumvent a single village enroute and reaching Edmoor just before sunset. Though their journey had been free of strange and dangerous creatures, they were due to run into something. The way his luck was going, the longer the wait, the bigger and deadlier the creature they eventually came across.

'Do we make camp here and carry on tomorrow?' Silva asked, already scouting out defensible sites.

'Not a good idea,' Shift said. 'The Temple of Champions is very much a night-life place. If we're going in, it needs to be when it's busy and we can blend in.'

'I think turning up when the place is closed might raise an eyebrow or two,' Auron said. 'Stealth and subtlety will be the key to this one. No Gornak stuff.'

'Who's Gornak?' Nicolas asked.

Auron thought for a moment then chuckled to himself. 'I'll tell you another time,' he said finally. 'You need to get that?'

He turned to follow Auron's pointing finger then cursed. T'goth had begun using one of the big mushrooms for a drum, and Nicolas had to rush off to prise the Deity from his new instrument. Sounding their approach with drumming was neither stealthy nor subtle.

'Are you now going to share your plan to allow us access to the temple?' Garaz asked Shift, who appeared to have been waiting to be asked.

'To get in, you need to be of a certain class and calibre.' Shift grinned theatrically. 'It's pretty exclusive, so we need to show that we fit in. Or more importantly, that I do.'

'We aren't coming with you?' Nicolas asked, slightly concerned.

'Of course. You don't lose me that easily.' They winked in his direction. 'It's just that you guys will be my retinue.'

'Your what?'

'So here's the plan, my friends,' Shift smiled. 'I turn up as a rich merchant looking for some, *entertainment*. I have a lot of coin and a mind to spend it. *But* I need to prove that I'm important. Having you guys with me will reinforce my status to help us get through the door. Once we're in Auron goes to find the vault, when he has we excuse ourselves, break into it and steal back a certain staff of a certain Deity. And we all live happily ever after.'

'As easy as that?' Auron asked.

Shift nodded eagerly.

'And what parts do we play in this little drama of yours?' Garaz asked.

'You and Silva are my protectors. Everyone who's anyone in there has muscle with them. An orc and a mercenary should prove that I'm pretty important. T'goth can be my soothsayer, seeing as we can't leave him wandering out here...'

'Saying sooth, I can sooth say as much as a soothsayer can say sooth.' T'goth danced, clearly happy with his assigned role and seemingly reinvigorated at least partially by his presence in the forest, just as Nicolas was.

'And Nicolas will be my manservant.'

'Your *what*?' he cried, to the general amusement of the group.

'Manservant.' Shift smiled. 'If I'm to appear to have status, I need at least one servant and well...we can't exactly pass you off as muscle, now can we?'

'Ha bloody ha.'

Bad enough I had to follow them around as an adjutant, now this?

'And what part do I play?' Auron asked, grinning at Nicolas's frustration.

'The haunting spirit.'

'I think I can manage that.' Auron nodded happily.

'I have a question.' Nicolas interjected.

'No, you can't swap roles.'

'Not that,' he muttered in annoyance. 'If we're to pass you off as a wealthy merchant, don't you need to...look the part? I know you can change shape, but your outfit doesn't exactly scream affluent.'

Shift looked down at their tunic and breeches. 'Gasp,' they exclaimed with mock hurt. 'You don't like my ensemble?'

'No, it's not...' He stumbled over his words before he realised that Shift was teasing him...again.

'Funny thing about that,' Shift said coyly. 'The plan isn't an original one. The crew I was running with a few years back had the idea, so we stashed some outfits and show money in the forest for when we made our move. However, the day before we'd planned to do so, one of our guys decided to refuse to pay his tab in a city tavern since the ale was like *'warm donkey piss'*. Offence was taken, swords were drawn, guards were called, and that was the end of my crew. The stash should still be here though.'

'What a delightful anecdote.' Garaz grimaced. 'At least their misfortune is our luck now.'

As it turned out, the stash *was* nearby and still intact. Within the hour, they were in their outfits and ready.

****

What were the chances their second attempt at sneaking in somewhere secure would go better than the first? This place was likely much more dangerous than the castle, and look how that had turned out.

As they emerged from the treeline, Nicolas let out an involuntary gasp. His surprise wasn't due to the temple at the edge of the clearing, but more what was around it—or not, in this case. The area directly around the temple had been cleared, stumps left in the ground like grave markers. How could someone take an axe to such a magical place? What sort of person would? It seemed...sacrilegious. And most of the destruction had occurred just to make room for a carriage park.

In a large, fenced-off area, carriages of various sizes and colours waited. The only thing that really linked them was that no expense had been spared to make sure everyone knew exactly how rich the people travelling within them were.

Instead of allowing his sadness at the wanton destruction to take root, he focused on the temple. It was old, ridiculously old, but he'd known that already. He'd just expected...more. The building was almost unassuming: a simple rectangular structure accessed by a pillared walkway and a set of steps. Covered in moss and vines that were equally ancient, the white stone was greyed with age. As far as he could tell, there were no intricate carvings in the stonework, but someone had placed a gaudy sign above the temple's entrance. *'The Temple of Champions'*. The bright yellow lettering stuck out like a sore thumb against the temples greying stone and there was a sword beneath the words, just to put an exclamation point on what this place was. It would look tasteless even in a city setting, here it was outright offensive.

Nicolas found himself shuffling around, smoothing his clothes as if something was amiss with them. Yes, they were new and uncomfortable, but that wasn't the issue. It was the temple. It gave off, he didn't know how to describe it, but his skin was crawling. This sacred place had been violated, and the temple knew it and was screaming it aloud in its own unique way. Finally he had to take his eyes away from the building to ease his discomfort.

There's just no end to the offences this Big Boss will commit.

'So this is *The Temple of Champions*?' he whispered to Shift, unclenching his fist. It was a stupid question, but he needed to distract himself from his outrage. 'I don't see an arena or anything.'

'Dwarfs dig down. It's what they do,' rumbled the deep, unfamiliar voice in reply.

'Big Boss is a dwarf?' Auron asked.

'Didn't I mention that?' Shift asked thoughtfully. 'I don't know if the title's supposed to be ironic, but I do know that dwarf's love their underground structures. That's where the arenas and everything else will be. The temple is just the entrance.'

Why is it all tunnels and underground lairs?

'I thought it'd be...well, more,' Nicolas mused. 'Even the temple itself.'

'This was a place to worship the source of life itself.' Garaz's voice was full of awe. 'It does not need fancy architecture.'

'Yeah, kid,' Auron added, 'people came here to pray, not *ooh* and *aah* at the finely chiselled vestibule or painted ceilings.'

'I believe we came here to do a job,' Silva suggested coolly.

With a deep breath, he started down the pillared walkway—in front of his master, as was expected. At the steps that led to the temple door were five men in black leather tunics, with a black mark under each of their right eyes.

No need to guess what those are.

The guards watched them approach with confident detachment. They had nothing to fear on their own ground. And he had everything to fear.

'Remember what we rehearsed,' Shift whispered in his ear as they came to a stop a respectful distance from the steps. One of the guards moved forwards to greet them.

Rehearsed was a stretch. Shift had told him his lines once and expected him to remember them—*and* they'd already been transformed into this rotund, dark-skinned gentleman wearing a multitude of skins and chains, which had been quite distracting.

'You've got this.' At least they were confident.

'It's really strange talking to you looking like that,' he grumbled.

His annoyance about his role combined with the usual paranoid concerns about what would likely happen if this all went wrong was making him very...tweaky. *Not* a particularly good head space to be in to try to convince seasoned thugs that you were there for some good old-fashioned blood sports, and definitely not to steal from them.

'I'm sorry you can't speak to me if I don't look attractive,' Shift retorted dryly.

He was starting to know a conversational trap when he was about to stumble into one, so he remained quiet.

'Go on, *manservant*,' Shift whispered playfully.

'Yes...sir,' he said, heavy on the sarcasm.

Stopping several metres short of the guard, Nicolas gave an elaborate bow, his servant's tunic—which was too tight—cutting him in several places as he did. 'Greetings,' he said with a flourish. 'My master Talan Talanir the Third wishes access to your establishment.'

'He isn't on the list,' the man replied simply.

'You don't have a list.' And that was his first mistake.

The guard's brow furrowed as he clicked his tongue thoughtfully. Whether from some sixth sense or his own anxiety, he had an idea this guy was weighing up the pros and cons of hitting him for answering back.

'Doesn't matter what I've got in my hand,' the thug replied finally. 'I know our guests, and your *master* isn't one.'

'Tell him: *My master heard Big Boss was welcoming of all wealthy patrons. If that isn't the case, we shall take our leave,*' Auron said.

Nicolas repeated the words before raising his hand and clicking his fingers.

Garaz stepped forward, doing his best to look like a more stereotypical orc. Reaching them, the orc presented the chest he carried, which Nicolas made a big display of opening before stepping back to let the guard appraise what was inside. Rough eyebrows raised at the stack of precious jewels, though really there were only a smattering of real ones atop a pile of forgeries. Garaz closed the chest quickly as it didn't do to have the contents scrutinised too hard. What the guard had seen did the trick, however, as he walked back to the temple, quickly jogging up the steps and banging on the door three times before gesturing for their party to come forward. The door itself was reinforced metal. Probably not part of the original design.

A small metal slot opened in it. He couldn't see who was on the other side.

'Get Lucas,' the guard said.

Without a word, the slot slammed closed again.

The thug made his way back down the steps to them. 'Wait here.'

The wait was very unpleasant. He kept watching the door, expecting armed men to burst forth and attack them at any moment. It was made much less bearable by Shift grumbling about the waiting and belittling him loudly for not hurrying their entry as he squirmed and fidgeted in his tight uniform. Shift was simply playing their role, but it was still annoying, especially as they played it so well.

Finally, the door to the temple opened, and he stifled a yelp. A figure taller and more muscular than Garaz emerged, having to duck slightly to even get through the double doors. Though he'd never seen a minotaur before, he made an educated guess from descriptions he'd heard that this was one.

Great, another cow monster.

Licking his lips casually, the minotaur approached the guard who'd spoken to them and listened as the man whispered in his ear. With a nod, the minotaur turned his bovine eyes to Nicolas and his companions and stomped towards them on hooved feet.

Staring from the thick nose ring to the large black horns, he fought off images of himself being impaled on them as he clenched his shaking hand.

'Relax,' Auron whispered. 'They just want to check us out. Do not blow this, kid.'

'You aren't on the list,' the creature rumbled as he glared down at them.

He didn't answer. It was for the best; he wasn't sure he could keep the fear from his voice. Instead, he again snapped his fingers. The case was produced, its contents flashed. The minotaur snorted. It could've been a positive or negative snort; he couldn't tell.

'Tell your master to step forward,' the minotaur demanded.

This time he had to speak. 'My master does not—'

'I do not deal with *manservants*,' the minotaur snapped, causing Nicolas's testicles to flee to somewhere around his chest.

Shift approached them. 'You may step away, Nick.'

Nicolas turned, bowing as he was shooed away by Shift.

'I'm Lucas,' the minotaur rumbled respectfully. 'Big Boss's Hand.' *Fist, more like.*

'Talan Talanir the Third,' Shift spoke in an almost foppish way. 'Spice trader, entrepreneur, and most importantly tonight, game enthusiast.'

'Forgive me,' Lucas boomed. 'But I've not heard of you around these parts.'

'Dear boy.' Shift chuckled heartily. 'That's because I'm not from around these parts. I'm from the east and usually like to keep it that way, but doing business locally, I heard tales of games here that piqued my curiosity. The *entertainments* back east have become so droll nowadays. Too many authorities enforcing the moral right, if you catch my drift. So I couldn't help but come here to satisfy my curiosity and hopefully bulge my purse.'

'We always welcome hopeful travellers,' Lucas replied. 'If you have the coin, we have the games.'

Shift gestured offhandedly to the chest Garaz was carrying.

'I think we can see our way to squeezing you and your party in.' The minotaur nodded. 'But understand that you are accountable for the behaviour of any of your retinue during your visit.'

'My people know how to behave, dear boy.' Shift smiled back.

The minotaur stood to one side and gestured for the group to head to the door.

'No carriage?' The question wasn't a casual one. The minotaur was as sly as he was big.

Shift didn't even pause. 'Another thing that's droll back east is the healers, my boy. They say my fine dining will be the death of me. I'm not about to change how I eat, I can tell you that, but I will do a bit of extra walking from time to time if I must. Though if I'd known how far the walk would be when my driver dropped me at the edge of the forest, I would've taken the reins and driven the wagon myself.' Shift laughed deeply as they patted their large belly.

'Quite,' Lucas replied, seemingly satisfied.

With that, the minotaur turned and led the way into *The Temple of Champions*.

Chapter 16

Almost immediately after entering the temple, they were stopped by a second set of equally formidable doors. Half of what could've been called a reception area was closed off by bars, beyond which sat a vast array of weapons, ranging from the practical to the exotic. With the odd disturbingly brutal one thrown in.

Lucas raised a palm the size of Nicolas's head. 'Check your weapons here.'

Thankfully, he'd left the *Dawn Blade* with the rest of their gear in the hollow tree where Shift's stash had been. A manservant carrying a sword wasn't in keeping with the character, it'd been explained to him. That was all right for the rest, as they'd gotten to take their weapons with them into the den of villainy. Until now. Maybe now they'd know how naked he felt without the sword. Although, come to think of it, his companions' weapons had been his last protection if something went wrong. He tried to put that to the back of his mind. No one would look at a servant, according to Shift, but if they did, they might ask questions if he were shaking like a leaf.

Garaz handed over his sword to the guard behind an opening in the bars in exchange for some kind of chip. Silva seemed less inclined to comply. The warrior's eyes narrowed, and for a moment it seemed she'd start using rather than surrendering them. One glance from her *master* was all it took to change the warriors mind, thankfully. Though Nicolas was surprised at the number of weapons she handed over.

Where does she keep them all? She barely wears anything...

The thought of Silva's flesh-to-armour ratio inspired some others that he quickly shooed away so as not to lose focus on the task at hand.

'You carry no weapon?' Lucas asked Shift.

'Oh Deities, no.' Shift laughed. 'Do I look like I fight? That's why I keep these with me.' Breezily, Shift gestured to Garaz and Silva.

Garaz did his best to look menacing; Silva did it naturally.

'Very well.' With a satisfied nod, the minotaur gestured for the guards at the door to open it. Though Lucas had been polite and proper so far, he would undoubtedly be a nightmare beast if provoked. Hopefully, they'd never have to find out.

With a grunt, the two men pushed the heavy double doors apart, revealing a large chamber that had obviously once been used for devotion to…whatever this temple was built for. Now it was devoted to gaming and sin.

The builders of this temple would be outraged if they saw it now.

The place must've been restructured, as the inside certainly didn't match the temple's simple look from without. It was almost as if he were in the grand hall of some castle. Actually, he'd been in a castle recently, and this was fancier.

Glowing orbs at regular intervals along the wall bathed the tables and their patrons in dim light. Each table hosted games of chance—cards and cups and some he didn't recognise. But where a game was played, money was wagered on the outcome.

Judging by the disgruntled looks and moans of despair, it wasn't a good night for the players. They'd come here eager to make money and were now just desperate not to lose what little they had left.

Why don't they just cut their losses and leave?

As they stepped into the room proper, Garaz wrinkled his nose in distaste. Nicolas knew his companion disliked being in *'seedy'* places. If this *establishment* didn't fit that description, then he didn't know what would.

Beyond the gaming tables was an area for entertainment with a large bar and various podiums on which scantily clad fairies danced with seductive pouts for leering patrons.

Focus on the task at hand, he chided himself quickly, looking away from the podiums.

'Tongue in, manservant,' Shift whispered, jabbing him with their elbow slightly.

Nicolas reddened as he saw Auron and Silva looking at him with matching displeasure, like disappointed parents.

'This way, please.' Lucas gestured to a desk just inside the entrance door, behind which sat a goblin with a long parchment and quill. 'We don't deal in coin at the tables themselves, or in the arenas below. If you give your chest to Grek, he will give you tokens for the games. You can send your manservant to the bar for drinks, and we have a food menu with many delicacies not native to Sarus.'

The term *manservant* rankled, but he couldn't have said why. He was playing a part, and there were consequences for breaking character. Besides, the minotaur could call him whatever he fancied if it meant staying on his good side.

'Ah, I am fond of a delicacy or two, that much must be clear.' Shift chuckled, rubbing their belly again.

'Quite,' Lucas replied. 'I recommend the Agleran Fish Stew. The cook does wonders with his spices.' The minotaur didn't seem the type for fine foods, but Nicolas wasn't about to say so to his face.

As Garaz took care of business with the goblin and the chest of fake jewels, the minotaur stomped away. Everyone gave his big form a wide berth as he made his way to the back of the room and ducked through a door at the far end.

****

Shift, with a bass whoop of delight, clapped their hands gleefully and reached out to scoop the pile of chips on the table's centre towards them as the dice roll once again favoured them. There were groans of annoyance around the table. Beside Shift, T'goth was content to fiddle with a chip, running it between his fingers as if hypnotised and thankfully quiet. For now. The powerless Deity looked almost lost in his reflection in the shiny token.

'Ah, 'tis a lucky night, my friends. A lucky night indeed,' Shift boomed as they arranged their winnings in front of them.

Watching the dice game like the dutiful servant was starting to become tedious, so Nicolas took in the other sights the room offered. The room was full of patrons intently concentrating on their games. He didn't want to even guess at how much coin changed hands in this place on a single night, but he was sure that Big Boss had a full vault because of it. It wasn't just the opulence of the place and amount of customers that suggested Big Boss was well off. He had a veritable army of men watching over his sordid little empire, all of them members of the Forged.

How are we supposed to rob a place this heavily guarded?

No. He had to trust that Shift knew what they were doing. It was the only way he could stay sane in the belly of the beast.

Another whoop of victory brought him back to the table. They'd been playing for half an hour now. Shift had suggested, in their professional opinion, that they play for a while, settle in, before snooping around for the staff. Shift believed they were being watched carefully as new patrons of the establishment, which he suspected was also the reason for their early winning streak. He suggested as much to Garaz.

'Of course it is,' the orc replied quietly. 'One does not cultivate wealthy new customers by draining them dry as soon as they enter the building.'

Some people here tonight wouldn't be leaving wealthy. Nicolas's gaze settled for a moment on Auron, who stood in the centre of the floor with his arms folded, content to let people walk through him. The red tinge of his aura spoke of his annoyance, as did the thunderous look on his ethereal features, like a Deity might look were they about to smite someone.

Why hasn't he gone to look around yet?

It wasn't like anyone would notice him missing. But best not to ask. They were hardly on good terms at the moment, and the spirit looked angry enough as it was.

'Not again! My luck must be vast this evening.'

Back at the table, Shift had won again, unsurprisingly. He had half a suspicion Shift was delaying them because they were enjoying themselves, plus making a nice little pile of coin.

'Curses, woman!'

The hissing cry made him, and most of the patrons in the immediate area, turn to the source of the sound. Behind Shift was an unhappy, wet-looking Serian. He'd only seen the reptilian race once, briefly, in Yarringsburg—a family leaving the city just after the vampire attack. This Serian was more well-built, obviously muscle for someone, and furiously attempting to rub a red stain from his tunic while glaring at Silva with yellow, slitted eyes.

'You bumped me when your master won, and I have spilled my drink,' the Serian continued when Silva failed to respond to his eye contact.

'I did no such thing,' the warrior replied simply.

At the table the Serian had been watching, the person Nicolas assumed to be his master turned around in annoyance, his other three guards making it clear they were ready to back up their comrade at a moments notice.

'You will apologise and buy me another drink!' the Serian demanded.

'I will do neither of those things.' Silva's voice was icy cold.

The Serian's eyes went wide. Evidently, his honour or pride or something had been offended, and it seemed he was unwilling to back down, especially now that he'd drawn a small audience.

Garaz stepped behind Silva as the rest of the room goggled at the show. Tokens changed hands and the audience spoke in hushed voices. Were they actually betting on who would win if a fight broke out?

'I'll tell you what you will do, woman,' the Serian said. 'You will get a towel and dry me, and then if you will not buy me a drink, I shall come up with another way for you to repay me.'

That did it. Within a moment, Silva was nose to extended nose with the Serian, her face contorted in a snarl. 'I will do nothing for you, you wet reptile, save give you a single chance to apologise for that remark.'

Nicolas wished he had some money to bet on Silva.

'I am not the one who shall be sorry, wench.'

Silva jumped back a step and crouched into a fighting stance. Nicolas was wondering what had happened when a metal glint caught his eye. The Serian had a knife. The betting around them became more fervent. The reptile smiled confidently as he proudly showed his weapon. Nicolas took a step back, hand shaking as different scenarios ran through his mind. In the forest Silva had jumped directly between him and danger, in the form of a knife wielding hunter.

Shouldn't I do the same?

Possibly.

Okay, probably. But the only part of him that seemed capable of movement was his shaking hand.

Silva's hand slid slowly down her leg towards the top of her knee-high boot. So she did have a weapon...and a very defined, muscular leg.

Dammit, I need to stop looking at her like that. What's the matter with me?

Why couldn't she still wear head-to-toe armour?

'What's it to be, wench?' the Serian hissed gleefully. 'How do you want to be stuck?'

The Serian's hissing chuckle became a cry of pain as a large hand engulfed his wrist, squeezing until there was an audible crunch. His knife hand went limp, and the weapon dropped to the floor, as did the Serian when the hand released its grip.

'No weapons allowed,' Lucas stated in a slow, low growl.

Where'd he come from?

Naturally, they'd all been distracted by the fledgling fight, but he couldn't believe someone so big could sneak up on anyone. The Serian's slitted eyes were wide with fear as he backed away quickly.

'And there's no fighting allowed in here either,' added a gruff voice.

Behind Lucas, flanked by two anvil-tattoo-sporting guards, was a dwarf who, despite his small stature, had a presence bigger than any of them. A sense of ownership and power wafted from him as proudly as wings on a dragon. Leaning forward over his cane, the dwarf regarded the rapidly paling Serian then looked at his master.

'Escee, is this how your people are going to behave in my establishment?'

The finely dressed Serian at the gaming table, Escee, shook his head slowly, very aware that he was in dangerous territory. 'He is new, Big Boss,' Escee replied with a feeble shrug. 'Just a second cousin of mine. He meant nothing by it.'

The dwarf stroked his elegantly plaited beard as he mulled this over for a moment. 'And how dedicated are you to family ties, Escee?'

The Serian's gaze alternated nervously between Big Boss and his second cousin, who looked terrified and pained. Finally, Escee gave the dwarf a half nod, half shrug. Two men promptly dragged the Serian with the broken wrist from the club while everyone else found other things to occupy their attention.

'Good choice.' Big Boss approached Escee, holding out his hand.

Tenderly, Escee took the hand and planted a slight kiss on the large signet ring on one of the dwarf's thick fingers. The hand was withdrawn, and Big Boss turned from the Serian without further acknowledgment.

Shift beckoned Nicolas over to help them rise from their chair. Though it felt pretty demeaning, it was part of the show they were putting on, so he helped his *master* to their feet, trying not to pay attention to the twinkle in their eye.

'Ah,' Shift bellowed with arms wide. 'You must be the Big Boss I hear so much about. Talan Talanir the Third, spice trader and gaming enthusiast. A pleasure to make your acquaintance.' Shift gave a shallow bow that was the best they could muster given their size.

Either way, Big Boss seemed pleased with the gesture.

'Pleasure to have you in our *humble* establishment,' Big Boss replied, gesturing to their surroundings with a wave of his hand.

If this is humble, what's fancy?

'Not at all, not at all,' Shift replied. 'It is I who am pleased to be here and pleased with your timely intervention.'

'Yes...that.' Big Boss cast a cold sideways look at Escee, who was currently scampering to the far side of the room with his other men as quickly as decorum would allow. 'I apologise. People will try to sneak in weapons no matter how many examples I make. Fortunately for your protector, I was on my way here already. It's good business to meet all new patrons, especially those from afar. Who knows what relationships you might cultivate?'

Big Boss produced a fine ivory pipe from his jacket, which one of his men lit. The stocky dwarf took several long tugs on the pipe before blowing enough smoke from his nose to impress a dragon.

'Indeed, indeed,' Shift said gleefully. 'As a man of commerce, I understand how important relationships can be. But I also understand the benefits of enjoying oneself after one's labours, which is why when I heard tell of this wonderful place, I just had to come see it for myself.'

'I hope we live up to your expectations.' The undertone being that if they didn't, you were to keep it to yourself. 'If you decide the main floor is a little too...uninteresting...for your tastes, we have more exotic entertainments on the lower levels. Gladiatorial combat is the main attraction of this place, though we also have other, less conventional games. If you need anything, just—' Big Boss stopped mid-sentence and turned to a couple of men who'd just walked past him. 'Hey, *you*.' The dwarf's voice was ice cold, silencing everyone in the immediate vicinity, all of whom became deeply interested in the contents of their tankards and glasses.

Both men stopped and looked around, smirking, for who was in trouble. Once they realised it was them, the colour drained from their faces.

'Um...yes...?' the man on the right asked, trembling.

'What did you just say?' the dwarf snarled.

'W-when?'

'Just then, when you walked by me.'

'I...I...'

'Did you say *short*?'

The man looked like a deer in a hunter's sights. His mouth moved up and down like a fish as his friend slowly stepped away from him. 'I...I...said that I'm a little short of coin. I w-was hoping my friend might loan me some more,' the man stammered, turning to look at his friend for support only to find he was no longer there.

'We don't use the *S* word here,' Big Boss snarled through gritted teeth. 'Never. Ever. *Lucas*.' The dwarf snapped his fingers, and the minotaur strode forwards, his facial expression suggesting that nothing friendly was about to happen.

Lucas grabbed the man by the hair and dragged him from the room. Firmly in the minotaur's grip, he cried and begged and screamed, but no one was listening.

Big Boss watched the pair disappear. 'Can't let people take liberties like that.'

'Of course not.' Shift's voice faltered slightly. They must've been nervous. 'No liberties should be tolerated at all.'

The dwarf watched the door for a moment before regaining his composure and turning back to Shift with a smile. 'You know what, Mister Talinar the Third? I don't think tonight has been the best example of our hospitality. Please allow me to ensure you don't pay for a drink the rest of the evening.'

Nicolas thought what just happened was a perfect example of Big Boss's hospitality.

'That sounds delightful. Many thanks,' Shift said with a wide grin, showing bright white teeth that contrasted their dark skin perfectly.

'We'll talk again later.' The dwarf stowed his pipe back in his jacket. 'Until then, good luck on the tables... Just not too good, eh?'

Both Big Boss and Shift laughed then Big Boss sauntered away with his guards in tow, leaving everyone to unclench.

Nicolas looked at Shift. Behind their grin, they were visibly shaken. It seemed Shift wasn't as breezy about this mission as they'd claimed.

Chapter 17

Apparently, the serving maid behind the bar didn't waste demure glances on a simple manservant. 'What'll it be?' she said snottily.

Not ten minutes ago, that would've annoyed him, but watching the minotaur drag a man kicking and screaming from the temple by his hair had caused Nicolas to invest completely in his role. 'Lispian wine, please. One glass,' he replied with a polite smile.

'Seems you've taken to being a manservant better than you have an adventurer,' Auron commented at Nicolas's side. 'Less Nick Carnage and more Nick *Carnigetyouanythingelsesir.*'

Normally, he would've taken this for the spirit's usual banter, but recently Auron had been sharp with him to the point of cutting. The remark had been delivered in a flat, cold tone, so it was no different from the rest. He remained silent.

'So, what do you think of the place then?' Auron asked, seemingly trying to lighten the mood a little.

'It's a seedy hole built to suck people's wealth into oblivion before spitting them out again,' he whispered with a shrug, aware that talking too loudly to what appeared to be thin air would draw attention.

'Not a gaming man,' Auron mused as he surveyed the place. 'Shocker.'

He was starting to get a little tired of the berating and digs. 'Shouldn't you be looking for the staff or something?'

'On my way,' the spirit said. 'Just getting the lay of the land and—'

'Making sure I don't mess up a simple drinks order and get us all caught?'

Auron looked at him and let out a slight chuckle. What he didn't do was deny the charge, so Nicolas was at least partially right. The spirit evidently trusted the senile, powerless Deity more than he trusted Nicolas. That stung.

'On the topic of tasks you struggle to complete,' Auron continued, dropping any pretence of levity. 'I wanted to talk to you about something somewhere you couldn't start flapping about it.'

Flapping about it? Not the best way to endear yourself to the person you wanted to talk to, in his opinion. But he let it go. Not the place for an argument and all that.

'You promised me once that you'd help me with my unfinished business,' Auron spoke seriously. 'And I know you tried, but you failed. Now, somehow, the woman who murdered me is our travelling companion.'

'Auron, we talked abo—'

'I know we talked about it,' the spirit snapped, that red tinge flashing in his aura briefly. 'But I wasn't satisfied with the outcome of that conversation. You need to honour your word to me. Am I to be stuck here forever while she wanders around? Silva needs to die. I cannot stand to have her just…there anymore.'

'That isn't Silva,' he countered. 'Not as you knew her. She's changed. She saved my life.'

Auron snorted. 'She's changed before. She's good at it. But she could switch back at any moment and kill you all in your sleep, and that will be on you…but that's okay, because she can just repent that too and it'll disappear, just like all the other bad stuff.'

There were so many things Nicolas was afraid of on this adventure, so many potential fates playing out in his mind over and over. And here, travelling with him, was someone logic told him to be wary of, yet he trusted her. That didn't make sense to him, not in the least. It just was what it was.

'I trust her.' He couldn't look Auron in the eye.

'Is that really it?'

'What do you mean?'

'I've seen the way you look at her… Such a lithe, muscular warrior woman must be impressive to a boy who knows little of the *real world*.' The intimation was clear.

'Hey,' he snapped a little too loudly, drawing odd glances from patrons nearby. Fortunately, everyone just went back to their drinks.

'Oh.' The spirit nodded knowingly. 'It's the other thing then. You know you aren't cut out for this, so you make sure your best chance at protection is kept as close as possible. To the Underworld with your friends and your word. Nicolas is happy to keep me damned as long as he's safe, right?'

His mouth opened. Closed. He couldn't believe what he was hearing. As plausible as it sounded, it was wrong. So wrong. 'I don't want to keep you anywhere. I want to help you, I really do, but—'

'You can take the boy out of the village, but you can't take the village out of the boy.' The tinge of red in his aura became worse, veins of crimson creeping slowly throughout his light form. He stared at Nicolas with a fury that made him feel as if he were falling into a pit.

'I won't kill anyone in cold blood. Not for anything.' Nicolas whispered the words, but from the impact they had on Auron, he may as well have screamed them at the top of his lungs.

'What happens next is on you,' Auron spat. With that, the spirit turned and disappeared into the crowd.

Shakily, Nicolas returned to the table with Shift's drink and presented it to his *master*. Shift took the glass and waved him away like an annoying fly. After bowing reverently, he took his place next to Garaz, who was keeping a keen eye on T'goth. The Deity was still playing sombrely with his token.

Did he age while I was at the bar? It certainly looked like it.

'Are you okay?' the orc asked with concern.

'I think we may have a problem with Auron,' he answered quietly, gesturing to Silva.

'She killed him, Nicolas, and now she travels with us,' the orc said, looking at the warrior woman. 'It must be terrible to bear, having your murderer standing before you, unpunished. It is a burden I cannot fathom. We just have to give him time.'

How many more cutting remarks do I have to suffer between now and then.

Until that time he could withstand it, hopefully. As long as Auron didn't do anything stupid.

He sighed. Auron's wrath would have to keep for now. They still had a task to accomplish here. 'How are they doing?'

'Not as well as earlier, but well enough,' Garaz replied. 'Hopefully, Auron will return soon with the location of the staff, and we can continue on our quest and get out of this...place. I find it troubling.'

'Same.' Nicolas couldn't get out of here soon enough.

In front of him, Shift groaned loudly, suggesting a loss. The pile of chips in front of his companion was less than when he'd left. The honeymoon period was over; time for the Big Boss to take his pound of flesh.

'Ahhhh,' Shift cried suddenly, making him flinch. 'My luck on this table is sadly spent. I must find a game with better luck lest I go home penniless.'

A few raised eyebrows from the other patrons gave a clear indication as to how they thought that would work out.

Shift raised their hand, letting it hang in mid-air. Nicolas was only peripherally aware of it until Garaz gave a polite cough.

Oh right.

Quickly, he helped Shift rise from their chair.

'Dally again, and you shall walk home on bare feet,' Shift chided, much to the amusement of those around them.

'Sorry, master,' he said in an apologetic tone.

'Maybe we should sample the entertainment while I decide what other games may take my fancy. Garaz, please collect my tokens while my boy shows me to a table. Come now.'

As the orc leant over and carefully picked up Shift's remaining tokens, Nicolas led them toward the back of the room. Silva followed closely, the ever-attentive protector, while T'goth brought up the rear quietly, looking pensive and rubbing his head every so often.

Weaving through the crowd, he caught a glimpse of Big Boss, sitting alone near the back wall. Several guards around him ensured that he stayed that way.

'Enjoying yourself?' he whispered as he escorted his *master*.

'What's not to love about having you at my beck and call...*boy*?' the rotund man replied with the hint of a smile.

Finding a table free, he led Shift to it and ensured they were seated properly. Silva and Garaz stood at their side, and T'goth took a chair silently next to them.

'He's getting worse,' Nicolas said, indicating the powerless Deity, who was muttering to himself furiously. 'He hasn't even tried to wander off or rambled about anything.'

'I have been thinking on that,' Garaz said quietly. 'I believe he is perturbed because we are close to the staff. I believe he can sense it nearby. He seems to be struggling with who he is now and memories of who he was. Either way, he is getting weaker.'

As distressing as that was, it was also a boon. Despite the opinion of a certain spirit, T'goth was the one most likely to give them away, so having him sedate was a good thing.

Is it good though? I shouldn't find any boon in another's suffering.

'Everything was shiny. Shiny and glowing. But why was everything shiny and glowing? Who shined it up so nice? Where did the glow go?' T'goth muttered to himself.

From the crowd, Auron reappeared, his bright form standing out like a beacon. He seemed pleased. 'It's here.'

'You have seen the staff?' Garaz asked.

'Not so much,' Auron admitted. 'But I found the door to a vault in a secret room. It has some heavy-duty magic runes protecting it, strong enough that I can't pass through it. But I could sense the power emanating from the other side. It's got to be there.'

Further conversation was interrupted by a burst of applause from the tables around them. A lithe fairy in an elegant, figure-fitting gown had emerged from behind a curtain, fluttering her wings coyly at the applause. For a moment Nicolas forgot there was anyone else in the room as she glided to the podium prepared for her. Her eyes scanned the room, and even though they locked with his for only a second, in that second he was more important than a king.

Once the applause died down, she began to sing, it was an old song about love and loss, and Nicolas was made to feel every inch of it through her melodious voice.

She isn't singing just to me. But...

A slap on the forearm brought him back from his daydreaming. Shift was watching him with a raised eyebrow from the chair. 'We do this now,' they said with resolve in their voice.

'Is that wise?' Garaz asked with concern. 'Is it not too soon?'

'I don't know how long our sham spice trader will last,' Shift said with authority. 'The moment they take too hard a look at the gems I traded for the tokens, we'll have an angry minotaur on our asses. Runes or not, I'm sure I can get the door open. We just need a distraction to slip away.'

Despite Shift's confidence, Nicolas couldn't help feeling they were missing a big piece of the plan. 'What about getting back out again?' he asked. 'Once we have it, they aren't just going to let us walk out with it.'

'That's the beauty.' Shift smiled. 'We don't.'

He was about to ask what they meant when Shift nodded towards T'goth, and he understood instantly. Once they had the staff and gave it to T'goth, they wouldn't need to worry about making an escape. When the Deity got his powers back, it was everyone who'd pissed him off who'd need to worry. Hopefully, they'd have time to reach a minimum safe distance before the smiting began, though part of him wanted to witness it.

Shift promptly picked up their drink and spilled it down their front. '*Stupid boy!*' they snapped, rising and clipping Nicolas around the ear, a little too hard. 'These clothes are the finest in Azra, and you knock my drink onto them.'

'I'm…sorry,' he replied with a whimper as he rubbed his sore head, which had been through enough on this adventure already.

'Clean me up, instantly!' Shift demanded, though it was unlikely anyone was listening. They were all too entranced by the singer.

After helping Shift up, he asked a passing serving girl for the washroom, which was apparently a level below them. Leading the party toward the door to the stairway, Nicolas unfortunately tripped just before they reached it, stumbling forwards and colliding with one of Big Boss's guards. With an annoyed grunt, the man pushed Nicolas off with the arm not in a sling before frowning at him. Nicolas carefully didn't make eye contact with the thug, instead focusing his attention on the fresh scar on the man's temple, which looked raw and pretty painful, before throwing his gaze to his feet as he mumbled submissive apologies.

The man huffed and stomped off toward the seating area.

That was too close.

'Well done, idiot,' Shift whispered.

'Sorry.' Briefly, Nicolas looked back to see what he'd tripped on. He couldn't see anything.

****

It didn't take long for Shift to reappear from behind the curtain as he knew them best. Thankfully, the loose fitting robe they'd worn allowed for the concealment of a spare set of clothes. Nicolas wasn't sure how they'd managed it, but he also didn't know how Silva carried so many weapons on her. Maybe he'd ask them later, right now it was just nice to see their preferred face again.

'I'd ask if this was better,' Shift remarked coyly, 'but I can tell from the way you're looking at me.'

'You wish,' he scoffed.

'Maybe if I was wearing skimpy armour with my abdominal muscles showing, you'd take more of an interest?' Shift smiled, passing him and flexing their bicep playfully.

Not them too.

Once Auron had given the group the all-clear, they emerged into a corridor, which according to the spirit was one of a network running beneath the temple. The whole place was impeccably built, and like the main hall, echoed the interior of a castle. So much so that Nicolas kept forgetting they were underground. He couldn't imagine the time, effort, or coin involved in getting the place looking like this, though he was sure it was being earned back in abundance.

'Right.' Shift appeared in their element. 'Garaz, you stay here and make sure no one disturbs your *master* while he cleans up. Silva, you'd better come with us in case we need some guards roughed up.'

'As you ask,' Silva replied, with just an edge of excitement in her voice.

With Auron's lead, it didn't take them long to get where they were going, a corridor a couple of levels beneath them.

Reaching a blind corner, Auron gestured for them to stop. When Nicolas peered around, two guards were standing on either side of a figure protruding from the wall, a statue of what looked to be an elf. Judging by the ancient and weathered look on the face's proud features, it predated the redecoration.

'They look like they're just watching the hall,' Auron explained. 'But really, they're guarding that statue. The hidden vault room's behind it. I think some of these tunnels were part of the original temple.'

'Drawing attention to it with guards.' Shift tutted softly. 'Sloppy.'

'Are you sure?' Nicolas asked. There was no obvious handle, but he supposed there wouldn't be. It was a door to a *secret passage.*

Auron caught his eye. The spirit's incredulous expression gave him a clear reply, *'I can walk through walls, kid. Of course I'm sure.'*

'The glow is bright, but I can't see it. I know it's there, but I can't see it. So close,' T'goth muttered angrily to himself. The powerless Deity was becoming progressively more agitated. They must be getting closer to the staff.

How horrendous must it be to be trapped in your own mind?

Nicolas had some experience of that lately, with the images of what had happened in Yarringsburg haunting him constantly, affecting even the simplest tasks. But what the Deity must be experiencing was way beyond that. At least now the end was in sight, for both of them. Once T'goth was restored, he was going straight home with a promise to never venture from it again.

'Silva, can you deal with those two?' Shift gestured to the heavy-set men watching the statue.

'Yes,' Silva replied.

'Quietly,' Nicolas added. 'We don't want to bring the rest of the guards down on us.' The image of a certain minotaur loomed over him, and he shivered.

Silva looked at Nicolas and screwed up her face slightly to suggest how ridiculous she found the question. Obviously, it was—she was a trained killer—but he had to say it anyway, just to be sure.

Without another word, Silva strode around the corner as the rest watched, save for T'goth, who was scratching his head in frustration.

'Oi,' one of the men shouted as soon as he noticed Silva. 'You can't be here.'

Drawing their swords, the two men approached the warrior. Silva didn't stop until she was right in front of them.

'That's close enough,' one of the men commanded. 'Raise your hands.'

Silva did, but quickly slipped them behind her neck, unclasping her armoured top, which fell forwards to hang around her waist. The guards' eyes widened as their swords lowered.

'Uh…' one of the men stammered.

He didn't get to finish his sentence. Silva cracked him across the chin with a vicious right hook, abruptly halting the momentum of the punch so she could throw her right elbow back into the temple of the second guard. As he stumbled away, Silva grabbed the first by the hair and slammed his head into the wall, with a dull thud of flesh on stone. His limp body fell to the floor just as the second guard came at Silva with a ferocious punch. The warrior ducked the oncoming fist while striking the guard in the throat. He hacked and gagged for a moment until Silva bounced his head off of the opposite wall. Even as his body slid to the floor, Silva redressed herself.

'Impressive.' Shift seemed in awe as they came up to Silva and admired her handiwork.

'Breasts will disarm most men,' the warrior said.

Nicolas looked at the two men out cold on the floor then at Silva. He promised himself he would never get distracted by her form again.

He failed two minutes later.

Shift approached the statue, cracking their knuckles then bringing their hands to an almost prayer position below their nose as they studied the carving. After only a couple of seconds, they reached out and tweaked one of the statue's pointed ears. Shift stepped back beside him as grinding stone signalled the door opening. 'I have skills too.' They were justifiably smug as the door opened. 'And I didn't have to flash anyone to do it.'

The open door revealed a long room with a large circular stone door at the end. Though the torchlight was dim, the runes carved into the door were big enough for him to see. There were other images carved into it's centre that he couldn't make out, set in concentric circles. They must've been similar to the carvings on the wall to their left. Despite the wearing of time, and the patterns of moss, he could see figures in the stone. Some were stood above others, as if being worshipped, whilst others seemed to lead their followers.

Garaz would love this place.

The other wall of the room was completely obscured by vines. The smell of the plants combined with the smell of old air contained for too long to create a musky odour that made his nose wrinkle.

At first Nicolas had put the tremors through his body as he entered the room down to fear, but that wasn't right. It was the power beyond the vault door. It was thrumming with energy which passed through him. They were definitely in the right place. Behind him, T'goth wept softly.

'The light.' The Deity pointed ahead of them. The old man was so weak he couldn't even point straight to the door, his finger shaking more toward the vined wall.

We're nearly there.

Nicolas was about to step forward when Shift's hand on his shoulder stopped him. 'Not so fast,' they cautioned. 'These old temples always have traps.'

'*Traps?*' He stepped hastily back.

'Yup,' Shift replied absentmindedly as they scanned the walls and ceiling of the room. 'Sometimes poisoned darts shoot from the walls, sometimes spiked pits…or maybe a giant boulder.'

He took another step back. If a giant boulder was coming after him, he wanted a head start.

Shift turned, noting his retreat with a smile. 'The most interesting fact though is that there's *always* a shut off on this end.'

'There is?' Silva asked.

'Uh-huh,' they replied as they walked to the wall. 'How else would the people who bury treasure down here ever get to it again?'

Slowly, they reached out to a bare-chested stone figure, another elf, judging by the pointed ears, who was pointing a sword at what appeared to be an army of orcs. Shift pressed their finger and thumb around the figure's nipple and turned it sharply to the side. Several clicks emanated from within the wall.

'Done,' Shift said, before turning to look at the vault door. 'I'm guessing a picture based puzzle lock. I haven't seen one in years.' They sounded almost excited as they strode toward the door. 'I'll have it open in no time.'

This was it. Job done. They'd made it here, and he hadn't gotten any of his friends killed. Sure, he'd had several near-misses, but it'd worked out okay. Soon, it would be time to go back to regular life. He would never be late for work again. He'd gratefully throw himself back into his routine. This was not his life. It wasn't him.

'Ho, ho, ho.'

The deep booming laugh made them all freeze until they slowly turned toward the vined wall as one. With a shimmer the vines vanished, revealing an extension on the room, where Big Boss waited, surrounded by Lucas and ten of his armed guards. One of the men, the one Nicolas had bumped into on the way off the gaming floor, stood in front of the rest.

'Don't recognise me, boy?' he snarled, gesturing to the scar on his temple.

Oh no. He wasn't even sure of the mistake he'd made just yet, only that he had made one. Then it came to him. The last time he'd seen that face was when the arm attached to it had him pinned to a stable wall—until Silva made a timely save.

How had he not noticed? Was he really that stupid?

Another thought dawned on him. *I've doomed them all.*

'You know him?' Shift asked, eyes wide.

'Yeah...he, um...yeah,' he stammered.

'You *idiot*!' Shift cried, not even slightly wrong.

'I gotta say, I admire the guts on you guys.' Big Boss laughed heartily. 'I would've been tempted to invite you to join my organisation, had it not been me you tried to steal this from.' From behind the dwarf's back, he produced a knotted staff almost as tall as him. T'goth gasped and began to walk towards it. It took both Shift and Nicolas to hold him back. He was surprisingly strong when given the right incentive.

'Well, well,' the dwarf said as he looked at T'goth. 'If it ain't the fool I stole the power to change the world from. Thought I left you wandering around that hill of yours?'

T'goth didn't answer, his eyes focused on the staff, fingers twitching as if he wanted to reach for it. Silva moved in front of them, ready to fight. Nicolas looked back towards the door, it was only now he noticed Auron wasn't with them.

Where'd he go?

Shift stared at Nicolas with a mixture of anger and confusion, and he wanted to apologise right now, a lot, but it wasn't the time. They gestured towards the still-open door of the room. It seemed the best plan they had was to make a run for it. They could make it before being cut off, if luck favoured them.

'Take them,' Big Boss ordered with a dismissive wave of his hand.

As the assembled guards charged forwards, Silva threw herself at them, the small knife concealed in her boot now in hand.

What's she doing?

They had a brief chance to flee, but she seemed bent on taking them all.

What do I do?

He didn't want to leave her, but taking on that many men was suicide.

'Go!' Silva shouted as she waded into the attackers, dodging blows and slashing with the knife.

Shift, who looked similarly torn, began to make for the door but was grabbed around the waist by a guard who'd been surprisingly fast. They kicked and struggled but were held firm and lifted from the ground.

'*Nick*! *Help*!' Shift cried.

Nicolas wanted to, he really did, but he couldn't move. His hands shook. His ragged breathing rasped in his ears as his temple pulsated like the veins were about to burst. He needed to help Shift, but his body was numb, hollow. The world around him was shrinking, and all he could do about it was watch. He'd frozen in the face of danger before, but this felt different, like his soul was vacating his body as it melted into the floor. As if claws made of pure dread were gripping his shoulders and holding him in place.

To his side, the clomping of hooves on stone grew closer. He turned, the scene blurring as his head moved, Lucas was advancing on him at a leisurely pace. His vision tunnelled until the minotaur was the only thing he could see, that grinning bovine face attached to the barrel-chested body that got closer and closer. Then the image changed, the large teeth becoming fangs, the horns moulding into bat-like ears. A scream was building in him that would burst him from the inside out if he didn't release it.

'Nonononononononono...' He backed away, holding sweat-slick, shaking hands before him.

The minotaur grinned as he closed the gap, and more leering, thirsty vampires appeared over his shoulder, goading him. The scene around him became a deep underground tunnel, the minotaur once again filling it with his muscular body.

Suddenly his legs were no longer there and he began to fall to the floor. The last thing he saw before everything faded to black was Shift being struck over the head with a club as numerous men overwhelmed Silva, raining down on her with fists, clubs, and boots.

Chapter 18

Up to a certain point in his life, Nicolas had easily managed to avoid two things. One was being rendered unconscious. Two was being locked in a cell. Within the space of a year, he was already in his second cage and had been knocked out, or passed out, enough times that he had to mentally rehearse his parents' names and birthdates to be sure he didn't have brain damage.

Shaking off the final grogginess and using the bars for support, he rose carefully. Even that slow movement made him nauseated and shaky, so he closed his eyes to settle himself. When he opened them again, he managed to look around at the jail. The place perfectly met his expectations of a jail, from the random straw on the floor to the pot in the corner for him to relieve himself. On the positive side, at least he wasn't alone.

In the cell directly next to his, Shift paced like a caged animal, grumbling to themselves. Beyond that sat Garaz, hands bound behind his back, looking sullen. In the cell adjoining his, Silva had both arms and legs tied in an uncomfortable-looking position. Judging by the muzzle over her mouth, the guards were taking no chances with her, even after the obvious beating she'd taken. Though, with that venomous look in her eyes, he didn't blame them. At the far end of the cell block, T'goth was curled in a ball on the floor, weeping.

'Look who's awake!' Shift exclaimed with open arms upon noticing him.

'I'm sorry.' This wasn't going to be pleasant.

Shift stared at him incredulously. 'You're *sorry*?' they exclaimed. 'What exactly are you sorry for? Not realising you'd bumped into an old friend? Or leaving me in the lurch to get grabbed and smacked over the head?'

'All of it,' he replied. 'You know that.'

Shift huffed derisively. Obviously, the apology wasn't accepted. Instead, they walked over and tested the door of their cell with a firm shake. It didn't give.

'Can't you make yourself into a child and squeeze between the bars?' he asked.

His companion turned and looked at Nicolas as if they were trying to work out whether that was a serious question. 'Have you actually looked at them?' they asked testily.

Focusing was still a slow exercise, but when he did, he saw that the bars of the cell were crisscrossed, instead of the vertical ones he'd seen before.

If I'm going to humiliate myself, where better to do it than somewhere I can't run from?

'If you remember, I can only change my size to a certain point either way. I'd have to be mouse-sized to get through there,' Shift continued, aggravated.

'What about you, Garaz?' he pleaded. 'You said you can throw a fireball now or something?'

'Do you seriously believe I could just melt these bars?' the orc replied glumly as he looked at his cage. 'You must know better than that? Besides, my hands are tied behind my back. I'd be more likely to hit you than the cage.'

The claws of despair dug ever deeper into him. That was it. They were trapped here.

Why are we still alive? Surely Big Boss should've just disposed of us? To what end is he keeping us prisoner?

Various hideous fates ran through his mind in staggering detail. Whatever was going to happen, there would be a terrible retribution at some point. He wondered if any of the others knew anything.

'So—' he began.

'Do not ask,' Garaz interrupted testily.

'Don't ask what?'

'You were about to say something to the effect of *so what do you think they will do to us?*' the orc replied. 'I have no wish to speculate on such possibilities, and you definitely should not.'

'What's that supposed to mean?' he asked, his voice rising slightly.

'Well, your disposition.'

'My what?'

'You know how you are,' Shift added absently as they continued to probe the bars.

'How I am is locked in a cage because a certain *master criminal* got cocky.'

Shift turned around slowly, eyes wide. 'I beg your pardon?'

'*Oh, we can just bluff our way in. Oh, let's just do it now when they least suspect*... Sound familiar?' he hissed back. 'And how did that work out exactly?'

'Are you just whining because you didn't like being my manservant?' Shift snapped. 'Still sore about that, are we, *precious*? Or maybe you're just trying to deflect from the fact that you're the reason we're in this mess. The plan was sound.'

'Was it?' he cried. 'For some of us, this isn't some fun jaunt. *Oh, let's go tour a treasury that got robbed. Let's go and steal something from a temple. That'll be a laugh.* There are consequences to this stuff, real ones.' He gestured to the room they were in as Shift glared at him.

'Is that what you really think of me?' they asked, face stern.

'It's…what you said.' Why did he feel on uncertain ground? 'You said you came to check out the vault out of…professional curiosity.'

'How dumb are you to actually believe that?'

I've got something very wrong here, haven't I?

'Yeah, I said that,' Shift continued. 'But that's not why I was in Sarus City. I was there because I saw the poverty people were being forced to live in because of the robbery. I saw people suffering, and because I met *you*, I couldn't just turn a blind eye to it. I was there to help…Moron!'

Every decision I've made to this point has been so wrong. The worst was the decision to come at all.

'I think the reason you're *here* is because he just doesn't have the stomach for this,' Auron cut in. 'I said you'd put them all in danger.' The spirit stood in the corner of the room, glaring at him coldly. 'Isn't that right, kid?' he continued. 'Up for the fun parts of the adventure, but when things get tough, out comes the whining. Out comes…*you*.'

'Auron,' Garaz chided. 'That is unnecessary. He cannot help…' The orc trailed off as Nicolas looked at him wide eyed.

'*How I am?*' he shouted. 'That's what you were going to say, right?'

'Some people just aren't tough enough.' Auron shrugged.

Heavy silence fell in the room, all eyes on him. Even Silva looked at him from the corner of her eye with something like disgust. Feeling their judgement, he turned away.

'I thought I could do it.' A tear ran down his cheek. 'I thought I could come with you. But since the vampires, I…I see them every night, haunting my dreams. Sometimes, I just close my eyes, and there they are. I jump at every shadow. The fear's in me all the time. It's been getting worse. When I saw the minotaur coming at me, I just…just…'

He couldn't finish the sentence, admit what shamed him so. He was sinking under it. They were right. He knew that. He'd known it all along.

Why in the Underworld did I agree to come on this adventure? Did I really think it would be a walk in the countryside, easy pickings?

He was a liability to the rest of the group, and he'd known that, and now they were all paying for it. If only he'd been able to help in the vault room...

Shift was right, this should've been simple. How had it gone so wrong?

That was easy. The guard, the one who attacked him in the stable.

If only I hadn't tripped and bumped...

A question came into his mind.

How did I trip?

The answer was so terrible he didn't want to believe it at first, but at the same time, it made complete sense. Yes, he'd been a coward, but one of them had done something much worse.

'I've failed you all,' he began slowly, 'and I am so sorry for that. But at least I didn't do it on purpose. Unlike you.' Nicolas pointedly looked at Auron, whose icy front broke slightly under his gaze.

'What do you mean?' Garaz asked.

'Did that drink just spill on the Serian on the gaming floor?' he asked. 'And what exactly did I trip over that made me fall into the one man who would recognise me?'

The spirit said nothing, but his ethereal face softened, his aura seeming to fade slightly as his jaw worked with no sound emerging.

'Dammit, Auron,' Shift shouted. 'What in the Underworld were you thinking?'

'She killed me,' Auron cried finally, pointing at Silva. 'She killed me, and none of you were doing anything about it. You just let her walk around. I couldn't...I couldn't handle it anymore. I thought if she got into a barfight... I thought...' Auron became quiet for a moment, eyes wide, but looking at nothing. 'I didn't think. The anger took me over and...I didn't think.' The spirit looked down at his feet. When his white eyes rose again, they were full of shame, surprise, and realisation. 'Oh Deities,' Auron whispered. 'What have I *done*?'

Before anyone else could speak, Auron disappeared through the wall, a faint puff of white smoke marking where he'd been.

Shift gave a disbelieving laugh. 'What a team we are.'

'Guys, I—'

Nicolas's words were cut off by the door to the jail opening. Four armed guards marched to his cell and opened the door.

'Out,' the lead guard commanded, pointing towards Nicolas with his club.

He did as he was told. There was no point prolonging the inevitable. It was wrong of him to be here at all, and now it was time to pay the price for that. Dejectedly, he followed the guards out of the room, head hung low so he wouldn't have to see the looks on the faces of those his cravenness had doomed.

****

Nicolas was unceremoniously shoved through an open door into a small, bare room. Instead of indicating where they wanted him to stand, the guards roughly dragged him to a spot in the centre of the room, one standing either side of him, holding his arms. One of the others grabbed a small stool, which he placed in front of Nicolas. That was strange. His enquiring look to the guard resulted in a derisive snort.

Several moments later, Big Boss sauntered into the room, removing his thick fur coat and handing it to a guard by the door. Rolling up his shirt sleeves, he stepped onto the stool so he was eye level with Nicolas.

The dwarf slapped him across the face.

'*That*,' Big Boss spat, 'was for sneaking into my establishment.'

He slapped Nicolas again.

'*That*,' he snarled, 'was for trying to steal from me.'

Again, the hand crossed Nicolas's cheek.

'And *that* was because I don't like you.'

After three strikes, his cheek felt pretty raw. The little man could hit hard. While his instinct was to rub the bruised flesh, his hands were held too firmly. So firmly, in fact, that his fingers were beginning to go numb.

'We need to talk.' Big Boss pointed a stubby finger in his face. 'And by *talk*, I mean I ask you questions, and you answer them.'

'Okay.'

He slapped Nicolas again.

'I didn't ask you anything yet,' the dwarf snapped. 'You don't talk until I say.'

Deep inside Nicolas each slap acted like a bellows, causing an ember of rage in the pit of his stomach to flare briefly. But it was immediately doused again by his lack of will to act on it. At least he now knew why they'd been imprisoned: the dwarf wanted something.

What can he possibly want?

'Where's the chicken?'

'*Chicken?*'

This time, he slapped Nicolas twice.

'You don't ask the questions!' the dwarf screamed, jabbing his own chest with a stubby finger. '*I'm* in charge here.'

He slapped Nicolas again for good measure.

'If I may?'

The voice was familiar and came from a corner Nicolas would've sworn was empty. Now, Wade LeBeck leant against the wall, half-smiling in the most narcissistic way. Lazily, the hunter pushed from the wall and approached them, prominently removing the large knife from his belt and running his finger slowly along its edge.

'We just want the chicken,' Wade said serenely. 'Give it up, and things will go easier for you.'

'Like you aren't going to kill me?' Nicolas asked sarcastically.

'Oh, you're gonna die, boy, you and all your thieving friends,' Big Boss said after administering another slap. 'It's the manner in which you die that will be determined by this.'

'Maybe—' Wade began.

'*Maybe,*' Big Boss interrupted, turning to face the hunter, 'I hired you to do a job and here I am, having to do it myself.'

The room turned icy cold for a second.

'There were unforeseen complications,' Wade replied smoothly after taking a moment to calm down, indicating Nicolas.

The dwarf seemed unimpressed. 'It's just a chicken, and he is just a boy.'

'If I could—' Nicolas began.

The stumpy hand slapped him again. 'If you could *what?*' Big Boss snapped. 'If you could *what?* You have something important to say? Let's hear it then, big man.'

That last slap stoked his anger into a defiant glare at his captor. *If only I could...* Then it was gone. He had nothing left to give. His head slumped to the mocking laughter of the dwarf.

'You know what?' Big Boss raised Nicolas's head by a scruff of hair. 'I think this boy likes being slapped. That right, boy? You like being beaten? Maybe you get off on it a bit?' The dwarf appraised Nicolas, getting so close he could smell the pipe smoke on his breath. 'I don't think pain is the best way to get you to talk, is it, boy?' he whispered. 'I saw that little display in the vault room, you turning craven when your friends needed you and collapsing on the floor. I think maybe fear would be a better motivator, or a combination of the two. But you don't seem scared of me or Wade. Not enough, anyway. So let's find something you are scared of.' Big Boss turned to address his men. 'The Pit.'

After one more slap for good measure, the guards dragged Nicolas back out of the room.

Chapter 19

Nicolas rolled across the hard floor as the guards unceremoniously launched him into the room. Limbs connected with stone, eliciting grunts of pain until he finally came to a halt, just as the thick double doors shut behind him.

Slowly, he stood, his aching muscles protesting but following his direction regardless. He appeared to be in an open oval room with stone walls, lit at regular intervals by torches, with another imposing door on the far side. Above him was a viewing gallery, from which a wealthy-looking collection of people watched him with interest, talking quietly with each other.

'Oh no,' he whispered.

Tell-tale patches of dried blood discoloured the grey stone floor and there were chips in the surface that could only have been made by weapons.

He was in an arena.

'I hope you feel honoured boy,' Big Boss chuckled from above, leant against the banister that ran the length of the gallery. 'This is my personal arena. Only the elite of the elite get to come here. And they'll all be wagering on you.' The dwarf thought for a moment. 'Well, against you, anyways.'

Panic enveloped him once more as he turned full circle, looking for any hope of escape but finding none, unless he developed Auron's ability to walk through walls. Very soon, it seemed, he would be developing a lot of Auron's abilities.

'I hope your bets are in, people,' announced the dwarf as he returned to his comically oversized throne in the centre of the viewing gallery. 'Because it's fight time.' Big Boss looked Nicolas right in the eye before he continued. 'Let's see how long our new contender lasts.'

His legs weakened and the room swayed around him.

The far door opened to a cheer from the crowd. A single figure strode into the arena, and Nicolas quailed. Beating his battered chest plate enthusiastically, the muscular warrior stoked the crowd into more cheers. His scarred face spoke of easy confidence and a killer instinct as he saluted the crowd with his spiked mace in the arena's centre. They lapped it up. Nicolas less so.

'Hey, boy,' the dwarf shouted from his throne. 'Do you want to talk yet or shall I let him have his fun?'

As much as it shamed him to admit it, he wanted to talk. He wanted to tell Big Boss everything, but he had no clue where the chicken was. The last time he'd seen the bird was when they left it in the forest. The damned creature had almost gotten them killed because of its presence, and now, ironically, he was going to be killed because it wasn't here.

'Fair enough.' The dwarf smiled before addressing his gladiator. 'I need him to talk so no killing him. Otherwise, enjoy yourself.'

The warrior bowed low before turning towards Nicolas and advancing.

It felt just like it had when the minotaur approached him, every sensation and hallucination repeated as the warrior bore down on him. The only part of him that would move were his hands, which were shaking so violently they threatened to come away from his wrists. Tears stung his eyes.

Of all the places in the world I could be, and I'm here, in a damned arena, about to die.

As the warrior's slow advance became a full-on charge, Nicolas finally began to back away but slipped instantly. He hit the floor with a spike of pain that travelled up through his spine, but still managed to scrabble away from the mace-wielding gladiator.

'Nonononononononono,' Nicolas cried as the warrior came so close, he could make out every nick in his armour.

Wanting to see no more, Nicolas closed his eyes as his limbs continued to work furiously to get him away from danger. Eventually, he'd run out of places to go.

Will I end up in the Underworld for endangering my companions or will I roam the world forever like Auron?

Either would be fitting.

Something bumped his flailing foot. There was a crash. And a wet sound. And a cry suddenly cut off. A collective gasp rose from the crowd. Then silence.

I'm still alive. That's not right. Well, okay, it is right because he was ordered to keep me alive. But why aren't I getting beaten?

Cautiously, Nicolas opened his eyes. He screamed and jumped to his feet, backing away from the bloody scene until he felt the cold stone of the wall at his back. If he had to guess, the warrior had tripped on one of his flailing legs, to fall directly onto his mace, which had ended up through his throat and face in several places. He gagged as he realised it was through one of his eyes too. Blood poured from the wounds. The gagging became so fierce that he had to look away.

The crowd booed.

Oh, no...is this not good enough sport for them?

Damn shame.

He was alive but judging by the rage on a certain dwarf's face, that was about to change.

'Remove that and get the next one in here!' the dwarf screamed.

There was a brief intermission while the dead body was dragged away, leaving a long trail of blood to tell the direction in which it had been taken. The crowd used their free time to pelt Nicolas with various food items, mainly nuts from the dishes they held.

From his chair, Big Boss raised his arms. 'Calm down, my friends.' The room quieted instantly. 'We all get lucky sometimes. Though *that* was some special kind of luck.' He paused for the laughter from the crowd. 'But the next opponent will put on a better show, so get those bets in now.'

Above Nicolas there was a flurry of activity as the door at the far end of the room opened again, people placing quick last-minute wagers.

He gaped at the figure who entered —a portly, bearded gentleman in a red turban. The man glided into the room as only a professional showman could. An expectant hush fell over the crowd. The silence prolonged as the man waited for his moment. The uncertainty of what was to come gnawed at Nicolas. *Who was he? What could he do?* Finally, with a dramatic flourish, the man turned with an open-armed gesture, fanning his robe out behind him to reveal straps crisscrossing his chest to which a multitude of small metal loops that almost looked like collars were attached.

This guy might not look like a warrior, but he was here for a reason. Personally, Nicolas would've preferred his opponent's deadliness to be more obvious. It seemed only polite.

'Ladies and gentlemen,' the man pronounced in an exotic accent. 'A week ago, I was naught but a humble travelling conjurer.' *Conjurer? Oh crap, he's a wizard.* 'And yet thanks to our most gracious host my fortunes have changed.' The Big Boss gave a regal wave as the crowd cheered. 'Now I stand before you, a master of the most amazing, powerful and twisted beasts so incredible, that not even your imagination could dream them.'

Even Auron would be envious of this guy's showmanship.

The crowd lapped it up, even his elaborate bow at the end, applauding and cheering as if possessed—which they were, by blood lust.

Beasts, was the word that stuck out to Nicolas the most. Terror renewed its grip on him as he imagined what sort of creature was coming to maul him. He didn't want to get eaten. He didn't want any of this.

How can people enjoy such a disgusting show?

He was a living person, and they were just…enjoying themselves. For a moment, his fists clenched. For a moment, the shaking wasn't fear.

The wizard ran his fingers up and down the collars on his belt, apparently quite at his leisure.

He can stand there fondling his collars all night if he fancies. I'm in no hurry.

'This one,' the wizard purred finally.

Nicolas jumped as the robe fanned suddenly, one of the collars flying from the wafting material to hit the floor near him. He looked up at the wizard, who smiled in a very *'I know what's coming and it's not good'* kind of way.

Nicolas backed away, ready for anything yet prepared for nothing. There was another flapping of robe and suddenly the wizard had a large whip in his hand. He swung it around his head several times before striking it to the floor with a sharp *crack.*

'Come forth,' the wizard commanded. Almost instantly swirling smoke formed around the collar, seeping out from it, before growing and taking shape. As it solidified into a form there was an impressed gasp from the crowd, and a whimper from Nicolas.

That explains where the strange creatures all went.

In front of him, and looking slightly confused, was the strange mating of a tiger and a bear, the collar firmly around its neck. It had to have been made by T'goth's stolen power. The creature squinted at the sudden light while the crowd whooped and cheered and placed more bets. The animal's instincts seemed to be to back away for safety—though who could threaten something like *that*? He made the mistake of looking at the razor-sharp teeth that would shortly be sunk into his flesh.

Please Deities, no.

The whip cracked again. 'Strike him down, my pet,' the wizard commanded, pointing to Nicolas. 'But do not kill.'

Despite him wanting to focus all his attention on the creature, Nicolas couldn't help but glance up at the Big Boss. He made these creatures to watch them fight and die.

Is there no low he won't sink to?

His eyes narrowed as he focused on the smirking dwarf. If he ever got the chance he was going to…

A low growling brought his attention back to the arena. The creature was staring at him, teeth slightly bared. The whip cracked again, the creatures collar pulsating as it did. The beast reared and let out an ear-splitting roar that the crowd cheered with enthusiasm. What a bunch of troll dicks.

Would they be cheering so loud if they were down here instead of me?

As the creature took a step forward, he took a step back…and something moved underfoot. The stone tile beneath him was broken. Quickly, he bent down and after a couple of fumbling attempts, removed the sharp corner, holding it up toward the beast like a man attempting to calm an oncoming storm with a twig. He had no idea what, if anything, he could do to a bear-tiger with his pitiful weapon, but having something in his hand gave him some forlorn comfort.

Which evaporated as the creature charged.

He ran.

How long can I outrun the beast?

Not long. But he was determined to prolong his life for as long as possible. Running in a large circle around the arena, he found himself coming back toward the wizard, the creature's padding feet hot on his heels.

He was gaining speed when the sound of the creature pursuing him stopped abruptly, and the crowd above him gasped.

It's jumping at me.

Spinning around, Nicolas slipped on the blood of his former opponent. His arms flailed in the air even as he fell, a dark shadow with flashing claws passed over him, missing by mere inches. There was a crack, and he struck the floor. The crowd roared with amusement.

What was that cracking sound? Not any of his bones, as far as he could tell.

Lying on his back, he looked up at the ceiling high above him, the impact of the landing continuing to reverberate through him. The room was deathly silent. With a groan he finally turned his head. He stifled a scream. The creature's head was right next to his.

Why aren't I being mauled right now?

Instead of attacking him, the creature seemed curious about something by his hand.

Moving his hand slightly, he saw the collar that the creature had been wearing, laying broken on the floor.

I must've struck it with the rock when I fell.

If it was that fragile, how it had survived being thrown on the floor in the first place was anyone's guess. The creature regarded the broken remains, sniffing at them with its large snout. Then the beast turned its head and looked Nicolas in the eye. For a moment, he could've sworn the creature nodded thanks to him, its eyes full of joy and relief.

The wizard died screaming moments later. No amount of whip cracking could save him.

Standing to a stunned silence, Nicolas looked away from the very gruesome image of a half-eaten wizard. Above him, Big Boss sat slack jawed on his throne. The bear-tiger lounged in the corner of the room, happily cleaning gore from its paws with its tongue.

Quite soon after it had killed its captor, the bear-tiger was put down by crossbowmen in the gallery above, that familiar look of relief on its face before it dissolved into a pool of green slime.

All Nicolas could do was watch it happen, and inside him, the ember of anger began to grow. Being thrown into this arena, made to fight, the shallow people watching it for entertainment, the betting on how fast he would die, the poor creature murdered for wanting to be free…it was disgusting. All of it, *disgusting*.

'Our new competitor is on quite the undefeated streak,' Big Boss declared to the crowd, an edge of annoyance in his tone. 'So let's give him a real test, shall we?'

After Nicolas's second *victory*, the crowd had become quite disgruntled. Obviously, a lot of people were losing gold betting against him. No one was brave enough to shout *fix* aloud, but from the faces in the viewing gallery, they were all thinking it.

'Let's see how he does against our arena champion!'

Those words whipped the crowd back into a frenzy, enough to make Nicolas shake again. Chants of '*Feshic, Feshic, Feshic*' permeated the arena as the doors opened for a third time. His eyes widened as a huge feline Kascat warrior strolled into the room with complete confidence, ignoring the crowd and their adulation. The warrior had a formidable, muscular form with off-white fur. He was far bigger than Nicolas. Coin changed hands rapidly in the viewing gallery. He doubted anyone was betting on him, despite his two fluke victories.

Prowling forwards on padded feet, the warrior came up close to Nicolas, green eyes glaring down at him with contempt. 'What is *this*?' it asked at last, in a deep and proud voice.

'Your opponent,' Big Boss shouted from the gallery.

The warrior looked Nicolas up and down with disdain. 'This is hardly a worthy opponent,' the warrior declared in an offended tone. 'It hardly qualifies as an opponent at all.'

Big Boss looked more than perturbed that no violence was taking place. 'Hey, you're paid to fight and put on a show. So do it!' the dwarf snapped.

The warrior took a couple of steps back from Nicolas, almost as if he smelled bad. The crowd murmured in confusion.

'This would not be a fight. It would be a slaughter, and I am no butcher. I am a warrior. You have others for that,' the warrior declared. 'There is no honour in fighting this scrawny thing, so I shall not.'

In the gallery, the crowd began to boo and jeer. Some went as far as walking out as Big Boss grew red with rage once again.

Inside Nicolas, the disdainful looks of the warrior had thrown the perfect kindling onto his burning anger. He remembered the disgust on Big Boss's face when he was beating him, and the way his companions had looked at him in the jail when confronting him with his cowardice. The beatings, the belittling, the constant threats and fear. The insults and put downs, especially from Auron. He thought of the poor cow-dragon he'd had to put down and the bear-tiger he'd seen killed. All those who'd died and were suffering because of scum like this *Big Boss*, the same scum who'd thrown him into an arena for people to bet on how long he'd live—only to find, ultimately, he wasn't worth killing.

The rage boiled over, and his breathing evened out into slow, dedicated breaths. His shaking hand closed into a fist again.

'I'm not good enough for you to fight?' he growled. '*Too scrawny*? *Too weak*? You know what…you don't have a choice now. If you won't fight, you're going to get your ass kicked.'

Nicolas tore at his shirt until he'd pulled it over his head and threw it angrily to the floor. Then, raging with defiance, he raised his fists towards the warrior. 'You best decide you want a piece of me,' he snarled. 'Because like it or not, you are getting one...furball.'

In his mind, multiple alarm bells tolled. What in the Underworld did he think he was doing? He'd nearly had a free pass, and now he was challenging the warrior to a fight. Was he insane? Had the rage about everything that had happened since a cow-dragon had descended on his village finally pushed him over the edge?

Maybe the furball comment was a bit much.

But it was too late, his blood was up, and there was no stopping now. He puffed his chest out and bounced on the spot slightly, shifting his weight from one foot to the other rhythmically. He didn't know why he was doing this, exactly. Maybe it would make him look like he knew what he was doing?

The warrior cocked his head to the side and looked at Nicolas before bursting out in deep, booming laughter that resonated around the arena. 'You amuse me, but there is no honour in killing you.'

'I'm not taking lessons in honour from someone who fights in *his* arena,' Nicolas snarled back, pointing a contemptuous finger towards Big Boss.

'Child, you must be insane if you think—' The warrior's words stopped short as Nicolas's fist connected with his abdomen.

Unfortunately, that was the only effect the punch had on the warrior, who stood looking at the fist as if he'd never seen one before. From Nicolas's perspective, it felt like he'd just punched a wall. His knuckles throbbed as pain stampeded up his arm.

Feshic gave Nicolas an impressed smile. 'I have seldom seen such courage in the face of inevitable destruction from warriors twice your size. You are braver than you look, my boy.'

He didn't know how to respond to this. Issuing his challenge had seemed so right, and then so ridiculous, and now...where was he supposed to go from here?

'My spirit honours the warrior spirit in you, boy, and I shall do no harm to such a kindred soul,' the warrior pronounced with a slight bow before leaning in to whisper to him. 'But you had best put your fists down before I take offence and change my mind.'

The crowd became riotous as Nicolas dropped his fists and shuffled awkwardly on the spot. On his throne, Big Boss was so red he might explode at any second.

'No, no, no, no!' the dwarf roared over the din. 'Nobody says no to me!'

The door from which Nicolas had been thrown into the arena opened, and four guards walked in, this time holding crossbows pointed at him, and by extension, the warrior standing behind him. A furious Wade strode after them, knife in hand.

'He's mine,' the hunter shouted as he thoughtlessly shoved one of the guards out of the way.

Though a push can be a simple thing, it can also have a drastic knock-on effect. In this case, the kinetic energy travelled through the guard's shoulder, down his arm, and to his trigger finger, which twitched slightly. Just enough, in fact, to pull the trigger. The fired bolt sailed over Nicolas's head and grazed the Kascat warrior, taking a small chunk out of his triangular right ear.

For a moment, the room was filled with an explosive silence. Turning, Nicolas saw Feshic shaking with rage behind bared teeth. He managed to duck just as the warrior launched over him with a mighty roar and proceeded to maul the guards with his very imposing claws.

As the guards, and Wade, tried to get away from the whirlwind of slashing claws—the crowd loving every second of it and placing new bets on the outcome—Nicolas slipped out of the open arena door.

Chapter 20

Now topless and still in great danger, Nicolas bolted through the corridors to get as far from the arena as he could. There seemed to be no immediate pursuit, which he attributed to the Kascat warrior keeping Big Boss's men busy. Hopefully, the warrior was okay. For a guy who fought in a gladiatorial arena, he seemed a decent sort.

Where am I going?

Running blindly around an underground building was no sort of plan, and he needed a plan.

What I actually need is an unoccupied room.

A couple of doors down, he found one.

After carefully peeking through the opening to check it was empty, he quickly slipped inside, closing the door behind him and leaning heavily against it, catching his breath. Directly in front of him were several racks of clothing.

My luck must be turning.

He began to rummage and found his luck wasn't as good as he'd hoped. The racks contained dresses that must be for the dancing girls in the main hall. Some of them were so revealing he might as well stay as he is. None of them would set the right tone for someone fleeing for his life, even if he could fit in them. Topless it was then.

Instead, he slumped down in one of the chairs, at a table strewn with make ups and perfumes, the combined smell of which was quite over powering. Briefly, he entertained the idea of disguising himself as a dancing girl but dismissed it quickly. He was learning quickly that disguises weren't proven solutions.

With a sigh he sat back in the chair before screaming and nearly falling from the seat. Looking back at him...was him. He'd heard of mirrors before, but only the very well to do had them. It was so strange looking at himself.

Deities, I look a mess.

His skin was pale, save for his red cheek, and his eyes tired. His hair was matted by sweat produced by both over exertion and fear. Adventuring definitely took a toll. Yet he was still alive.

He brought his fist up and studied it. 'You punched that warrior.' His voice was awestruck. 'The punch sucked, but at least you did it.'

He needed to talk through his options. With the mirror in front of him, the only person to do that with was himself.

'So,' he began with a deep breath. 'First job is to free our friends.'

'That's the first place they'll expect us to go,' his reflection replied.

'Well, yeah,' Nicolas scoffed. 'But we can't just leave them.'

'They were jerks to you earlier,' his reflection pointed out.

'Firstly, I deserved it, and secondly, that doesn't mean we just leave them here.'

'True.'

'What we need is a distraction.'

'Oooh, like the fire in the necromancer's fort?'

'Exactly, but I don't think starting a fire here is a great idea. We're underground and don't know the way out.'

'Fair point.'

'What have they got here that we could use?'

'Big Boss has dancers, plenty of guards, patrons, fighters and a mean slap.'

'Very true. That doesn't help though. Although, he doesn't just have fighters in that arena…'

He had an epiphany. It was a bit of a long shot—who was he kidding? It was a massive longshot—but if everything worked as planned, the shot might land. It wouldn't be easy, but if he could pull it off, it was certainly preferable to trying to fight his way through Big Boss's guards…shirtless.

With renewed purpose, he stood and walked towards the door.

Where am I in relation to the jail?

His only modes of travel here had been being dragged or fleeing in terror, making it difficult to piece the complex together mentally.

As he concentrated on trying to chart a way back to the arena, Nicolas absentmindedly opened the door without checking first. As soon as it was open wide enough, a hand shot through and grabbed him by the neck. The follow-up hand pushed the door open before striking Nicolas in the face, sending him reeling back into a rack of dresses.

'I am done messing around with you, boy,' Wade snarled as he drew that knife again. 'You're going to tell me what I need to know, then I think I might skin you just for the inconvenience you've put me through.'

Shaking off the wooziness from the hunter's strike, he looked at Wade, who had a very bloody claw mark on his left forearm.

Well done, Feshic.

Fresh blood on the hunter's blade suggested the fight hadn't been one-sided. Hopefully the warrior was okay.

'Staining my reputation,' the hunter muttered as he advanced. 'And all over a chicken.'

'What is it with that chicken? Why does everyone want it so badly?' Rising, he backed away from the hunter, who had the manner of a predatory animal. To say that he wasn't happy with Nicolas was an understatement.

'I was paid to get it by short stuff back there, who lost it and has upset some very bad people because of it. Got a bit big for his boots and thought about ransoming it off, broke a deal, so he brought me in to make it right. Should've been really simple but, you...' Wade wagged the tip of the knife towards Nicolas.

Nicolas bumped into a dressing table. 'Why the heck would a famous hunter like you bother with a chicken?'

'Fun part about being a hunter.' Wade grinned. 'It gives you a taste for exotic cuisine. I've hunted and eaten all sorts of rare and endangered creatures, but I waived my fee on this job for the opportunity to taste Chicken *à la King*.'

The hunter finally closed the gap between them and raised his knife until the tip of the blade sat under Nicolas's chin, pressing painfully into the skin.

This would normally have been the part where Nicolas blacked out or nearly soiled himself. Instead, a calm sort of anger overtook him as the pain from the blade registered, as well as the wetness of the blood where it'd broken the skin. His hand shook for a second, but he closed it into a fist and forcibly suppressed it. He'd really had enough of being threatened, poked, and otherwise pinned to walls.

'So then, boy...' Wade said. 'Where is it? You're going to tell me before I— *Ow!*'

The aforementioned chicken had slipped into the room behind the hunter and driven its beak right into the back of his leg above his boot. For a second, the hunter wavered, stooping slightly, the tip of the knife dropping. Nicolas, who'd been subtly reaching behind himself while Wade prattled on and was thoroughly fed up with the guy, gripped the first thing he found—which turned out to be a small dish containing powdered makeup—and slammed it into the hunter's face. Wade cried out as the powder went into his now-furiously blinking eyes. As the hunter tried to wipe the powder away, cursing, Nicolas saw no reason not to kick him directly in the balls. The hunter crumpled, uttering a high-pitched *'wooooooo.'* Clasping both fists together, Nicolas swung them with all his might into the hunter's cheek. Wade was knocked backwards by the impact, spinning and falling face first to the floor.

Nicolas hit him with the nearest chair, just to be sure he stayed down.

Breathing heavily, Nicolas doubled over as he tried to overcome the shaking, attempting to reclaim his body. With some deep breaths, he gained control of himself. As he did so, he found the chicken staring up at him.

'How do you keep sneaking into places?' he asked with a laugh, grateful that the creature had.

'You'd be surprised how few people look down at their feet unless they have a reason to.'

There was a moment of stunned silence.

'Of course you can talk.' Nicolas sighed as he looked at the chicken. After everything he'd seen so far on this adventure…*why not.*

'I feel the need to explain wh—' the chicken began.

'We'll get to that later,' he interrupted, holding up a silencing hand. 'I have friends to rescue first.'

'Very well,' the chicken replied. 'I shall aid you in this endeavour.'

'Fantastic, because you've been really unhelpful to this point.'

'I stopped him killing you,' the chicken said, sounding put out, as it pointed its beak at Wade.

'Then we're even for the few times you nearly *got* me killed.' He didn't know why that made him smile. The very notion of dying because of a chicken was ridiculous, and yet his life was still in danger because of one.

Before he left the room, he stripped Wade of his waistcoat and knife. No way was he running around here unarmed and bare chested. Maybe one day he would have the physique to pull off topless adventuring, but it certainly wasn't today. Taking a moment to look at himself in the mirror, he found he quite liked how he looked in the waistcoat, though he needed some more muscle on his arms to really pull it off. Semi-clothed, he went off to find his friends, the talking chicken following dutifully.

Though careful to look for signs of anyone as he made his way through the complex, Nicolas and his strange companion still managed to bump directly into Auron. Figuratively, of course. The spirit, who was walking frantically in their direction, stopped dead as soon as he saw Nicolas. Well, deader.

'Kid...' The spirit's white eyes were full of regret. 'I...'

Nicolas raised his eyebrows and waited for the deceased hero to continue.

'I am so sorry,' Auron continued. 'I betrayed you. Everyone.' The spirit sagged slightly. 'When I first saw Silva in the stable I nearly lost myself again, just like in the necromancers fort. But I fought it away, kept control. At least I thought I did. Instead the rage dwelt deep inside me, growing and eating away at me until...' Despite what he'd done, Nicolas hated seeing him in so much pain. 'I shouldn't have tried to put killing Silva on you. But when you kept refusing and she was still there...the fury was consuming me, and...she just had to die...and I just...lost control.'

'I get it,' he replied with a half-smile. 'If I were in your situation, I'd be the same.'

Auron studied him for a moment. 'I don't think you would, actually.'

'Too weak?' Nicolas asked.

'Too decent,' Auron smiled. 'Once I'd calmed down and realised what I'd done, to you, to the others, I came looking for you—'

Nicolas held up a silencing hand. 'You know what? Not the time nor the place.' It could keep. 'I have people looking for me and can't stand around here too long.'

Auron gave him a half smile. 'You got away, so you're doing alright so far.'

'I saw myself in a mirror just now,' Nicolas replied. 'I know I don't look alright.'

The spirit whistled. 'They, have mirrors here? Fancy.' He then looked Nicolas over again. 'I'm sure Garaz can fix you up when we break him out. And hopefully we can find you some better cloth...oh, the chicken found its way in then?'

For a moment Nicolas was half tempted to tell Auron that the bird could talk. But the guy *had* been pretty unpleasant to be around lately, so why do him any favours right now. 'He gets everywhere,' he replied instead, before continuing on his way.

Auron followed after him after a moment of confusion. It was probably strange for him, being the passenger when he's used to being the driving force of events

'So what's the plan?' the spirit asked.

'We need to break the rest of the guys out,' Nicolas said. 'But they'll be waiting for that, so we need a distraction. I just came from an arena. There was a wizard there who had a load of creatures made by T'goth's power under his command, but I'd bet anything that Slappy the Dwarf has more of them caged around here somewhere for his fights. I'm going to find where he keeps them.'

'Then what?'

'Let them out.' Nicolas smiled.

Auron mulled that over for a moment. 'I'm impressed, kid,' he said finally. 'Nice plan. Very crazy and very daring. I must be rubbing off on you.'

'I just beat up a hunter with a chicken and some powdered makeup,' he replied with a broad grin. 'I'm all about the crazy and daring today.'

'Very *Nick Carnage* of you.' His companion smiled.

'Thanks, Aaron,' Nicolas replied.

'That's not my name,' Auron shot back quickly.

'I know.' He smiled. 'Annoying, isn't it?'

'Well played, kid.' The spirit badly suppressed his own smile.

They found their way back to the arena with what Nicolas assumed was more luck than any sort of innate skill. The same luck also provided them with an empty arena. The only signs that anyone had been in there at all were the bloodstains on the floor and a discarded chunk of ear. At the far end of the arena, the opposite door stood wide open.

'This definitely qualifies as *too quiet*.' Auron looked around sceptically as they walked across the open ground towards the door.

Almost as if Auron saying it aloud had caused some power of the universe to look down on them, notice they were having it too easy, and rectify the situation, a guard appeared in the gallery above. The man walked casually towards Big Boss's throne, whistling a merry tune to himself. After picking up some item that had been left on the table by the side of the throne, it looked like the ivory pipe, the guard turned and proceeded to walk back out again.

Nicolas—and the chicken—stood completely still, watching the man, praying to that same power that he wouldn't turn and see them. But in a moment of cursed fate, the guard gave a nonchalant glance over his shoulder followed by a double take. Then the shouting began. By then, Nicolas was already at the far end of the arena and nearly through the door.

Beyond it were stone corridors with no visible markings, save the odd claw mark and bloodstain, to indicate which way to go, so Nicolas simply ran in a straight line until a better option presented itself. Once he reached a junction in the wide corridor, he stopped and listened. Hearing a feint howling to his left, he turned and ran towards it, closely followed by his companions.

After zigzagging down several corridors using this method, the group entered the upper level of a vast cavern. In front of them, a set of wooden steps led down to the main floor and various cages with a crazy assortment of unnatural creatures, keening and howling and hissing. Nicolas saw a dog with crab claws, a large snake with bat-like wings, a sheep with an armoured turtle's shell, and so many more, and so much worse. There were several guards in the room, but they were all sitting around a table on the far side of the cave playing cards.

'This must be why we haven't seen any running around the plains.' Auron looked at the imprisoned creatures. 'He's been gathering them for his games.'

'What about the ones we have seen?' Nicolas asked, thinking back sadly to the cow-dragon.

'Fallout of taking T'goth's power? Escapees?' Auron mused. 'Who knows?'

Creeping down the stairs with care, each step making a creak that could've woken the dead, they somehow made it to the animal cages unseen. One of his worries with this plan had been that the odd creatures would give them away by reacting to their presence and making noise, but they seemed more curious than anything. Worse than that, they seemed sad.

'We need keys,' Nicolas whispered, glancing towards the guards. He didn't like his chances four on one with a single knife, albeit a bloody big one, and a chicken for backup.

Beside him, Auron eyed the monstrous creatures dubiously. 'Are you sure about this?'

'I'm kind of hoping they show appreciation for freeing them by not eating me.' Based on his encounter with the now-deceased wizard, he guessed the creatures would be more interested in punishing their jailers, but they were unnatural creations.

Can they even feel things like gratitude?

The cow-dragon had, but... Maybe this wasn't such a good idea. If he could get back to the jail...

'There you are!' Big Boss shouted from the cavern entrance above them.

The dwarf's presence certainly got a reaction from the caged beasts, who banged against their bars, spitting and hissing and snarling at Big Boss as his men spread out on the stairs and landing above, pointing crossbows at Nicolas. His plan seemed sounder now, which was good, because he was most certainly committed to it.

Across the cave, the guards at the table suddenly became aware there was an intruder, rising from their seats and drawing swords. They were surrounded, a fact Big Boss noted, judging by the smug look on his bearded face.

'And you brought the bird.' He laughed at the chicken cowering behind Nicolas's legs. 'Great stuff.'

Nicolas had really had enough of that guy. Of course, he hadn't been fond of him before now, but every time he saw the dwarf, he found some new facet to hate about him.

'You're a pest, boy,' Big Boss continued. 'And I would *love* to take my time killing you, but I have a busy schedule and places to be, so I'll have to settle for watching you shot to death. Don't worry, I'll still enjoy it plenty.'

'Those locks look pretty old and rusty, you know, kid,' Auron observed as he inspected the cages at Nicolas's side. 'And that knife you have looks pretty tough.'

Nicolas didn't need a second invitation. Before anyone could react, he struck the padlock of the nearest cage, which snapped in two. There was a general gasp of shock as the large snake with bat wings crashed through the door of its unlocked cage, knocking him backwards. With a flash of scales and a flap of wings, it flew straight past him towards Big Boss with its venomous fangs bared. The dwarf shouted at his men frantically.

Crossbow bolts flew both at the snake and Nicolas as he ran from cage to cage, breaking locks and freeing creatures. It seemed his guess had been right, and they were grateful to be released, or at least they hated their captors so much they were willing to ignore a side snack. Flashes of fur and hide and scale whizzed past him as the creatures dashed frantically for the dwarf and his men. It was such a blur that most of the time he didn't even properly see what he was freeing, which he was quite pleased about. Some of the creatures were truly disconcerting.

Big Boss fled back down the corridor, followed by the few guards who weren't currently being gnawed on. The four guards who'd been approaching Nicolas from behind were now too busy dying to do anything to impede him. Within moments, the room was empty save for those last couple of creatures left happily chomping on the remains of the guards.

'That worked well.' Nicolas was as surprised as anyone.

'Time to get our friends then,' Auron said with a proud smile.

On their way back to the jail, the empty corridors took on a chilling feel with roars and screams echoing from unknown directions, coupled with fresh bloodstains on the walls. Suddenly, the shadows between the torchlight seemed potentially deadly and each corner was a risk. More of a risk.

But it had succeeded in not only leaving the way open but the jail unguarded.

Chapter 21

With Auron to lead them, the trio made quick time back to the familiar door to the jail—where Nicolas saw the results of his plan first hand.

Beside the fortified door was a large toad, around the size of a wolf, with bear paws and razor-sharp teeth. The toad's chin bulged with pleasure as it finished... Well, Nicolas wasn't entirely sure what it had done. If it had planned on eating the guards, there were a lot of leftovers, but if it had been planning on simple violence, why were so many body parts missing? He couldn't help heaving at the bloody mess around the door but at least managed to do so silently. The creature hadn't noticed them, and he had no wish to get its attention, lest it fancied dessert. He concealed himself back around the corner and waited. Luckily, he wasn't kept waiting long as, goal accomplished, the creature hopped away laboriously, suggesting it was very full.

Approaching the door, he found himself having to tip toe between blood stains and body parts while trying not to be sick. It was quite the juggling act, and he nearly failed several times. But his sheer determination not to slip and fall into the mess that had once been men saw him through.

'There are the keys,' Auron exclaimed, pointing to a pile of gore as he walked anywhere he fancied. Not really touching the ground meant not worrying about stepping in…stuff.

With a sigh, Nicolas bent and delicately picked the ring of keys out of a pile of red goo and held it between two fingers, shaking it carefully to dislodge…whatever the bit of red stuff hanging off it was. This time, he was sick.

'Can I go on one adventure with you where you don't vomit?' Auron asked dryly.

'Easy to say when you don't have to touch this stuff.' The words came from a burning throat. Nicolas cleaned his mouth with the edge of his new waistcoat.

After finding the correct key, he quickly opened the door to the jail.

'Nick?' Shift cried, standing bolt upright. 'You're alive!'

'Thank your human Deities.' Garaz sighed with relief. 'We all feared the worst.'

'I had a lot of worst,' he replied, 'but I made it here and look.' Jangling the keys in his hands, he was warmed by his companions' smiles. Even Silva, whose mouth was still covered by the muzzle, had a hint of pleasure in her eyes.

'I'm sorry about letting you guys down,' he said awkwardly. This wasn't the ideal time for it, but if he didn't address it now, he might never.

'I think freeing us again makes us good.' Shift smiled.

'Balance has been brought.' Garaz chuckled.

'About that...' Auron began sheepishly as he entered the room.

'You're in a lot more trouble than he is,' Shift said with mock severity, pointing at the spirit.

'Indeed,' Garaz added dryly. 'But I think we understand. We can most certainly forgive, provided you have come to your senses now?'

'What he said,' Shift added with a nod.

'I have it under control now.' Auron's voice was full of emotion. 'I don't think I realised how bad it was getting until I did what I did. It was a wakeup call, and it won't happen again, you have my word.'

Nicolas hoped he could keep it. He seemed to be ruled by some other force when it came to Silva.

'I see you found him too.' Shift pointed at the chicken as Nicolas approached their cell to unlock it. 'How does that thing keep turning up?'

Nicolas looked down at the chicken and nodded towards his friends.

'Well, ahem, I have quite the story when we have the time.'

He almost laughed at the open-mouthed expression on their faces. It was nice to know something they didn't for a change.

'Of course.' Shift laughed. 'We have a shapeshifter, an orc, a ghost, a drowned mercenary, a wet-behind-the-ears-village boy, and a senile Deity...why wouldn't we add a talking chicken to the mix?'

'Not a ghost,' Auron mumbled grumpily.

'You are when I'm mad at you,' Shift snapped as Nicolas opened their cell door.

'Told yeh that chicken weren't natural,' T'goth cried, pushing himself up against the bars of his cell and glaring at the animal with a slight growl.

Shift approached Nicolas and was almost awkwardly silent for a moment. There was something in their eyes that he couldn't identify. It vanished as soon as it had appeared. 'Are you okay?'

'I'm good.' He smiled at them.

'I think you might just be,' they replied, punching him playfully on the arm.

One by one, Nicolas released his companions, opening the cells and unbinding them where necessary. Garaz gave him one of his ridiculously tight hugs, and T'goth expressed his pleasure in some sort of interpretive dance. Silva gave him the slightest of nods.

'We are sorry for how we treated you.' The guilt was evident in Garaz's voice. 'When they took you, we thought we would never see you again. The things we said were out of line, and I, for one, take it back.'

'It's okay.' Nicolas let out a small chuckle. 'You weren't wrong, but we need to get out of here. Fast.'

'How did you deal with the guards?' Shift asked.

'He let a herd of crazy creatures loose in the building, and they're eating them all,' Auron replied, as if telling them the most exciting thing in the world..

'Oh,' Shift looked at Nicolas wide-eyed before being distracted by his clothing. 'Isn't that Wade's waistcoat?'

'Yup.' Nicolas modelled the garment briefly. 'Blinded him with makeup then kicked his ass. Well, kicked his balls, actually. Hit him with a chair as well.'

'Good,' Shift said with a huff.

'Impressive,' Garaz added.

'Can we go and find the light now?' T'goth asked in a childlike manner.

'Yes, yes we can,' Nicolas confirmed.

* * * *

Outside the jail, Nicolas's companions looked at the carnage on the floor and up the walls around the jail door.

'Wow.' Shift whistled. 'You really did set a load of crazy creatures loose.'

'That'd be a weird thing to lie about,' he replied.

'Your tactic seems highly…effective.' Garaz looked a little queasy at the sight.

In all honesty, as much as Nicolas was enjoying the fact he'd actually impressed his companions, he didn't really want to hang around here too long. In between the smell and the visual component, he wasn't sure how much longer he could hold off the nausea threatening to blast from his mouth at any moment. Again.

'So I take it the plan remains the same as before we got put in cells?' Shift said as they moved off.

It made sense. Get the staff, and this would all be done. He was sure they'd have a straight run to the vault now.

'Are we going back towards the light?' T'goth asked, following directly behind the chicken as if he didn't want to let the bird out of his sight ever again.

'Yes, well, you're going towards the light. Not us, hopefully.'

Will getting to the vault really be as easy as that?

'Excellent,' T'goth said gleefully, before adding, 'And don't worry. I'm watching it.' The powerless Deity tapped his nose with a wink and pointed towards the chicken.

'Okay,' he replied.

The group travelled in silence from then on, wanting to stay alert in case their voices drowned out the hissing or growling of some nearby creature about to strike. Auron carefully checked each corridor before they moved down it, so the group only saw the odd flash of movement and the disgusting aftermath of the creatures passing. Apparently, many of them felt the need to defecate as much as possible in the place where they'd been held and forced to fight.

'We need to find the stairs,' Shift told him as they rounded the next corner. 'You were unconscious at the time, but after they captured us they brought us down to the jail.'

That explained the hard bruises peppering the backs of his legs. He must've been dragged down the stairs. Another one for Garaz's ever growing list of his injuries that needed tending. He stroked his chin where Wade had nicked him with his knife. His thumb came away bloody. Ahead of the group, Auron had come to a stop. 'Okay, guys. Good news, the stairs are just around the corner.' His expression added the term *bad news* for him. He placed his intangible finger over his lips and gestured to the group to come to him quietly.

The bad news turned out to be a creature with the tusks of an elephant and tail of a scorpion, including the vicious stinger on its end, standing directly in front of the door to said stairs. The creature skittered agitatedly around the body it was playing with.

Maybe letting them all out wasn't the best idea?

He'd gotten a little caught up in the moment in the cave, smashing locks with wild abandon and not really looking at *what* he was releasing.

'I could just go and try shoo it away,' Nicolas suggested as they concealed themselves again. 'They responded to me before. Or at least ignored me.'

'Yeah, because they were too busy trying to get to their captor,' Auron said. 'Now, their blood is up, and they've tasted the old *man flesh*. I doubt they'll make the distinction between you guys and anyone they don't like.'

He looked back down the corridor. The, whatever it was, had a severed arm in its pincer which it was waving around, coating the nearby wall in splatters of blood. Maybe going for a chat with it wasn't a sensible move.

'I shall go and slay the beast.' Silva was striding forward even as she spoke, blade taken from the dead guard's hand.

That seemed like suicide, even as skilled as she was. The creature nearly filled the corridor and its hide looked leathery and thick. It would be no simple kill and a minor miracle if she succeeded with all her limbs intact. She certainly wasn't going to distract it with her boobs.

Nicolas grabbed her wrist. Silva reacted as if she'd been hit by lightning, swinging round and looking at the hand that gripped her as if it were the most surprising thing she'd ever seen. Or as if she were about to rip it off. But though she terrified him, he didn't let go.

'I don't think that's a good idea,' Nicolas told her nervously.

'You don't think I can slay the beast?' Silva replied coolly.

'I'm sure you can,' Nicolas said. 'It's just that I'd rather you didn't take the risk unless we really have to. It's kind of big, and you could…get hurt.'

Silva tilted her head to the side slightly and looked at him as if confused. 'Very well,' she said finally.

'It would appear we need another idea,' Garaz said.

An idea came to him. 'Auron.'

'Yes?'

'No, not Auron as in *hey Auron*,' he said, getting excited at his idea. 'I mean Auron as in *Auron*.'

'I fail to see the difference.' Garaz raised an eyebrow.

Why is it so difficult to explain myself sometimes?

Taking a breath, he collected his thoughts. 'He can poke stuff, right? How about Auron goes past the beast and taps the wall. The beast will hear it but not see where it's coming from, and he can lead it away.'

Shift looked at Auron. 'How about it? You up for some poking?'

The spirit gave an immature smile. 'That's what the princess of the nomad tribe of Gellia said. After that, we—'

Nicolas rolled his eyes. 'Not the time.'

'Later then.' Auron looked almost dreamy at whatever memory he'd conjured up. 'Back to the matter at hand then. Crazy scorpion-elephant monster.' For a moment or two, the spirit seemed hesitant.

Nicolas gave him what he hoped was an encouraging look.

Finally, Auron nodded firmly. 'I think I can manage that. If poking things is all I can do then poke stuff I shall.'

With a confident stride Auron walked down the corridor and past the beast, taking a second to make a totally unnecessary rude gesture. Once he was on the far side of the creature, he approached the wall and, with a look of intense concentration, poked at it with his smoking finger. Without a sound, the finger disappeared into the wall. Auron stood up, letting out what would've been a sigh if he could've breathed. Leaning forward again, he made a second attempt. There was no sound. Auron turned away from the group and appeared to be talking to himself, psyching himself up. Fierce exertion creased his ethereal features as he poked the wall again.

Tap.

Instantly, the creature turned towards the sound, barking a challenge. When it saw nothing, it looked around warily. Auron moved up the corridor slightly and poked the wall again.

Tap.

With a snarl, the creature stalked forward, lowering its body to an attack stance and raising its quivering spiked tail.

Twice more Auron tapped on the wall, and the beast grew infuriated at not being able to see what was making the noise. The next time Auron tapped, the creature attacked the spot from which the sound had come, its tail striking with lethal precision, taking a chunk from the stone wall before coiling back for a follow-up strike.

Now Auron had the creature enraged, he moved faster up the corridor, tapping more frequently as he did. The creature roared and charged in pursuit of the noise, eventually disappearing around the corner and out of sight.

After a few moments, Auron reappeared and jogged towards his companions. He looked visibly drained, his aura dimmer than usual, but he smiled with pride.

'Nice one,' Shift said with an impressed nod.

'Saving the day is what I do,' Auron replied without a trace of humility.

Without further ado, the group ran to the door, and after Shift had worked their magic on the lock, they ascended to the higher levels of The Temple of Champions.

****

Muted voices echoed down the corridor, causing the group to move with greater caution. Around the next corner was a set of double doors with a single guard. Even from here, Nicolas could see the way the man's crossbow shook in his hand as he looked around. Quickly, he ducked back in cover as the guard glanced in their direction.

'How do we…' His question was cut off by Auron sauntering past him with a theatrical wink. The spirit walked up the corridor, past the guard and after a pause for dramatic affect, tapped the wall with his finger.

Instantly the guard turned, crossbow aimed and ready as he scanned the corridor beyond him. Nicolas saw a flash of movement as Silva charged past him, moving completely silently. Within seconds she was upon the guard, arm around his neck. Moments later the man's body became limp and he was lowered to the floor before Silva gestured them forwards.

The double doors looked heavy, but they could still hear the voices beyond them. Someone was angry. Tentatively, Shift turned the handle and eased the door open enough that they could see beyond.

Inside the room Big Boss paced up and down, staff in hand, addressing a cadre of his men—too many to simply storm in and take the staff. Plus, they had a minotaur, who stood menacingly behind his master, arms folded.

'We've sealed off the lower levels, where the creatures are mostly contained,' one of the men explained in a slightly shaky voice.

The dwarf's face was dark as he stopped abruptly. 'Define *mostly*.'

For a moment, the man seemed reluctant to continue, but Nicolas doubted the dwarf would take being ignored well. 'One of the creatures got onto the temple floor,' the goon admitted finally. 'It made quite a... mess of the place before we put it down. But the rest are contained in the lower levels. We locked the doors to the stairways, so they're trapped down there. Unless they can pick locks.'

Crap. Maybe they should've relocked the stairway door. Nicolas looked at Shift, who shrugged as if to say *whatever*. No sense worrying about it now, he supposed. They had more pressing concerns.

Big Boss turned and glared at his thug before looking at the staff in his hand. Generally, the thing would've looked unremarkable, save for the eye carved into its top, but the power pulsing off it raised the hairs on the back of his neck. The dwarf seemed to be mulling something over, but then he levelled the staff at the man who'd spoken. Coursing red energy shot from it, engulfing him just before he could scream. His physical form writhed and altered as the energy surrounded him, transforming him into what appeared to be a large potato.

'Chip this idiot up and see that he's on the menu the next night we're open,' the dwarf barked, striking the bottom of the staff on the floor. The assembled men jumped at the loud crack, eliciting a chuckle from Lucas. Big Boss may have been short, but he made up for it in presence.

'I don't just want this contained,' Big Boss snarled. 'I want those creatures put down, each and every one of them. Get that wizard guy, Oleg-*whatshisface*. He can blast the stupid things to death. *Then* I want the place ready for business by tomorrow night. I also want that little runt who let them out. And I am going to say this carefully so no one can misunderstand, I...want...him...*alive*. Maimed, I don't care, but I want him breathing so I can properly punish him for all this dung he's levelled on me.'

Aw, I upset Big Boss? Good.

The group of goons all nodded their understanding. None of them seemed willing to speak aloud and draw attention to themselves.

'As much as I wanna do this myself, I gotta go to the meet.' Big Boss stroked his beard thoughtfully. 'I can't keep him or my destiny waiting. When I get back, I want this all to look like it never happened. Creatures dead, arenas ready, kid alive and in chains, and that blasted chicken roasted on a plate. Understood?'

'Yes, boss,' the men barked in unison.

Nicolas was so engrossed in the scene that he hadn't been keeping a proper eye on T'goth, who suddenly pressed his face into the gap between him and Shift.

'The light,' the Deity croaked as he caught sight of the staff.

Nicolas pulled him back, but it was too late. The door jerked suddenly, just enough to be noticed by the deadliest person in the room.

'*There*,' Lucas shouted, pointing towards them.

The assembled men turned quickly and raised their crossbows. Shift slammed the door shut as Nicolas yanked T'goth back. Just as the door closed, there were a number of *thunks* and several arrowheads appeared through the wood.

'Go,' Auron shouted.

The group turned to flee, though it hadn't really needed saying. Seconds later, Lucas ran through the door. Literally *through* it. The formidable wooden door was turned to a pile of kindling by the minotaur's muscular frame. For a brief moment, Nicolas locked eyes with the beast, yelping as Lucas kicked his hooved foot on the ground and charged.

The group sprinted down the corridors, often colliding with walls as they rounded corners without slowing down. The burly minotaur practically filled the corridor as he ran them down, the clacking of his hooves on the stone floor ominously bouncing from wall to wall. Lucas's head was tilted downwards as he charged, thick black horns ready to impale them.

Why do I keep looking back?

'He's gaining!' he cried in between pants.

'How's something so big so fast?' Shift asked, glancing back too.

The gap was closing as the number of seconds his life could be measured in lessened.

They rounded another corridor and…the way was blocked. The tusked, scorpion-tailed thing must've managed to get the door open and follow them up the stairs. It stood with its back to them, doing whatever strange creatures did when they weren't eating people.

'Don't stop,' Auron called. 'Go to the sides.'

The creature was large, this was going to be tight. Both Silva and Shift slid under the creatures legs in a way he knew he couldn't recreate. Even Garaz, the largest of the group, threw himself over the monster's legs, rolling to his feet on the other side of it as if he'd never been off of them. Auron just ran through it. That left him.

Pressing himself as close to the wall as he could, he charged past the creature, who was already beginning to move in pursuit of the meals that'd been presented to it. He collided with one of the creature's scuttling legs, almost stumbling and falling, but by some miracle he managed to stay on his feet. The beast cried in surprise, a sharp scream that made him wince.

It knew he was there now, but all he could do was keep running. Ducking down, he closed his eyes, praying that a pincer wouldn't cut him in half any moment now. The creature let out a hiss, one signalling that it was ready to strike.

This was followed by a terrible shucking noise, the sound of a collision, and an inhuman cry of pain. Risking another glance back, Nicolas found himself coming to an abrupt halt. The minotaur had obviously been too intent on getting them to watch where he was going. It was hard to tell from this angle, but it looked like Lucas had impaled the creature with both of his horns. There was a struggle as the beast whipped and thrashed in its death throes, and he assumed the minotaur fought to free himself, cursing loudly. Finally the scorpion tail fell limply to the floor as the creature succumbed to its wounds. Auron had told Nicolas once that sometimes people voided their bowels when being stabbed to death in battle. He hoped the same was true for bizarre hybrid monsters, because Lucas was stood directly behind it.

But he won't be for long.

Graphic death threats hounded him as he ran to catch up to his companions. They'd been given some time, best make the most of it.

Chapter 22

The screaming patrons fleeing the temple as creatures from their most twisted nightmares rampaged around made escaping a relatively simple exercise. By the time the group made it outside, there were carriages everywhere, desperately trying to get their passengers away before they were eaten but managing to get in the way of every other carriage trying to make its getaway. This created a jam which the drivers were attempting to solve by shouting at each other with rather graphic insults. As the guards tried and failed to contain the chaos, Nicolas and his friends slipped between the carriages to avoid being seen, before finally breaking away and disappearing into the natural concealment of the forest.

Returning to the clearing where they'd stashed their gear, they all took a moment to breathe. Ditching his stolen waistcoat—he didn't suit the bare-armed look, after all—he happily put his own clothes on again. He was also glad to have the *Dawn Blade* back on him, the weight of the sword reassuring him that he wouldn't have to resort to dishes of powdered makeup to defend himself.

Sitting on the grass, finally resting his weary legs, Nicolas took in the luminescent tranquillity around him.

Does the forest itself have healing powers?

His body and spirit already felt reinvigorated. Above them, beyond the leaves and branches, it was deepest night, yet the forest was light, the mushrooms and flowers of Edmoor glowing brightly enough to make the shadows around them unthreatening. Considering how often he imagined dangers in the shadows, this was a big thing for him.

He let out a satisfied sigh. They'd made it out relatively unscathed. The only exception was T'goth, who was curled in a ball and muttering to himself in a frustrated tone, rocking slightly. He looked even paler and older.

How long does he have left before his body gives in to its frailty?

It was clear he was running out of time.

'That was pretty intense.' Nicolas rubbed his aching legs and tried to distract himself from his ailing companion. 'I thought that—'

'Nope,' Shift said. 'No small talk. Not until we get an explanation for *that*.'

His gaze followed Shift's pointing finger to the chicken, who somehow looked sheepish under the scrutiny. After a moment of hesitation, the animal slowly walked into the centre of the group, like an actor taking the stage.

'Okay,' the chicken began with a ruffle of its feathers. 'I suppose the best place to start would be an introduction. I am King Silus of Sarus. Known as *King Silus the Unwilling*, if you must.' The bird took a small bow, which looked so comical that Nicolas nearly laughed aloud. How else could he react?

Of course he was surprised, they all were. The chicken, was a *king*. Even Silva had let her guarded exterior crack as she looked wide eyed at the chick...King Silus. Funny, if this had happened a few days ago Nicolas would struggle getting his head around it, but he'd seen so many strange things since going to the village square with his parents that he was coping with it rather well, in his opinion.

'Wow,' Shift said finally.

'His name rhymes,' T'goth spat venomously. 'Never trust a leader whose name rhymes with his country. They end up doing bad things. Also never trust a ladybug with odd-numbered spots.'

Offering the troubled Deity an indulgent smile, Nicolas gestured for the king to continue. 'I don't know how long I've been a chicken—I have difficulty keeping track of time since the change—but I remember how it happened. I was making my daily pilgrimage to the treasury when the walls changed to vines around me. Next thing I knew that blasted dwarf and his men entered, waving a staff around.' Silus gave a gesture with his feathers that could've been interpreted as a shrug. 'Then I was a chicken.' The king inspected his small body as if he'd never truly looked at it before.

'I have...many questions,' Garaz said hesitantly, obviously in very unaccustomed territory.

'Why do you go to the treasury daily?' Nicolas asked, guessing that was one of the more obvious questions. 'Do you like counting money or something?'

The chicken...king seemed reluctant to answer but spoke up after a moment. 'Well, this is quite embarrassing, but I go to the treasury to be alone.' He clucked. 'It's the only place where I can get away from…everyone, really. Even in my chambers, I have servants going to and fro. It's the only place where I'm not under scrutiny or expectation. The gold doesn't need anything and doesn't judge me.'

'What?' Shift looked incredulous. 'Surely being a king is awesome. Money and power and castles.'

'I can assure you it is not,' Silus replied. 'Hence, the *unwilling* moniker I've been given. I hate being king. People demanding things from you all the time, giving you opinions, expecting action and answers. It's terrible. You're never alone.'

'But are you not prepared for those responsibilities from birth?' Garaz asked thoughtfully.

'Not me,' Silus wailed, becoming quite impassioned. 'I was never supposed to be king. But King Ragus goes and gets himself, his wife, and his heirs lost at sea, and lo and behold, the line of succession somehow points straight at me. *Me*, of all people. I gamble and drink and like fine company and then *boom*, king. No more freedom, and all the responsibility in the world.'

'I thought you'd done so much good work, though?' Nicolas said. 'Didn't you clean up the streets or something?'

'Yes, the kingdom was becoming prosperous.' Silus conceded. 'The criminal element led by that thrice cursed dwarf was being driven out and the dens of vice they created closed. For the first time in a long time, the city was a decent place to live, and the country as a whole was growing. People were happy again…but Chancellor Lorca did that. Not me.' The chicken king sighed. 'He suggests stuff, and I sign the papers to make it official. Even at council meetings, I look for his nod before I agree to anything. I'm not even a proper king. I'm a giant puppet who nods and shakes his head on command. But things get better, and everyone loves me for it. I keep telling Lorca to let me abdicate so he can be in charge, but all I get is *it's important to keep the royal bloodline intact.*'

'Please get him back to the point of him being a chicken,' Auron said testily. 'Specifically, what happened afterwards.'

Nicolas conveyed Auron's wishes in a politer way.

'Like I said,' Silus began, 'they turned me into a chicken, which was quite the shock, I can tell you. Seemed like it was a shock to the dwarf's men as well. Everything was a bit woozy, as you may understand, but I did hear one of them ask his boss why he wasn't just killing me like he'd agreed to do. Ransom, apparently. So the dwarf said.'

'How did he expect anyone to pay your ransom when he was robbing the entire treasury?' Nicolas asked.

'Criminals like that tend to be greedier than they are smart.' Shift shrugged. 'If there's even the slightest chance to squeeze some extra gold out of it, they will.'

'Anyway, they tried to take me. Obviously having just changed into a chicken and now being chased was unpleasant, so I was making quite the ruckus. My Kingsguard heard and came running. They are very good men. There was a fight, of course, and in the confusion, I slipped away.'

'How did they get the treasure out if they were busy with your guards?' Shift asked. 'That much gold takes time to remove.'

'While his men chased me, the dwarf used the staff to give the chests and other treasures legs and they ran out. The kingdoms entire wealth *walks* out of the treasury, just like that.'

'Why did you not stay at the castle?' Garaz asked. 'You were in a village when we came across you.'

'Ah that.' The king's clucking voice betrayed his shame. 'Well, the truth of it is that after the shock wore off, I found that...I quite liked being a chicken. No responsibilities, no people telling me to do this or that, no one following me around constantly, no more of those Deity-forsaken meetings. Just me being a chicken, doing chicken things. I knew people were looking for me, as I'm sure the guards must've worked out what had happened, especially as I was running around in circles shouting, *'You can't do this, I'm the king,'* so I ran. I was going to leave the kingdom, until I came across you.'

That certainly explained why the people of Sarus were so passionate about their chickens. If word spread that one was on the loose who happened to be the king, people would be quite temperamental when it came to a chicken being abused by a crazy old man.

'Chicken nearly got us lynched,' T'goth spat, miming his neck being stretched by a hangman's noose.

Nicolas bit back his retort.

'I didn't wish you harm, just so we're clear,' the king said indignantly. 'Everyone was looking for me, so I was heading to the border to leave the kingdom when I crossed your path. You seemed like a group who would interfere, and I didn't want that so I tried to run you off, impede you as much as I could. If you got to the dwarf, I would be changed back and go back to a life I didn't want. I'm sorry.'

'So why did you help us escape? Why not let the dwarf off us?' Shift asked.

'I wanted you out of the way, not dead,' Silus admitted. 'Besides, while following you, I realised that you're good people trying to do the right thing, and I couldn't stand by and let harm come to you. Hearing you talk about the state of the kingdom and seeing first-hand what was befalling it, I found I wanted to help, just like you're doing even though you're not even citizens of Sarus. Seeing you put yourselves in harm's way because it was the right thing to do, well, it changed my perspective.'

'Lotta that going around.' Shift gave Nicolas a sideways glance.

'They must have hired Wade to hunt down the chicken—sorry, king—after he escaped,' Garaz said. 'That would explain why the men at the tavern took exception to us. They saw the same quality the king did and wished to stop us from interfering.'

'Wade said he was going to eat him.' Nicolas winced at the memory. 'Apparently, he has a thing for exotic delicacies and thinks eating a chicken who was a king would be quite the meal.'

'Well, that's just thoroughly psychotic.' Auron scoffed.

'When I was fighting Wade, he mentioned Big Boss had upset some bad people by not killing the king outright. It seemed there was some sort of deal that he'd gone back on,' Nicolas continued. 'He must've hired Wade to make it right.'

'Deity-power-stealing criminals is one thing, but breaking a deal, that's just *low*.' Shift chuckled.

'So someone… What? Helped the dwarf steal a Deity's power so he could assassinate me and make it look like a robbery gone bad? Why not just do it themselves?' Silus cried.

'Maybe that person, or persons, needed someone obvious to take the blame for the crime, someone plausible,' Garaz mused. 'Criminals are supposed to rob treasure vaults.'

Auron furrowed his ethereal brow. 'Avus Arex.' Just the use of the necromancer's name sent a cold shiver up Nicolas's spine. 'He mentioned he had friends when Nicolas fought him, friends who would make it seem like he was the hero of the story and make him famous or whatever in the Underworld he actually wanted.'

'King gets snuffed out by third party, and everyone thinks all's well when that third party is brought to justice,' Shift sounded the idea out. 'What about it, Silva, ring any bells?'

There was remorse in the warrior's face. Silva looked down for a moment, her forehead creasing with concentration. 'I am sorry,' she said at last. 'I remember much of what I did, but parts of those events are...patchy. I remember the necromancer, and I remember I did not work for him specifically...but nothing beyond that.'

'At least she's useful in a fight.' There was no small amount of sarcasm in Auron's words.

'I was wrong,' King Silus spoke suddenly and passionately. 'I didn't realise the kingdom was in this kind of danger. I just thought...I thought they would be as better off without me as I would be without them. That they didn't really need me. Just let Lorca sort it all out. I believe that may have been very silly of me.'

'I would not be so hard on yourself,' Garaz said. 'I think whoever tasked Big Boss with your assassination would be unlikely to let it lie if he had failed.'

'That's a fair point,' Nicolas said encouragingly. 'At least you're alive. All we have to do is get that staff, and we can undo all of this and hopefully get some answers.'

'The dwarf said he was off to a meeting,' Auron reminded everyone. 'I bet that meeting is with whoever set this up.'

'But how do we find it?' Nicolas looked around him. 'It could be anywhere, and all we have to go on is that there's a meeting...somewhere.'

'As much as young Nicolas is being pessimistic about our options, he is also sadly right,' Garaz said.

'Yeah, but his negativity still makes him a sourpuss.' Shift shrugged playfully.

'East.'

Everyone in the group looked at T'goth, who was absentmindedly drawing an arrow pointing east in the dirt with his finger.

'How do you know that?' Nicolas asked.

'Shiny light,' T'goth answered as if that explained everything.

'*Shiny light?*' Silva asked sceptically.

'The little fella had light in his hand. My light,' the Deity continued. 'I saw the light and now I can see the light always. It moves east. If that direction is east,' he finished, pointing a bony finger.

'Are we really going to use a senile, powerless Deity like a homing bird to find the location of a meeting where a dwarf with the power of said Deity is going to meet the shady person or persons behind an assassination attempt on a king?' Auron asked.

'Unless you have a better idea?' Nicolas shrugged.

'Actually, I think it's a brilliant idea.' The spirit smiled, ushering them up. 'Adventure time, people. There are asses to be kicked and wrongs to be righted.'

'What about it, Nick?' Shift asked with a half-smile. 'You up for a bit more adventuring?'

Though he'd known that question was coming, he still had no immediate answer. He wished he'd properly dealt with what had happened during his last adventure. Knowing he was struggling and hoping it would just pass in time wasn't the way to handle it, and people had nearly died because of it. He'd thought he could go off on another adventure and just pretend all that stuff wasn't festering inside him. In the end, it'd broken through, taking his usual anxious disposition and turning it into something that had crippled him when his companions needed him most.

Can I continue? Will I choke at the wrong moment again? Am I just a coward at my core?

No. He'd survived. He'd survived last time, and he'd survived this...so far. People needed help, and no one else seemed to be doing a damn thing about it. He looked at his hand, and it was still. Testing it, he clenched his fist several times, flexing his fingers as his hand opened. No shakes.

He nodded slowly to Shift.

'You're okay, though?' Shift asked. 'I mean, really?'

Nicolas thought about that for moment. 'I don't think I realised exactly how much the things that happened to me around Yarringsburg affected me.' Admitting it wasn't easy. 'I mean, I knew it had, but I just thought it'd...go away with time.'

'You thought it'd...' Shift rolled their eyes. 'Who'd you talk to about all that stuff when you got home?'

'No one, as far as we can tell,' Auron cut in.

'So, you thought you could go from a being village boy to facing a bloody city full of vampires and just *walk it off* or something?' Shift laughed. 'Jeez, Nick, you were tweaky enough before all that happened.'

'You cannot just shut those things away, Nicolas,' Garaz added. 'Whether you believe it or not, it affects you, and you have to face that. Preferably when our lives are not on the line,' the orc finished with a half-smile to show no hard feelings.

'Yeah, it may not have been my best idea. But I'm past the point where it'll control me now.' Nicolas looked at his still hands. 'Besides, I'm eager to deliver some comeuppance to a certain dwarf.'

Shift, Auron, and Garaz seemed to approve.

'What about you, Auron?' Garaz enquired, indicating Silva.

The spirit looked at the warrior, it was a cold gaze. 'Like the kid, I let my something eat away at me until it took over,' he said firmly. 'But me and her aren't done. At some point, there will be a reckoning. There has to be. But until then, the quest is more important. You'll have no issue from me.'

Silva gave one of her slight nods. 'I understand,' the warrior said. 'And I agree. Once this is done, my life shall be yours. Until then, I will fight with you. It wouldn't be the first time...' Silva's voice trailed off under Auron's fierce glare.

It appeared there was a story or two he didn't want the group knowing.

'Seems like we're ready to go then,' Nicolas declared, wanting to break the tense silence. 'Who can hope to stand against us?'

'It is certain no one would expect a group such as us.' Garaz chuckled.

'They have a minotaur,' Shift pointed out.

'Pfft,' Nicolas scoffed. 'Big deal. We have a talking chicken.'

'I don't mean to interrupt,' the chicken said gingerly. 'But are you all talking to someone I can't see?'

Chapter 23

Upon reaching the boundary of Edmoor Forest, the party found that crossing the country back to the city was going to be a lot more difficult than they'd first thought. There was just enough moonlight to make out the creatures roaming the dark plains, small bursts of unnatural movement catching the eye.

'They escaped the temple.' Nicolas gasped, hoping they hadn't spread to any nearby villages. Anyone they hurt would be because of *him*. All the more reason to get the staff back as quickly as possible.

'They must have found some other exit, or burrowed their way out,' Garaz mused. 'Unless they are mostly nocturnal, as we had suggested.'

'This is definitely a flaw in the plan, kid,' Auron said.

'It's not like I had it planned down to the finest detail,' he protested. 'I was in a stressful situation and trying to think on the fly.'

'Got, any of that *on the fly* thinking for us now?' Shift asked sarcastically.

'Nothing springs to mind, no.'

'The light.' T'goth began to stumble forwards in an almost dreamlike state before Silva and Nicolas pulled him back in. He was going to get himself eaten.

What will the other Deities do if I let one of theirs get eaten by some crazy creature? That thought knotted his stomach. *Maybe they aren't interested? Surely if they were, they would've intervened by now? In fact, would it hurt one of them to lob a single lightning bolt at a certain dwarf?* He sighed. Trying to discern the motivations of Deities would send him cross-eyed.

'Any advice would be gratefully received,' Garaz said to Auron.

'Move quickly and quietly,' the spirit said with a shrug. 'Unless you have some kind of invisibility spell you've conveniently forgotten about until now?'

'Alas, I wish that were so.' The orc chuckled. 'But my magic is sadly lacking in that area.'

As much as that would've come in handy, having all the abuse his face had taken healed by the orc was a great second best. Perhaps at some point these fireballs Garaz claimed to be able to throw would show themselves. They may be needed if stealth fails.

With no other option, the group followed Auron's advice, moving quickly and quietly between what cover lay across the plain—a tree here, an outcropping there—always moving with purpose. The only problem was T'goth, who seemed eager to dash off in search of his light, no matter how many times they impressed the need for silence on him.

'I could knock him out?' Silva whispered the third time the powerless Deity tried to run off on his own.

It was tempting. 'If you do, he can't guide us,' Nicolas said reluctantly.

Moving from concealment to concealment was time-consuming and played heavily on the nerves. The tension was as palpable as the silence. Thank the Deities none of the creatures could see Auron, who would've basically been a massive beacon with his aura lighting up the surrounding area. At least he offered them some extra light to travel by, ensuring that none of them slipped or tripped.

'The creatures seem to be dispersing,' Garaz whispered as the group found shelter behind a tree, the orc's breath fogging in the cold night air.

Or is it early morning now? He'd lost all track of time. The orc was right though, the creatures were rapidly moving out of the area. He really hoped they weren't fleeing anything.

'They must be going to look for food,' Shift said. 'Lucky for us, they didn't fill up on guards before they wandered out here.'

'That's one explanation.' Auron looked at the horizon with narrowed eyes. 'The other would be that they're moving off because this territory's been claimed and they're getting the heck out of here before they incur the wrath of whatever claimed it.'

Maybe *fleeing* had been right? 'That's nice and pessimistic.' Worry boiled in Nicolas's stomach. He looked around carefully.

'I really hope it's my option and not yours,' Shift added quietly.

Auron's instincts proved correct. As they crested the next rise, a giant shadow was using claws as thick as a hand to tear up the form of another strange beast. Moving around its kill, moonlight finally found the creature. Nicolas's stomach knotted. Its body had the quality of a large cat, but there were tufts of fur interspersed with scaled flesh across its muscular form. A set of sharp fins jutted from it's back, and it had a long snout filled with teeth. It looked like death.

Finally finishing off its prey, whose only crime happened to be that it was in the wrong place at the wrong time, the creature roared in triumph, raising its head to the sky in a feral howl that reverberated across the plain, its message clear: *'Piss off, or else.'* Satisfied, it prowled the area, marking its kingdom.

'I take it our path goes straight past it,' Garaz said dryly.

By way of answer, T'goth just pointed straight ahead, mumbling something dreamy and incomprehensible.

Or is his voice just that weak now?

'We could go around?' Nicolas suggested.

'I get the impression this thing is king of all it surveys, so that could take hours we don't have,' Auron replied, not unsympathetically.

'If we try to go through its kingdom…that's a lot of open ground.' He looked at the dead creature ahead of them and the blood drained from his face.

'I do not fancy our chances if that thing decides to come after us,' Garaz stated.

'Me either,' Silva added in a rare moment of both humility and actually contributing to the conversation.

Why's Shift so quiet? He turned to look at them, and they were sitting sullenly with their jaw set, looking pointedly away from the rest of the group as if trying not to be noticed.

'You okay?' he asked.

'*Fine*,' Shift snapped in response. 'Fine, I'll do it. But I'm not bloody happy about it, Nick.'

'Do what?' he asked warily as the rest of the group homed in on their conversation.

'I know what you want,' Shift replied, waving their arms. '*Get the shapeshifter to turn into a similar creature and draw it away.* I don't want to do it, but as you point out, I'm your only hope so it's up to me to bail you all out.'

'I never said—'

Shift put their finger up to his lips. 'I said I'd do it so you can stop trying to strong arm me.'

Rolling his eyes, he said no more. If they wanted to use him as a scapegoat to do what they were going to do, he wasn't about to argue, even though he *was* worried about what might happen to Shift. As annoying as they were, he was quite fond of them.

'Do you think that's the only—' Auron began.

Shift held up a hand to silence him. 'I'll do it,' they said firmly, before adding sheepishly, 'I just need you all to look away. If I change into *that* wearing *this*, my clothes will get ripped to shreds and I'll need them when I change back. Nick can carry them, seeing how this is his stupid idea.'

As much as he wanted to protest, he didn't. This seemed foolhardy and dangerous, but apparently the whole thing was his idea and no one else seemed to be raising any objections.

'Are you sure you can change into a similar creature?' Garaz asked warily. 'It is very...unique.'

Shift took mock offence. 'You doubt my abilities?' they gasped before adding, 'If I've seen it, I can copy it. Just be quick off the mark when I draw the thing away. No dillydallying. I'll meet you at the city gates.'

'City gates?' Nicolas asked.

'The capital of Sarus is directly east of here,' Shift replied. 'There's no way that isn't where the meeting is.'

'Good point,' Auron said. 'It is that way, and that can't be a coincidence.'

He looked east, back the way they'd come, and sighed. This adventuring lark consisted of a lot of travelling backwards and forwards. Just like with the necromancer—up the mountain, down the mountain, up again, and then through it. *If*—and that was a huge if—he ever adventured again, he'd invest in a horse.

'Turn around then,' Shift said testily, looking at the rest of the group.

They turned.

Nicolas shuffled uncomfortably. It was really awkward knowing that someone was getting undressed right behind him. He fixed his gaze on the horizon, and there it would stay until it was safe. Something hit him in the back of the head and he nearly turned. Pulling at the item that now hung around his neck, it turned out to be Shift's shirt. More garments hit him. Those that he couldn't catch he let fall to the ground, lest he bend down to pick them up and accidently see...something.

Once Shift had finished lobbing garments at him—including their unmentionables, which he picked up without looking directly at them – everything went quiet. Then he heard a soft padding on the grass behind him. Still he didn't look back, just in case. Shift, now almost identical to the creature on the plain, moved lithely around him, taking a playful snap at him, causing him to jump back and nearly drop their clothes.

It was strange seeing his companion in such an inhuman form. He'd seen them in various genders and ages before, even as himself once, but never...this. Shift looked at him through alien, reptilian eyes, and thinking he should do something, but not sure what, he settled for giving them a reassuring pat on the snout. Shift, even in that form, was blatantly unimpressed, shaking their head and uttering a sound not dissimilar to a tut.

'Good luck,' he whispered as Shift turned and began to pad away.

Shift looked back and gave him a dismissive snort before bounding away at speed in the direction in which the creature had gone.

The group waited tensely, making sure to give them ample time to find the creature and lure it away from both their current position and the way they were travelling. After several minutes, which felt like a lot longer, a howl reverberated across the plain — no, it was two distinct howls overlapping each other.

'I think that's the signal,' Auron said grimly, obviously as concerned for Shift as Nicolas was, despite the brave face he was putting on.

Tentatively, the group left their cover. Though they were still careful, the general belief was that the way would be clearer now that the creature had driven off all competitors. That belief held true.

****

By the time the party were within sight of the walls of Sarus City, morning had come to Etherius, the rising sun casting a beautiful red border across the horizon, framing the city it rose behind. A slight mist had descended on the plain, turning it into a white sea from which random islands of green rose—along with the walls of the city of Sarus. A ring of torches surrounded the city, which he assumed were to ward off the creatures, their flames finally being allowed to die out as daylight came.

'Now to get in,' Auron said, as if getting past that wall was the easiest thing in the world.

They made for a small hill to get the lay of the land. As the group climbed, the sprawl of the city came into view before them, a feat of human creation at odds with the nature around it. The only city Nicolas had visited before was Yarringsburg, and he'd never seen it from this vantage. It was impressive, to say the least.

How many thousands live here?

Really, right now though, there was only one person he cared about.

Where's Shift? They should be back by now.

'I think entering the city will be tricky considering the ending of our last visit,' Garaz said, looking at the gate and the numerous ant-like shapes moving around it.

'I'm confused,' Nicolas said. 'Why can't we just walk up to the gate and have him let us in?' He pointed towards King Silus, who dropped the worm clutched in his beak and shooed the writhing pink creature behind him with his clawed foot.

'Well, yes, I could just command it, of course.'

'There can't be that many talking chickens in the world, so they'll know it's him,' Nicolas added.

'I think that idea may be more complicated than you think,' Garaz replied knowingly. 'You seem to have overlooked the fact that the dwarf knew exactly when the king would be in the treasury. We cannot rule out the idea that whoever is behind this has confederates inside the castle, close to the king. Until that person is revealed, it would be wise to tread with caution.'

'It's the High Chancellor,' Auron said as if it were obvious.

'What?' Nicolas scoffed. 'How do you know that?'

'Hero instincts, kid,' the spirit replied casually. 'Plus, evil advisor to the king. Classic hero stuff.'

He raised his eyebrows. 'Of course, I forgot the law of *classic hero stuff*.'

'You'll see,' Auron said flippantly.

'It is difficult to believe the High Chancellor would be involved in the attempt to assassinate the king,' Garaz said.

'Lorca?' Silus clucked loudly. 'He is my closest advisor and has been instrumental in aiding the kingdom. It makes no sense for him to try to assassinate me. I offered him the job on numerous occasions.'

Auron seemed unperturbed by any of the objections to his theory. If he was proven correct, he'd be unbearable for a good long while.

'Either way, we might be walking into a trap if we alert anyone, which could be pretty fatal,' Auron said thoughtfully before adding, 'Well, to you lot, anyway.'

'The light shines bright.' T'goth, skin grey and dry, moaned as he reached a hand towards the city, grabbing at the air as if he could hold it.

Before, T'goth had just been a senile old man. Now he understood what he'd lost, there was a sadness to him and his fading form. It was just like the cow-dragon, knowing it shouldn't exist, that something was wrong. Thinking of the creatures again, Nicolas anxiously glanced at the horizon for any sign of Shift.

'They'll be fine,' Auron whispered, expertly reading his expression.

'Were you worried about me?'

Making a very unmanly sound, Nicolas jumped out of his skin as Shift's voice appeared directly beside his ear. He tried to ignore the chuckling of Auron and Garaz...and Silva's eyerolling.

Is my place in the group the quest jester?

Behind him, Shift had a broad, self-satisfied grin. He was sure they would've given themselves a round of applause had they not been holding a pair of branches in front of themselves to satisfy their modesty. He was so pleased to see them.

'Was that really necessary?' he asked.

'The real question is *'was it funny?'* Shift replied with a sly wink. 'And the answer is, yes, it was. And also, what was that noise you made?'

'Are you okay?' Garaz asked his companion.

'I would prefer to be clothed before I answer any questions, if it's all the same, big guy,' Shift replied. 'So how about it, Nick? Got my clothes?'

'I should've thrown them in the mud,' he replied testily, producing the clothes from his backpack and placing them behind the tree Shift indicated with a nod of their head.

'Only because you want to see me walk around naked.' Shift blew him a cheeky kiss.

He really hoped his face wasn't flushing right now, because it certainly felt like it was. Shift carefully manoeuvred behind the tree, keeping the branches between their bare skin and the others eyes. After a few moments, Shift was redressed and rejoined the group.

'To answer your question,' they said as they brushed creases from their clothes, 'I'm fine. I led the creature away easily enough. Apparently, it saw me as a female and fancied its chances.'

'You didn't—' Nicolas said, slack jawed.

Shift looked at Nicolas in horror. 'No, I bloody did not, Nick,' they cried. 'I'm not that kind of shapeshifter, so keep your grubby thoughts to yourself.'

'Very smooth, kid.' Auron laughed.

'What?' he said with exasperation. 'I just wondered.'

'Maybe you ought to keep your musings on such matters to yourself,' Garaz said dryly.

This time his cheeks definitely flushed as he looked around for support. T'goth was busy staring at the horizon and Silus was busying himself with the worm that he'd recaptured. He finally looked at Silva.

'I do not know how any of you achieve any sort of mission with all of this *camaraderie*,' Silva said simply before continuing to sharpen her blade.

'It is only our second outing.' Garaz shrugged.

Shift walked over to him and tussled his hair playfully.

'Please always be so easy to mess with,' they said with a half-smile.

'So back to how we get into the city then?' he said in a dry tone, keeping Shift's gaze.

'The same way we got out the first time,' Shift replied, equally dryly but with a pinch of sarcasm.

By the time they'd circled the city to get a view of the graveyard, their fledgling plan had already failed. The site—specifically the gravestone from which they had emerged to freedom—was now surrounded by guards.

'I said we should have taken care of the witness,' Silva said with distaste.

'That's your input on this?' Shift asked. '*I told you I should've killed someone.*'

'You want to redeem yourself?' Nicolas asked testily. 'Then it starts by not killing random innocent bystanders that happen to be an inconvenience to you. Do you want to be a better person or not?'

For a moment, Silva seemed furious at the rebuke, maybe a little inclined toward a violent response too. However, after a moment, she relented, her body sagging slightly with a hard breath out. 'You are right. I came to you to learn,' the warrior admitted. 'Therefore, I should listen.'

'Maybe a diversion would be useful?' Garaz suggested, ignoring Silva and Nicolas's interplay.

'I don't know,' Auron said thoughtfully. 'I doubt we would draw them all away, and all it'll take is one to raise the alarm and we'll have an army on us.'

'He has a point,' Silva said as she squinted to view the guards, most likely calculating the odds of taking them all before the alarm was raised.

'They don't exactly look attentive,' Nicolas noted as he watched the soldiers himself.

And they didn't. Several of them were sitting playing a game while others lolled on the grass, some lying across graves in a very disrespectful manner. These men were hardly the elite of the Sarus military. Had they not been in uniform, he may not have taken them for soldiers at all, and said as much.

'Unfortunately, much of the corruption in my city extended to the army,' Silus said as he scratched the ground. 'Many took money to look the other way or act as muscle for this *Big Boss*. As we cleaned out the city, they all went to ground, and it became nearly impossible to work out who was corrupt and who wasn't.'

'Maybe the reason they attempted to have you killed?' Garaz mused.

'I'm telling you, it's the High Chancellor,' Auron said, stubbornly standing behind his—frankly silly—idea.

'It can't be,' Shift argued. 'He helped clean the place up. What possible motive could he have?'

The spirit shrugged. 'Who knows? Maybe he wants to take over Big Boss's *businesses*? I don't really care. I just know it's him.'

Nicolas rolled his eyes and looked at the soldiers again. 'Even if these guys are bad ones, we still need to get past them. Any ideas?'

'We could wait for them to go to the toilet, and Silva could take them out one by one. She likes ambushing people when they have their trousers down.'

'Seriously, Auron?' Shift said.

'Sorry.' There was little indication that he actually was. 'I accept her being here, but it's still difficult, and that's going to slip out from time to time. You don't like it, tough. At the end of the day, she does need to die.'

When Nicolas looked at Silva, she was peering over his shoulder, her head cocked slightly to one side. 'And so I shall.'

Before anyone could ask what she meant, Silva leapt up, covering the distance between her and Nicolas in a single bound, shoving him aside and behind her.

He stumbled away, falling to the grass. 'Silva, what in the Underworld...' The bloody tip of a crossbow bolt exploded out of her back, and she sagged towards him. '*No!*'

He vaulted up and caught her before she fell, gently lowering her to the grass. His attention was drawn by a whistling sound an instant before something flew from the foliage: two balls connected by a long rope. The balls circled each other, held together by the rope as they pirouetted past him and caught around Garaz's neck. The orc made a choking sound as the rope tightened, drawing the balls in at speed until they struck the orc on either side of his head. With a moan, Garaz fell to the grass, unconscious.

'No more playing.' Wade stepped out of the foliage, crossbow aimed.

Nicolas didn't need to follow the hunter's eye line to know his target. Leaping up with a speed that surprised even him, he shoved Shift aside just as the bolt passed where their head would've been. The hunter cursed in frustration, throwing his spent weapon at Shift, the heavy crossbow striking them in the head and knocking them to the floor. Nicolas watched in horror as his companion's body sprawled out on the grass beside him.

Uttering his own cry and drawing the *Dawn Blade*, he charged the hunter, swinging wildly to take his head from his neck. Wade caught Nicolas's sword arm at the wrist and struck him hard in the stomach, driving the wind from his lungs and crumpling his body. Drawing back, Wade struck him hard across the jaw, the impact shaking his teeth, possibly loosening several as he reeled back, the world blurring into a mass of flashing colour. Hitting the floor, dazed, he realised he'd dropped the sword, but his vision was still too hazy to see where.

Roughly, he was turned onto his back, and a great weight struck him in the chest. As the world came into focus once more, he saw the hunter sitting atop him, grinning wildly, holding the knife that had until moments ago been in his own belt. The knife came down towards him, its deadly tip closing on his neck at speed. Then it stopped.

It wasn't mercy from Wade, but a wrinkled hand had reached out and grabbed the hunters wrist. Another swung around, gripping Wade's throat so tightly that his face became red in seconds. His eyes bulged as his hand opened and the knife fell to the grass. As the veins in the hunter's temples began to protrude, he attempted to cry out. A stifled, wheezing sound came from his mouth instead.

T'goth hauled the gasping hunter into the air. 'You mean to keep me from the light. I cannot have that,' the old man said casually, before throwing Wade into the nearest tree so hard that the entire trunk shook from the impact.

As Wade's limp body fell away from the tree, there was a visible dent in the bark. His body collapsed to the grass, covered by the leaves the blow had dislodged from their branches. T'goth joined him on the grass a second after, falling to his knees, eyes becoming vacant as his skin went a lighter shade of grey.

'There must still be some Deity juice in him,' Auron said, appearing over Nicolas. 'You okay, kid?'

He raised a shaky thumb, though picking himself up from the ground took more than one attempt. His chin throbbed and his stomach burned badly enough that he couldn't stand up straight. Three of his companions lay around him, and he had no idea how bad they were or what to do. Silus was eagerly pecking away at the rope around the orc's thick green neck, and Shift was beginning to stir, though they had an angry bruise on their forehead already. That left Silva. He hobbled to the warrior and knelt beside her, his hands hovering over her as he tried to figure out what to do with them. Her torso was covered with blood and the end of the crossbow bolt still protruded from her chest.

'Grab something and apply pressure to the wound,' Auron told him.

Thinking fast, Nicolas took off his top, wrapping it around the area where the bolt had struck before pressing down hard. Silva groaned, her face becoming whiter by the second. There was a strange expression of almost satisfaction on her face as she looked at him from beneath half-closed lids.

'I didn't think I could do that,' she said quietly. 'I am glad I was wrong.'

'Stop talking like you're already dead,' Nicolas cried.

Silva chuckled slightly, a weak wheezing sound. 'It's not like I don't deserve this.' She smiled, a small trickle of blood running from her lips. 'It's an ironic end, really. That I should go the same way I murdered Auron.'

'Please,' he said, feigning brevity but failing miserably, 'you have way more atoning to do before you die.'

Silva raised an eyebrow weakly.

'That is true.' Garaz's voice was a croaky whisper as he came to Nicolas's side. 'So we had best ensure you live to do so.'

For a moment, it looked like Silva would protest, but instead she passed out, head lolling onto the grass. Quickly reaching inside his cloak, Garaz produced several small pouches.

'Do we pull it out?' Nicolas asked, looking at the shaft emerging from Silva's chest.

'No, Nicolas.' Garaz gestured for him to remove his hands from the now blood-soaked shirt. 'Many arrow heads are designed to break from the shaft upon impact. We need to find and remove it before it displaces and causes a deadly infection.'

He wanted to help, but he didn't have the skill. The best he could do was let Garaz work and be on hand if he needed assistance. The orc traced the line of the shaft with his finger and gently pressed Silva's skin around the wound.

'There,' the orc exclaimed finally, removing a small, fine blade from his robe. 'I am going to have to make an incision to remove the arrow properly. Once I am done, you will need to reapply pressure to the wound.'

Staring at the pooling blood on Silva's chest, he found himself becoming almost hypnotised by the nausea-inducing red liquid.

'*Nicolas!*'

'Yes, yes, got it,' he confirmed, snapping out of his trance.

He really didn't want to watch this, but he couldn't help if he shut his eyes and looked away. Garaz opened a small incision just below the shaft of the arrow with more grace than seemed possible for someone with such large hands. As blood pumped from the new cut, Garaz reached in with another delicate tool and, after a moment of tweaking, removed the blood-covered arrowhead. After discarding the tip of the weapon, Garaz removed the rest of the shaft quickly, and the unconscious Silva let out a moan as her body spasmed. Quickly, Nicolas applied pressure to the now-open wound.

Gesturing for him to move again, Garaz poured some form of powder around Silva's wound—which, judging by the warrior's cry, burnt more than a little. He then rested his big green hands over it and chanted, closing his eyes so he could focus. The gap between Silva's body and Garaz's hands glowed with bright white energy and his features creased with exertion. After a few moments, Garaz fell back on the grass, panting heavily.

The wound was now closed, though it looked raw and angry and her upper torso was still caked in drying blood. She appeared to be alive, a slight colour returning to her skin.

'Amazing,' Nicolas gasped.

Though he'd seen Garaz heal the various cuts and bruises the group had amassed during their adventures, he'd never seen it done to this extent. It seemed to have taken quite a bit from the orc, who'd already been dazed from Wade's weapon. As Nicolas helped him up slowly, Garaz knelt beside Silva, checking her over carefully.

'Will she be okay?' Shift asked, gently dabbing at the large purple and blue mark on their forehead but seeming otherwise okay.

All Nicolas could offer by way of an answer was a shrug.

'Time will tell,' Garaz said as he continued his work. 'The wound was deep, and she lost a lot of blood. I believe that the internal damage is minimal, and she is strong. Whether her will to fight and live is strong…Well, we shall see.'

The warrior had only just offered up her life to Auron, and now she'd nearly spent it saving his. Despite the things she'd done, he didn't want her to die.

At his side, Shift looked at Silva lying prone and bloody on the grass for a second more then moved away without a word. Nicolas heard thumping noises behind him, accompanied by male groans of pain.

Give him one from me.

Finally turning away from Silva, he caught Auron's gaze. The spirit had been standing next to him wordlessly the whole time. He should've looked pleased, but his ethereal face was unreadable.

By the time Nicolas got to him, Wade was securely tied to the nearest tree. The hunter's face was a mass of bruises and several of his teeth littered the ground beside him. One eye wasn't visible underneath swollen purple skin. Shift had given him quite the beating.

Well done.

'Has he talked?'

'I haven't asked him anything yet.' They shrugged, glaring at the hunter, whose head lolled drunkenly from side to side.

'You going to?' he asked.

'Oh yeah,' Shift said fervently. 'I reckon if anyone knows who can be trusted in the city, it's him. He managed to enter it when it was on lockdown *and* get to us in the treasury, so I think someone has friends.'

'Tell...you...*nothing*...' Wade's voice was weak but defiant.

'You're gonna talk, big fella,' Shift snarled. 'Or my chicken friend here will peck your privates clean off.'

'I *will*?' Silus sounded shocked, though not as shocked as Wade looked when he realised the chicken could talk.

'He was going to eat you.' Nicolas was happy to play along, hoping it didn't get to the point where they had to make good on the threat. Some things you could never unsee.

'Yes, but still...' Silus replied with distaste.

Shift, acting as if they'd heard nothing, knelt on the grass and put their face close to Wade's, which, judging by the fear in the hunter's only working eye, was intimidating him quite a bit. 'Yeah, he will,' they said slowly. 'And if he doesn't, I'll turn into something much bigger and do it myself.'

Shift gave Wade a menacing smile with a mouth filled with terrifying fangs. They growled, low and primal.

The hunter whimpered and began to talk.

Chapter 24

The troop of soldiers marched in perfect formation towards the graveyard. Would he look as grand wearing the plumed helm of their commander, which bobbed in time with his footsteps? After some contemplation, he finally decided he would look ridiculous in it, stationary or moving, and most likely feel very awkward wearing it. A normal helmet had been bad enough.

It took a few minutes for the soldiers in the graveyard to notice the approaching men as they continued to lie around in lackadaisical fashion. Standing to attention quickly and ensuring they looked as presentable as possible, they waited for the other party to reach them.

Nicolas really wished he could hear what was being said as the commanders of the two groups exchanged words. This was a big gamble, and it wasn't playing well with his nerves.

Maybe all that anxiousness isn't just to do with the graveyard?

Briefly, he looked at Silva, who was still being tended to by Garaz and evidently not out of the woods yet.

'Things are getting tense,' Shift whispered.

Turning back to the scene below, he didn't need to hear what was being said, the body language was obvious. Judging by the way the leader of the soldiers guarding the graveyard had his arms folded, he was not impressed with what he was being told. Behind him his men milled about uncertainly. The leader of the newcomers said something else, to which the man shook his head defiantly. Within a second the leader of the newcomers was in his face, talking animatedly and pointing back towards the city gates. Nicolas didn't understand much about identifying military ranks, but assumed that the bigger the helmet plume, the more important the person, and the guy in charge of the men in the graveyard was very much out-plumed. Eventually, and with great hesitancy, the graveyard soldiers upped and left. Once they were finally out of sight, Nicolas and his companions revealed themselves, walking down the slope with their palms on show at all times. This situation could still turn bad very quickly.

'Captain Carris?' Shift said as they approached the leader of the group of soldiers, who was looking at them with every ounce of suspicion he had.

Nicolas tried to not notice the hands clenching on weapons as they approached. Not that he was surprised. They were likely wanted criminals for that nonsense in the treasury.

Is there a price on my head? How much would it be?

He'd broken into the castle and threatened the chicken king at crossbow point. Surely that would make him worth triple figures.

Why am I even thinking about this?

'I take it you're the people responsible for the *message* I received?' the captain asked, weighing each of them up in turn.

Really, Auron had been responsible for the message. Once Wade had told the group who couldn't be trusted amongst the Sarus military, Silus had selected a captain whose loyalty he could be certain of and who was most likely to be curious enough to follow the directions of the message. It was just a matter of contacting him—and Auron's newfound ability to touch things came in useful again.

'That was us,' Garaz replied levelly, cradling a limp Silva in his arms. They hadn't wanted to bring her with them, but there was little time and Garaz was sure that leaving her in her weakened state would be worse. 'We were not sure you'd understand, or even come at all.'

'Yes, well,' the captain began hesitantly, 'when I hear insistent tapping on the seal of the king and then on the city map in my quarters directing me to this graveyard, it arouses my curiosity. I come here to find those layabouts shirking in their duty to the crown and lo and behold, once I dismiss them, you appear. At the moment you still have my curiosity. What you say next depends on whether or not your *party* end up being shackled and escorted to the city dungeons.'

Auron looked unbearably smug at the captain's words, despite the threat. He'd surely earnt the right, but that didn't mean he had to be.

'Because it is your king who summoned you,' Silus said, stepping from behind Nicolas's heel and into the light, albeit hesitantly.

Seven grown men simultaneously bending the knee to a chicken was a very strange sight, but then, these were strange times. He'd chatted to a tree.

'My liege,' the captain said as he looked towards the grass. 'I heard what had happened, and I didn't believe it, but…now I see that the stories were true.'

'Yes, Captain,' Silus replied. 'I am so glad that you…Can you all stand up now, please?'

The soldiers rose. As they looked at their king in all his poultry glory, a definite awkwardness descended over the troop. However, the soldiers dealt with it well enough, certainly better than Nicolas had thought they would. Though, on reflection, he'd dealt with it well himself. Pretty well, actually. He continued to surprise himself.

'Very good,' Silus continued. 'As I was saying, I am glad you took the message seriously enough to come. It is no exaggeration to say that we have dire need of your services.'

The captain puffed out his chest very slightly. 'Whatever my king commands.'

'These friends of mine are helping to find the men who've done this to me and make it right.'

'Then I, and the whole kingdom, are in your debt,' Carris said with a nod to Nicolas and his companions.

'We need you to allow us access to the tunnel so that we may bring these men to justice and undo the mischief they have perpetrated,' the king continued.

'Begging your pardon, my liege,' the captain interrupted hesitantly. 'But if you know who and where these men are, can we not just go and arrest them?'

'There are deeper concerns,' Garaz interjected. 'Your king was the victim of an assassination attempt from someone close to him.'

'This troll dung,' Shift said, indicating Wade, who they'd dragged along behind them, shirtless now Nicolas had taken his top to replace his own blood stained shirt, 'indicated that certain of the city guard are corrupt, which is why you're here.'

The captain didn't seem surprised to hear that some of his fellow soldiers weren't entirely honourable. 'Never fear, my lord,' he declared. 'These traitors will be rooted out and made to pay.'

'That's the spirit, Captain.' Silus clucked happily. 'However, we need to know who is behind this before we can purge the ranks, and that can only be achieved by a certain amount of stealth and subtlety.'

The captain thought about this and nodded. 'Of course, my liege,' he replied finally. 'We shall hold this gate and ensure that none follow.'

'You can also take this trash off our hands.' Shift shoved the beaten Wade towards the men. 'He's responsible for the murder of several city guards, so be careful and feel free to make him as uncomfortable as possible.'

From the eye that wasn't a swollen black-and-blue lump, Wade glared at Nicolas and Shift, but was smart enough to say nothing as two of the soldiers took him away.

'We also need you to tend to our injured friend,' Garaz began. 'She was—'

'No.' Silva's voice was weak but firm. Slowly, her pale face rose. Sweat had matted her hair to her head, but her gaze was fierce and determined. 'I will not stand idly by while you throw yourselves towards danger.'

'You've done enough,' Nicolas said, hoping to talk some sense into her. 'You saved my life, repeatedly. Rest.'

Through sheer force of will, or stubbornness, Silva wriggled free from Garaz's grip and stood tall—well, as tall as she could, given the recent arrow to the chest.

'If you are not careful, you will aggravate the internal damage and—' Garaz began to protest.

Silva held up a silencing finger and took a couple of staggering steps towards the entrance of the tunnel to the city before turning slowly back to the group. 'Are you coming?' she asked, jaw set.

Nicolas looked at his fellows. Shift shrugged at him, and he returned the gesture. Garaz looked furious and muttered to himself as he followed Silva. Though he couldn't make out exactly what the orc was saying, he heard the phrase *'absolutely ridiculous'* several times.

Silva turned to continue to the tunnel access but found her way barred by Auron. The spirit stared at Silva with an unreadable expression, his incorporeal arms folded. After a moment, Auron offered her a slight nod then stood aside to let her pass. Silva hesitated at first, her mouth a thin line in her pale face and her eyes full of emotion, but returned the nod and continued.

'Good work with the message,' he said as he passed Auron, hoping to lighten the mood.

'Who knew I could be so useful in death?' the spirit replied.

'Perhaps we should stop calling you *The Dawnblade* and call you Auron *Magic Fingers* instead?' He realised how wrong it sounded as soon as he said it.

Beside him, Shift screwed up their face. 'Ew.'

Auron leaned in close to Nicolas. 'Many maidens already call me that,' he said with possibly the smuggest grin in the history of Etherius.

'Ew,' Garaz said, screwing up his green snout.

****

At the city end of the graveyard tunnel, Nicolas and his companions realised they'd overlooked a very important detail.

'I hear voices,' Garaz whispered, holding up his hand to bring the group to a halt.

Garaz was right. There were definitely men speaking nearby. Whoever they were, they sounded at ease.

'They guarded the other end of the tunnel.' Shift cursed.

'We're so close to the light,' T'goth moaned feebly from the rear of the group. It was getting more and more of a struggle for him to move. The Deity really didn't have long left.

'Well, we can't go back,' he said. 'This is the best way in.'

Three of his companions gave him the *'well, obviously'* look he was beginning to hate with a passion.

'I'll scout it out.' Auron was already moving towards the mouth of the tunnel.

'There are five guards,' Auron told the group upon his return. 'They're sitting around a table by the opening, but none of them are really paying attention to it. Judging by the empty bottles, they've been drinking for a while.'

'What if they're loyal soldiers and not corrupt?' Nicolas asked.

'The drinking on duty suggests that they are less than ideal soldiers,' Garaz noted.

'So we go through them.' Before anyone could stop her, Silva was charging towards the tunnel mouth with more vigour than she should've been capable of.

He was going to shout after her, call her back, but he closed his mouth quickly. All she had was the element of surprise. Instead, he sprinted after his companions, who were already following in her wake.

By the time he emerged from the tunnel opening, one of the guards was already on the floor and Silva was busily cracking the jaw of a second, who fell sideways from his chair. One of the guards made to rise, drawing his sword. Silva kicked down on the hilt to force it back into the sheath before striking him across the cheek with a backhand blow, followed by a fierce cross to the jaw. As the guard fell, Silva launched herself over the table at the other two, who were reeling from a bottle Shift had thrown at them. Garaz made sure that the first guard, who was starting to rise, stayed down. The second was already nearly back on his feet and cursing, until Nicolas struck him on the back of his head with the hilt of the *Dawn Blade*. The guard didn't try to rise again. By the time he'd done this, Silva had unleashed a flurry of kicks and punches at the final two guards and rendered them unconscious, using one's head to break the end off the table. She stood over their limp bodies, panting heavily.

'How did you get to be such a good fighter?' he asked with awe.

'One day I shall tea—' Silva collapsed onto the table, crashing against it before sliding to the floor.

He rushed around the table, took her muscular arm, and helped her to the nearest chair, trying not to think about the size of the bicep in his hand. Silva nodded gratefully, though the look on her face suggested disappointment. It was then he knew.

'I've worked it out,' Nicolas whispered as Garaz approached to check Silva over.

'I don't kn—'

'You should be resting, but you won't,' he interrupted. 'And now you charge into a fight with five armed men when you are nowhere near one hundred percent. Every chance you get, you throw yourself against impossible odds. Did you need to put yourself between me and that crossbow bolt? Or could you have just pulled me aside?'

Silva looked at him, enough emotion in her eyes to tell him he was right.

'You say you want redemption, but I think you just want to die.' Even without Silva's expression, Nicolas knew it was true. 'I think you want some kind of glorious death to right your wrongs, and to get it, you're going to throw yourself into every stupid situation you can until someone finishes what the river began.'

Silva looked at the bodies on the floor around her. 'You...are—'

'Right,' he said. 'But you know what? You don't get to do that. You've done bad things, so you don't get to take the easy way out. If you really want to change, start acting like it. If you want to atone, do the hard work... Live. Be better one day at a time and prove yourself worthy of redemption.'

Silva held his gaze intensely for a moment. Long enough for Nicolas to feel awkward that he was still holding her arm and let it go.

'You are right,' Silva admitted. 'I am going for a quick fix, and it is not right. I shall...do better.'

'That is sage advice,' Garaz said reproachfully to the warrior as she rose again.

'Nicolas gave sage advice?' Shift feigned surprise.

'Surely a sign that the end of the world is in motion.' Auron chuckled.

Nicolas cussed each of them before moving to the window of the warehouse to ensure that no one had heard the commotion.

****

T'goth seemed almost in a hypnotic trance as he led the group through the backstreets of Sarus City's warehouse district, muttering to himself vehemently as he shambled on. Though he should've been questioning whether letting the senile Deity lead them was the right thing to do, he had faith. Not the religious faith one had in a Deity, though that would've been understandable given the circumstances, but faith that T'goth's desire to be whole again would overcome his issues with sanity. Plus, they had no better idea.

His faith in Silva had paid off, even though letting her join the group had seemed to demonstrate issues with *his* sanity. He was less happy that she was with them now. Every glance told him how weak she still was, but no matter how much they tried to talk sense into her, Silva wouldn't be left behind, much to Garaz's continued frustration. Unable to convince her otherwise, the orc settled for following his patient closely, much to her frustration. It would've been funny, if not for the seriousness of the situation.

'The light is close,' the Deity said in a trembling voice as he rounded the next corner.

T'goth's skin was starting to look thin now as his fading continued at an alarming pace, though knowing that his power was so close had returned the twinkle to his eye.

Before the group lay the city docks. Living in a village in the middle of fields of farmland, Nicolas was impressed by the sprawling wooden piers that jutted from the land to stand tall in the water. Beside the piers, large ships floated, thick masts rising high with draped sails waving casually in the breeze. He'd never seen such feats of construction before.

How does something so big even float on the water?

It made no sense. The thought of being on one made him shudder.

'Merchant ships bringing in goods to trade,' Auron commented as he observed the ships nonchalantly.

'Don't fancy their chances of making much here,' Shift whispered conspiratorially in Nicolas's ear. 'I hear the city is broke.'

'Really?' he replied with slight outrage.

Shift gave him a playful half-smile in response.

By that point, they'd all been around T'goth enough to know when he was going to run off, and noticing the signs, Nicolas and Garaz grabbed the Deity. Despite his withered frame, T'goth fought them with more strength than they'd credited him with, even after that business with Wade.

'The light is there,' T'goth protested. 'Unhand me, goat monster. Unhand me, boy.'

Though there was no one around—that he could see, anyway—any sort of scene could get them the wrong kind of attention.

'I know,' he soothed, standing in front of T'goth, staring into his ageing eyes. 'And we will get you to the light. That's what we're here to do. But we must be careful. Bad men have it, so we can't just rush in.'

Understanding formed in the Deity's eyes, and he slowly calmed—or ran out of energy to continue fighting. T'goth placed his hand on the side of Nicolas's head gently. 'You're a good boy.' His wrinkled old eyes pleaded for help, salvation. Nicolas was going to give it to him.

With the Deity now calmed, he led them through the docks, towards an area fenced off from the rest of the facility.

'This section of the docks is reserved for diplomatic craft,' Silus said, looking around. 'There should be guards everywhere.'

'They got sent away.' Beside the fenced-off section sat a small boy, feet dangling over the edge of the dock as he attempted to attach some wriggling bait to his fishing rod. 'You've got a talking chicken,' the boy noted simply, looking at Silus. 'That's cool. My friend Johnny reckons the king was turned into a chicken, but he says stupid stuff like that all the time. He once said he saw a six-foot dwarf.'

Nicolas knelt next to the boy. 'Hey, kid, I'm Nicolas.' He offered the kid a hand.

The boy shook it enthusiastically. 'I'm Brin Ju.' The boy smiled. 'And this is my pet, Kai.' Reaching down beside him, Brin produced a small lizard, which sat calmly in his hand, flicking its forked tongue rhythmically. 'He doesn't talk or anything like your pet, but he flicks his tongue out sometimes and that's pretty neat.' The boy imitated the tongue flicking.

'That is neat.' Nicolas smiled. 'I see you've been here a while fishing—'

'Caught nothin',' the boy interrupted.

'Maybe you saw what happened to the guards?'

'Some official-looking guy came and shooed them away,' Brin said nonchalantly. 'Then some guys came and went into the warehouse there. They had a minotaur with them. I've not seen one before. He looked *angrrrrrry*. Then that ship turned up a couple of minutes ago.'

There was a single ship docked on the diplomatic peer. Compared to the other ships around the dock, this one looked fast and fancy. It was certainly no merchant vessel. There were signs of movement on board, but nothing he could make out clearly.

'That ship has no heraldry or any identifying marks at all,' Auron said, scrutinising it.

'I've never seen it before,' Silus offered.

'The light, the light.' T'goth moaned longingly.

'Is your friend okay?' Brin asked, indicating the powerless Deity.

'Yes, he's fine. He just doesn't like the sun too much. Sensitive skin,' Nicolas said before adding, 'Thanks, Brin, you've been a great help.' He took a coin out of his pouch, which he tossed to Brin, who caught it with a big smile.

'No guards on the door works for us.' Shift walked to the gate and worked the lock with their hair clip. Within moments, it clicked, and they were granted entry to the secure pier.

CHAPTER 25

With the guards relieved of their posts, it was easy for the group to approach the single large warehouse on the secure dock. That didn't mean they could throw caution to the wind, though. After moving around the building to find a quiet side door, they had Auron check to ensure no nasty surprises waited behind it, before Shift again worked their thief magic on the lock while Nicolas kept a close eye on T'goth. Shift had the door open in seconds, and Nicolas and T'goth followed them in. Silva, who looked as determined as she did pale, and Garaz, who was practically carrying the warrior, followed. Just before Shift closed the door behind them, Silus slipped in, feet scratching against the wooden floor.

A wall of stacked crates and shelving meant the group could only see a few feet in front of them. Some of the crates seemed to form walkways that quickly disappeared around sudden corners. None of the party would've had any idea where to start, but muted voices in the distance at least gave them a general direction to head in.

Staying together, they entered a wooden maze that twisted and turned. But the swelling voices told him they were on the right track. Eventually, they emerged behind a large piece of shelving on the open water side of the warehouse. Finding a gap between the crates, he peered through it to see what was happening beyond.

Big Boss paced the floor in an agitated manner, staff in hand, while a handful of his men, and Lucas, watched him silently. The moment T'goth saw the staff again, he reached toward it and opened his mouth. Nicolas caught him at the last second and soothed him to silence. The old man was clearly aching for his power to be returned but getting them caught again wouldn't further that goal. The Deity looked like he was on his last, infirm legs.

'Making me wait. *Me?*' the dwarf huffed. 'Not only is he hours late, but now he sits out there like he's got all the time in the world. He's just tryna show who's boss, make sure

I know my place. I'll show him my place.' The dwarf looked out towards the water and gave another large huff of annoyance. 'Who does he think he is?'

'You know who he is,' interjected a nasally voice outside his line of sight. 'And why he's here. You also know why we need to get this over with quickly.'

'Hey,' Big Boss shouted, pointing at the unseen figure. 'You don't tell me what I do and don't know. I have the power here.' The dwarf shook the staff to prove his point.

'And don't forget the people who enabled you to achieve this power…and what you were supposed to do in return.' That statement took the wind out of the dwarf's sails, deflating him slightly but not removing the defiance from his eyes.

'We'll find the chicken and finish it,' the dwarf replied sourly.

'Once this *distraction* is out of the way, you had better.' The figure emerged from the shadows.

Fancy robes were all well and good, but there was such a thing as overdoing the tassels and braiding.

Yes, it's very obvious you're important. No need to rub everyone's noses in it.

The man's plump face was stuffed full of its own self-importance, and his embroidered hat of office was gaudy in the extreme. He was certainly overdressed for a dockside warehouse meeting with criminal elements.

'Chancellor Lorca,' Silus whispered angrily. 'The backstabber. The traitor. The judas.'

Behind Nicolas came a wave of smugness. No need to guess who that emanated from.

'Told you,' Auron said in a self-congratulatory tone.

'Trust me, Lorca,' Big Boss replied, 'this won't take long, and once it's done all my attention is on the chicken.'

'It should've been from the get-go,' the chancellor huffed. 'Indeed, there should've been no chicken to begin with.'

Both the man and dwarf glared at each other until another of Big Boss's men sprinted into the room. 'He's coming,' he announced, before taking his place with the others.

'That's my cue to exit then.' Lorca gave the door of the warehouse a look of distaste. 'I shall find you once your business is concluded.'

As the last flap of the High Chancellor's long robe disappeared through another side door, one of the main doors to the warehouse opened and a party entered. The majority of them must've been muscle, though muscle who wore finer clothes than Big Boss's men. The two giant cyclops were most certainly muscle, each scanning the room thoroughly with their single eyes. The large brutes stood to either side of the charge they were escorting into the room.

Small, wizened yellow eyes took in the room with casual disinterest as the goblin shuffled in on his jewelled cane.

'The High Chair,' Shift whispered, sounding slightly starstruck.

'Whose chair?' he asked.

'The *High Chair* is a title, dumbass,' Shift said with a withering look. 'One used by the head of the Criminal Guild. That goblin controls all crime in the Nine Kingdoms and beyond.'

'*Him?*' He looked at the frail goblin and his slicked-back white hair incredulously.

'If I have learnt anything from you, Nicolas, it is that looks can be deceiving,' Garaz said quietly.

Is that sarcasm? It didn't sound sarcastic. *Maybe I should take it as a compliment?*

Coming to a halt a few paces away from Big Boss, the goblin extended a wrinkled green hand with a large gold ring resting on one of his long fingers.

'If you think I'm kissing that, you're going to have a long wait,' the dwarf snarled.

'So then,' the High Chair replied in a slow, husky voice, 'you finally take a stand.'

Taking some unseen cue from their leader, the High Chair's men drew handheld crossbows from inside their jackets. Big Boss's men reciprocated, and we had ourselves a standoff.

'I knew your disrespect ran deep,' the goblin continued, unfazed. 'But I didn't believe you would dare be so brazen about it. Robbing a kingdom's treasury and trying to assassinate the king without permission from me or the council. *Tut tut.*' He wagged a scolding finger.

'I don't need permission,' the dwarf boasted. 'This is my territory.'

'It was, until the *law* drove you out of the city with your tail between your legs.'

The dwarf's face reddened. 'Well, now I'm taking it back. And much more besides.'

The goblin shook his head like an exasperated parent. 'I blame myself, you know,' he said with a slight shrug, 'Many said I was wrong to promote you, that you were too defiant. But I liked your ambition, and you always had a good eye for making gold, more than your people are famed for. Your ruthless streak meant you didn't care what you had to do to get it. I hoped that gratitude, if not loyalty, would keep you in check. But it seems your worst quality is your memory. You seem to forget that this is all my territory. I simply allow you to work it.'

'*You allow*,' Big Boss scoffed. 'I made myself. You didn't do me any favours. You didn't deign to notice me. I made it so I couldn't be ignored. And yet you're still too arrogant to acknowledge my status and what it really should be. You summon me here like I'm some kind of lackey when I am so much more.'

'Yes, yes, you are the *'Big Boss'* now, aren't you?' the goblin said dismissively. 'And you've found yourself some new patrons. But giving yourself a fancy title and finding some new friends doesn't give you the keys to the kingdom.' The High Chair shook his wrinkled head sadly. 'I had such high hopes for you, Gorin Thundabrig. I suppose if I can't keep you in your place, I can at least use you as a cautionary tale.' The goblin tapped the tip of his cane on the wooden floor. 'Krell, Kull, rip his arms and legs off.'

The two cyclops growled in affirmation and rumbled forward. Lucas kicked himself off the wall and growled. Big Boss watched the two cyclops bear down on him dispassionately. Before the pair could complete their task, things changed dramatically. With a flick of the dwarf's arm, lightning shot from the staff, engulfing both cyclops, who cried out feebly, trying to swat it away. Not two moments later, both had been transformed into surprised-looking cats. The High Chair took a step back in surprise. The rest of his men began to look very uneasy.

'Nice kitties,' the dwarf said, crouching to stroke one of them. The cat nuzzled his podgy hand. 'You guys look so hungry. Let's do something about that.'

There was another flick of the staff, and moments later, a small mouse emerged from the High Chair's fallen cloak. The dwarf, laughing, pointed the little rodent out to the cats, who bounded after it hungrily as it attempted to scurry away to freedom. It didn't make it. The goblins men watched the scene in horror, crossbows still raised but unsure what to do now.

'Seems like there's been a change in management,' Big Boss said simply as he played with the staff in his hands. 'So it's time to pick a side, boys.'

It took a second for the men to lower their crossbows.

'Good call.' Big Boss grinned.

Nicolas was so engrossed in what was happening that it took him a few moments to notice Shift tapping him on the arm. When he finally did, he turned to them and to the four crossbows pointed directly at him and his companions.

'Enjoy the show?' one of the guards sneered.

* * * *

'There they are!' Big Boss cried as Nicolas and his companions were escorted from their hiding place, encouraged by prodding from the business end of crossbows.

Nicolas had his hands in the air. Shift and Garaz couldn't as they'd been bound and gagged. Garaz, so he couldn't cast any magic and Shift because they'd suggested that a man's mother lay with trolls. Another carried Silus firmly in his arm, escorting T'goth roughly with his free hand. Beside Nicolas, Auron was frantically looking around, trying to think of something, anything to help. The only one missing from the group was Silva, who he assumed had managed to slip away. Or maybe she'd finally succumbed to her wounds. He hoped not. *Huh.* There was a time when he'd hoped she would've. Times had changed.

'Isn't this a great day?' the dwarf continued, almost dancing on the spot. 'First, I get a promotion and now the pests that have been eluding me fall into my lap. And I get the chicken too. I must be blessed.'

'You wouldn't be blessed if he had anything to say about it.' Nicolas snorted, indicating T'goth.

The Deity struggled uselessly against the grip that held him, desperate to get to the staff. The last of his real strength must've been expended on Wade.

'Shame that he can't do anything about it.' The dwarf chuckled. 'But I suppose we're in a bit of a stand-off. I can't exactly kill him or I'm sure to attract the attention of the rest of those pompous Deities and get myself royally smote, and he's too weak to do anything to me. So, he gets locked away somewhere deep, dark, and remote. Luckily, with the rest of you, I don't have to show such restraint. Firstly, I get my revenge on you for all the issues you caused me and the damage to my temple. After that, I get revenge on the king who made it his business to drive me and my interests out of his precious city. Today is a good day.'

Nicolas, Shift, and Garaz were lined up along the waterside of the dock, just a single step back from the water and parallel to a group of Big Boss's men and their loaded crossbows. T'goth and Silus were held off to the side, unable to do anything but watch.

'Three pains in my ass.' Big Boss smiled as he surveyed them. 'You especially, boy. You've cost me a lot, so I'm going to savour this.'

'Villains and theatrics.' Auron tutted to himself as he continued to look for a way to help. Considering the spirit could barely interact with his environment, Nicolas didn't hold out much hope.

'Do I let my boys finish you, or shall I have some fun with this?' Big Boss held up the staff thoughtfully.

'You gain the power of a Deity, and all you can think to do with it is become a better criminal?' Nicolas asked in disgust.

'A better criminal?' The dwarf laughed. 'I've just become the High Chair, boy. I am *the* criminal now. I've taken this power and turned it into near infinite power and riches... All mine.'

'Kid.' Auron's voice distracted Nicolas from the dwarf as he continued to rant about how amazing he was. The spirit was pointing towards the side wall of the warehouse. Looking over, he saw Silva concealed behind some rickety shelving. The warrior gestured to him in a way that Nicolas assumed meant to stall for time.

How am I supposed to do that?

His mouth was dry from fear and his brain running a hundred miles an hour and incapable of logical thought. Then he looked to his side. Next to him, Shift and Garaz were both grim but determined, though they couldn't do anything in their bound state. In front of him, T'goth looked as if he might crumble to dust at any moment, despite Big Boss's assertion that he should live. Then there was Silus, who'd only wanted some peace. It wasn't just his life on the line. His friends would suffer, along with all the others the dwarf would likely harm during his tenure as the most important piece of furniture in the land.

No. He would damn well make sure that didn't happen. With that determination came an idea. It was off the cuff, most likely stupid, but if it was their only hope then so be it.

'So now we get to the *any last words* part of this drama,' Big Boss said, once he'd finally finished his self-aggrandising. 'Seeing as only one of you can speak,' the dwarf sniggered to a lot of muffled sounds from Shift, 'that just leaves the boy to say something.'

Taking a deep breath and steeling himself, Nicolas took a single step forward. 'I do have something to say to you before I die.'

'This ought to be good,' the dwarf said to his chuckling men before gesturing to Nicolas. 'Please, say your piece. I'm sure your last words are going to be epic, though unfortunately I am without quill and paper.'

The assembled men laughed indulgently at their boss's joke.

Now that all eyes were on him, he began to panic. His dislike of being the centre of attention threatened to overwhelm him, jumbling his thoughts and stalling his words. Yet despite this, looking at the smug dwarf in front of him and thinking of his friends in peril, he found his voice.

I know exactly how to rile you up, Gorin.

'Should I just keep this *short*?' he asked.

Instantly, the chuckling men were silent. Big Boss looked at him with a raised eyebrow. '*What* did you say?' the dwarf asked incredulously.

'I was just wondering how long I should make my last words. I don't want to fill it with too much *small* talk.' As much as it didn't really sit well with him to make fun of his height, Big Boss's issue *was* his inferiority complex. And if he could just poke that wound long enough...

'Be careful...' Big Boss threatened.

Quickly he raised his hands. 'I am so sorry,' he exclaimed. 'I forgot about your *short* temper.'

The dwarf's face reddened and the staff shook in his hand. He took a threatening step towards Nicolas.

That's it, get angry. Come closer.

Nicolas glared at the dwarf defiantly. 'I'd ask for mercy, but we all know how *short* you are on that.'

Big Boss cried in anger, stepping closer. Nicolas knew he was being neither smart, nor heroic, but he was using all he had left, and it was working. One more ought do it.

'Despite our falling out, I'm glad you got promoted. If anyone needed a *high* chair, it's you.'

That did it. '*I am not short!*' the dwarf roared finally, stomping up to Nicolas and pointing the staff right in his face. 'You like jokes?' the dwarf snarled from between gritted teeth. 'The jokes they tell about what I'll turn you into will last *centuries*.'

The staff was in reach. Nicolas readied himself to grab it even as the red energy collected at its tip. It was either win or lose now. Grab the staff and save the day or end up being transformed into...he didn't want to think about it. The real question was whether or not he'd bought Silva enough time.

With a creak that echoed throughout the warehouse, the large rack of shelving began to wobble then fall towards Big Boss's men, who cried out in surprise before scattering in all directions. First the crates tumbled from the shelves, thankfully catching a couple of men too slow to realise what was going on and knocking them out cold. Then the shelving itself struck the floor with a thunderous crash, throwing up a mighty dust cloud. The only thing he could see was the glowing staff in front of him. While the dwarf was distracted, Nicolas made his move, grabbing the staff and moving it away from his face in the same motion, the impact of which caused it to fire. Energy bounced from the ceiling of the warehouse and out a nearby window.

'Run!' he shouted to Shift and Garaz, barely thinking now, just acting. Probably the best way for him.

Launching himself as hard as he could as the dust cloud began to retract, Nicolas threw himself forwards, trying to push the Big Boss over so he could take the staff. But the dwarf had a lower centre of gravity than him, instead stumbling backwards into his men with Nicolas in tow.

Is throwing myself into a group of armed men a great idea?

Not really, but if it stopped those men from pursuing Shift and Garaz then it was worth it.

Colliding with several of his assembled men, Big Boss finally fell, toppling backwards but stubbornly keeping his grip on the staff. Frantically Nicolas tried to wrench it free from the dwarf's grip, but Big Boss pulled it back with just as much force. But there was no time for a prolonged bout of wrestling over the staff, as Nicolas soon found crossbows pointed at his head. Releasing his grip, he raised his hands as Big Boss was helped back to his feet.

'You're tenacious, boy, I'll give you that.' The dwarf chuckled as he rose. 'And it was a good try, but it was never going to work.'

'It was worth a shot,' he replied, raising his hands in the air as he stood.

'Speaking of *shot*.' Big Boss smiled, brandishing the staff.

Whatever the dwarf had been about to say was interrupted by a new commotion. Doors all around them were kicked in as soldiers of Sarus rushed into the room, bearing crossbows of their own and shouting commands for everyone to drop their weapons. Another standoff ensued as the soldiers surrounded Big Boss and his men, with Nicolas slap bang in the centre of it all.

'What in the…' the dwarf began.

Behind the soldiers, High Chancellor Lorca and his ridiculous cloak swept into the room. 'In the name of the Kingdom of Sarus, you are all under arrest,' the chancellor announced, making sure he stayed behind the armed soldiers.

'You dirty snake,' Big Boss snarled. 'You dare double cross me?'

'I am here to bring assassins and thieves to justice.' Lorca smiled. 'And if you move even an inch, I shall have no qualms in having my men administer that justice right here.'

Big Boss cackled harshly. 'Like you're letting us leave here alive anyway.'

'Criminals who robbed the treasury and assassinated the king, dead in warehouse raid,' Lorca mused. 'Does have a nice ring to it, doesn't it?' It was then that Lorca noticed Silus, who'd managed to escape his captor in the confusion but froze when the soldiers entered. 'The chicken,' Chancellor Lorca cried with glee, clapping his hands in a foppish manner. 'Finally.'

'Filthy traitor,' Silus spat at his chancellor.

'Cease your futile clucking' Lorca snapped back. 'You didn't even want to be king. You should be thanking me. Well, what you should've done was stayed gone, but your mistake, my advantage. Kill them.'

In that split second, fingers tightened on the triggers of crossbows all around, the staff glowed, and the minotaur flexed his neck. Nicolas watched it all unfold in slow motion, seeing every micromovement around him as he wished for something, anything, to get him out of this situation.

Then the warehouse became chaos incarnate.

A rumbling shook the building, dislodging loose planks from the ceiling and causing shelves to topple. The water beyond the dock rose, forced upwards, before parting to reveal a large, scaled body, followed by a large, snouted head and angry red eyes. The creature grasped the end of the dock with a large, clawed hand, flicking its tongue out as everyone slowly backed away in disbelief. Its roar caused them all to clap hands to their ears. High-pitched ringing muffled all other sounds once the roar receded.

Instinctively, Nicolas stepped back. Opening his mouth, his ears popped suddenly and sounds came flooding back to him.

'What in the underworld is that?' one of the soldiers cried.

'Kai Ju,' Nicolas answered with a gulp, recognising the lizard from the boy Brin's hand, even though it was now supersized. This was really escalating quickly.

I hope Brin is okay.

'The blast from the staff that went through the window must've found a target.' Auron looked intimidated despite knowing the creature couldn't harm him.

'I'm not fighting that,' Nicolas said, indicating the creature. *No, sir.*

'You don't need to fight that,' Auron said. 'You just need to fight him.'

Big Boss was standing directly at his side, a stunned look on his face as he took in the mighty creature.

'Kill it!' Lorca screamed in a shrill voice, waving his arms in the air. 'Kill the creature, kill the chicken, kill them all.'

As crossbow bolts fired in all directions, Nicolas threw himself at the dwarf again. The two men beside their boss were quick off the mark, trying to grab him despite the arrows flying everywhere. Thankfully, the timely intervention of Shift and Garaz, who appeared seemingly from nowhere and were now unbound, rendered that problem moot.

Resuming his tussling with the dwarf, he winced as Kai roared again, a cry of anger at those who'd fired the bolts stuck into its thick, scaly hide. Comparing the size of the crossbow bolts to the size of the creature, they would surely need thousands to actually take the creature down. His train of thought was interrupted as Big Boss yanked on his hair, reminding him he was in a fight.

As the dwarf used his superior weight to roll him over, the lizard raised its giant, clawed hand in Nicolas's peripheral vision. The hand crashed straight through the wooden floor of the warehouse, throwing up a huge wave, which washed through the room, throwing people everywhere and causing the two men who'd been standing where the hand had landed to disappear completely.

As the wave hit Nicolas, everything around him blurred, the impact pushing him backwards across the slippery floor. For a moment, he remembered falling from a bridge and nearly drowning, and he fought frantically against the water that washed over him, as if trying to rise to a surface that wasn't there. His heart raced and his lungs burned as he held his breath, despite the assertion of his mind that the wave would recede at any moment. As it did, it took the fear with it, Nicolas regaining control over himself. If he took anything away from all of this, it was that he was learning to manage his fear.

Rising carefully, still disorientated, he found himself surrounded by wet, hacking figures he couldn't immediately identify. One, who may have been either a soldier or one of Big Boss's men, raised his crossbow to fire. Moments later, his top half vanished with an audible crunch. As Kai's mouth rose again, the pair of bodyless legs stood for a moment before falling to the floor. Nicolas retched.

The lizard rose, its head crashing through the ceiling of the warehouse, raining debris down on them. Through the arms he used to shield himself, he watched the creature turn and make its way back towards the rest of the city. Someone grabbed Nicolas, and he spun around, fist raised and ready.

'Calm down, Nick,' Shift said, soaking wet but somehow smiling, then they gave him a strange look he couldn't read. 'Short jokes?'

He shrugged awkwardly. 'I was improvising.'

'Don't be embarrassed.' Shift smiled. 'A couple of them were pretty funny. You're so…'

'What?'

Shift smirked. 'Doesn't matter.'

Forgetting his situation for a moment, he hugged Shift tightly, glad his friend was still alive.

'I know you can't control yourself around me, but this is neither the time nor the place.' Shift chuckled as they pushed him off. 'We have bigger fish to fry… Well, lizards… Well, a lizard. But a bloody big one.'

Looking back towards the open end of the warehouse, he saw Kai moving away with a triumphant roar. As it dissipated, he could hear the screams of fearful people and cries of alarm in the distance it had drowned out.

'That thing will wreck the city,' Shift said.

'Then we have to get that staff,' he replied urgently. 'And quickly.'

He thought back for a moment to Yarringsburg and the destruction that city had suffered. Even after they were victorious, the city had been devastated. He wouldn't let the same happen to Sarus, the kingdom and its people had been through enough already. Well, he would try his best to stop it.

'Working out where the staff is would be a good start,' Shift said, looking around the room.

'It's over there,' Auron said, appearing next to them, looking annoyingly dry.

The spirit was right. Nicolas spied the tip of the staff poking out from beneath a fallen crate, and it seemed they were the only ones who'd noticed it. The problem was that they themselves had been noticed. Both Big Boss's men and the soldiers had managed to pick themselves up and get over the shock of a giant lizard suddenly appearing, only to realise that some of the people they were supposed to kill were sitting in plain view.

Pulling Shift with him, Nicolas jumped behind a crate just as the warehouse became the scene of a mass of flying arrows. There were the distinctive *thunks* as they struck wood, and distinctive screams as they struck flesh. Peeking out from cover, he saw six soldiers—with Lorca cowering behind them—between them and the staff. There was no way they could make it to them before they reloaded, and he doubted they could subdue them all if they did. They needed some kind of miracle.

The miracle arrived in the shape of a giant green tail. Even as Lorca pointed them out to his men, grinning inanely, Kai's tail crashed through the roof of the warehouse in a single destructive flick before doing the same to the floor, just where Lorca and his men stood. For a second, he saw that inane grin become a look of sheer terror before Lorca disappeared.

'Serves him right,' Nicolas exclaimed. Yes it was a little petty, but Lorca *was* a bad guy. 'Way to go, Kai,' Shift cheered.

Even though the tail flick had been no more than an animal impulse, they were pretty damned grateful. Even Auron was slack jawed at the fortuitous twist of fate. A miracle indeed. That, and the fact that the warehouse was still standing. Judging by the strained creaking of the wooden structure, though, that could change at any moment.

He'd just begun to believe that luck was on their side when the minotaur hit him. Roaring, Lucas knocked Nicolas aside like he was nothing. He struck the floor hard, his shoulder audibly cracking, causing him to cry out with the white hot pain.

Dazed, he writhed on the floor clutching his throbbing shoulder. *Maybe I can just lie here a moment.* No, there was a rampaging minotaur on the loose.

Slowly and carefully, he got back to his feet. Something in his shoulder was grinding painfully as he rose, he was sure the bone was broken. But there was no time to take stock, Lucas was holding an unconscious Shift in his large paw, the other raised to strike. Every ounce of self-preservation evaporated instantly.

'Hey!' he shouted at the minotaur. 'What's got two horns, is full of bullshit and ugly as sin?' His sense of self-preservation returned quickly as the minotaur's head swung towards him. 'You're not even going to guess?' he finished shakily.

Snorting angrily, Lucas dropped Shift and charged him. 'No more stupid jokes!' Lucas bellowed over the clomping of hooves on wood.

This time, he didn't freeze. This time, he was ready. He knew what he had to do. With determination, he reached for his belt. It was only when his hand closed on itself that he remembered that Big Boss's men had taken his sword.

'Oh crap,' he whispered as the minotaur bore down on him.

He saw the big fist swinging at him and ducked. Instead of taking his head off, Lucas took a chunk out of the wall of the abused building. Furiously Nicolas threw punches at the minotaur's ribs with his one good arm, but he might as well have been trying to punch down a stone wall. With a snort, Lucas grabbed him by the throat, plucked him from the ground and drove him into the wall. Everything jerked nauseatingly as his head cracked against the hard wood, then his broken shoulder struck it and the pain was so great that he couldn't even scream. Lucas pulled him forward and did it again. As he impacted the wall a second time blood spat from his open mouth and he briefly forgot his own name. His limbs dangled limply from his body as the minotaur sneered at him.

'You're so difficult to kill,' the raging minotaur snarled directly into his face, 'that when I'm finished gutting you, I'm going to demand a raise.'

Lucas reared his head back. It looked like he intended to deliver the final blow with one of his horns. Nicolas had barely anything left to give, but a glint caught his eye and he had an idea.

Reaching up, he took hold of the gold ring protruding from Lucas's nose and pulled with all the strength he had left. It was enough. Flesh tore and he was splattered with blood as the piercing was ripped from the minotaur's nose. Lucas roared in pain. The grip on his shirt slackened, but didn't yield completely.

What to do now?

He had no weapon and no more ideas.

With a defiant caw, Silus landed on the minotaur's snout, pecking and slashing with his claws. By the time Lucas had grabbed the bird and thrown him off, the minotaur had one less eye. Blood poured from the wounds on his face as he held his now empty socket and snarled in frustration.

'Damn you all!' Fearsome rage emanated from his remaining eye, which looked directly at Nicolas. The minotaur stomped his hoof on the floor twice, about to charge again.

'Finger poke of doom,' Auron said flatly as he appeared beside Lucas and drove his spectral finger deep into the minotaur's only functioning eye.

Lucas stepped back, crying in pain again as he clutched his ruined eyes. As the minotaur thrashed and cursed, Garaz walked up to him calmly, chanted a single word Nicolas didn't catch, and unleashed a fireball from his cupped hands that engulfed Lucas's head. This time, the minotaur's scream didn't sound even vaguely human as he fell to the floor, rolling around to smother the flames. This gave Shift a good opening to finish Lucas with a crossbow bolt straight between where his eyes had been.

'Thank the Deities for that,' Shift said, looking much worse for wear.

'Nice fireball.' Nicolas grinned, equally pained.

'It did the job,' Garaz replied modestly.

'Never mind that,' Auron said, staring wide-eyed at Nicolas, 'You ripped out his nose piercing.' The spirit shuddered as if it were a terrible thing to do.

'And you poked him in the eye,' Nicolas smiled, leaning heavily against the wall. 'It was a team effort. Though, *finger poke of doom?* Some of us can actually hear you, you know.'

'You've got to name your finishing move, kid,' Auron replied smugly.

'Lucas!'

Big Boss crawled out from beneath some debris on the opposite side of the warehouse, looking bloodied and bruised even from here. Evidently, he'd emerged just in time to see his top guy sent packing to the Underworld and it had left him slack jawed. Around the warehouse, a handful of Big Boss's men were regrouping, with the High Chair's men and the soldiers with Lorca either seeming to have fled or died. As the men stood by their stout leader, their crossbows either gone or spent, they drew small knives from belts, or picked up pieces of wood that would make passable clubs.

Nicolas and his companions stared at the group of thugs, who stared back at them to the background noise of Kai's continued path of destruction. They were running out of time. Once the monster was through with the docks, it would make its way into the city proper and the death toll would be enormous.

Can I even do this? I'm half dead already.

Yes, he could. He wasn't about to take a rest when people were in danger. Slowly, he pushed himself off of the wall. He was a mess, but none of the bad guys looked any better.

'Shall we?' Garaz suggested, holding an improvised club of his own.

'Let's,' Shift said with a half grin. 'Nicky gets the staff. We get the goons.'

'Deal.' Nicolas stretched his aching back and flexed his damaged arm tenderly, needing to be as ready as possible for what was to come. It was painful, but just about usable. But at the mention of the staff, he couldn't help but briefly glance towards it, a gesture the dwarf noticed. Big Boss saw the staff, and that he was closer to it. His bearded face broke into a pleased sneer.

'Get them!' the dwarf cried, already scrambling to his feet and beginning his dash for the staff.

He couldn't let the dwarf get it first. This had to end now. Nicolas ran, and Shift and Garaz charged forward as well, shouting oaths at the men who were closing on them.

Though the dwarf was closer to the staff, Nicolas had longer legs. As he threw himself across the hole made by a giant lizard's tail, Big Boss leapt toward his prize. He grabbed the staff. So did Big Boss.

'Let go!' the dwarf cried, pulling the staff from its concealment and finding Nicolas's hands attached.

'I was going to say the same,' he shouted back, yanking against the dwarf's iron grip. One of his arms was very weak, but determination drove him onwards.

Again, he ended up rolling around the wet, hard floor with the dwarf, with no less at stake than the power of a Deity. With each tug at the staff either by him or the dwarf, Nicolas winced as his shoulder screamed in pain. Unable to pry the staff out of the dwarf's hand, he resorted to throwing punches and kicks at Big Boss, which were returned in kind. His kicks were better, due to his long legs, but the dwarf had plenty of muscle to throw a mean punch, and several times he was dazed enough to nearly loosen his grip on the staff. Neither yielded.

I...won't...let...go.

Finally, Big Boss ended the standoff by biting Nicolas's hand. The dwarf's teeth sank deep into his skin as he did his best to take a chunk from his hand. Nicolas screamed in pain as blood poured from the wound. Enraged and thoroughly fed up with the dwarf, he took a leaf from his companion's book, driving his finger straight into the dwarf's eye. Now it was Big Boss's turn to scream.

'Damn you, boy!' the dwarf roared, his head snapping backwards.

As Big Boss fell back, his arm gave one last yank—one that was too much for Nicolas's damaged hand. Involuntarily, his grip slackened, and he let go. But the wet wooden staff also slipped from Big Boss's grip as he crashed to the floor clutching his eye.

The staff slid across the floor until it hit Garaz's foot. The orc threw aside the man he'd been beating before leaning down and picking up the staff. Four armed men charged him from either side, knowing he had their boss's prize.

'Garaz, pass it!' he cried, holding out his good hand and getting ready to run.

For a fleeting moment, Garaz didn't acknowledge him. Instead, the orc stood there, studying the staff.

He's going to throw it, right?

Beyond them was a mighty crash that could only have been a giant lizard levelling a building, which seemed to bring the orc back to the present moment. Garaz reached back then launched the staff towards Nicolas, who wasn't entirely certain of his catching skills but hoped for the best. To his side, the dwarf ran at him, ready to tackle him to the ground. The piece of wood circled through the air...to be intercepted by a wrinkled, nearly transparent hand.

'The light,' T'goth exclaimed in a dreamlike state.

CHAPTER 26

Blinking the residual light from his eyes, Nicolas regained consciousness.

What happened? Why am I not standing where I was standing? Actually, why am I not standing at all?

Slowly, hazily, the memories returned. T'goth had caught the staff. There'd been a light so bright it hurt his eyes and a concussive force that threw him back like a leaf in a storm. And then the flash of impact.

Using the wall for support, he stood up, feeling as if his entire skeleton had been shaken. Spots of light still danced in front of his eyes. Before him stood T'goth, and not the crazy old man he'd become accustomed to. This was T'goth as the statue had captured him, though it had completely missed the raw power and divinity that radiated from him. His skin prickled and stung from the energy coursing through the warehouse. Struggling to look directly at the Deity, and not sure if he even wanted to, he snuck a glance instead. The Deity didn't look happy.

'You!' T'goth boomed in a voice that seemed to occupy the entire room.

Just to the side of Nicolas, Big Boss was desperately trying to crawl away, only open eye bulging with fear. As he watched, the dwarf was propelled screaming through the air until he came to a sudden stop, floating before an unimpressed T'goth.

'You *dare* strip me of my power and trap me in a withered mortal form?' T'goth snarled in a way that made even Nicolas squirm. 'The sheer audacity of you. The gall.'

Big Boss attempted to speak, mouth flapping like the wings of a distressed bird, but nothing came out.

'So you like chickens, do you?' the Deity asked with an evil smile. With a swish of his hand, T'goth conjured a chicken, which stood at his side, looking very confused at being suddenly brought into existence in the middle of a dockside warehouse. 'So you don't like being small, do you?' the Deity said through gritted teeth, practically frothing at the mouth.

Nicolas was terrified, so he couldn't imagine how the dwarf felt.

With another swish of T'goth's hand, Big Boss began to shrink, his crying voice becoming more high-pitched the smaller he got, until he was no bigger than a pea, at which point T'goth plucked him from the air and casually threw him to the chicken, whose beak caught the falling dwarf, swallowing him whole.

With purpose, T'goth crouched beside the chicken. 'Do not think I am done with you, dwarf,' the Deity declared. 'Once you have enjoyed your ride through the chicken's innards, I am going to spend a good couple of centuries coming up with more and more inventive punishments for you.

'And do not think I have forgotten about those guilty by association,' the Deity snapped, waving his hand again. Those of Big Boss's men that remained were instantly turned into worms. Standing, T'goth looked down at the chicken again and nodded in the direction of the worms. 'Reunite them with their master,' the Deity commanded.

Hungrily, the chicken charged away to obey the command as the pink creatures wriggled and writhed helplessly on the floor.

Nodding with satisfaction at his work, the Deity looked over his body as if it were new. He probably would've done the same had he been stuck in an old man's body. The Deity only looked back up again when a distant feral roar rocked what was left of the warehouse.

'Oh yes,' the Deity said absentmindedly. 'That.'

Slowly, he walked to the open part of the warehouse where he looked out at what Nicolas assumed was Kai, who sounded like he was busily tearing his way through another building. The roaring ceased instantly at a gesture from T'goth, which made the screams and cries from those affected by the lizard's rampage audible again.

'This is a bit crazy,' Shift whispered, coming up beside him.

'I've seen a lot of crazy stuff,' Auron said, 'but this is quite far above most of that.'

'I have never seen a Deity in its true form,' Garaz added.

'Nor have you now, orc,' T'goth said, apparently having heard every word, even though he was far away with his back to them. Turning, T'goth approached the group, sweeping across the gap between them at inhuman speed. 'This form,' he said, indicating his body, 'is not my truest form. This is just a...suit I wear that makes me more palatable for you mortals. Perceiving my true form would drive you insane, if you managed to live through it at all.'

Nicolas had no words, and it seemed his companions had none either.

T'goth looked at the assembled group in front of him. 'One of you is missing,' he mused, clicking his tongue.

Scanning the room, the Deity eventually stopped at a pile of crates on the floor, dismissing them with another deft hand-flick and revealing Silva, lying prone on the wet wood. She wasn't moving.

No. Please don't let her be dead. She can't be.

Whether she'd had her warriors death or not, Silva had definitely atoned in his eyes. Nicolas sagged as the grief punched him in the gut. All they'd been through and...

Silva's body rose from the floor and floated towards them.

'Such tenacity,' T'goth said as she reached him. 'A chequered past, to be sure, but I cannot deny the fact that she helped me.'

'Can't you just let her die so I can move on?' Auron asked, slightly petulantly.

Ignoring the remark, the Deity placed a large hand over Silva's abdomen. Beneath the hand, a light flashed, and when he moved it, the warrior stepped to the ground, her colour returning . Silva looked herself over, seemingly unsure how to react. Then her eyes fixed on Auron. Facing him, the warrior looked directly into those white eyes for what Nicolas assumed was the first time.

'I'm...I'm sorry.' Her voice was low and trembling. 'I'm sorry for murdering you. I haven't said it yet because I couldn't admit to it. It is hard to take ownership of terrible things you have done. But I know that I did it. I wish I could take it back, or trade my life for yours, but I cannot. All I can offer is my apology. I expect no forgiveness, because I deserve none. But I need you to know that I regret it, with all my heart.' Her voice and face were so sincere that Nicolas believed every word.

Auron seemed to believe it too, though he appeared less than impressed. At least she'd finally said it.

'Keep him safe, follow his example, and we are as good as we can get.' Auron indicated Nicolas with his thumb.

What does that mean? Why would I need to be kept safe?

His adventures were done. He was never doing this again. Ever.

'Maybe it will be like old times again.' Silva seemed to regret those words the moment she said them, looking away from Auron, who seemed equally upset by the comment.

What's their history?

Judging from the way they both reacted, it was a bitter one.

Not elaborating, Auron instead waved his hand in front of his face a few times. 'Not passing on then.' His tone was grim and his face weary. 'The sorry wasn't enough for that, I suppose.'

'You assume she is your unfinished business, Auron of Tellmark,' T'goth said with a knowing half-smile.

From Auron's expression, he wasn't pleased with the cryptic remark, nor the possibilities it might unlock. But judging by the look on T'goth's face, there would be no follow-up information, which must've frustrated Auron no end, though he didn't let it show.

'Can you heal me too?' the spirit asked hopefully instead.

The Deity laughed, a deep booming noise that shook the eardrums. 'There is only so much I can do with regards to interfering in mortal affairs, hero.' He chuckled. 'Deities are bound by laws as much as any other being in the universe. Why do you think our messages to mortals are so obtuse? Also, you burned your body to ash, so sadly, I cannot undo your death.'

Auron looked deflated. 'Worth a shot,' he muttered.

'However,' T'goth continued, 'I am allowed to interfere in events that my power was directly involved in creating. Such as that lizard creature, and this...'

The Deity clicked his fingers, and another chicken that had been watching the scene cautiously from the edge of the room suddenly became a large, naked, and very flustered man.

'Your Highness,' Garaz said with a formal nod, turning his eyes away awkwardly.

Nicolas didn't blame him, looking in any other direction than at Silus.

'Your...royal sceptre,' Shift said diplomatically.

'Um...thank you,' the king said as he quickly found some pieces of wood to cover his...personal matters. His body jostled and jerked as if he were unused to it. Though until recently he did have wings instead of arms.

'Do not sound too grateful.' T'goth snorted before he craned his head to listen to something. 'Soldiers are starting to storm the docks,' he declared finally. 'That lizard made quite the mess, and I do not wish to be here when they arrive. Apparently, I must now spend my time travelling around undoing a large number of unnatural creatures thanks to that little snot. *Big Boss*, indeed.'

'Um.' He didn't really like the idea of talking to a Deity directly, but there was a matter to address. 'There's a tree by your shrine. Can you...take care of that first? Please.'

T'goth looked at him silently for a moment. 'I know the one, and it shall be done. But first, this.'

Raising his hand, T'goth—Deity of growth, change, and evolution—breathed in deep and a flash of light appeared in his open hand. For a moment, Nicolas wondered what had happened until he realised that his hand and shoulder and...rest of his body no longer hurt. He also felt the familiar weight of the *Dawn Blade* on his belt again. He felt invigorated, and it looked like he wasn't the only one.

'I owe all of you.' The Deity's words caught as if he were unaccustomed to being indebted to mortals, which he most likely was. 'And I have no desire to be in mortals' debts. So I have granted you each a gift. Shift, in your pocket you'll find a lockpick that will open any door. Just press it to the lock and it shall open. The chain around it will grow and shrink in parallel with whatever form you take.'

Shift rummaged in their pocket and produced the small key-like item with a chain around it. 'I was already pretty good at this,' they began, before noting T'goth's raised eyebrow, '...but thanks. It's brilliant.'

'Garaz,' the Deity continued, with a slight smirk. 'I think it is only fitting you have your own staff. It shall help you channel your power.'

In his hands, the orc held a long wooden staff which hooked around at the top, almost like the crook used by goat herders.

Was that intentional?

'You have my thanks.' Garaz bowed, casting a slightly unimpressed look at the top of the staff, obviously coming to the same conclusion as Nicolas.

'Auron,' T'goth seemed almost contrite. 'I cannot give a boon to those who are not living. But I can offer you some counsel. Continue with your practice. If you do, you shall do far more than just *poke* things.'

Though he wasn't entirely sure what the Deity meant, and neither was Auron, it seemed, the spirit appeared pleased at the possibilities it promised.

Behind them, Silva looked quizzically at the group.

'I have healed you, woman,' T'goth snapped, as if hearing some unspoken question. 'You have done many bad things, so you are lucky I even did that.'

The warrior blushed a little but kept quiet.

'And you.' T'goth looked at Nicolas with meaning. 'You I owe most of all. You guided me and were patient with me. Maybe the stick was right to choose you.'

He didn't feel as if he'd been that patient, but okay.

Wait...

What did he mean about the stick? That stupid ceremony was completely random...wasn't it?

The idea that maybe he'd been chosen on purpose sent a shiver down his spine.

'So, Nicolas Percival Carnegie, what can a Deity do for you?' T'goth asked before adding, 'Within reason.'

Though it seemed like a huge question, and one he should give careful consideration to, he already knew the answer. 'I'd just like to go home.'

That was the dream. Stick or not, he had no business being out here, and he'd pushed his luck far further than he ever ought to have. The quiet life called to him, and he was ready to answer with gusto.

'That sounds nice.' Shift smiled. 'I would love to see where you live. Count me in.'

'What?'

'His mother is an excellent cook,' Garaz remarked, rubbing his chin thoughtfully. 'I should also like to visit them again.'

'These people are the only ones who can see or hear me, so I'll join that little trip too,' Auron said with a nod.

'Where Nicolas goes, I go,' Silva declared simply.

'Wait, guys...' What was happening? 'I'm not having a party or anything—'

'You are now,' Shift replied with a wink.

T'goth seemed to think upon this for a moment. A long moment, in Nicolas's opinion.

What's he even considering?

Eventually, when the Deity's eyes reopened, something in his expression worried Nicolas.

'I will send you where you need to be,' the Deity declared finally.

Nicolas breathed a sigh of relief before he realised something.

'Wait, that does mean that you'll send us home, right?'

The Deity smiled.

Before Nicolas could say anything else, a beam of light engulfed him and his body was pulled into the air yet again—even though his feet felt rooted firmly to the ground. As his body stretched and elongated, it also seemed to twist and warp. The world around him went upside down then inside out, and he felt everywhere, but nowhere. All was coloured light then all was black.

****

There was a sound.

Was that...cawing?

Why is there cawing?

There was another sound.

Waves?

Are waves crashing?

Why are waves crashing?

Opening his eyes, Nicolas could see nothing. It took him a good few moments to realise this was because he was lying on his stomach. Quickly rising, he spat out mouthfuls of sand. The coarse stuff covered his lips, nose, cheeks, and hands. Furiously, he rubbed it off. Why was he covered in sand? He was then sick. Repeatedly.

Everything was spinning slightly as he pushed himself off the floor. Was he sweating because he was so disorientated or because it was so hot?

Why is it hot?

Looking down, he saw the handprints he'd left in the sand. He was so confused.

He got cautiously to his feet then took a moment to let the world around him settle, shutting his eyes again as the glare off the sand blinded him.

Raising a hand to shade his eyes, he finally opened them properly. His head screamed in agony, and he began to question whether his eyes and brain were working properly. Slowly, he turned to get a full three-hundred-and-sixty-degree view of his surroundings.

'I'm on an island,' he muttered to himself wearily, before crying aloud, 'Dammit!'

Epilogue

King Silus shut the door to his personal chambers, taking a moment to ensure that no stray servants were around before allowing his regal manner to drop and slumping against the door. The meeting with the Council of Lords had been horrendous, and it had lasted most of the day. So much shouting. Accusations were thrown left and right as councillors took the opportunity to try and incriminate those they had grudges with, suggesting they'd either known of Lorca's machinations and said nothing or outright participated in the plan. Now that Lorca was dead, no one would ever know for sure who'd been in on his scheme, or why he had done it at all. Even most of the corrupt soldiery had managed to slip away. Those who'd acted directly with Lorca at the warehouse were either dead or in the wind, and their fellows were keeping their heads down.

It saddened him that though this tragedy should've pulled the lords together, instead the room had been full of hate. Everyone was more bothered with who was accountable instead of how to move forwards. The real truth, that Lorca was behind the whole affair, would be kept from the people. This kingdom was already teetering on the brink. To find out the High Chancellor was behind an assassination attempt on the king...there would be civil disorder and who knew what else?

So what if we leave him out of the official story?

They still had that cursed dwarf to blame, who was primarily responsibly anyway. Though as far as the people seemed to be concerned *'dwarf'* meant any non-human who resided in the kingdom. He'd received a report today of black garbed men in the streets preaching hate.

Not in my city.

In the morning, he'd look into having this element removed. Riling up the people would do no good when they needed to pull together to rebuild. Yes, he would see they were run off. He would also remind the people that an orc, of all things, was partly responsible for helping both him and the kingdom.

But despite all of this, he was relieved. As daunting as the meeting had been, he'd asserted himself, taken charge, acted like a king for the first time. The treasury had been restored, which they would desperately need to repair the damage to the city that thrice-damned lizard monster had caused. Many of the old guard had gasped at the idea of sending soldiers into the enchanted forest, citing the ancient laws that forbade such actions.

Will ancient laws feed my people and reopen trade?

It was what had needed to be done. *The Temple of Champions* was shut down and anyone found therein arrested. Trials and executions would give the public a sense that justice was prevailing, seeing as all the ringleaders were beyond punishment, either dead or being tortured by a Deity who knew where. They had Wade, but Silus had decided he could rot in a dungeon for the rest of his life.

Planning to eat me indeed.

It had felt strange not having Lorca beside him at the Council, whispering suggestions in his ear. But he was pleased not to have needed it. Through this ordeal he'd found a fortitude he hadn't realised he possessed, thanks to them. Now he intended to put it to good use. He would be the king they all thought he was, the one they needed.

I can do this.

He reached for the decanter on the table before staying his hand. It was a reflex. He hadn't really wanted a drink, and he certainly didn't need one.

'No,' he said to the decanter, closing his hand and pulling it back. He was not that man anymore, nor would he be again.

I will be better.

His train of thought was interrupted by the sight of his breath fogging up as it left his mouth. Giving the fireplace a sideways glance, he saw the raging fire within.

So why's it so cold in here?

Shivering slightly, he pulled his cloak tightly around himself.

What's going on?

Suddenly, he realised he wasn't alone.

'Greetings, reluctant king,' came a voice from behind him, a gravelly, soft tone that seemed like several overlapping voices. 'Please do not be alarmed.'

Too late. Turning in the direction of the voice, Silus was very alarmed. He didn't have the words to adequately describe what he was looking at, but he knew it terrified him. First his legs felt shaky then they were unable to support his weight. He fell to his knees.

'Who are you?' he asked, trying not to look directly at the figure before him.

'That is not the question you want to ask,' the whisper replied.

Silus took a moment to form the sentence on trembling lips. 'What are you?' he asked finally.

'Better,' the voice soothed. 'I am...complicated. Too complicated for you. As far as you are concerned, I am...a fixer.'

'Fixer?' the king repeated in confusion.

'Yes,' the voice replied. 'He who commands me sends me where things need fixing.'

'What needs fixing here?' Silus asked, fearful that he already knew the answer.

'You,' the voice answered as if it were the most obvious thing in the world.

King Silus's breeches became warm and wet. 'I'll call the guards,' he cried, starting to crawl away from the...whatever it was. 'They're just outside the door.'

'You misunderstand,' the whisper interrupted, holding up a hand, if that was what the appendage could be called. 'I am not here to kill you, but I will kill any guard who sets foot in this room. Though, of course, they cannot hear you. The room has been proofed against unwelcome ears. This is between the two of us.'

He looked desperately towards the door. Beyond it were five well-trained men. Good men, who would die if he called for them. He was sure of it. They had no chance against...that. He couldn't summon them to their doom.

'I am here because you are not supposed to be,' the voice continued, seeming sure he wouldn't call for help. 'Great effort was expended to remove you from your position, yet here you are.'

Silus sagged. His inevitable end was nigh. 'You *are* here to kill me.'

'No,' the voice said with a slight chuckle that chilled Silus to his core. 'We are unfortunately past anything so simple.'

'What do you mean?'

'The people who tried to kill you are all gone,' the voice replied. 'If you die here now, in your chambers, it is obvious that others remain. These matters will be looked into, and we cannot have that. It is not...neat. We require another solution.'

'So this was bigger than Lorca?' Silus asked.

'Lorca was a part of something much bigger, yes,' the voice confirmed. 'He played his role well, and it should have been that you died during a robbery, but the dwarf got greedy. Such is the nature of mortals. Still, he caused enough chaos that our goals are still achievable.'

'I don't understand,' Silus wailed. 'Lorca helped me, he helped the kingdom. Why do that just to try to usurp me anyway? He could've had the throne. I would've given it to him. I kept offering, and he kept refusing. Why do all that? Why do all that good work just to kill me? The man made me.'

'Hope is a powerful tool,' came the reply. 'Your kingdom was in the grip of corruption and vice, and the people knew no better life. But if you build people up to understand what a better life can be, give them hope for a brighter future, and then snatch that away from them, they become...malleable to certain ideas.'

'Like what?'

The figure raised a single long finger and waved it from side to side. 'I cannot tell all. But you will see.'

'So, I do get to live?' Silus asked, not sure where this was going but sure it would be bad.

'After a fashion.'

Silus gulped before he asked his next question. 'What does that mean?'

The figure reached behind him and produced a small creature. It sat in the fingers of an unnatural hand, a small writhing mass of tentacles no bigger than a cup.

'Using you is simpler than killing you,' the figure said, stroking the creature, which made small, pleased gurgling noises. 'So instead, this will bond with you. It will be a part of you, whispering in your ear as Lorca did and making sure you make the correct decisions. Sarus will be rebuilt, and you will become a strong king, a legendary king.'

Silus's ire rose 'You expect me to give up my freedom like that?' he cried. 'I will do nothing to hurt my people.'

'Hush,' the voice commanded in a harsh bark.

Silus shrank under the will being pressed upon him.

'If you do not comply then you *will* die,' the voice continued. 'A fire in the castle would be best. Many of those who live and work here will die too, but so be it. It would be an inconvenience, nothing more. But if you force my hand, I shall do what I must. Or those people can live and you can let my pet do its work. It can forcibly bend your will, but it would be so much simpler if you just comply.'

'But you will—'

'Make your kingdom stronger,' the voice interrupted. 'That is the will of he who commands me.'

Silus looked at the creature again and weighed his options. Calling the guard was pointless. He could throw himself through the nearest window, but he doubted it'd make a difference to whatever these people wanted.

Can I attack the figure myself?

No, the very idea made him sick with fear. He had no options bar one…comply. Comply and hope he could find a way out of this at some point. Dead, he could do nothing. Alive, maybe he could do something.

Then an idea hit him, a single sliver of hope for the future.

'One question,' Silus said.

The figure gestured for him to continue.

'Nicolas and his friends. What of them?'

'Ah, them,' the figure mused. 'They have interfered. That cannot be permitted.'

Silus took a deep breath and steeled himself before he replied, 'I guess you can just put that thing on me, and it will suck my will regardless. But if you guarantee that my people will not get hurt and that Nicolas and his friends will be allowed to live, I will surrender to it willingly. If not, I will fight it every single day. You hear me? *Every. Single. Day.* I will become more than just an *inconvenience*.'

The face of the figure did something that could've been construed as a smile.

'We may make a strong king out of you yet.' It chuckled.

'So?' Silus pressed.

'I will make you this offer, good king. Nicolas and his companions get a free pass. Once. But they cannot be permitted to interfere in the agenda again. If they do, that pass is void, and we shall do what we must.'

Am I likely to get a better deal than that?

He doubted it. The figure didn't look like the haggling type. But he'd achieved one goal, giving Nicolas and his companions a chance. He'd followed them, watched them. He knew their hearts were in the right place and they already had an idea this thing may be bigger than it looked. If anyone could stop...whatever this was, it'd be them. Hopefully, they would do something great with the time he was buying them.

Slowly, he nodded, looking down at the floor beneath him. 'Very well.'

'Wise decision.'

Though he couldn't see, didn't want to see, he heard the figure rise and move towards him. It grew colder the closer it got. Eventually, its shadow loomed over him, and a long, bony finger reached down, opening his shirt and revealing his bare neck. After a second, something wet was placed onto his shoulder, and a small tentacle caressed his neck gently.

Be brave, Silus. Brave like they were.

There was a crunch, and Silus screamed.

ACKNOWLEDGMENTS

I remember a much younger version of myself who dreamed of publishing a book one day, and here I am, 39 and about to publish my second!

That would seem insane to me, but upon finishing my first book, *The Simple Delivery*, I fell in love with my characters. How could I not continue their adventures? In truth I have just recently completed the first draft of book 6 of the series. Oh, dear lord I am putting my guys through it (I do really love them...honest). Sometimes it's hard, and sometimes it's easy, but every time I sit down to write, I love it.

And I hope that you're loving the series so far. I am so excited for what's to come, both from the perspective of me writing it, and you reading it.

But as much as the story is written by the author, I couldn't have published this book without help. Firstly, of course, is my mum, Christine, my stalwart alpha reader who also got promoted to proof-reader for this second instalment. But before the spellings are checked, the content always needs going over, and for that I have my amazing editor, Dani. Not only did she polish up my work and offer me some very solid pointers, she also managed to temper my over enthusiasm so that what I wanted to write was appropriate in the world in which it was set (long story). And once you've gotten the content right, you also need a pretty package for that content, and for that I give the team at Miblart a huge thank you. I asked for a minotaur on the cover, and I got one. They've done an amazing job with the covers for the first three books in the series and I look forward to seeing what they continue to produce for the rest.

What's that I hear you ask?

'Hey Andrew, how did you manage to fund these amazing professionals?'

Excellent question. And the answer to that is Kickstart. To everyone who contributed to my Kickstart campaign to get this book produced, thank you. I am truly touched that so many of you took a chance on this new author. It's folks like you that drive me to make these books the best they can be.

So, to you reader, and everyone out there who loves a good adventure...I hope you enjoyed the book and are eager to find out what's going to happen to poor Nicolas and company next!

Until book 3...keep adventuring!

About Author

Andrew Claydon is a UK author from Somerset, and writer of the *Chronicles of the Dawnblade* series. Currently, he writes from a desk in the corner of his kids' bedroom, trying to ignore the glares of the cat who likes to sleep in there during the day whilst he types away.

When he isn't writing, he loves to read sci/fi and fantasy novels. It's one of the things that inspires him to write himself. He also enjoys playing Warhammer 40,000 and is a keen wrestling fan.

He has degrees in both history and psychology, as well as black belts in several martial arts. When he isn't creating vast fantasy worlds and populating them with good guys and bad guys to run around fighting each other, he works as a supermarket baker.

Subscribe to my newsletter for the latest publishing news (and get a FREE prequal novella) at: www.andrewclaydonauthor.com
Or follow me on social media:
Facebook: Andrewclaydonauthor
Instagram: @authorandyc
Tiktok: @authorandyc

If you enjoyed the book, then please leave a review on Amazon and/or Goodreads. Reviews are really important to indie authors to help them get their work out there. If you do take the time to leave a review, thank you.

Also By

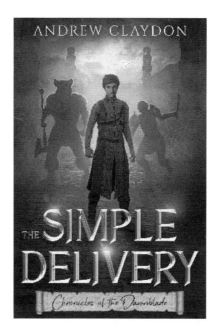

The Simple Delivery
Chronicles of the Dawnblade Book 1
Available now at all great retailers!

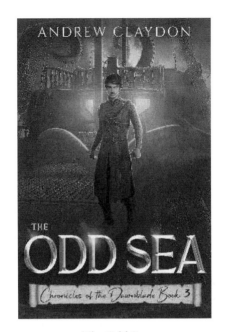

The Odd Sea
Chronicles of the Dawnblade Book 3
Coming 2023!

Printed in Great Britain
by Amazon